RUN. LEAVE YOUR FRIENDS—
THEY BELONG TO JUSTICE NOW.

The dwarf blinked rapidly.

Go, and warn those like yourself.

The knight's glare gleamed in the dwarf's terrified eyes like sunlight off ice.

Tell them Shadowbane watches Downshadow. Tell them I wait for them.

And with that, he jerked the scabbard away and sent the dwarf scrambling with a shove. Without even looking back, the thug vanished into the everlasting night, choking and sputtering.

ED GREENWOOD

PRESENTS

WATERDEEP

FORGOTTEN REALMS®

ED GREENWOOD
PRESENTS
WATERDEEP

DOWNSHADOW

ERIK SCOTT DE BIE

Ed Greenwood Presents Waterdeep

DOWNSHADOW

©2009 Wizards of the Coast LLC

Cover art by Android Jones
First Printing: April 2009

9 8 7 6 5 4 3 2 1

ISBN: 978-0-7869-5128-4
620-24025740-001-EN

U.S., CANADA,
ASIA, PACIFIC, & LATIN AMERICA
Wizards of the Coast LLC
P.O. Box 707
Renton, WA 98057-0707
+1-800-324-6496

EUROPEAN HEADQUARTERS
Hasbro UK Ltd
Caswell Way
Newport, Gwent NP9 0YH
GREAT BRITAIN
Save this address for your records.

Visit our web site at www.wizards.com

DEDICATION

According to Stephen King, writing is a kind of telepathy, where the words that I transcribe convey a thought from my head indirectly into yours. It is this very connection I'm going to try to use right here, right now, when I say this book is for *you*.

Usually, you pick up a book, flip to the dedication page and say "John and Sue? Whatever." But not this time. This time, this book is for you, right there—right now.

(Yeah, I'm talking to you.)

I dedicate this book to you, gentle reader, for having faith in me and in our Realms.

This one's for you.

ACKNOWLEDGMENTS

This book is the result of a great support network consisting in no small part of an excellent team of Realms scribes. First and foremost, I wish to honor my fellow Waterdhavians Ed Greenwood, Steven Schend, Jaleigh Johnson, and Rosemary Jones—thanks in no small part to whose hard work our beloved Realms soldier on.

Special thanks to Ed, without whose tireless and prodigious efforts I could not have written even half of this book.

Thanks to the many Realmsians who've given me advice, support, and friendship over the years: Bob Salvatore, Paul Kemp, Elaine Cunningham, Richard Lee Byers, Ed Gentry, Brian Cortijo, George Krashos, Brian James, and dozens more. Special thanks to Elaine for her great poesy—may Danilo Thann ever live on! He will in my heart.

My editor Susan Morris deserves a great deal of the credit (or blame) for this novel. She's done an excellent job on the Waterdeep series, and continues to be one of the Realms' best allies.

Thanks also to the sages/scribes at Candlekeep—to Alaundo and Sage and Kuje and Wooly and all the rest—without whom even the strongest swimmer would drown in the ocean of Realmslore. Thanks for the faith, guys, and please keep it up. We need you more than we will ever know.

Thanks also to an intrepid band of online writers and adventurers—Mari, Laws, RW, Jeggred, Wraith, Grim, Pred, Gem, and Lady C—who give me hope for the future of our genre.

And, as always, my lovely companion in arms, Shelley, without whose constant support, unconditional love, and especially fine editing skills I would be lost for sure.

INTRODUCTION

I t's all too easy to blow up the moon.

It's even tempting, if you have the power—and in a world full of magic, the stroke of a pen can always muster power enough.

Which is why the first of the firm, written rules decreed by Jeff Grubb, the brilliant designer who was the first "traffic cop" of the published FORGOTTEN REALMS®, read as follows: "Don't blow up the moon."

Jeff's last rule was: "Remember: Don't blow up the moon. I mean it."

It's a credit to Jeff's vigilance (and that of his successors in the post, which some have compared to being sheriff in *High Noon*), that the moon still serenely glides along in the night skies of Faerûn. (Which must be a great comfort to the moon goddess.)

Not everyone can resist such temptation. That's why fantasy readers get to read so many multi-book sagas where the fate of the world hangs in the balance as gods grapple, armies march, seas open up to swallow clifftop castles, dragons crash down into cities, and, yes, the moon blows up.

Exciting, stirring stuff. (I know; I've written some of it.)

Not everyone can resist the temptation to read it, either. Yet just like a steady diet of ice cream, or any other culinary treat, it palls after a bit. It should be special, and kept for special occasions.

Which leaves the rest of the time, when we need darned good storytellers to leave the armies unmustered and the dragons slumbering in their lairs and tell us gripping, exciting, fun-to-read stories about this particular character, here, or that one yonder.

Stories that look over the shoulders of people who dwell in Waterdeep and live out their daily lives without ruling it, or leading armies.

Stories that vividly bring to life what it must be like to be a member of the long-suffering City Watch. And a paladin, living by a moral code that places strict limits on what you can do—and that gets sorely tested, all too often.

And to be torn between two loves. Or three. Or four. All under one roof with you.

A story like this one, *Downshadow*, which is a delight of a tale. Full of fights and duels, chases, a splendid revel, long-sought and bitter revenge, sinister secrets, at least one deadly hired slayer, a little dungeon-delving, and faithful love.

Want to really feel what it's like to tramp the streets of Waterdeep? Read this book.

Want to get caught up in a story that really zips along? Read this book.

Want to read another one? Hope this powerful, funny writer pens another Realms tale as delightful as this one.

I created Waterdeep, and just as I felt thirty years ago when I opened a book by Elaine Cunningham called *Elfshadow*, I opened this one and felt right at home. This *is* Waterdeep, brought to life vividly all around me.

Gosh, I wish I'd known these characters earlier.

I'm buying four copies of this book. I know I'm going to wear them out reading *Downshadow* over and over.

Ed Greenwood
November 2008

PROLOGUE

Black rain lashed the city, pounding away at ragged cobblestones and blurring the glow of street lamps to a haze. Buildings that towered majestically by day became, by drenching night, idols of stone and shapeless mountains. Such a rain dampened the City of Splendors, changing its romantic luster into something much colder—much darker.

Such a rain made the city resemble the world below.

Beneath the slick streets, in the nefarious passages of a legacy of old Faerûn, lay Downshadow. Under the city, under the mountain, sprawled treacherous halls that knew no light except that which men made.

Once, this labyrinth had been called Undermountain, the dream of a mad wizard called Halaster, and the deeper levels still teemed with his warped whims and creations. The shallow stretches, however, had become a home for the cruel, the desperate, and the scarred.

Some said Downshadow tainted its inhabitants; some claimed the reverse. Regardless, what once had been dungeon was now desperate homeland—where once had been monster, now was man.

In one unlit chamber, a man crouched amid a circle of foes, flaming steel in hand. Leering faces surrounded him, half-illumined in the light of his sword. Blood and sweat dripped from his worn leathers. Numbness choked his arms and legs but he gave no sign of it. His left hand held him aloft, and his body was tensed like a cornered wolf. His head was bent and his sword low, but he was not broken. A knight in shadow.

A darkness, he thought. I will make for myself a darkness in which only I exist.

Six men stood around him, growling and glaring. At first, ten had threatened, but now the other four lay crumpled and moaning

1

against the walls. Shadows flickered among them, cast by the glow of the brilliant sword, which dripped silver fire onto the floor.

He'd given them a chance to surrender, and they'd laughed.

Now, their mirth had faded. The biggest tough—a burly wretch whose hoglike features and olive skin spoke of orc blood—spat on the stone floor at the downed man's hand. The yellow spittle landed on his steel gauntlet.

"Picked the wrong gang to push, crusader," said the half-orc. He slapped the haft of his nail-studded morningstar with his free hand. "Drop the steel and we kill you quick."

The man smiled through the slit in his full helm. Numbness crept through his body, and his lungs burned as though he breathed smoke. But he would not fall.

"Take it from him, Dremvik! Take it!" others of the gang shouted.

Yes, the knight thought as he focused past the pain in his lungs. Take it.

The leader—Dremvik—was a tyrant, the knight knew, but he wasn't stupid. Warily, the half-orc feigned a stomp on the knight's sword hand and kicked instead at the helmed face.

Rather than counter, the knight dropped his sword on the ground and jerked his thick gray cloak over it, stealing its light from the chamber and blinding them all. He shifted toward the kicking foot and pounced, wrapping his arms around the half-orc's leg.

Cries went up in the darkness but the knight ignored them. He wrenched to the side, toppling Dremvik to the ground with a satisfying thump of head against stone, and sprang away.

"Help!" Dremvik moaned. "Kill the bastard!"

"Get 'im!" one of the thugs cried, and they all started stomping and kicking. "Get 'im!"

The half-orc bellowed. "Not me, you bastards, not—" Then a boot crunched his face and ended his commands in a moan.

Deprived of their leader, lost in the lightless chamber, the thugs scrambled, lashing out at anything and everything that touched them. One squealed as a club smashed his head against a wall, and he fell nerveless to the ground. Jabbing knives opened flesh and wrenched forth screams—none of them the knight's cry. Finally one of the thugs managed to jerk the cloak away, revealing the sword and returning light to the chamber. The four remaining toughs looked around, trying to reason where their quarry had gone.

The knight, clinging to the wall just above their heads, whistled. They looked up to see his pale eyes blazing down at them. The eyes seemed to have no color, like diamonds.

"Four left," he said, and he leaped into their midst.

His booted feet took one in the face, and he lunged off the falling man to slam his iron-wrapped fist into a second's face. The two fell in opposite directions, and the knight whirled in the air to land on his feet, knees bent, near his sword.

An axe chopped toward him, but he tipped up his sword with the toe of his boot and flipped it into his hands in time to block the strike. He bent under the force, compressing through his knees—one hand on the hilt, one halfway up the long blade. The axe-man—a gigantic brute whose size bespoke orc and even ogre blood—held him in place, straining.

A blade stabbed the knight through from behind, but he barely felt it. The studs in his leather deflected the thrust just enough that it opened his ribs but missed his lung.

The knight twisted, throwing the axe wide, and slammed the pommel of his sword into the half-ogre's jaw as he stood. The big creature stumbled back and the warrior followed. The blade slid from his back with a splash of blood but not so much as a grunt came from his throat. The knight shoved the half-ogre against the wall and elbowed him in the ear.

The brute went down and the knight pivoted to face the one who'd stabbed him. With a gasp, the man looked down at his treacherous sword.

The knight smiled behind his helm.

As the thug lunged, the knight twisted his sword point down, then stepped forward to thrust from above. His block and his counter were a single movement; every parry was an attack unfolding. The silver-burning blade glided through the man's chest, dropping him to his knees.

The knight had miscalculated, though, for his sword wedged in the man's ribs and resisted when he tried to pull it free. He gripped it firmly and tugged it loose, but too slowly.

A club struck his face. It snapped his head back and sent him staggering. The sword fell from his numb fingers. The club-wielding dwarf sported a wide red mark on his face in the shape of the knight's gauntlet.

Then a larger body crushed him against the wall—the half-ogre. He felt the pressure but little of the pain. Trapped fast against the heavier brute, he could only struggle to no avail.

Two thugs still stood: the dwarf, who clutched a broken jaw, and the half-ogre, who didn't seem much hurt. The man who had caught both feet with his face wasn't getting up, and the backstabber was choking and gasping. All told, he'd downed eight of the gang of ten.

The knight made a note to take more care with those of ogre blood.

"Damn, damn!" moaned the dwarf, his words wet in his mouth. "Bastard done break me face, Rolph. And stuck Morlyn for good an' all."

The enemy he had skewered coughed and moaned. Blood trickled from his wound but did not gush. The knight knew he wouldn't die of that injury, but he wouldn't be fighting any time soon.

"What we do with 'im?" asked the half-ogre. He squeezed the knight's helm against the wall until it started to give.

"Break 'is head off?" suggested the dwarf.

At that moment silence fell and there was a sense of suction from high in the chamber—above and between them. The dwarf opened his mouth but the chamber exploded in blue light, blinding them, bathing them all in a light brighter than the sun.

When the knight could see, he blinked at a woman floating in midair—a woman cloaked in crackling, blue-white flames. They did not burn her, but seemed to clothe her. Her feet trod upon nothing but air, and long hair floated around her. He could make out little in that bright light—everything was blue and white and dazzling.

She blazed like an angel of Celestia, he thought. Like a *goddess*.

She was saying something, but the words were nonsense to his ears.

She screamed and sobbed in a tongue that sounded like the blackest whispers from the foulest dreams. Her eyes scanned things he could not see, and she seemed to be fighting invisible demons.

Then, just as abruptly, she vanished. The light died as though it had never been.

"What?" said the dwarf.

At that moment, the half-ogre howled—the bellow started low, then grew in volume and pitch until it became a scream. The beast clutched at himself where the knight had kneed him in the groin. The half-ogre tipped and fell with a tremor that shook the underground chamber.

The dwarf started to cry out but the knight slammed him against the wall and pressed his empty sword scabbard under his chin.

"Don't!" the dwarf gurgled, but the knight just shook his head. His voice was cold as ice and sharp as lightning. "Run."

"Uh?"

"Run," the knight said. "Leave your friends—they belong to justice now. I have told the City Watch where they will be found. Go, and warn those like yourself."

The dwarf blinked rapidly.

"The Eye of Justice watches Downshadow." He pressed the dwarf harder. "Tell them."

"I don't understand!"

The knight's glare gleamed in the dwarf's terrified eyes like sunlight off ice.

"Tell them Shadowbane waits." He narrowed his eyes. "Tell them I wait for them."

And with that, he jerked the scabbard away and sent the dwarf scrambling with a shove. Without even looking back, the thug vanished into the everlasting night, choking and sputtering.

The world seemed so heavy—and cold. Shadowbane watched the dwarf flee down the tunnel, then turned his head heavenward.

A bowshot above, through thousands of tons of stone, rain would be falling on Waterdeep. Rain that would shatter against his steel helm.

He knew he would barely feel it, thanks to the spellplague.

He felt, instead, only a creeping numbness—the absence of feeling. The surfaces of his thighs and arms had become like natural armor, like frozen leather greaves and bracers. It left his flesh filled with senseless nerves. His fingers, however warm, perpetually felt frostbitten to his touch, and his legs, as much as he pushed them, felt disconnected. His skin felt like dead flesh.

The spellplague had stolen feeling from Shadowbane, as it had stolen so much from the world. In time, it would take his life as well. He could only hope it would give him long enough.

"Long enough," he whispered, "to do what I must."

He thrust the scabbard through his belt, turned down another passage, and ran through the darkness below the world.

ONE

24 TARSAKH, THE YEAR OF THE AGELESS ONE (1479 DR)

Araezra Hondyl sighed heavily, smiled, and silently counted to six. The ranking valabrar of the Waterdeep Guard despite her tender twenty-odd winters, she exercised the iron-clad control of her passions that had secured her so many early promotions.

Despite her firm grip on the reins, patience was fleeing her. She put her fingers to her temple where, Kalen saw, a vein had risen beneath her skin.

"Once again." Her long tail of braided black hair trembled under the strain. "Slowly."

Kalen Dren, vigilant guardsman and Araezra's chief aide, took notes in his small, tight script, spectacles balanced on the end of his nose. His plume scratched quickly and efficiently, and his face remained carefully neutral. He had his duties as a scribe and fulfilled them scrupulously. Not that they were on official business, exactly, but it was his job.

Araezra's best friend, Talanna Taenfeather, loitered casually nearby. She had bent to examine some of the wares in a shop window. The "fashion" spikes wired out of her orange-red hair bobbed behind her head as she nodded and murmured to herself. She wore the uniform of her office but was off duty, and was present for the same reason as Araezra: to part with coin. They'd stopped after morning patrol out of South Gate, only to find a situation requiring their attentions.

"A fine sun that brings you through my door, lady," said Ellis Kolatch, a greasy, unpleasant man who sold jewelry and fine silks—also knives, flints, and small crossbows, if the rumors were to be believed. "And timely, for I have need of the Watch!"

"Guard," Kalen corrected indifferently, but no one seemed to hear. He continued scribbling down the merchant's words and those of the accused thief: a small half-elf boy.

"I tell you, this little kobold pustule is stealing from me," Kolatch said. "He's been in here twice in the last tenday, I swear—him, or someone like him. Always some half-blood trash that's lashed me with his tongue an' stolen my wares!"

"Blood-blind pig!" The half-elf grinned like the scamp he was. "I've never been in this place afore—you must think all the pointy ears be the same, aye?"

"You!" Kolatch raised his fists threateningly.

"Goodsir." Araezra's voice snapped like a whip. "Have peace, lest I arrest *you*."

Nothing about the valabrar's fine face—widely and fairly thought to be one of the best in all of Waterdeep—suggested impatience. Here was the controlled seriousness that had won her the respect and love of the Guard, the Watch, and much of Waterdeep. One who knew her well, as Kalen did, might see her fingernails straining and failing to pierce her gauntlets as if to draw blood from her palms.

"Aye, my apologies." Reining himself, Kolatch put his hands behind his back and cleared his throat. "I am sorry, gracious lady Watchman."

"Guardsman," Kalen murmured, but kept writing.

The distinction meant less and less, these days. The City Guard had become a division of the Watch, and while the guardsmen might be—as professional soldiers—better armed and trained than the average Watchman, the names meant little to the ordinary citizen. Kalen, who had been an armar in the Watch proper two months before, didn't mind.

Araezra had commissioned him as her aide based on his record as a lion who had to be lectured more than once regarding his "impressive but nonetheless embarrassing zeal."

Now things had changed, though she couldn't have known they would do when she called him to service. His debilitating sickness had been his first confession, and he knew he'd become a disappointment to her: he was a kitten and not a lion.

But Araezra had a great love of kittens, too. He smiled.

"*Sst*—Kalen!" Talanna hissed.

Kalen looked around to find Talanna poking at him. He hadn't felt it, of course—because of his sickness—but he heard her quite well. He raised an eyebrow.

The red-haired lass held a sapphire necklace to her throat. "What of *this*? Aye?"

Kalen sighed and turned back to his parchment booklet.

"And you, boy?" Araezra asked the half-elf accused of thievery. "Name yourself."

He bowed his head. "Lueth is the name my father gave me, gracious lady."

Kalen noted this, recalling that "Lueth" meant "riddle" in Elvish. A false name? The boy was unremarkable, forgettable in face and form, but for the sharp gray eyes that peered up at Araezra with intelligence, wit, and bemusement. Something was not quite right about him. Kalen's neck tingled.

"What have you to say?" Araezra asked.

"Naught but what I said, good lady," said Lueth. "This stuffed puff of a blood-blind don't know what he seen. Was just admiring the baubles and gewgaws, and he done accuse me of stealing." The boy spread his hands. "Why'd I need jewels, aye? They'd better laud your beauty, good lady." He blushed and winked.

Kalen saw Araezra stiffen and recalled the one time he had brought up her looks on duty—and the blackened eye he had suffered. Not that she minded being beautiful, or being beloved of half the Watch (and half the magisters, merchants, and lordlings of the city), but when she ceased to be taken at her word because of her face, it tended to . . . *irritate* her.

Araezra hid her feelings behind a cool, lovely mask. "If there is no evidence," she said, "then I cannot arrest you, boy."

Lueth stuck out his tongue at Kolatch, who glared at him. Then the merchant turned his glare on Araezra. Talanna giggled. Kalen smiled privately.

"On your way, child," Araezra said to the boy. She gave him a little smile. "And in the future, best not to admire gewgaws with your hands, aye?"

Lueth flashed a wide, pleased grin and skipped toward the door, where Kalen stood.

Casually, Kalen swept out his hand and caught the boy's arm. "Hold."

"Ay!" The boy struggled, but Kalen was deceptively strong. "Why stay me, sir?"

Calmly, Kalen transferred his notebook to his teeth, then reached down and tugged on something in the boy's sleeve. A bright red kerchief fluttered forth, studded with gold and silver earrings and a large, dragon-shaped brooch. The fat merchant gasped.

"That," young Lueth said. "I can explain that."

Kolatch blinked as Kalen continued to pull. Tied to the end of the kerchief was another—this one the blue of the sea after a storm—that also sparkled with jewels. Knotted to it was a long scarf, and finally a puffy pink underlinen, such as a lady of the night might wear beneath her laced bodice, had she the coin for silk.

"Ay," the boy said. "That—"

"My jewels!" Kolatch shrieked. "Thief!"

"Hold, you!" Talanna said from where she stood trying on bracelets. "I've got him, Rayse!" She leaped forward, the spikes in her hair bobbing and the half of her orange-red mane left unspiked dancing around her shoulders.

The boy gave an *eep!* and twisted out of Kalen's grasp, shedding his patched and frayed coat as he did. He caught at the red kerchief as he ran, tearing it and sending jewels tumbling across the room. Kalen lunged, but phlegm boiled up in his throat and he coughed instead of grasping the thief. Lueth darted out the door, Talanna in immediate pursuit. Kolatch, puffing and red in the face, stormed after them.

Araezra stepped toward Kalen, eyes worried, and put her hand on his shoulder. "Kalen?"

"Well," he said under a cough. "I'll be well."

He didn't meet her gaze and tried to ignore the pain in his back.

He could feel her hand only because it fell on a bruise—it felt distant, far removed from his empty body.

They stepped into the street. A furious Kolatch shouted and cursed after the distant red head of Talanna, who was running westward like a charger after the boy. They turned south along the busy Snail Street, cutting back into Dock Ward.

"Think he'll escape?" Kalen asked softly.

"Unlikely. Tal's the fastest lass in Waterdeep."

"And this Lueth is only a boy," Kalen said. "Short legs."

Araezra smiled and laughed.

Kolatch, hearing their voices, wheeled on them and glared. "Smiling fools! That knave has taken hundreds of dragons from me!"

"The Watch will return your good when the thief is caught," Araezra said. "We know his name and face—have no fear."

"Bane's breath," Kolatch cursed. He stared at Araezra and his lip curled.

Kalen felt a familiar tingle behind his eyes: cruelty hung in the air. Araezra seemed to sense it too.

"Though it's to be expected," the merchant said, wiping his sweat-covered brow in the morning sun. "Those damned pointy ears—can never really trust 'em." He spat in the dirt.

Kalen hid his contempt. Waterdeep was a free city, one where any blood was accepted so long as the coin was good, but there existed some few who held these sorts of views.

"I'm not sure I take your meaning, *goodsir,*" Araezra said.

Kolatch sniffed. "One day, thems that buys from pointy-eared, thin-blooded freaks like them, or the spellscarred, what should stay down below in Downshadow," he said. "One day, the taint on that coin'll be seen. And on that day, we'll rid ourselves of the whole lot. Keep 'em away from our homes and our lasses—" he grinned and stepped toward Araezra, who narrowed her eyes.

"That will be enough, goodsir," said Araezra.

Kolatch spread his hands. "Just trying to watch over you, ere you find a husband."

"I hardly need your protection." Araezra fingered the sword at her belt.

"Just a concerned citizen," Kolatch said. "But as you wish. And if a handful of those tree-blooded elves or those spellscarred monsters winds up . . . *uncomfortable* in sight of my dealings, I'll make sure not to protect them either, eh?" He pursed his lips. "All for *you,* sweetling."

Kalen knew the man was dangerous. But he had confessed nothing, so they could do nothing against him. Kalen knew how that would infuriate Araezra—she, who would take good and justice over the law of Lords any day of any year.

The fat merchant gave her a "what are you going to do, wench?" grin.

Kalen heard a roar beginning in Araezra's throat and started toward her. "Araezra . . ."

Kolatch looked over at the unassuming Kalen. He said nothing, but his eyes were laughing—asking what a beautiful woman was doing trying to wear a uniform and sword, and whether Kalen was going to defend her honor.

"The day goes on," Kalen said. "Let us leave Goodman Kolatch to his coin gathering."

The merchant gave a little chuckle, and Kalen could see the arrogance in his eye.

Araezra turned smartly on her heel and started down the Street of Silver.

Kolatch grinned after her. "And of course, sir and lady," he said, "if you catch the thief, I shall lower my prices for your custom—for the service you do me."

Araezra bristled, and Kalen braced himself.

"My thanks," she said tightly. "But bribes tend to insult me rather than flatter."

Kolatch's smile only widened. "Well, have it your own way," he said. "*Lass.*"

Araezra's eyes narrowed and Kalen knew she wanted to say something—loudly—but stopped herself only by virtue of her discipline.

"Come," Kalen said, placing a gentle hand on her arm. "We must let justice work itself at times." He smiled at Kolatch.

The merchant gave Kalen a little nod and the sort of sneering smile nobility-striving merchants reserved for men they thought lower than themselves.

After they had walked half a block down the Way of the Dragon, Araezra uttered a sharp curse that would have startled an admirer of her self-discipline.

"You should have hit him," she said. "Not as a guard, of course, but . . ."

"Araezra," Kalen said.

"Hells, *I* should have hit him," she said. "Not out in the street, of course, but . . . we could have brought someone from the Watchful Order to wipe his memory, aye? No harm done, aye?"

Kalen smiled and shook his head.

She sighed. "You're no help." She looked down the street where Talanna had run. "Reckon we should follow?"

"You know how I am on my feet." Kalen coughed.

"True," she said. "I imagine Tal can handle one little scamp. Aye." She shook out her long black braid and yawned. "Forget the barracks—let's go to the Knight for a quick morningfeast. Feel like a stroll?"

Kalen put out his arm and Araezra, with a smile, took it. They turned back down the Dragon toward south Dock Ward. She leaned her head against his shoulder briefly, almost without realizing it. Kalen was familiar with her habits.

He could feel a cough boiling up inside and bent all his focus to stop it.

Araezra yawned again and stretched. "If Jarthay gives me patrol duty outside the walls one more time, I swear I shall fall asleep in the saddle, or fall out of—Kalen?"

Trying and failing to fight it, Kalen coughed and clutched at his burning chest.

"I will make of myself a darkness," he whispered. He cupped his hand over his ring, which bore the sigil of a gauntlet with an eye. "A darkness where there is no pain—only me."

"Feeling well?" Araezra's face was concerned. "Kalen? Kalen, what's wrong?"

Only me, he thought, and tried not to taste the blood on his tongue.

It subsided—his last meal slowly sank back to his belly.

"Well enough," he said. He reached down, fingers trembling, and found Araezra's hand. Numbness stole the feeling from his fingers, so he squeezed her hand only gently—he couldn't be sure how hard he was clutching her. She didn't seem pained, and that pleased him.

Araezra's eyes searched his face. "These morning duties are hard on you, I can tell," she said. "I'll speak with Jarthay—move us to a less nocturnal schedule."

"I'll manage," Kalen said, as he always did.

Araezra smiled. They walked on, each in their own space this time.

"Thank you, Kalen," she said. "Back there . . . you know how I can be."

"I know," he said absently, and he laid his hand on her shoulder. His touch was brotherly. "Your coin at the Knight?"

"Agreed." She smiled at him. "Come, aide—lead the way."

"Sir," he replied.

As they walked south, Kalen reviewed his mental note of the jewelry—surely cheap, likely fenced—that he had seen in Kolatch's shop. Kalen's sharp eye had noted it all: three earrings, a ruby-eye pendant that would be easily recognized, and the dragon brooch. He studied it in his mind, making sure he remembered it keenly.

They reached the Knight 'n Shadow, at the corner of Fish and Snail streets, after a brisk walk. The bells of Waterdeep's clock (named, by its uninspired dwarven builders, the "Timehands") chimed: one small bell past dawn.

Kalen guided Araezra through the door of the tavern and waved for a pair of ales.

TWO

The Knight 'n Shadow was a two-story tavern, connected by a long, poorly lit staircase that spanned two worlds: Waterdeep above, and Downshadow below.

The Sea Knight tavern, which previously occupied the site, had utterly collapsed in 1425. Whether the result of a wizards' duel or a bout of spellplague (the accounts of locals differed), no one could ever say for certain. Some enterprising miner had dug out the cellar and discovered its connection to Undermountain. He built stairs, platforms for sitting, and a rope ladder, hired burly, ugly guards with spears to keep the monsters and coinless hunters at bay, and the shadow—dark half of the tavern—was born. The knight above ground grew shabby and dingy, like a sheet of parchment soaking up blood from below. It absorbed the stink of Downshadow and became the same sort of place: a squatting ground for unsuccessful treasure hunters, coin-shy adventurers, and other criminals.

Men like Rath.

The dwarf savored the tavern's duality. It reminded him of himself: smooth faced, even handsome on the surface, but hard as steel beneath. Perfect for his line of work.

Quite at ease in his heavy black robe despite the moist heat of the shadow below, Rath sipped his ale, ignoring the two dwarves who—like all dwarves who approached him—had come to test their mettle. Like all dwarves in every wretched land he visited, he mused.

They had seated themselves, uninvited, at his table, and had stared at him without speaking for the last hundred count. The first—an axe fighter with a thick black beard tied in four bunches that brushed his hard, round belly—sipped at his tankard. The other—a dwarf with a thick red-gold beard that spilled over his wide chest—was trying hard not to let Rath catch him laughing. He'd cover his mouth so as not to erupt with laughter, but the sounds that escaped his fingers were reedy and almost girlish—grating in Rath's ears.

Finally, when the stench of the dwarves had grown too much for his nose, Rath said, in a mild, neutral tone, "May I help you gentles in some way?"

The two dwarves looked at one another as though sharing some private joke.

Blackbeard smirked at Rath. "Lose a bet?"

It was the smooth face. Dwarves could respect a bald pate, as many went bald at a young age, but to have no beard was practically a crime against the entire dwarf race.

The red-bearded one let loose a loud burst of his childish laughter, as though this was the funniest jest he had ever heard, and slapped the table. Rath's tankard of watered ale toppled, spilling its contents across the grubby wood and into his lap.

Anger flared—hot dwarf anger that was his birthright. Immediately he rose, and the pair rose with him, hands touching steel. Their eyes blazed dangerously.

"Now, now, boy," said the smiling Blackbeard, hand going for a knife at his belt.

Cold swept through Rath, smothering his natural reaction. It was a trick, he realized, so he did not meet their challenge. Instead, he waved for more ale, then sat down and began picking at his black robe, unable to keep the disdain from his face. He'd just had his clothes laundered.

The dwarves watched Rath warily as he sat, and he knew their game. That had been a move calculated to provoke a brawl. Now, though, their trick spoiled, they stood uneasily, halfway to their seats, half standing. Rath found it amusing and allowed himself the tiniest smile.

"You're just going to sit there?" asked Blackbeard. "After I insult you?"

"Obviously," said Rath.

Redbeard chuckled, but Blackbeard scowled and cut his companion off with a hiss. He leaned in close. "What kind of dwarf are you that won't rise to fight?"

"A kind more pleasant than yours, it seems."

Blackbeard's face went a little redder, and his red-bearded friend stopped laughing. The eyes in the tavern turned toward them and Rath could hear conversations subsiding.

Rath wondered if these were native dwarves or foreigners. The dwarves of Waterdeep were few enough, but trade and coin were good in the city. Thus they came, those more accustomed to the merchant's scales than hammer and pick. Plenty of mining went on to employ those with traditional skills, in the bowels of fabled Undermountain or in the new neighborhoods popping up all over the city. In Undercliff, beneath the eastern edge of the old city, dwarves sculpted homes out of the mountainside (illicitly or not). Or in the Warrens, where they could dwell amongst others their own size.

Rath had never considered going to either of those cesspools, and he had no drive to dig or mine. These two did not look like builders or diggers—more like fighters. Foreigners, he decided—sellswords or adventurers, the kind who itched for trouble. He could see it in their bearing and in their confident glares. Besides, had they been Waterdhavian, they might have heard of the beardless, robed dwarf who stalked Downshadow and thus known better than to bother him.

The beardless *dwarf*, for true, he mused. He hadn't thought of himself as a dwarf in some time—not since he had shaved his beard on his twentieth winter solstice, forty years gone.

"I don't like being ignored," Blackbeard said finally, unable to hold back his anger. "You get on your feet, or Moradin guide me, I'll cut your throat where you sit." He drew his knife.

The red-bearded dwarf gave the same wheezing giggle and reached for his own steel.

Rath opened his mouth to speak, but a murmured "sorry" stole the dwarves' attention. The serving lass with her bright red hair and high skirt came and left his ale, sweeping up the coppers he'd set on the table. Rath thanked her without looking up—without paying her the slightest attention. The other dwarves ogled her, as sellswords are wont, and Rath felt queasy.

"You going to say something?" asked Blackbeard. "Or am I going to say it for you?"

At that, Rath had to accept that they weren't going to go away. He took up his tankard and sipped. Nothing for it, he thought, but to deal with the situation.

"Your Moradin," he said softly over his tankard, "weeps for his people."

The dwarves looked surprised at the sound of his gentle voice.

"Care to say that again, soft-chin?" said Blackbeard, his voice dangerous.

Rath set his ale on the table and folded his hands. "Do you know why so many of your gods have faded and died since the world before?"

The two dwarves stared. Redbeard uttered a nervous giggle that died halfway through.

"It is because of faith like yours—that of weak, unquestioning dwarves," said Rath. "The gods thrive upon courage, and when you fear the truth, the gods become weak."

"What?" The black-bearded dwarf was aghast, and the other's face was turning red as his beard. "How *dare* you?"

"You bluster and boast, but I see fear in your eyes—cowardice that would shame your fathers. You have never questioned your heritage, but accepted it without thought, and so you do not know what it is to be a dwarf. I know this, and I choose not to accept it. You . . ." Rath looked at them directly for the first time, "you do not *deserve* to be dwarves. You are nothing."

His speech had exactly the effect he had expected—expected, not merely hoped for. Rath was not a dwarf given to hope.

The black-bearded dwarf drew his dagger and spat at Rath, hitting his tankard. "You beardless thin-blood," he snarled. "You take that back, or you draw and fight me."

Redbeard giggled again—malevolently.

Rath picked up his tainted tankard and looked at it distastefully. He made no move to draw his sword—sacred to his order—from the gold-leafed scabbard at his side.

"It is simply the truth," he replied.

Blackbeard growled low like a murderous dog. "You insult your blood, smooth-face. Take it back!" He prodded at Rath with his blade. "Take it!"

"As you wish," he murmured.

Rath flicked his half-filled tankard in the air to draw their eyes. They looked.

In a blur of motion, Rath twisted the dagger out of the black-bearded dwarf's hand and plunged it—to the hilt—into his companion's right lung. Redbeard looked down at the hilt sticking out of his ribs and his giggle turned into a wet cough.

Blackbeard just watched dumbly as the tankard fell and clattered to the floor, splitting open and sending ale over his boots.

The dwarf looked mutely at his unexpectedly empty hand, then at Rath, then at his companion, who gaped down at his injury. As if on cue, the red-bearded dwarf's eyes rolled up in their sockets, and he slumped in his chair.

"Really," Rath said. "Why would you stab your companion like that?"

The dwarf looked at him again, eyes wide, and they went even wider when Rath smiled. It was not a pretty smile—handsome enough, but cold and sharp as drawn steel. The dwarf didn't bother to catch his ally but turned and ran for the stairs.

Trembling hands pawed at his side. Rath glanced down at the panting, wheezing dwarf and looked at him indifferently. The dwarf, mouthing pleas for help that went unanswered, fell to the floor with a wet burble that might have been a laugh.

Rath waved for more ale.

"Here's for the tankard—and the blood," he said, pressing silver into the terrified serving woman's palm.

>———W———<

In a secluded corner, behind the half-closed velvet curtain drawn for private dealings, a pair of gray eyes set in a feminine half-elf face sparkled as they watched, with some bemusement, the beardless dwarf defending himself against his assailants. A trifle unsubtle, that one, but some matters did not demand subtlety.

"That," said her patron, indicating her breast with one languid, silk-gloved finger, "is a passing fair brooch."

"It pleases?" Fayne ran her delicate fingers over the edges of the dragon-shaped brooch. "I just obtained it today. Had to elude the fastest red-haired chit of a guard, but I managed it."

She went back to watching the beardless dwarf, and she giggled when he drove one antagonist to the ground and scared the other away with a glance. Hesitant tavern-goers stepped forward to recover the bleeding dwarf—Rath did not so much as acknowledge their presence.

That sort of man, Fayne thought, could be very helpful in certain situations. She would have to see about acquiring hold of his strings—coin-pouch or breeches. Either. Both.

"Whence?" Her patron pointed at the brooch.

Time for business, it seemed. Fayne turned to him. "A bumbling old fool of a merchant up on the Dragon," she said. "I've been robbing him blind for two tendays now."

"Different faces?" Her patron's tone was mild.

"What am I, dull? Of *course.*" She rolled her eyes. "Art is pointless if you don't *use* it."

"Quite right."

Her patron rubbed at his cheek, where she could see two small scratches that were the only flaw on his otherwise smooth, ever-bemused face. His elf cheekbones were thin and high, his nose sharp without being aquiline, and his eyes a rich gold that matched the soft hue of his skin and his deeper golden hair. He wore a fashionable doublet and coat, rich but not attention grasping, and several rings over his white silk gloves. Each high, pointed ear bore several jewels, and though a great flounce of lace hid it, she knew he wore a thin silver chain around his throat with a locket that she'd never seen him open.

He bore no weapon, but Fayne knew he needed no such thing.

"So to business," Fayne said. "Who shall I ruin this time? Another lordling, perhaps? You'll read about the Roaringhorn girl on the morrow." She smiled at the memory.

He nodded. "Someone more important." Plucking a pink quill from nowhere—it might have come from his sleeve or from the air—he wrote three words, two short, one longer, on a scrap of parchment, without benefit of ink. This he pushed across the table to her.

"Who——?" Fayne furrowed her brow in thought. Then her

eyes widened. "You don't mean it." Her hands trembled in her excitement.

He straightened his gloves. "You've prepared for this for some time, yes?"

"Decades," she said. "Suppose that doesn't mean much to you. Just a wink of an eye."

He smiled and handed her a scroll bound with a burgundy leather thong and his seal, a silver shooting star surrounded by a ring of tiny flames.

"I'll do it." She stuffed the instructions into her bodice. "Besha's tits, I'd do it for *free*."

He put a hand up, and she froze as though he'd smitten her with a binding spell. "Have a care upon which goddess's bosom you swear, dear one," he said. "And mind: as much as you've looked forward to this, take care." He slid his fingers along her cheek. "Do not grow careless."

She smiled. "You know me—I am the picture of care."

He didn't look convinced. "I am very familiar with hatred, my little witch," he said. "And I know well the damage it can cause. Do not let it control you."

She closed her eyes and laughed. "I haven't spent half a century sculpting myself to fail now. Don't—" She looked up, but he was gone as though he had never been there.

Fayne sniffed. His abrupt comings and leavetakings had startled her in her youth, but then she'd started to wonder how to do it herself. She hadn't quite mastered that power—yet.

She put her small belt satchel on the table and waved for ale. The serving woman nodded and held up three fingers. Fayne shrugged, took out a small mirror, a quill and ink, and a bit of parchment, and began writing.

When next Fayne looked up, the woman was standing over her, hands folded in front of her apron. "Aye, lady?"

She was a pretty thing, the serving lass, with hair that fell in ruby ringlets to her midback. Fayne liked her looks—had worn such herself, once upon a tenday.

"Take this"—Fayne pressed the note into the girl's fingers, along with a disk of polished platinum—"and a bottle of your best amber brandy to yon beardless gentle."

The young woman looked where Fayne pointed and blanched. "You don't mean . . . Arrath Vir, aye? Oh, lady . . . unwise, methinks."

"What?" Fayne flicked blonde hair out of her eyes. "He's not one for the ladies?"

The serving lass shook her head, then slid into the booth opposite her. " 'Tis said he's a mystic or some such, heartless and cruel. Hails from a temple of some sort of . . . emptiness? Void? Sommat the like. Only"—she leaned closer to speak softer—"only he tired of his brethren, killed 'em all, and now he sells his sword for coin. He'd slit your granddam's throat for a copper nib. Him, or one of the Downshadow folk what worship the ground he treads."

"Mmm," Fayne said. "Sounds perfect." She could feel her heart in her throat and a heat in her belly. "I wonder at his skill with his blade—perhaps I'll sample it myself."

The woman didn't look convinced. " 'Ware, goodlady—his in't the sort you ought toy with. And his taste—" She looked down at Fayne's clothes and bit her lip.

Fayne understood. Beneath her greatcoat, she wore the immodest working clothes—low-cut, high-slit—one might expect of a Dock Ward dancer. The shirt was frilly, the vest cheap, and the skirt revealed more than it hid: the wares of a lady of negotiable virtue at best. In truth, the crass garb did ride Fayne's rather fine curves and lines very well—at least, in the body she'd made for herself with her flesh-shaping ritual.

She'd just come from scandalizing one Sievers Stormont in a Dock tavern, luring him into just the sort of irresponsible play that would cast a pall on his upward-bound older brother, Larr Stormont. Not that she had any idea why—she trusted her patron to keep his own counsel regarding the cut-and-thrust of the nobility (and of those who yearned to join them, like Stormont). This, of course, hadn't stopped her from spending a night in the elder Stormont's bed and acquiring evidence that led her to believe he was a Masked Lord.

Which, of course, only helped in writing her next tale for the

Minstrel—one of Waterdeep's most caustic, sarcastic, and thus widely read broadsheets. A lass has to earn a living, she thought, and if she did it by ruining the wealthy and self-important, then so be it!

The serving woman was staring at her, Fayne realized. For a reply, and yet, something more . . .

"I like your *hair*." Fayne leaned across the table and fingered the lass's red curls. Then, impulsively, she kissed the woman on the lips. Then: "Go to, go to! Enough eyes on my chest."

Blushing fiercely, stammering some kind of reply, the serving lass hurried off.

Fayne put the quill and ink away and looked in the silver mirror. She pulled from her belt a thin wand of bone and waved it across her forehead. Her blonde hair shifted into a strawberry red, then a vivid scarlet.

There. Just like the servant's. Only—there. Fayne's hair shortened until it just kissed the tips of her shoulders. Perfect.

Still looking in the mirror, she pressed the wand to her cheek. A scar crept onto her face: not *caused* by the wand, but rather revealed by it. The wand peeled the magic back.

She remembered that day. A thumb to the right, and she wouldn't be sitting there at that moment.

"Oh yes, bitch," Fayne said. "I remember you—I remember you quite well."

THREE

Shadowbane crept through a Downshadow passage, taking great care to attract no notice. He stole past natives as quietly as a ghost, leaving barely a footprint.

Huts and lean-tos crowded Undermountain's stale interior, packed into ancient chambers like the carcasses of freshly cleaned game in a butcher's window. The structures were built mostly of bones, harvested cave mushrooms, and scraps scavenged from above. The folk rarely stayed in one place long, skulking from chamber to chamber to avoid the underworld's inherent dangers. The knight in the gray cloak picked his way between the huts and barriers like a wraith.

Cook fires released greasy smoke into the air and coalesced at the ceiling. There, it escaped through holes and cracks and dispersed into the night above. Visitors to Waterdeep often claimed that the streets smoked, but they did not know why.

Long ago, in the old world, heroes and monsters had struggled in death-dances in these very halls. Now life filled the place: folk too scarred or poor to live in the light above. The last century had seen an influx of warriors, sellswords, treasure seekers, and what many might deprecatingly call adventurers, all of them with more prowess than coin. Waterdeep required coin, so they lived in Downshadow, where the only requirement was survival.

Downshadow was far from healthy, and even farther from pleasant. As he slipped through a chamber the width of a dagger-toss, Shadowbane nudged against something wet and cold near the door, and he stepped quietly back. The corpse of a hobgoblin, its face and snout twisted in terror, sat at his feet, the marks of three dagger wounds livid in its naked chest. The knight stepped over the body and continued stalking through the tunnels, cowl pulled low.

Downshadow was a complex, interwoven system of warrens in

passageways and chambers, only one of which held any kind of permanent encampment. The southernmost cavern of the complex, it had once been a breeding and warring ground for monsters, but the adventurers who moved in had cleared most of them out. The newcomers built shacks and shanty huts that huddled against walls or stalagmites until the place resembled a clump of city. Perhaps a thousand souls lived there—the population ever shifting as would-be heroes braved the lower halls of Undermountain, which still held hungry creatures that skittered and stalked.

Shadowbane paused to consider Downshadow "proper." The shanty town was an unpleasant reflection of what Waterdeep could become, were it sacked and burned by a marauding army and rebuilt by bitter, impoverished survivors.

Once he gained the smoky interior of the great cavern, Shadowbane shifted his travel to the walls, rather than the floor, swinging between familiar handholds and stalactites. Downshadow was quiet this night—many of its inhabitants gone to the world above for the hours they thought their due. Climbing allowed him to survey the most dangerous part of the underground world from above—safer and largely unnoticed as he looked for trouble.

Trouble was why he had come—why he came every few nights.

The great cavern was the first area settled in Undermountain, and Downshadow's reach had expanded from there, gradually encroaching on the monsters year by year. Those who lived nearest the surface made some attempt at civilization, forming tribes built on mutual protection. Those who could make food from magic did so for the benefit of their tribes. Other food came from harvested mushrooms, slain monsters, thieves working above, or from trade with the black-hearted merchants who visited below.

The tents and lean-tos hosted exceptionally seedy taverns, dangerous food markets, and shops that traded equally in hand-crafted wares and stolen goods. These establishments sometimes disappeared at a heartbeat's notice. Some of the folk had become sufficiently organized to establish a fire patrol of spellcasters, though residents had to bribe them for protection.

As in Waterdeep above, trade ran the city, but barter in

Downshadow took the form of illicit services and stolen goods, rather than hard coin.

Most folk of Waterdeep had never seen Downshadow—they knew it mostly from hushed tales in taverns, and repeated those stories to frighten children into obedience. The Guard ventured down on occasion, but only at need and only in force. Guardsmen hated such assignments, preferring tasks like gate watch or midden duty. More than a few merchants made a killing in these halls—literally and figuratively. When surface folk spoke of "driving the thieves and swindlers underground," they weren't speaking metaphorically.

One of those thieves, Shadowbane meant to visit that night. Ellis Kolatch was his name, and in Downshadow he brought back clothes and jewels he'd sold on the surface a tenday before, then had stolen cheaply. He met with his hired thugs in an alcove not far from the lower half of the Knight 'n Shadow tavern.

"Threefold God," Shadowbane murmured, running his fingers over the hilt of his bastard sword. It bore an inscribed eye in the palm of a raised gauntlet. "Your will be done."

As though in answer, Shadowbane felt that same ancient weakness inside him—the numbness in his flesh that gave him power and stole life from him little by little.

He did not beg for strength, for he would not beg.

Never again.

"I think there's been some misunder—*oof*," Fayne said, then dropped to her knees in the wake of a punch to her stomach that cut off her last word.

The torchlight flickered, casting wavering shadows against the chamber wall.

"You do this to yourself," said Rath. "Simply give me the gold." He nodded, and the half-orc bruiser who'd put his knuckle prints on her stomach hit her again—with his foot.

Breath knocked out of her, Fayne went fully to the ground, curled like a babe. She cradled her midsection, struggled to breathe, and glared up at the handsome dwarf she'd come to meet, and whom—until two strangled breaths ago—she'd hoped to hire. Her mistake, she supposed, was to trust him to meet her alone in an isolated chamber of Downshadow.

He'd brought four men. One—a bowman—kept watch down the tunnel. A second, a lanky human with pasty white skin and yellow hair, stood impassively at Rath's side. The other two—a half-orc and a very ugly human who might have passed for a half-orc—had gone to work on her shortly after Rath demanded more coin than she claimed she'd promised. She called it a misunderstanding. He disagreed.

"Can we," Fayne panted, "can we talk about this . . . with words?"

Rath stopped them with a raised hand; Fayne could have kissed him. He stepped forward, and the grace with which he moved stunned her. He cupped her chin in two fingers, and her body went cold and rigid as though he pressed steel to her throat. Slowly, he raised her to her knees.

"Until I see the gold," Rath said, "fists and feet will have to suffice."

He stepped away, pulling his hand from her chin so fast she thought he might draw blood. The ugly man, whose arms were wider than Fayne's chest, punched her cheek and sent her into the wall. The punch disoriented her so that she didn't even feel herself hit the stone.

Beshaba, she thought, where do men learn to *hit* women like that?

Before she could ponder that deep and relevant question, a hand grasped her red hair and wrenched her head up, the better to slam it against the wall. The half-orc took his turn as well, kicking her stomach and sides. Stars danced across her vision, and Fayne finally felt the cold steel of a knife against her jaw.

"Getting personal, are we?" she murmured.

"Hold," Rath said, and the thugs did—as obedient as dogs. "Little girl, you must understand—I do not hurt you out of malice. This is merely business."

"Aye," she said, and she spat blood from her split lip. "I understand. And my reply is: Bane bugger you all."

Rath sighed and waved.

Crack.

Fayne didn't even know what they'd done to her. She felt staggering pain, and then she slumped against the wall again. Every part of her hurt.

"You're a pretty thing," said the thug. "Be a shame to peel your face off."

"I agree." Fayne looked right at him, as directly as she could with the dizzying stars in her eyes. "But where I'd grow a new one, I don't think you have that luxury, pimple pincher."

The thug snarled, reversed his blade, and brought the pommel down hard on top of her head. He shoved her to the floor.

Serves you right for antagonizing him, her inner monologue noted.

She made squishing sounds as she tried to rise. Dungeons were worse than gutters. Sludge—mostly dust, mud, and human waste—covered her hair and leathers.

Do business with scoundrels, her patron always said, expect to be dunked in shit.

"Big man," she murmured lazily. "Big arms, big knife . . . little blade, I'm guessing."

The thug's face went red. "This one's keepin' her mouth shut, boss," he said. Fayne knew that look in his eye—that of a man eager to prove a manhood sullied. Mostly by unsheathing it. "Bet I could make her squeal for you, if only—*uhn!*"

Fayne looked up, head swimming, and saw the ugly-faced thug slam into a puddle of filthy water three paces distant. Rath rose from where the man had been standing. The dwarf had thrown him *that* far?

"Do not embarrass yourself," Rath said to him.

The thug sat up, shook his head, and snarled. "You hrasting worm, I'll . . ."

And Rath leaped across the intervening distance and drove his fist down across the man's face. Bone cracked, blood spattered the ground, and the thug curled into a quivering lump.

Fayne blinked. "That's . . . ooh."

Rath turned toward her, and his eyes gleamed in the torchlight without the slightest remorse. He might as well have stared at her with polished emeralds.

The half-orc, Fayne saw, was looking at him with fear in his eyes.

"Give me the coin you promised," Rath said. "Do not, and there will be consequences."

She couldn't help it. "Like punching me to death?"

Rath looked down at the thug, and Fayne saw his lip curl. "His crime was worse than yours and deserved greater punishment. You made a simple error of judgment. He exposed his own cowardice and weakness, which in turn dishonors me, his employer."

"So you won't just kill me," Fayne said. "No profit in that."

Rath shook his head.

"In *that* case . . ." She smiled dizzily. "Piss on the graves of your fathers, beardless dwarf."

With a sigh, Rath waved to the sickly pale man at his side, whose fingers were studded with rusty, iron claws like fingernails. Gauntlets, perhaps? The man stepped forward.

"Your wight is supposed to frighten me? I'm a grown woman, dwarf."

"Hold," Rath said.

The sallow face glared at her.

"You've come to your senses, girl?" asked the dwarf.

"A few more blows and I just might." She coughed. "It's just working so *well*."

Rath waved, and the half-orc charged forward to kick her in the side.

"That was irony!" Fayne whined in vain.

The half-orc drew back his leg to do it again, but Rath held up a hand and spoke a word Fayne didn't understand. The hobnailed boot didn't meet her belly, so she decided it was her favorite word of the year.

"Rath?" said the half-orc.

"Our sentry approaches," replied the dwarf. "Silence."

"Thank the gods," said Fayne, "that more hitting would be accompanied by further cries of pain."

Rath gestured to her. "Stifle it."

The half-orc kicked her in the stomach. The world blurred.

When her eyes worked again, a stick-thin man with a strung shortbow in hand and a quiver of arrows at his hip appeared in the corridor that led to the larger cavern. His eyes flicked to his dead comrade, but wisely he held his tongue.

"Battle," he said. "Attacked a merchant, downed his guard—didn't kill 'em, though. Probably itchies in Downshadow, looking for coin to scavenge or deeds to do."

Itchie, Fayne recalled, was a term for a sellsword, and most of those brave—or stupid—enough to live in Downshadow were something of the sort. Poor, hungry, and angry. *Itching* for a fight.

"Who?" Rath asked.

"Kolatch," said the sentry. "Awaiting a trademeet, probably." That name swam around Fayne's head—sounded familiar. "The fat merchant hisself is coming this way, wild eyed. Babbling sommat like a shadow attacked him, or the like."

Fayne was about to speak but was spared the commensurate blow by the damnably late arrival of her common sense and the appearance of a figure in the tunnel: Kolatch. When he stumbled into their chamber, she knew him—the merchant from earlier that day. His eyes rolled and his hands shook. Even if he weren't so maddened, he wouldn't have recognized her from the shop—not with a different face and a different gender.

Not seeming to notice the corpse, Kolatch scurried toward Rath and cried, "Save me—the black knight—save me!"

His hands never touched the dwarf. Rath stepped low in a crouch and threw Kolatch into the wall with a shrug. The merchant slumped. Fayne almost laughed at the way his frog lips burbled, but she suspected that making sounds would bring pain.

The thugs looked at one another, seemingly confused at the merchant's ramblings.

Kolatch's eyes focused on the tunnel and he whimpered. "The knight! The black knight!"

Fayne saw a cloaked man silhouetted against the crackling torchlight of the corridor, striding toward them. His worn cloak fell around him like a gray waterfall. She could see no face in his cowl, but she could feel his eyes upon her—upon them all. She shivered.

The figure stalked forward like a great black cat.

"I have no quarrel with you folk," he said in a cold, direct voice, muted only a little by his full steel helm. He pointed at Kolatch, who gasped as though struck. "Only him."

The knight's gaze shifted to Fayne. The torches flickered as though from his glance.

"Leave that woman be and flee," he added.

The self-assurance in his voice made fear—and excitement—rise in her stomach. He might as well have been delivering the words of a god.

The merchant gagged. "I'll pay all the coin I have!" he cried to the men around him. He pointed at his attacker. "Just save me!"

"Bane's blessing." The half-orc left Fayne and drew his steel. "I'll take that offer."

The helm began to pivot as the half-orc charged, scimitar high.

They moved almost too fast for Fayne to follow. The knight raised a scabbarded sword high, caught the scimitar, and stepped around, bringing his pommel down across the half-orc's face. The thug staggered a beat, snorted, and slashed again.

The knight ducked, moving with all the grace of a master tumbler, and punched the flat of his sword into the half-orc's gut. He could have unsheathed the blade and disemboweled his foe, but instead he slammed the pommel into the thug's lowering chin. The half-orc spun senseless to the ground.

Fayne could have cheered to see her attacker thus beaten, but she saw the sentry nock an arrow and draw the fletching to his cheek. "'Ware!" she cried.

The knight turned toward her, taking the arrow in the shoulder instead of the throat. He staggered back a step, and Fayne's heart sank. The archer laughed—then cursed as the knight, undeterred by the wound, bounded forward. The archer fumbled with a second arrow.

As he charged, the knight shifted his grip to the sword hilt. He closed and whirled, blade coming free of the black lacquer scabbard in a silver blur. The sword slashed the bow in two, and the scabbard took the hapless archer in the jaw. He dropped like a stack of kindling.

The pale-faced man fell on the knight, lunging with his sharp nails stretched forth like knives. He'd been waiting arrogantly for his moment, and now it had come. Blue lightning arced around the man's claws, and Fayne realized—horribly—that they were one with his fingers, and not part of his gauntlets at all. A spellscar, she realized—the spellplague had bound razor steel into the man's hands and enhanced it with magic.

As Fayne watched, the malformed hands closed on her rescuer's steel helm, seeking to wrest it off. The knight wrenched free, but the man caught his left arm. The claws tore into the black leather, and Fayne saw smoke rising from the rent and smelled burned flesh. The pale man's face was rapt in frenzied glee. It was over, Fayne realized— such a wound would stun the knight, and then the spellscarred man would gouge out his throat.

She knew the knight would be in hideous pain, but he did not show it. Instead, he glared into the spellscarred man's face and the ugly smile faded. Then the helm slammed forward, crushing the 'scarred man's nose and sending him moaning to the ground.

The knight whirled back to Fayne. In one hand, he held the gleaming sword, which flared like a wand of silver flame. His left hand thrust the empty scabbard through his belt, then reached up to snap off the arrow in his shoulder. He winced only a little and made no sound. Through it all, Fayne never saw his eyes waver. They stayed cold and solid as ice.

She stood slowly—no sudden dramatics, and certainly not reaching for the knife she kept in her boot. When the knight didn't react, she realized he wasn't looking at her.

"Draw your steel," he said.

Across the chamber, Rath shrugged. He stepped forward from where he had been leaning on the wall—as he had throughout the duel. His smile was easy as he idly touched the hilt of his sword in its red lacquer scabbard. "Another time, if you prove worthy."

Rath moved to the center of the chamber. His posture did not threaten, but neither did he seem cowed.

"Stop," said the knight.

"I have done nothing," said Rath. He pointed to Kolatch, crawling toward the tunnel. "I think you have more pressing matters."

With that, the dwarf turned and—bending low in perfect balance—leaped into the air. He grasped the edge of a hole in the ceiling at least a daggercast above the chamber floor. Fayne blinked as he swung up into a tunnel shaft she had not seen before.

How could a mortal creature *move* like that—jump so high without a running start?

"Ye gracious gods," she said.

The knight looked after him a moment, then turned to the exit corridor.

"Kolatch," he said. His voice did not rise.

The merchant squealed, grasped his chest, and fainted dead away at the word.

Then Fayne watched, eyes widening, as the knight in the gray cloak bent low, tensing his legs, as though to follow Rath upward. Magic, surely—she thought. But . . .

She gave a wheezing sort of sigh and stumbled against the chamber wall, sliding down into the ever-present dungeon refuse. "Ooh, my head."

The knight appeared over her and his hand caught her under her arm. He cradled her like the helpless victim she only half-pretended to be. She felt such strength in his hands.

"Are you well enough to stand?" The cold voice broke her thoughts. "Are you bleeding?"

"My pride, perhaps," Fayne said, "and I shall need a new coat." She plucked at the garment, which was more muck than cloth, grimacing.

"Well," the knight bid her, and he turned.

"Wait!" Fayne caught the edge of his cloak and knelt at his side. "It could have gone worse for me. How can I thank you, my hero?"

As she spoke, her fingers brushed her necklace gently and let her illusory face shift ever so slightly. The bruises remained—his eye would stay on those—but her cheekbones rose higher, her eyes became a little larger and softer, and her lips swelled just a bit. She spoke more softly, her words weak and afraid.

In all, she became a bit more enticing—more the grateful damsel. She played upon his need—the need in all men—to protect. To feel strong and in control.

"Not necessary," he said, but she could feel his body relaxing as he considered her.

"How," Fayne pressed, "can I thank you?" She stepped closer—into his arms, should he raise them to embrace her. Most men wanted to, when she plied her charm—and most men did.

Her savior, to her brief disappointment, was not most men. He stepped back, out of her reach, and his sword hand moved toward her, interposing sharp steel. Its fierce glow had dimmed, but the blade still glimmered faintly.

"Does your blade call me dangerous, saer?" she asked, using the form of address for a noble knight of unknown rank. She looked him down and up. "Perhaps you should listen to it." She could see nothing of his face, but she was sure his cheeks would be reddening. Unless he had no shame—which she wouldn't mind either.

"These men." The cold voice startled her—the voice of a killer. "Do you know them?"

Before she could begin the explanation that came naturally, he held up a hand. "You are far too capable a woman," he said, "for this to be random."

Fayne grinned. "You noticed."

The knight's mask was impassive.

"Yes," she said. "I had arranged to meet their ignoble master— the dwarf, Arrath Vir, known to his friends and foes as Rath. Or so I'm told, at least." She kicked the nearest thug—the half-orc—who groaned. "These triplings I do *not* know."

The knight nodded, once. "And that one?" He pointed at the slain man.

Fayne shook her head. The truth was easy. "Our friend Rath dealt that death with his empty hand. However"—she smiled and stepped closer—"your hands need not be empty this night. My talents are other in nature—but no less moving."

The knight sheathed his sword. "You are rather forward," he remarked.

"Better than backward," she said, and she reached for his helmet.

The knight caught her arm and held it with a grip like steel. "No."

Fayne bristled at being thwarted but only smiled. "How am I to kiss my champion?"

"That would be difficult." He shoved her away, though not hard enough to hurt her. He turned and tensed his legs to leap.

"Wait!" she said. "At least a name!"

He looked over his shoulder.

Fayne shifted her weight and wrung her hands in a way that was very like a demure maiden. "Your name, saer, to remember for my prayers—and to ward off other knaves. A name to call in the night"—she laughed—"when I'm attacked, of course—so that you might save me."

He hesitated. "Shadowbane," the knight said.

She shivered in all the right ways. "Well met," she said. "I am Charl."

Shadowbane paused, and she got the distinct sense he was smiling. "No, you aren't."

Fayne put her hands on her hips. "And why would I lie?"

"I don't know, *Charl*atan," Shadowbane said. "Why would you?"

Fayne licked her lips. True, that had been an easy riddle. "Care to find out?"

He held her gaze for a moment, then jumped, blue-white flames trailing from his feet.

There was magic in his leap—of that Fayne had no doubt. It propelled him up like a loosed arrow. She knew that blue light—had seen it just a moment before: spellplague magic.

Spellscarred, was he? This Shadowbane? How intriguing.

Fayne couldn't help but marvel as he reached the ceiling and pulled himself over the ledge where Rath had disappeared. His movement was athletic—whereas Rath moved with unnatural grace, like nothing human or dwarf or anything like—Shadowbane moved very much like a *man*. Near the peak of human achievement, yes, but a man nonetheless.

Watching him, Fayne found breath difficult. She hated men who resisted her charms, and yet this Shadowbane lingered in her thoughts. She wanted another chance at him, when she could better prepare. He was a man who presented a great challenge.

Gods, how she loved challenges.

She looked to Kolatch, barely awake, who lay moaning and terror-dumb, and smiled.

She loved tricks as well.

FOUR

"Corrupt merchant attacked and magically disfigured!" shouted the boy who carried broadsheets at the corner of Waterdeep Way and the Street of Silver. He held up his wares: copies of the *Vigilant Citizen*. "Vigilante menace spreads in Downshadow—Watch denies all!"

Cellica, who could pass easily for a human girl in her bulky weathercloak, chuckled ruefully and shook her head. The halfling paid a copper nib for one of the long, broad scrolls—printed on both sides with ink that would smudge in the rain—and glanced at it. Apparently, some fool named Kolatch had come away with purple hair and beard yestereve.

She giggled.

"Brainless Roaringhorn heiress caught in bawdy boudoir!" cried a broadcrier for the acerbic *Mocking Minstrel*. "Scandal rocks house; says Lord Bladderblat—'typical'!"

"Undead stalk the nobility!" shouted a third, this one a girl for the infamous *Blue Unicorn*. "You can't see, you can't tell—they survive by bedding the living! Interviews and tales!"

Cellica skipped through Castle Ward, giggling at the worst news that was apparently fit to print. Most Waterdhavians called the drivel in the broadsheets ridiculous, but that hardly stopped them reading it. The printers would never go out of business as long as there was drink and stupidity and nobles to indulge in both.

She strolled west, then north along Waterdeep Way, breathing deeply the refreshing air of the bustling city. Waterdeep grew busy just after the gates opened at dawn, the streets choked with laborers and merchants, commoners and nobles alike. She bought a jellied roll and hopped up on a bench in Fetlock Court—in the shadow of the palace and Blackstaff Tower.

This was one of Cellica's favorite pastimes: watching folk. She watched nobles in particular, because they amused her. She found the way they walked comical: shoulders back, chest forward, staring down their noses at commoners, laborers, merchants, and any they saw as inferior. She giggled at the sharp tongues of lords and ladies in the street, took note of arguments, and laughed aloud when a seemingly delicate old lady seized a younger male relation by the ear and hauled him, flailing and protesting, to a waiting carriage. The gaggle of lordlasses he'd been striving to impress giggled until they saw Cellica also laughing. Then their laughter died and they stared coldly at her.

"Go on, off with you," Cellica said. Her lip crooked. She repeated, more forcefully: "*Go.*"

The young noblewomen stiffened, peering anxiously at one another. Then they shuffled away as though compelled, looking flabbergasted.

Cellica giggled. Folk tended to do what she said, if she said it forcefully enough.

The city raced by day in the warm light, and wouldn't sleep until long after the sun had gone down. Trade was the blood and bile of Waterdeep, as it had been for centuries. And everyone, regardless of country or creed, was welcome in these streets—so long as they brought good coin and a fair hand.

A fair hand was the less consistent of the two, and something Cellica read about every day. Setting aside the remains of her morningfeast, she unrolled the broadsheet—the *Citizen* was the most reputable—and read every tale of news, politics, and commerce in detail. Who was offering fair deals? Who stood accused of dirty trade or slavery? Who might be a spy for the Shades or Westgate or even the defunct Zhents?

This research was largely on behalf of her partner—gods knew he wouldn't do it *himself.* Looking for a target wasn't his firewine of choice; once he fixed on one, though, no man or creature could stand in his way.

So long as he had the right woman directing him, of course.

He would probably be getting back from his nightly ordeal now—collapsing into his bed at their tallhouse, not to wake until evening.

She worried that he rested enough, but she also knew that worry was futile. Damned if he would take her advice anyway.

Cellica finished with the *Citizen* and bought a few more broadsheets, including the *Daily Luck, Halivar's,* and even the *Minstrel.* This last (a bitter cesspool about corrupt Waterdhavian politics, lascivious noble houses, and shadowy merchant deals) hardly ever yielded anything of use. That day, its reporting of the Talantress Roaringhorn scandal—as told by the oh-so-noxious Satin Rutshear—curdled Cellica's stomach, so she crumpled the sheet and tossed it aside.

She much preferred the *North Wind,* which featured her beloved illustrations of fashionable garments and easy-on-the-eyes models, in addition to plenty of gossip about circles far above hers. As the *Wind* reported, the annual costume ball was upcoming at the Temple of Beauty on Greengrass, five nights hence.

"Oh, to be noble!" Cellica sighed, clasping the broadsheet to her breast. "Or at least rich."

After fantasizing a few moments, she polished off the last of the watered wine in her beltskin and hopped down from the bench.

With the business of "keeping atop Mount Waterdeep" done, she cut east down alleys and turned north up the Street of Silks, deeper into Castle Ward. These were narrow, less crowded streets—filled with fewer folk and more broken crates, rotting sacks, and other refuse. The people who lived here were poorer, many of them huddled in doorways and beneath raised walks. They looked at her with hungry eyes, and she fingered the crossbow-shaped amulet that hung at her throat. Others waved to her from festhalls just opening for the day.

Cellica pulled her hood lower to attract less attention. Few small folk appeared in this part of the city—gnomes and halflings usually kept their distance. Cellica happened to know, however, that her people were less a minority than the eye suggested. She slipped among the taller people, trying not to touch anyone. No one batted an eye or stayed her.

"Doppelgangers infiltrate houses of ill repute!" cried a small figure who appeared to be a human boy. "Welcomed by festhall madams for their general skills and adaptability!"

Cellica made her way toward the crier, who was not a boy but a round-faced halfling. Anyone who knew Waterdeep might see through his disguise, based on his wares. He was selling *Pleased Toes,* a set of tales written, printed, and sold exclusively by his kind.

"Good to see you, Harravin," she murmured to him. "Mum well?"

"Aye, Cele," he said. "When you coming back to do some more o' that cooking?"

"Soon." Cellica leaned against the wall next to him and took a broadsheet from his stack. She unfolded and began to read. While she did, coin changed hands.

"You can pay me back this month, aye," said Cellica.

"Cheers." Harravin grinned, then called, "Doppelganger whores! Some reported missing—test your husband to make sure he's your own!"

Cellica hurried down the alley. As she went, she heard a sound and looked up at the edges of the roofs above her. Water dripped off split, moss-covered roofs—old rainwater fell on her forehead and she wiped it off. She thought she'd heard . . . but no, of course not.

She gave a little smile and turned to look down the alley. A trapdoor, covered by a heap of dirty cloths and broken crockery, was set into the cobbles. She bent down. A soft thumping sounded from below, like a machine working in the distance.

She pulled open the trapdoor and a dozen bright eyes blinked up at her from smoky candlelight. Farther in, she saw a frame press working, turning out *Pleased Toes* and lurid chapbooks. A halfling turned toward the sudden light and wiped his forehead, removing a thick coating of black soot.

"Philbin," she said, nodding to him.

"Well," he said. "S'bout time th'tyrant of a paladin lets you out. Ready for second print!"

"Celly!" came a cry. The small ones within started cheering and hopping up and down.

"Well met," Cellica said. She climbed down a stout ladder, closed the trapdoor behind her, and joined her adoptive family.

The little halflings crowded around her, cooing and yipping like puppies. She saw their mother, Philbin's wife Lin, cooking a meal over the steaming frame press engine: eggs and sausage and toasted thin loaves. Her stomach growled.

"You've come for more coin, I take it," Philbin said. "And our free food too, eh?"

Though the gruff halfling patriarch didn't look it, he was one of the wealthiest merchants in Waterdeep—partly because he was such a skinflint.

Cellica drew a bottle from her satchel. "I brought wine."

Philbin rolled his eyes.

"Just in time for morningfeast!" said one of the little brothers, Dem.

"Silly!" said a halfling girl—Mira. "*Second* morningfeast!"

Cellica found peace among the halflings of the Warrens, one of the cities beneath Waterdeep. It wasn't home—that was the ruined city of Luskan, far to the north—but for a time, she could pretend.

At least until her tasks called her back.

FIVE

Perched on the corner of the desk, Araezra said, very clearly, "Ellis Kolatch."

"Ellis Kolatch." Kalen's monotone gave no indication of recognition.

Araezra sighed. Of *course* Kalen would be indifferent. The damned man was a stone.

They'd been taking their evening leisure hour—waiting for the Gateclose bells to sound, signaling the shutting of the gates for the night—before going out on another inspection. They were alone in the room, pointedly not speaking.

Though Kalen seemed calm, Araezra had been boiling with anxiety, wanting to talk but not to be the first to speak. Her nerves manifested in anger that went undirected at either Kalen or herself. Instead, she turned it against their commander.

Damned Commander Jarthay, who'd declined her request for day work. Twice-damned Jarthay, who'd argued so logically that more villainy would be afoot by night than day!

What she wouldn't give for a good invasion or riot to thwart—preferably incited by Shadovar spies or Sharran cultists or any of a thousand enemies of goodness in Faerûn. But no, it was a time of relative peace, and peace meant schemers and conspirators.

She'd take Kalen, of course—and Talanna, if she was at liberty—but she couldn't speak freely with Kalen then. She could now, though, if only he would pay attention to her.

Araezra set aside the locket with the half-done miniature she'd been painting in it: a gilded chamber, with light filtering through a flower-laced window. It was an amusing hobby—one perfectly suited for boring hours at the barracks between patrols.

She fixed her eyes on Kalen—on his hard, grizzled face with the constant layer of stubble, framed in the brown-black hair that fell in spikes. His oddly colorless eyes, like slits of glass, avoided hers, but she was not about to let go now that she'd got a reply out of him.

"Ellis Kolatch," she said again. "The crooked merchant we met yestereve."

"Ah." Kalen pushed the spectacles up his nose.

He'd been looking through Watch ledgers all day, much to Araezra's chagrin. He hadn't told Araezra why, and she hadn't asked.

"I'm told . . ." Araezra shifted her position so Kalen had to look at her. "Kolatch presented himself at the palace today in a frightful state—clothes a mess, eyes puffy—and demanded we lock him up for trade violations and dirty dealing."

Araezra's mouth turned up at the corners in a way she knew her admirers adored.

"You wouldn't happen to know aught of this?"

Kalen shrugged. He moved the ledger away from her and kept working.

Araezra frowned, then draped herself across his ledger, setting her face level with his. "Seems his hair and beard had turned the most frightful shade of purple as well. No?"

Kalen's eyes met hers, and she saw a little flicker in his face—a tiny tic in his lips. Was that anger, or a smile?

"Araezra," he said chidingly, "I'm working."

No one called her by her full name—no one but him, always so damned polite and cold.

She hated his formality when they were supposed to be at leisure. To set an example, she wore her uniform breeches and boots but not her breastplate or weapons. With her hair unbound and cascading in liquid black tresses around her linen chemise, she knew damn well how good she looked, and yet—confound the man—Kalen hadn't even noticed.

She'd never had this sort of trouble with a man. Usually, it was the opposite, and required a stout stick to fend away unwanted hands.

"Who are you looking for so intently?" she asked.

He looked at her over the rim of his spectacles. "Arrath Vir—a dwarf. No beard—turned his back on his blood, I suppose.

Suspected of crimes against the city and citizens."

"Why the interest?" she asked.

Kalen kept reading. Perhaps she was irritating him, or perhaps he was simply ignoring her—she had no way of knowing. Kalen kept his own counsel.

She tried again. "That scar, on your arm." She pointed to a long red-and-white mark, as though from a burn, visible out his left sleeve. "How did you come by that?"

He shrugged. "Clumsy with the simmer stew," he said. "At times it burns me and I don't realize, because . . ." He trailed off.

"I'm—I'm sorry," Araezra said. "I didn't mean to mention it."

"It's naught." He adjusted his sleeve over the burn.

Araezra sighed and looked at the ceiling. She wished she could talk to him without putting her boot between her teeth. And his illness . . . she wondered if he would feel it if she hit him in frustration. Likely not.

She tried a third time. "Kalen, there's a costume revel at the Temple of Beauty on Greengrass," she said. "I was hoping—er, I think a guard presence might—"

"If that is your order, Araezra."

Trying to hold in a scream, Araezra tapped her painted nails on the darkwood desk. Kalen turned back to his ledger, adjusted his spectacles, and scritch-scratched another note. She marked the ring on the third finger of his left hand—with a sigil of a gauntlet—but he turned another page and obscured her view before she could observe it more closely.

Frustrated, she picked up her locket and the delicate little brush and set back to work on painting the light through the window. Kalen's pen scratched. Araezra's teeth clicked.

Finally, she could take it no longer.

She rolled her eyes, threw the locket down on the table, and raised her hands. "Gods, Kalen! It's *Rayse*. How long have we worked together? You can't call me that?"

"If that's an order, Araez—"

"*Rayse*." She grasped him by the shoulder and he winced. "Bane's black eyes, Kalen—after what we've been through? After we . . ."

She cut herself off. Oh gods, had she almost just said that? Talanna was going to *kill* her.

But gods-burn-her, she couldn't help it. She—a woman infamous for her calm, unreadable face—just went to pieces around him.

"Araezra." Eyes calm, Kalen gave her a half-hearted attempt at a smile. "Must we?"

Her heart started beating faster. "Kalen, we should talk about this," she whispered.

"And say what?" He looked back at the ledger. "You were the one who ended it, not I."

"Only because—" Araezra scowled. "Kalen, only because you wouldn't . . . stlaern."

She expected him to correct her language, but he only shook his head. "Rayse, I told you about my illness," he said. "You know I don't . . . I can't. You knew that."

"You wouldn't hurt me." Araezra put a hand against his cheek. "I wouldn't let you."

He gave her a half smile. "It wasn't because I didn't want—"

The door opened, and his hand darted away from hers. Araezra almost fell from her seat but caught herself and stood, straightening her linen chemise and cursing herself for taking off her armor. The silvered breastplate lay on a nearby chair, next to her helm, the five tiny gauntlets denoting her valabrar rank staring at her like five sly, winking eyes.

She composed herself in a flash, exercising her iron self-discipline to the fullest.

Into the room came Talanna Taenfeather, still sporting the wild rack of horns woven out of her vivid hair. On her breastplate, she wore three gauntlets, identifying a shieldlar.

Talanna would have been fine company, but behind her strode an older man—thirty or so winters, brown hair, bright eyes, bemused smile—whom Araezra recognized only too well. Bors Jarthay's badge depicted a single gauntlet clutching a drawn sword—the sigil of a commander.

Talanna froze and looked first to Araezra, then to Kalen. Her smile curled in the way it did when she was about to say something particularly cutting. "Ooh," she crooned. "We're not interrupting aught, are we, Rayse?"

Araezra opened her mouth, but Kalen grunted no without looking up from his work.

"And what a shame that is," Bors added. He nodded to Araezra's breastplate and helm. "Taking our ease, lass?"

"My steel is always near to hand." Araezra smiled tightly. "Do I need to don it?"

"Your breastplate against *me,* Rayse? Nay!" Bors grinned. "I would hardly want to discomfort two of my best lady Watchmen." He nodded to Kalen. "Good day, Vigilant Dren."

Kalen looked up. He started to rise, stiffly, as though to salute, but Bors waved him down. The commander grinned at Araezra, but she refused to look at him.

"Need you aught, sir?" she started to ask, but Talanna rushed to Kalen's side.

"See this, Kalen?" On the forefinger of her left hand she wore a ring of interlocking golden feathers. "A gift of Lord Neverember." She smiled wryly. "The Open Lord's *passionately* in love with me, you know."

"Oh, don't be a dolt," Araezra said. "He knows your inclinations."

Talanna whirled, heat in her cheeks. "But a little banter hurts no one, aye?"

Araezra winced. Jealousy had prompted her tongue, she knew—she longed secretly to marry someone with power like that of Neverember, but *greater.* She wanted to wed one of the Masked Lords; the greatest, if possible. And then, with her husband's power, she could make right all the ills of the city. Rewrite laws to trap the guilty. Put together a secret wing of the Guard, who would reshape Waterdeep into a cleaner, safer, ordered place. Expunge the traitors, slavers, and other evils of which she knew very well. Little things.

She realized she'd lost herself in thought for a breath, and Talanna and Bors were staring at her. Kalen had gone back to work.

"Aye," said Araezra, "what prompted the gift of this ring, Talanna?" The use of her full name—rather than her pet name, Tal—was meant as a warning.

The red-haired woman grinned. "Well, I'm told the spell within is a safeguard if I fall from a great height—some call it 'feather light,' or 'feather float,' or something of the sort—that of course being a jest about—"

"—your last name, aye," said Bors. "But what occasion? Have I missed my sweetling's nameday?" He ruffled Talanna's hair, making the wires in the spikes click. "These are so glim."

"Damn them, then!" Talanna ducked out of his reach and began ripping the wires out. Araezra tried not to wince; Talanna was always so rough with her appearance.

"There," Talanna said when her wavy red tresses fell freely around her face. "As I said, 'tis a gift from Lord Neverember after my accident tenday before last."

Bors and Araezra winced.

Kalen, who looked up when the talking ceased, blinked at Talanna. "What happened?"

"She was chasing a thief from Angette's in Dock Ward," Bors said, "when she fell—"

"Jumped!" Talanna corrected. She indicated the ring on her right hand that gave her the power to jump great distances.

"—jumped from a building and broke her ankle," Bors said. "The Torm priests healed her, but not before the story got out. It was the talk of the city—our favorite little flame-haired Watch-lass, having taken a frightful spill."

Kalen nodded slowly. He looked to Talanna. "You caught the thief?"

"Faith!" she cried. "Why do you think I jumped? The fall broke more in him than in me."

Kalen nodded casually. "What of the thief at Kolatch's from yesterday?"

"Never caught that one," Talanna admitted. "Damned guttersnipe outdistanced me."

Araezra tapped her fingers on the desk, unhappy at being ignored.

"Getting slow in your old age?" asked Bors, gesturing at Talanna.

"Getting soggy in yours?" asked Talanna, gesturing at his midsection.

Araezra let loose a cough, more exasperation than throat clearing.

"Ah, yes," Bors said. "What brings us to your fine abode this eve? First, I need to borrow Kalen for a late evenfeast and thereafter. In his place, you will take Talanna to visit the walls."

"What?" Araezra asked. "But Kalen's *my* assistant."

"Second," Bors said without pause, "it has come to my attention that you need some aid in asking Vigilant Dren a certain question, Valabrar Hondyl."

Araezra's iron will broke. "What?" She looked wide-eyed at Talanna, who giggled. This was some jest of hers, Araezra realized.

Bors turned his eyes to the ceiling and swept his hands wide. "Can it be that the fair Araezra might be doomed to disappointment and apt to weep herself to a sweet, tender, and no doubt *lonely* sleep this night?" he asked. "Might not I be of some assistance in this—"

Araezra threw back her hair—an impressive flurry—and glared at Bors. "For the last time, Commander, nay. All the poetic words in the fair Realms couldn't get me into your bed."

Bors dropped a hand to the pouch that hung at his belt. "Even if I brought diamonds?"

Araezra glared even harder.

Bors moved his hand. "Well, then, I simply must woo you, lovely Araezra, with prodigious adoring looks." And he got right to it.

"Go on, Commander," Talanna said to Bors. "Tell him, already!"

"Tell him what?" Araezra looked at Talanna and mouthed: *You didn't.*

Talanna beamed innocently at her.

Araezra thought her face might explode. Kalen, gods burn his eyes, seemed nonplussed about the whole situation. He looked up calmly.

"Kalen, son," Bors said, puffing up to his fullest height.

"Commander?"

"I've been told Rayse will be on duty at the costume revel at the Temple of Beauty."

Araezra glared at Talanna, who smirked.

"Regarding the instructions of these lovely ladies," he said, "and knowing as I do that Rayse intends to ask you to go along as her escort, I've come to order you . . . don't go."

Araezra's mouth fell into a perfect O. "What?"

Talanna laughed aloud and slapped her knee, her jest completed.

"Sir?" Kalen asked.

"Honestly, if you took Rayse to the ball, it would be disastrous for morale," Bors said. "You can't imagine the number of broken hearts and spoiled nighttime fantasies I'd have to deal with. And no one wants weepy guardsmen." Bors shuddered. "So don't take her, even if she asks. I'm ordering you."

"Ah . . ." Kalen nodded. "Aye, sir."

"Now wait just a breath—" Araezra started, but they ignored her.

"Now that that's settled, Kalen," Bors said, "if you're finished up here, let's go have a drink at the Smiling Siren—just the two of us."

"It's never 'just two' at a festhall," Talanna quipped.

Araezra couldn't manage to produce words. She felt that if she spoke, she might explode.

"Away, good Kalen!" said Bors. "Unless, of course, you lovely ladies care to join us?"

Araezra fumed—at Bors, at Kalen, at everyone. "Mind yourself, Commander."

The commander winked at her. "Just us, Kalen. I'm sure the ladies can amuse themselves without us here. Though"—his voice lowered—"I'd love to watch that, wouldn't you?"

Kalen shrugged.

Araezra plucked up Kalen's discarded ledger to throw, but Bors was out the door—Kalen in tow—before she got the chance.

SIX

Night had fallen in the world above, but below—in the tunnels that ran rank with the creations of the mad wizard Halaster—darkness persisted regardless of the movement of sun or stars.

Shadowbane stalked from chamber to chamber in Downshadow. While he did not share any of the special visual acuity of elves or dwarves, his eyes were accustomed to the gloom, and in the presence of even the faintest torch down a corridor, he could see well enough. He could also, of course, create his own light by drawing his sword.

Hand on the worn hilt of Vindicator, he paused and listened. He heard footsteps, harsh breathing, and gentle words ahead, in a chamber that had once been some manner of living quarters. Who could have dwelt this far north in the Undermountain of the old world, he did not know—one of Halaster's legendary mad apprentices, no doubt.

He peered in and saw a single moving figure—a woman in a gray cloak—among several sprawled, moaning bodies. When her attention turned away from the corridor, he ducked into the chamber and climbed to a better vantage point. There he crouched, balanced atop a moldering wardrobe, and watched.

He'd been following the cloaked woman for some time, since she had entered by one of the northern shafts into Downshadow. He'd glimpsed her several times before and knew how to anticipate her comings and goings. This was the night he had chosen to catalogue her doings.

Likely she was a crooked merchant, seeking to peddle stolen goods. But if so, where were her warders? She could be here for no other reason—why would a citizen of the world above come down to Downshadow, alone, if it were not for some vile purpose?

Anyone other than himself, of course.

He watched from the secure, unseen top of the wardrobe as she went about her tasks. Here camped a band of delvers who had seen better days. Two men in armor wheezed pitifully, and a lad in leathers clutched at a torn belly and choked back sobs.

Only three. Shadowbane knew the ways of sellswords: they usually roved in packs of four or five. That meant they had left at least one of their number in the depths.

"Buh-back," the boy murmured. "Back away, lest I . . . I . . ." His hand feebly raised a dagger, then dropped it clattering to the floor.

The two armored men beside him only groaned.

As the woman knelt beside the bleeding boy, Shadowbane tensed, ready to spring to his defense. Adventurers were just as likely criminals as anything else, and his vigil in Downshadow did not include saving those who had brought a harsh fate upon themselves. Still, he would not watch idly while anyone murdered those who were weak or helpless.

She was casting a spell, he realized, but he recognized the words as similar to those of a healing chant his old teacher, Levia, had used many times. He relaxed his grip on Vindicator, though he kept his legs tensed, ready to leap.

Sure enough, healing radiance suffused the woman's body. Shadowbane watched, awed, as she pulled back her hood, revealing a fine-boned face of about forty winters and a forest of beautiful, red-gold curls. Such beauty could touch only a Sunite celebrant, he thought.

The priestess bent to kiss the injured lad on the lips, and healing radiance spilled from her and into his young body. The boy coughed and retched, and Shadowbane saw the wound in his belly close, to be replaced by smooth—albeit bloody—skin.

Jaded as he had become, Shadowbane still smiled at the beneficence of some folk.

The boy looked up in wonder at the priestess who had healed him. "My—my thanks, lady," he said. "I thought for sure, once we lost Deblin . . ."

She shook her head and pressed the boy's shaking hand to her cheek. "Sune watches over us all," she said. "I am Lorien. While I see to your companions, speak: what befell you?"

"A roving spell," the boy said. "It drains your strength away, so you can barely carry your own bones." As he spoke, the priestess healed the first man in armor, who hugged her around the knees, then promptly fell to a snoring slumber. "We escaped that, but then we ran afoul of a pair of those mad panthers with tentacles—the ones who aren't where you think."

Shadowbane knew such creatures: displacer beasts radiated magic that bent the light, making them dastards to strike. And with the lashing tentacles that grew from their shoulders, one needed to strike them quickly.

Lorien nodded as she bestowed a healing kiss on the second of the armored men, who coughed and stammered his thanks. "Are there more of you?" Lorien asked.

The boy's face went pale. "Deblin, a priest of Amaunator—he died when the beasts attacked—and our wizard, a girl called—called . . ." He sniffled, and Shadowbane saw his eyes fill with tears. "I was holding her hand when one mauled me. She disappeared. Can't be far!"

Lorien smiled and cupped his chin. "Never fear," she said. "I shall look for your lady love, and where love shines, there Sune shall guide us."

Shadowbane bit his lip. He'd found little enough of love—or Sune's guidance—along his path. Beauty often surrounded him, he admitted, but he allowed it only so close. He'd made too many mistakes.

The priestess pulled down her cowl and hurried down the tunnel where the boy had pointed.

Shadowbane followed, smoothly and silently. The weary delvers could only blink and question whether they had really seen a figure pass.

―W―

The priestess hurried north along a tunnel, heedless of traps. Shadowbane shook his head. What if an accident befell her in these depths? If he weren't following, how long would it be before someone found her?

Lorien paused abruptly, and Shadowbane had only an instant's warning to press himself into a crevice before she looked back, searching.

Impressive, that she'd heard him—perhaps she'd once been an adventurer herself.

A blue light flashed in a chamber at the end of the corridor, and the priestess turned to follow it.

Shadowbane pursued—at a greater distance this time.

As they moved, he got the distinct sensation they weren't alone in the tunnel. Something else was there—something hidden. Several times, he looked over his shoulder but saw no one. He kept his hand tight on Vindicator's hilt.

Finally, Lorien passed into the chamber where they'd seen the blue light. Shadowbane saw her stiffen, then creep cautiously toward something he could not see.

He picked up his pace, heedless of making sounds.

The chamber was wide and roughly square, lit by luminous pink and blue mushrooms. It had partly collapsed some years ago, and great shards of rock stuck out of the formerly smooth floor like stalagmites. A second entrance gaped in the west wall. The chamber was otherwise plain, except for two bodies in the northeast corner. They looked whole, though he could not be certain from his distance.

Strange. Though the room smelled thickly of blood and animal spoor, he saw no beasts, displaced or otherwise, that might have attacked the wounded adventurers. That was odd—why would monsters leave two perfectly good bodies lying in the chamber? Why, if they'd been somehow warded off, had they not chased the wounded and weak adventurers south?

A crude jest around the ante table was that one only needed to run faster than one's slowest delving companion.

He saw his answer, then: against the far wall were two bloody, ashen outlines of creatures like great cats. Shadowbane wondered what manner of magic had done *that*.

"All's well," Lorien was saying. "I'm here to help—not to hurt."

Shadowbane turned, but he could see only that Lorien was approaching someone. He heard another voice—younger, also female—speaking words in a tongue he didn't know. She sounded terrified and, he realized, familiar. He couldn't place the voice.

"Wait!" Lorien said. "Let me help you!"

He saw a flash of blue light, and then the speaker—whatever it had been—was gone. Shadowbane peered closer and saw Lorien kneeling to examine a blood-stained woman, heavy in build and wide of face, who lay in a puddle of blood-spattered robes. Something was odd about her skin, too—it seemed puckered and red as though burned by fire.

Lorien gave her a kiss of healing, and the wizard murmured wordlessly.

Then the back of Shadowbane's neck prickled, and he knew they were not alone.

Lorien looked up, though Shadowbane thought it impossible that she'd sensed him. She looked instead deeper into the cavern, where a short, wiry figure in a black robe perched atop a rock, contemplating her with his chin in his hands. The light of the mushrooms bathed his face in a cruel, fiendish light: Rath.

Shadowbane drew his sword halfway.

"Well," said the dwarf. "Now *that* was impressive. How did you hear me, I wonder?"

"I have a guardian, to serve me at need," Lorien said with a defiant toss of her curls.

At first, Shadowbane thought she must be speaking of him, but then he saw it, finally, in the light shed by the mushrooms. A shadow, unattached to anything else, seemingly of a tall and broad man, flitted across the floor, moving fast toward Rath.

Rath calmly raised a hand and spoke a word in a tongue Shadowbane did not know. Light flared from a ring he wore, bathing the room in a white glow. Lorien shielded her eyes.

The shadow hesitated, then fled into the darkness, and Shadowbane saw it no more.

"Simple enough," the dwarf said. "When one is prepared."

Rath stepped toward Lorien, his hand on his slim sword.

The priestess backed away, spreading her arms in front of the wounded woman.

Shadowbane cursed. He knew revealing himself was unwise, yet he couldn't just stand and watch. He stepped into the room, hand on his sword hilt. "Hold."

Lorien looked up at his appearance and her eyes widened. She gaped.

Rath hardly looked surprised. "Ah," he said. "Come to see if I shall fight you this time?"

Shadowbane drew Vindicator, whose length burst into silvery white flames. "Face me or leave this place," he said. "This lady is under my protection."

Rath eased his hand away from his sword hilt, but Shadowbane could see the violence in his eyes. "Very well," said Rath. Unassumingly, he walked forward.

Shadowbane drew back into a high guard, ready to slash down hard enough to cut Rath in two, but the dwarf just ambled toward him as though unaware of the danger. Shadowbane couldn't help feeling a little unnerved, but instinct seized him and he struck.

Rath stepped aside, fluid as water, seized Shadowbane's grasp on the sword, and elbowed him in the face. The blow would have been hard enough to shatter Shadowbane's nose and cheekbones, if not for his helm.

Stunned, Shadowbane staggered back, empty-handed, and the dwarf admired Vindicator in his hands. The sword's silvery glow diminished but did not go out.

"How amusing," Rath said, as power pulsed along the length of the sword, "that you think yourself worthy of me."

Shadowbane's helmet was ringing, or maybe that was his ears.

"Here," said the dwarf, lifting the blade in his bare hands. "Yours, I think."

Not thinking, the knight groggily reached out to take it.

Rath leaped, twisted over the sword, and kicked him once, twice, in the face. Shadowbane fell to one knee, while Vindicator clattered to the stone near Lorien.

The dwarf barked a laugh, then turned to Lorien. "Now, woman," he said. "We shall—"

But Lorien had seized the sword and tossed it toward Shadowbane.

The knight was already running forward, and he seized the blade out of the air. Rath leaped, and only his speed kept Shadowbane's slash from taking one of his legs. The dwarf landed two paces distant and Shadowbane pressed, slashing and cutting high and low. Rath ducked and weaved and snaked aside, dodging each swing.

Then Shadowbane saw irritation flash across the dwarf's face, signaling that the duel no longer amused him. The dwarf dropped low, knees bent, hands at his stomach. Shadowbane pulled Vindicator back to block.

Putting all the force in his compact, powerful body into one blow, Rath slammed the heels of his palms into the flat of Shadowbane's sword as though it were a shield. The blade slammed into Shadowbane's chest, and the force sent him back through the air and onto one knee. As though with a great maul, the dwarf had knocked him a full dagger toss away.

His face calm, Rath looked down at his black robe, where Vindicator had cut a single slash below his simple wool belt. He fingered the cut, frowning.

Shadowbane coughed and levered himself up on the sword.

"You yet stand." Rath rose, a smile on his smooth, handsome face. "Good."

Calling on the power of his boots to enhance his leap, Shadowbane lunged, crossing the distance in one great step, and slashed down, as though to cut his foe in two.

Vindicator sliced only air and sparked off the stone as Rath leaped. The dwarf wrapped his legs around Shadowbane's head, twisted, and tossed the knight back—this time even farther. Shadowbane rolled as he landed and kicked onto his feet.

The dwarf landed lightly and beckoned with one languorous hand.

Shadowbane obliged. He darted forward, sword reversed as though for a high thrust. Rath sidestepped, just as Shadowbane expected. Exploding out of the feint, he spun toward the dwarf, slashing out and across rather than thrusting.

He had not expected the dwarf to be so fast. Rath ducked and, capitalizing on his low gravity, plowed into Shadowbane, driving him out of his spin and onto the ground.

The knight tried to rise, but Rath leaped onto the flat of Vindicator, which lay across his chest. He shifted his feet, caught the sword between his toes, and kicked it away, where it skittered into the shadows, its light still blazing.

Rath's eyes weren't amused. He bent down, pulling back his fist to crush Shadowbane's head against the stone. "Enough of this," he said.

"I agree," said a feminine voice from behind them.

Rath and Shadowbane looked, and there stood Lorien Dawnbringer, divine radiance shrouding her. If she had been lovely before, she was now truly beautiful—fantastically so, glowing with a force and grace not given to mortals. Shadowbane could not look directly at her.

The dwarf danced off Shadowbane and leaped toward her, but then stopped and lowered his fist, unable to approach her aura of majesty.

"Run," Lorien said, and her words bore the weight of royal command. "Flee this place as fast as you can, and do not stop running until your legs fail you."

The dwarf shivered, fighting against her will.

"*Run!*" Lorien commanded again.

With an angry snarl, the dwarf turned and streaked toward the east tunnel. He moved so fast and with such grace that Shadowbane could hardly believe him a mortal creature.

He looked up. The priestess's figure no longer seemed quite as bright, but she was still almost blindingly beautiful. She reached toward him. "Lorien," she said.

"Shadowbane." He stared at her proffered hand.

"Come," she said. "I shan't hurt you—you just saved me, did you not?"

"You—" he said. "You're not going to command me to remove my helm, or the like?"

She laughed then, and the sound was like cascading water in a nymph's cove. "Of course not," she said. "If you're wearing that helm, then you must have your reasons. Though"—she pursed her lips—"though it isn't horrible scarring, is it? That would almost be a chapbook, right there. The priestess and the masked horror."

She grinned, and Shadowbane realized it was a jest. Warily, he put his hand in hers, and she helped him to his feet.

"You're hurt," she said. She pursed her lips. "I can heal you, if—"

Shadowbane tapped his helmet.

"Aye," she said. "Well then, my good knight." She curtsied girlishly, but thanks to the divine grace that lingered about her, it seemed straight out of the palace court.

"Well done," he murmured. "Though you might have cast some of those dweomers *before* he kicked the piss out of me." His cheeks felt hot. "Forgive my rough manners."

"I can swear like a sailor in my rages," she said. "It's unlikely 'piss' will offend my 'virginal' ears. Speaking of which—" She hugged him tightly before he could elude her.

"Ah, lady?" he asked, confused and more than a little uncomfortable.

"My thanks," she said against his chest. "If you hadn't delayed him so long, I couldn't have cast as many spells as I needed to send him away."

"I delayed him?" Shadowbane said. "You mean—with my face?"

"Aye." She hugged him tighter. "That."

To distract himself from how good she felt against him, Shadowbane looked at the injured wizard, who was breathing regularly, then at the burned shadows on the wall and wondered what might have done that. Could that wizard lass have managed such a spell? It didn't seem likely, if her band had fled from the displacer beasts.

He considered the dwarf and Lorien's shadowy defender. Rath's ring had only scared the creature away, not harmed it. And where had that shadow come from?

Too many questions, and he couldn't decide which to ask.

Shadowbane's ears perked up, and he became aware of footsteps coming toward them. "Lady Lorien?" came a distant, male voice.

"Oh, shush! She'll just *hide* from you." The voice was feminine, closer, and familiar.

"Shush, both of you!" came a quiet command.

Time to go. Shadowbane pulled away, but Lorien caught his hand.

"You saved me, and for that I am grateful," she said. "If I cannot give you a kiss, as the tales demand, then"—she pressed a small, pink scroll into his belt—"my temple is holding a revel a few nights hence, and I should be honored if you would attend."

"Lady," said Shadowbane, but she put a finger to his helm, over his lips.

"It is a costume revel," she said. "Famous heroes of the old world and the new—come as yourself, if you will. The invitations have no names, so even I will have no way of knowing you, saer." She smiled. "Your secret is safe."

Shadowbane wasn't sure what to say. He put his hand over hers.

Then, when he heard a gasp from behind them and reached for his empty scabbard, he realized he hadn't reclaimed his sword from the shadows.

SEVEN

Araezra hated these sorts of assignments, down in the dark and dank. But the Watch had been doing less and less duty in the sewers and Undermountain, leaving it to the more highly trained—and paid—Guard. She was serving the city, in a way, though she really wished nobles wouldn't get these crazy ideas and go vanishing down into the underworld alone where the Guard had to go fish them out.

She and Talanna trudged along the musty corridors of Downshadow, along with two other guardsmen, Turnstone and Treth. Best that Kalen hadn't come—he'd have been out of his element, and Araezra worried about him in these situations. It wasn't his spirit or his heart, but his body—his illness, after all, didn't permit much in the way of peril.

Not that Turnstone or Treth made her feel much better in a desperate battle. Gordil Turnstone was a wise and stolid guardsman, but well past his prime. His hair and great mustache were white from decades on the streets. Bleys Treth, on the other hand, was a skilled—if overeager and quick to draw—swordsman, but he'd seen well over forty winters. He'd been a hired champion in his youth, called "the Striking Snake" for his speed, and still retained some of his youthful charm and dash, but all the smiles in Faerûn didn't make up for age.

Araezra and Talanna were the youngest and most vigorous of the four. Talanna wore her light "chasing" armor, styled for running and leaping. Her long sunset hair was unbound, in contradiction of Waterdeep fashion, for two reasons, both to do with Lord Neverember. For a first, he liked to point her out to dignitaries by her red-burning curls. Second, he liked to see it tumble when they flirted, which they did shamelessly.

Araezra was glad to have the shieldlar at her side. She valued

Talanna's company and her martial skills—in spite of her oft-rambling tongue. As at that moment, for instance.

"Honestly, Rayse, you should be more careful who you wink those lovely black eyes at," Talanna said. "The men of Waterdeep can take only so much, you know."

Araezra groaned. Talanna always thought her choices could be better. Not that Talanna ever advised prudishness in romance—only selectivity.

"I welcome your words, but I shall keep my own counsel as regards affairs of my heart," she said.

"Heart? Nay—I was hardly speaking of such lofty *affairs*. I was aiming a bit lower."

Talanna made a sly and scandalous sort of gesture, and Araezra shot her gaze to Treth and Turnstone. The men seemed, conveniently, not to be looking.

"For true, though," Talanna whispered, "you ought to ward yourself. I have seen how you look at Kalen, and I've told you time and again . . ."

" 'Romancing anyone in the Guard, Watch, Magistry, or Palace is a grave mistake as well as improper,' " Araezra quoted from the Talanna Taenfeather rulebook. She'd learned well the value of dampening jealousies and avoiding entanglements among the city's elite. "I'm well—you needn't worry, *Shieldlar*."

Talanna pinched up her face. "Ooh, citing rank, are we? I see someone's a bit touched."

Araezra ignored that. It wasn't particularly proper, this repartee on duty, but their friendship ran too deep. It was like sisterhood.

"He's just a man, Rayse," Talanna observed.

"Who?" Araezra's blush belied her feigned ignorance.

"Don't try to deny it," Talanna said. "You're still sweet on him."

"Look, it's over, aye?" Araezra said. "Just let it pass."

"Honestly, though—is it him? Poor bedroom play, I think."

"No," Araezra said. Then, blushing more, she added, "I mean, no, I wouldn't know, because we never—"

"Right, right," Talanna said. "And that's why you get so flustered whenever I ask."

She signaled Treth and Turnstone to halt and caught Araezra's arm. She leaned in closer.

"Just tell me one thing, aye? Is it yea—" She held up her hands, about the length of a dagger apart—"or yea?" She brought her hands closer together.

"That's . . . that's none of our business," said Araezra. "Gods curse you!"

"Ooh," Talanna murmured. She brought her hands even closer. "Aye?"

"I am not having this conversation," Araezra whispered. She looked back, where Treth and Turnstone were watching them closely. "Belt up, men!"

Turnstone coughed and looked down, as though interested in his boots. Treth snickered.

Talanna poked her. "So I'll just have to seduce him myself if I want to find out, aye?"

Araezra blushed fiercer than before. "I'll have you flogged in the public square for this."

"Better not have Jarthay do it." Talanna grinned. "He'd enjoy it a bit too much."

"I mean it," Araezra warned.

"Ha! No, you don't." Talanna laughed.

Araezra scowled. "No, I suppose I don't."

Talanna squeezed Araezra's hand reassuringly. "Love is for fools, sweetling!"

"Good thing I'm not a fool." She waved to the men. "Swords forward!"

As they crept through the tunnel, Araezra wondered if Talanna's words didn't hold a ring of truth.

She remembered very clearly when first she had met Kalen Dren, on a raid in Uktar last year, back when he'd been a Watchman on the streets of Dock Ward. In her six years in the Guard, since she had joined at fifteen, never had she seen a man so determined and deadly—at least, not on *her* side of a raid. In his full helm, he'd waded into combat unhindered and unafraid, his eyes cutting through as many men as his sword. During the battle, he had saved her life from a stray arrow by taking it in his own chest.

She hadn't seen his face before the healers had taken him away, but his eyes haunted her dreams for nights after. She learned that Kalen had survived his wounds and was resting at the barracks, healing naturally. When she'd protested, his superiors had explained that letting him heal without magic was a rare reward for valor in the raid; he seemed to loathe anything but emergency magic, and only grudgingly accepted the Watch healers. He preferred to live with his scars, it was said, as a mark of pride.

She visited his bedside and was surprised at his youth: he was hardly older than herself. She'd talked with him for the day and into the night, long after aides had told her to let him rest. Kalen had merely waved them away, so they could speak in private.

In Kalen, Araezra had found someone like herself—someone who burned with the desire to fix the ills of Waterdeep. He wanted nothing more than to find and punish the guilty. He told her of a vow he had made to himself as a child—never to beg. All the while, his eyes had stared through her to the frustrated soul beneath—weighing what they found there, like something more than human. His eyes had made her shiver, but not with fear.

Was her desire really so surprising?

She'd been due for promotion to valabrar—the youngest ever to hold the rank—and she insisted Kalen come with her as her aide. For a time, she thought they could be much more, but he had refused her every attempt in that regard. When finally she confronted him, he told her of his illness, and Araezra's heart broke. She would have stayed with him thereafter, but his eyes were so sad—so frustrated—that she had let their short-lived romance fade.

She remembered his vow and knew that for her to beg would shame him.

As his physical prowess diminished, she'd kept him in service as her aide, thinking that he would want the post but would never ask. She'd thought it would do him honor, but now she wasn't sure. As a caged lion might relax but still see the bars, so might a wild beast waste away at the center of his pride, knowing that he has outlived his days of ferocity.

Nor was she sure that her motivations had been entirely selfless in awarding that assignment.

She had confessed to herself that she still desired him—confessed it every day. It was not love, exactly, but she wanted him to crave her, too—to show her anything but cold distance.

"I see that gleam in your eye," Talanna said. "Honestly—'twas but a simple question . . ."

"This isn't the time," Araezra snapped. "You're sure the boy pointed in this—"

Then she almost jumped out of her mail breeches when Bleys Treth cupped his hands around his mouth and shouted, "Lady Lorien!"

"Shush!" snapped Talanna. "She'll just hide from you."

"Aye, Shieldlar," Treth said sourly.

"Shush, both of you," Turnstone said. "You'll only call monsters or thieves."

Giving a duelist's sneer, Bleys spread his hands. "Let them come—I've my steel." He tapped the heel of his hand smartly on his sword hilt.

"Shush, all of you," Araezra growled. "Did you see yon radiance?"

A bright white light flashed in the chamber at the north end of the tunnel. They heard the clash of steel—a duel, she thought. She put her hand on her sword hilt and nodded. The others did likewise, and Talanna plucked a pair of throwing daggers from her belt.

Araezra waved, and they picked up their steps. She heard two voices, one a familiar soft soprano, the other a rolling bass.

Araezra and Talanna stepped into the chamber. A man in black leathers and a tattered gray cloak stood before them. His face was anonymous, hidden behind a full steel helm. In his arms was the very noblewoman they sought, the priestess Lorien Dawnbringer.

Araezra gasped.

"Away from her, knave!" shouted Talanna, hefting her daggers to throw.

"Hold!" Araezra said, half a heartbeat too late.

The man shoved Lorien down and dived to the side. One of Talanna's blades whistled harmlessly past where the priestess had been, and the other sank into his left bicep. Unhindered and unarmed, he ran toward them.

"Hold!" she shouted. "Down arms—you too, Talanna!"

No one listened. Bleys Treth snapped his blade out and lunged with the speed that had once earned him his moniker, but his target parried with an empty black scabbard. Treth twisted this out of his hands with an expert circle and cut back at his hip, but the man leaped like a noble's stallion over the last fence before the finish.

Araezra watched, gaping, as he soared over their heads and darted down the south tunnel.

"I've got him!" Talanna ran, drawing another blade as she went.

Araezra and Turnstone ran to Lorien. Turnstone searched warily for another foe, while Araezra knelt at the priestess's side.

"Are you well, my lady?" Araezra asked without ceremony. "Did he hurt you?"

"No," the priestess said. "I came here to spread Sune's healing, and yon knight protected me." Her cheeks were flushed. "Shadowbane . . . he means us no ill."

Shadowbane. Araezra shivered.

She considered whether the priestess had been deceived. They might have just saved her from a charming—but very dangerous—attacker. Or perhaps he truly had aided her.

Regardless, he had run, and in her experience, innocent men didn't run.

"Come with us," Araezra said. "We will deliver you safely to the city above."

The guards nodded and Araezra looked to the tunnel, considering what to do next.

"Wait!" Lorien pointed to the north wall. "His sword."

There lay a shimmering blade of silvery steel, a hand and a half longer than a typical adventurer's sword. Araezra's eyes widened and her hand drifted toward it unbidden.

Then she heard Talanna's triumphant cry from down the tunnels and remembered herself. "Confiscate that," she ordered, and Turnstone moved to claim the sword.

Araezra looked between the two guards, frowning.

"Well?" she asked, pointing. "Which of you jacks will go after them?"

Treth ran his hand through his hair. "A snake strikes at short distances, not long ones," he said. "At my age, I'm like to be no faster than Gordil, here. In fact—"

Turnstone, with his grim face and white mustache, shrugged.

Araezra sighed. "Well, *well*." She pulled at the clasps of her breast-plate, thrusting it open to the belly. Turnstone's eyes almost popped and Treth just smiled. "Turn, jacks."

They did—though she could swear Treth was still watching.

Araezra shrugged out of her coat-of-plate, revealing her sweat-plastered chemise. It was a thin, short affair that kept her cool under her uniform armor—to which the padding was attached—but it was hardly modest, particularly when sweaty. She rolled her eyes and positioned the straps of her harness where they offered the most cover—and the best support. Sometimes, Araezra wished she'd been born a boy.

"Well," she said, tying her hair back.

The guards turned. Turnstone had the decency to blush, while Treth snickered. Araezra threw her armor at the Snake's chest, blowing the air out of his lungs.

"Ward her well," Araezra said, nodding at Lorien. "Deliver her to the temple, then meet at the barracks. Unless you happen across Talanna or me—in that case, aid."

She seized the silvery sword out of Turnstone's hands and looked to Treth. "Scabbard."

Treth handed her Shadowbane's scabbard.

Araezra sheathed the sword and stuck the scabbard through the straps on her back, securing it with her belt. She made sure that her hips could move freely. She wasn't sure why she needed Shadowbane's sword, but something compelled her to take it. Then, tapping her watchsword hilt smartly in an ironic salute, she sprinted down the corridor where Shadowbane and Talanna had gone.

Talanna would catch him, all right, unless he could outrun the fastest woman in Waterdeep. Araezra wasn't sure, though, what would transpire when she did catch him. Likely, she would need support, and quickly.

This was ridiculous—running through Downshadow so indecently. If this didn't end terribly, she would look into a new suit of armor: a light, balanced harness like the sort Talanna wore, crafted for speed and mobility.

For the moment—well, Araezra only hoped the chase wouldn't take her where any citizens might be.

EIGHT

Araezra ran south after the sounds of footfalls. She prayed to Tymora that she'd picked the right direction and wouldn't end up a dragon's late-night meal. Fortunately, she saw Talanna's bright orange hair fly around a corner twenty paces ahead, so she ran on.

Shadowbane tried to flee deeper into Undermountain, but Talanna was chasing him back toward the main chamber of Downshadow.

Good, Araezra thought—at least we won't lose him in the tunnels.

Ye gods, but they were fast. Talanna and Shadowbane tore through chamber after chamber, brushing past the injured delvers they'd found, careening through empty rooms, denying Araezra the chance to gain on them.

Not once or twice but *thrice* they startled sentries and adventuring bands in tunnels and chambers Araezra and the Guard had avoided. Every time they caught the eye of a sentry and blazed like hellhounds through the midst of their camp, the sellswords and rogues would scramble up only in time for Araezra to appear. They met her with blades, cudgels, and even spells a-ready, confusion running through their ranks.

"Waterdeep Guard!" she cried for the first such band, and they managed only fumbling swings at her as she ran past, panting, her long tail of black hair flying. "Stand aside!"

She drew her sword but didn't bother to block or parry—she kept running, heedless, and leaped the delvers' cookfire to scramble down the opposite tunnel.

The second such band actually stayed her a moment, where a quick clash of swords and a well-placed kick to the nethers laid low an agile hunter. As she tore open the door Talanna had left swinging, the archer of that group fired an arrow that rustled Araezra's hair and shattered harmlessly off the wall. She had no time to delay.

The third band, composed almost entirely of young noble fops and a single plain-faced lass in the boiled leather of a delver scout, just stared at the flesh Araezra had bared from under her armor. As she ran past, thanking Tymora they had not attacked, Araezra saw the young woman slap one of the lordlings across the face. It didn't break his stare.

As she ran on, the valabrar cursed inwardly, cheeks burning, and wondered how many dreams of the next few nights would star a dark-haired, half-naked swordmaid.

These thoughts stole her concentration. Bursting into a new chamber, panting, Araezra slammed into Talanna, who had halted in her pursuit. Shadowbane, whom she had cornered, darted into an eastern passage as the women fell atop one another.

"Aye, Rayse!" said Talanna. "He's getting—" Her startled eyes drifted to Araezra's all-but-naked torso, and her cheeks went bright red. "Uh. Sorry!"

They fumbled apart and Araezra scrambled up. She forced her legs to carry her after Shadowbane. She saw his gray cloak flick around a corner and darted that way. Talanna, being much faster, caught up quickly.

They sprinted from chamber to chamber. Most were empty but for abandoned lean-tos and rubble, but in some they flew past sword-swingers and spellweavers, packs of monsters and flaming traps. Every time, they barely glimpsed Shadowbane ahead, disappearing around this corner or that. If they slowed even a touch, he would escape.

They crossed through an especially long chamber filled with clashing blades, screams of pain, and trails of sparks and lightning. Half a dozen warriors wielding the various steel of a rag-tag collection of dungeon delvers were fighting a whole horde of shambling, mindless zombies. Blood and limbs spattered the walls—much of it undead, some of it fresh. The adventurers fought and howled against the walking, flailing dead.

The room was outfitted with two rows of thirteen thrones stretching the length of the room. Zombies that stitched themselves together every time they were destroyed would make their way to the thrones. Three of the great chairs had been blasted to rubble over the centuries, and the zombies that approached those only flopped disconsolately to the floor.

Araezra recognized that hall from whispers among the Guard—the Sleeping Kings, it was called. Most sensible folk avoided the room, but few of the sellswords who descended into Downshadow were sensible.

"This is madness!" Araezra shouted to Talanna.

"Look!" Talanna pointed at Shadowbane, who was creeping along the fringe of the room unmolested. The brawl had slowed him, though, and he was only twenty paces ahead.

With a tight nod, Araezra and Talanna plunged into the thick of it, hacking their way through the undead to continue the chase. Swords bright with firelight, blood splashing everywhere, they fought their way across.

They had no sooner stepped near one of the thrones than Araezra heard a grinding of ancient gears. "Rayse!" Talanna cried.

The floor dropped out from under Araezra's feet, and she would have fallen had not Talanna grasped her wrist. Adventurers screamed and tumbled down, draped with the moaning, wrestling corpses animated by the room's fell magic.

Looking around, Talanna could see that most of the floor had dropped away, leaving the thrones on their bases standing like islands around the chamber. From the appearance of the floor and the sounds of the machinery, the trap had been designed as part of the original room.

Araezra dangled over the pit, clinging desperately to Talanna's hand. Her watchsword had slipped from her grip and fallen into the pit along with the trap's other victims.

She looked toward the exit—only two thrones away—where Shadowbane stood watching them. Inexplicably, he had paused in his flight, as though deciding whether to flee or stay and aid them. Araezra tried to catch his eye, but he looked away.

"Ready?" Talanna asked, teeth gritted. The strengthening gauntlets on her wrists glittered, enhancing her natural power.

Araezra realized what she meant to do. "What? No! Don't you even *think*—"

But Talanna strained, swung Araezra back, then threw her toward the next platform. Araezra uttered a tight scream but caught herself at the throne's base. It blew the air from her lungs, but she hauled herself up to discover a zombie shambling toward her, its eyes jaundiced yellow.

Leaping through the air, Talanna kicked it in the head, driving it off the platform and into the pit. Araezra pulled herself up and they stood on the platform, shaking and panting. Shadowbane waited on the opposite ledge, cloak fluttering around him.

"What's he doing?" Araezra asked. "Why isn't he running?"

Talanna shook her head. She gestured at the gap, which was as long as a dagger cast. Araezra nodded. As one, they braced for it, ran, and leaped.

With the aid of her magical ring, Talanna made the jump easily enough, but she slipped on loose rubble and fell with a crash. Araezra's feet faltered on the edge and she reeled back over the pit. Her heart froze.

Then a gauntleted hand caught hold of her arm and steadied her.

She looked up into Shadowbane's face, covered by his helm, but he averted his eyes. He pulled her away from the dangerous drop-off.

The three paused for many heartbeats—Araezra panting, Talanna kneeling and flexing her sore arms, Shadowbane standing aloof. He didn't seem able to meet their eyes.

"Don't run," Araezra said. She felt the hilt of Shadowbane's sword at her hip, slung crosswise across her back. "We mean you no—"

Talanna lunged from behind him, but Shadowbane eluded her hands. He whirled, slapping her in the face with his cloak, and ran into the next tunnel.

Talanna and Araezra looked at one another, then bounded after him.

>=W=<

On Shadowbane's heels, they burst into the chamber they had descended to reach Downshadow—a vertical shaft beneath a popular, centuries-old tavern.

Other than the Knight 'n Shadow, this place saw the most traffic into and out of the caves and tunnels. The hounds of Downshadow who stalked the Waterdeep night didn't use such a visible entrance, so the bottom of the shaft was empty.

Shadowbane leaped up, bounced off one wall and then the other, and grasped the harness at the end of a long rope that was used to lower folk into Undermountain—often at the Watch's behest for crimes against the city, but sometimes by request for fools with more greed than sense.

Shadowbane dangled a moment, twenty feet over their heads, then began to climb.

"Tal!" hissed Araezra, but the shieldlar was already moving.

Talanna hurled two daggers into the opposite wall. The fine adamantine edges sank into the stone easily, one at chest level, the other higher. She bounded up one, then the other, then pulled a third blade from her belt and stabbed it into the wall above. She grasped the knife below and snaked it up to jab higher. In this way, wiry arm muscles bulging, the red-haired guard pulled herself up dagger by dagger, as Shadowbane scaled the rope.

It was a bow shot to the top of the well—a long, hard climb.

At the bottom, Araezra shivered, panting at the speed of the chase. She wanted to pursue, but she was helpless without means to climb—or fly.

She seized the lowest of Talanna's daggers from the wall and felt for Shadowbane's sword on her back—still tightly secured. Then she looked up.

Long breaths dragged on, and she heard the click and scrape of Talanna's daggers as she climbed ever higher. The strength of that woman . . .

Shadowbane gained the tavern first, of course, and Araezra heard distant, startled murmurs of patrons at their drink. Talanna reached the top and pulled herself over the lip of the shaft. "Waterdeep Guard!" came Talanna's shout. "Lower the harness! With haste!"

Araezra winced, thinking of the stir she would cause when she appeared, half-dressed as she was. "Tal!" she shouted.

Sounds of a scuffle followed, then a feminine voice swore loudly. A red-fringed head poked over the wall far above. "Rayse! He's going to the street—I'll stop him!"

"Don't even think it!" Araezra shouted. "That's an order!"

Talanna bit her lip, then disappeared back into the tavern.

"Damn it, Tal!"

The harness came slithering down. Grasping the dagger between her teeth, Araezra rubbed her hands together, then leaped to grab hold. She hung on as it was pulled slowly—too slowly!—toward Waterdeep.

As Araezra reached the top, she swung free of the harness and planted her feet on the tavern floor. She ignored the startled and curious looks of patrons as she ran to the door. Talanna was nowhere to be seen, and if she didn't know better . . .

One of the patrons—a white-faced noble lad—gawked at her and pointed out the door. "They—they were fighting, lady, and—and they ran that way!"

Araezra pushed through the door of the Yawning Portal tavern and looked down the dark street—and cursed. "Oh, Hells."

She watched as Shadowbane leaped from one roof to another, running east along the rooftops toward Snail Street. Talanna, her red hair gleaming in the moonlight, sprinted after him.

Araezra darted into the chilly Waterdeep night and streaked after, following along the city streets.

>===W===<

Waterdeep's sky was clear that night, and an almost full moon and Selûne's tears shone down to light the streets. The night was very late—or very early, depending on one's perspective—and drunken lordlings were making their way back to their villas, where servants would aid them (perhaps along with new-met lasses, or possibly other nobles) into their beds. Meanwhile, the common folk—who had to earn an honest living—were rising to begin the day, making dough for the ovens or gathering eggs to sell at market.

Dawn was naught but a small bell distant, and pale light glowed at the eastern horizon. It was still a time for rest before the gates opened and the important business of coin gathering—and spending—began anew.

In Dock Ward, however, there was no such tranquility.

"You stupid, stupid—Tal!" Araezra shrieked as her friend leaped over the narrow thoroughfare between Belnumbra and Snail Street.

Talanna barely made the jump, tumbled, and got up to run again. She turned south to follow Shadowbane, and they ran down Snail Street. Despite its name, nothing was slow about the street that night.

Araezra, heart thundering in her throat from weariness and terror, ran on, panting. The damp chill of Waterdeep clung to her sweat-soaked, bare shoulders.

Talanna leaped from rooftop to rooftop in pursuit of Shadowbane, whose gray cloak streaked behind him like a pair of wings. Gods, the man was fast, if he could outpace Talanna. Araezra knew magic had to be at work, probably in his boots—no living man could run that fast or jump that far. Sure enough, she saw a slight blue glow lingering around his feet.

The few folk on the streets—laborers, mostly—peered at her curiously, but Araezra put her head down and forced her legs to carry her. At least she was in Dock Ward, where frenzied chases and loud drunken disruptions were common in the early hours of pre-dawn. In the finer wards, Araezra would be reprimanded for disrupting the peace, for sure.

Gods, she was tired.

They ran past the Sleepy Sylph tavern on the left. Araezra's heart almost stopped when Shadowbane seemed to fly across the alley between two buildings, and Talanna didn't hesitate to make the jump after him. Still, they continued their chase.

Araezra ran on, narrowly avoiding pedestrians and carts and broadcriers who were just setting themselves to morningfeasts of simmer stew in round loaves. At the sight of her, the older folk gawked and the younger giggled. This, more than anything else, made her cheeks burn.

They passed another tavern, The Dancing Pony, and then Ralagut's Wheelhouse, where Araezra ran up an unhitched wagon and jumped off the other side before pounding her way down the street. Her lungs felt like fire in her chest, but she kept running, her eyes scanning on high.

Shadowbane leaped over the next street, Talanna just behind him.

Surely she was tiring. Araezra thought she could hear the woman panting and wheezing for breath, even from so far away. They were going so fast and leaping so far . . .

At the end of the block, Snail Street curled east and south. At that juncture, a street from the west—Fish Street, named for its vendors, the finest place for a stringer of the morning catch—met Snail Street. It was a broad intersection, much wider than . . .

Gods, Araezra realized. "Tal! Tal, 'ware!"

Shadowbane ran across the roof and leaped—soaring like nothing human—all the way to the other side. The roof was lower there, and he barely caught the edge. Araezra saw him land and roll, and he looked back at his hunter.

"Tal!" she screamed. "*Stop!*"

Too late.

Talanna reached the edge of the building and leaped, and for one heart-wrenching moment, Araezra thought she might make it.

Then she slammed into the edge of the opposite building at chest height, and rebounded to plunge into the open Fish Street, where a few men with their nets were passing. Araezra could only watch, heart frozen, as her friend tumbled like a discarded doll toward the ground.

Then she slowed, and drifted down gently like a fluffy cottonwood seed. Araezra realized Tal was wearing Neverember's ring—the ring the Open Lord had given her to mock her name.

"Tal!" Araezra shrieked, and she pushed herself forward. She slammed into a fisherman rounding the corner, and they both rolled on the wet, grimy cobbles.

Talanna settled gently to the ground and lay there, unmoving.

Araezra cursed, forced herself up, and hobbled to Talanna. She fumbled for a healing potion in her belt, only to prick her half-numb fingers on a shard of glass. Her belt was damp and she realized her potions had broken somewhere in their hectic flight.

The hairs rose on Araezra's neck as Shadowbane dropped next to her, his cloak billowing wide. Two throwing knives—Araezra recognized them as Talanna's—stuck out of his shoulder and forearm, but he appeared not to feel them. Blue smoke wafted from his feet—the remnants of whatever magic he'd used to run that fast and leap that far. His cold eyes gleamed at her—seemingly colorless in the moonlight—then at Talanna. Those eyes looked somehow familiar, but in her terror for her friend, Araezra did not care.

"Away!" Araezra shrieked, falling to her knees at Talanna's side. "It's your fault! *Away!*"

Shadowbane put up a hand to silence her.

Araezra recoiled as though slapped. How dare he—how *dare* he treat her like a child! She remembered Talanna's adamantine dagger in her hand and she lunged forward, driving it toward Shadowbane. He twisted his arm around hers, ignoring the wound along his forearm, and dealt her wrist a slap with his other hand. The dagger clattered to the street.

Then he twisted Araezra's arm, driving her to her knees. His eyes gleamed down at her. He could break her wrist without resistance.

Instead, to Araezra's surprise, he let go. She scrabbled back a pace, cradling her wrist. It didn't seem broken, or even to have suffered serious harm.

Shadowbane bent over Talanna, spreading his hands wide.

"What are you doing?" Araezra demanded. She drew Shadowbane's sword—the only weapon she had left—but the hilt burned her hand and she dropped the blade to the ground. It lay, smoldering bright silver, on the cobblestones.

Shadowbane laid his hands upon Talanna's unmoving chest.

Araezra watched, stunned, as white light flared within his fingers and spread into Talanna. The red-haired woman's eyes fluttered and she curled into a pained ball, coughing.

Shadowbane rose and faced Araezra. She tried to meet his eyes, but he looked away—toward his sword. She stepped protectively before it, daring him to attack.

The man hesitated only a moment, then leaped away into the night.

"Gods, Tal!" Araezra knelt beside her friend and hugged her.

"Geh . . . almost . . . almost made it, eh?" Talanna said. "That jump?"

Then her eyes closed and she moaned, consciousness leaving her.

They were beneath the eaves of the Knight 'n Shadow, Araezra realized. She saw folk standing in the street around them, surprise and concern on their faces.

In particular, a half-elf lady with red hair caught Araezra's eye. She was dressed elegantly in a crimson half-cloak over a gold-chased green doublet, and was staring at them intently. Of all the onlookers, she was the only one who didn't look up. Araezra found her gray eyes unnerving. The woman turned away and disappeared into the tavern.

Araezra cradled Talanna tightly. "Help!" she cried. "Someone *help!*"

A chill rain began to fall.

NINE

Cellica was stirring the simmer stew from the eve before, reflecting that it might require a few more herbs, when she heard a thump near her tallhouse window.

Leaving the long wooden ladle in the pot on the fire, she turned toward the sound and saw the latch on the window rise—pushed up by a blade slipped between the shutters. She touched the crossbow-shaped medallion at her throat and waited silently.

The blade teased the latch up, bit by bit, until finally it scraped open. Then the shutter pushed inward and a man in a torn gray cloak tumbled through with a crash. He had clearly been leaning on the window from without, as though injured or weak.

Releasing the nervous breath she had held, Cellica rushed to his side, heedless of the rain blowing inside.

"Are you hurt?" she asked. She ran her hands over his chest and scowled at the knives standing out of his shoulder and his left arm. They stuck mostly in leather, she saw, but there was blood, too. "What passed?"

"You locked the window," Shadowbane said. "I couldn't—" He coughed harshly.

"It was raining. I guess I didn't think," said the halfling. "Curse it, you used your healing on someone else—you *fool*. How many times have I told you? If you need it, you need it." She grasped his helm. "Here. Let me—"

Without meaning it, she let compulsion slip into her voice, but he resisted her influence. He shoved her hands away, then wrenched the helm off by himself. Cellica glimpsed a little blood in the mouth guard before he cast the helmet away to crash, with several loud bangs, off the wall and floor. It rolled to the corner and stopped.

"I can't—I just can't." Shadowbane put his hands to his face as though he would weep. "I made a mistake, Cele. I didn't . . . I didn't mean anyone to be hurt."

"Aye." Cellica didn't know what had taken place, but she recognized the despair in his voice. "I'm sure you did what you could, Kalen."

His colorless eyes gazed at her, wet. He started coughing and retching then, and she could barely hold him up. He'd pushed himself, she knew—running and fighting and leaping. Magic boots or no, strengthening spellscar or no, a man was not meant to push so hard.

"Rest, now," Cellica said. "All's well. All's well."

She could feel his body relax as it bent to her will. Whatever god had blessed her voice with a touch of command, she thanked the fates.

As Kalen coughed and trembled, she held him as she had since they had been children on Luskan's cruel streets. When he'd been hurt or she'd woken with night terrors, they'd embraced each other like this—brother and sister, though not by blood.

After a while, Cellica spoke again. "You don't have to do this," she whispered.

He shook his head and limped to the table. "We'll talk come morn," he said.

"It *is* morn," Cellica said.

He sighed. "Highsun, then."

Cellica gently tugged the knives free and unbuckled Kalen's armor. His thick chest and shoulders swarmed with scars from years of this sort of activity. He wore as much blood as sweat.

"These are bad," Cellica said. "I could fetch a priest, and—"

"No," Kalen said. "Only needle and thread."

She shivered. Of course he wouldn't want magical healing. He wanted the scars to remind him—as though he deserved them. One scar for every drop of innocent blood. Cellica shivered.

Cellica worried at how Kalen didn't seem to feel the needle or thread as she stitched his wounds. He only winced when she touched the deepest bruises.

"You're so stubborn," Cellica said. "Haven't you atoned enough?"

Kalen started to reply, but his words became a coughing fit. He spat blood into his hand.

"You shouldn't worry." He coughed more blood. "Not much longer, I think." He took a mashed scroll from his pocket and handed it over. "Throw this out, aye?"

Cellica took the scroll—which smelled of both perfume and sweat—and frowned. "You shouldn't push yourself like this," she said. "Your body will only fade faster, you know."

"I know." He coughed. "I felt it hard tonight." He winced, but not from the needle.

"What if Rayse calls today?" Cellica asked. She snipped off the thread with her teeth.

He stared at the table a long breath. Such pain marked his face—so many shadows that the halfling knew were only his own.

His eyes closed and he sighed. "She won't," he said finally.

Cellica thought she glimpsed another shadow near the window that couldn't have been his, but it vanished when she looked more closely.

Trick of the dawn light, she thought.

TEN

Rath's eyes narrowed.

That was the only sign of unease he allowed himself—a slight squint—at her appearance. Otherwise, sitting back in his booth at the Knight 'n Shadow after a night of drinking, an open bottle of brandy before him, the dwarf might have seemed perfectly at ease. No one could see the conflict inside him, which he drank to pacify.

"You," Rath said.

"Me," she replied.

The red-haired half-elf slid casually onto the bench across from him. She was quite fetchingly attired in flattering black breeches and a green doublet trimmed in gold, puffed at the throat and wrists. The lady threw her legs—long, sinuous, smooth legs—across the edge of the table and leaned back on her right hand. Her left hand, still in view, danced along her knee. Her deep gray eyes appraised him wryly.

Rath couldn't deny a stir in his loins. Strange that she would affect him so. The curve of her hips, the lines of her face—perhaps that was simply her way. Mayhap it was the drink.

The dwarf silently inclined the bottle of brandy toward her.

"No, my thanks," she said with a sweet smile.

He poured himself another. "You're taking an awful risk coming to me."

"What can I say? I'm brave." Fayne waved to the serving lass for wine. "All passes well in Downshadow, I trust?"

Rath only stared at her silently.

When the wine came in a chipped bowl, Fayne raised it to her lips and drank it down greedily, more like a beast than a woman. Rath liked that, too.

"Aye?" Fayne blushed and adjusted her seat. "You're wondering about me?"

"Weighing you." Rath ran his hand across his grizzled chin. He hadn't shaved, he realized, and took his hand away. To look anything but impeccable filled him with self-loathing. "Judging, specifically, whether you purposely arranged matters for me to meet Shadowbane. It seems very much in character."

Fayne put a hand to her throat. "My *dear*," she said. "Certainly not. Why, I would never so much as go *near* that foul creature, even for a thousand dragons. The very idea!" She gasped in mock offense, then went back to smiling. "And have no fear of any tension between us, either: Ours was a legitimate disagreement regarding coin. We are both professionals—I bear no grudges, and I trust you do not either."

Though she smiled broadly, her eyes betrayed nothing.

Rath shrugged. He drained the last of the brandy from the bottle and waved for another.

"You ought take care with such strong drink," Fayne said. "Or does your dwarf stomach ward you from its ill effects?"

Ill effects, Rath mused. It would be worse if he did *not* drink.

The second bottle came, and he snatched it from the tavern wench with a scowl.

He hated this—hated his occasional and inconsolable desire for drink. It reminded him of his dwarf blood, and that heritage was one of the things he most hated about himself. Also failure and his urges. He hated that he could not master himself.

The need for drink had first come before he had shaved his beard and fled his homeland for the monastery hidden deep in the mountain. Training among the monks had suppressed this desire to connect with his hated blood—for a time, at least. He had drunk himself to a stupor just before he killed the masters of the monastery, took their most sacred of swords, and fled to Waterdeep. And for a while, with the blood he spilled almost as easily as breathing, he had not felt the urges.

Until this night—until that thrice-cursed *Shadowbane*.

Was this the third time he would drink to excess?

"Rough eve?" Fayne asked, pointing to the empty bottles—three of them.

Hard as it was—and it was hard, indeed—Rath set the bottle back on the table and pulled his gaze away from it. He still thought about it—craved the sweet fire on his tongue and in his belly, dulling his base impulses—but she could not see his mind.

"What do you know of it, girl?" Rath asked. "I am a master at my art—I have never been defeated, or I would be dead." He was saying too much. It was the liquor in his stomach, saturating his blood and making him weak. Making him into a dwarf, when he should be free.

"And yet," Fayne said, "you look like a man who bears a vendetta. Against a foe who left you alive, perhaps?"

Rath would dance to her steps no more. "What do you want?"

"The question," Fayne said, "is more correctly, do I know what *you* want?"

The dwarf waved. "I want nothing."

"Oh, I wouldn't be so sure." Fayne took a slip of parchment from the scrip satchel she had set on the table and showed it to him. It had a single long word on it. A name.

He read the parchment and his eyes narrowed. "You know this man?" he asked. "Not just know of him, but you *know* him?"

"Indeed!" She nodded. "It's only a matter of time before I have his face, too—and I'm sure that would be worth something to you." She reached across the table and laid her fingers across his wrist. "And perhaps I can think of a few other things, aye?"

Rath looked at her hand on his arm. His face remained expressionless.

"I had thought," he said, "that your inclinations did not match mine." He nodded to the serving lass, who was delivering a heavy tray of tankards to a group of half-orcs. "From your kiss with yon wench of yesterday."

"You noticed," Fayne said. "Would you like to see it again—perhaps in a more intimate setting? Waterdeep is the city of coin, after all."

"You mean—" Rath grimaced. "How disgusting."

"You'd be surprised," she said. "Call me . . . free of mind. I can do many things—even dwarves." She winked. "*Especially* dwarves."

Rath curled his lip. "Offer me coin, or begone—I'll have nothing else of you."

Fayne pouted. "What a pity."

Rath drank his brandy down and poured another. Fayne took out a second parchment, this with two words written on it, and passed it across the table. He looked at the name.

"Interesting," he said. "The first shall be my reward for this? Why?"

"This is personal," she said. "Someone I've hated for a long, long time." Her face and voice were deadly serious. "You are a professional—I do not think you could understand that."

It was Rath's turn to smile—yet it might have been the brandy. "*You'd* be surprised at what I would understand." He chuckled. "I am very familiar with hatred."

Fayne paused at that. "Mmm," she said. "Well. I shall deliver your payment—as noted on that parchment—upon completion. Aught else?"

As quickly as a snake might lunge, Rath reached across the table and seized the lace at her collar, wrenching her face close to his own. Fayne went pale.

"You are afraid," he whispered. "Why?"

Fayne blinked. Her face was calm, but her eyes were fearful. "Release me," she said. "Release me, or—"

"Or you will strike me?" Rath smiled. "I could kill you in a heartbeat."

To demonstrate, Rath gave her face a flick with his fingers, splitting open her upper lip. She didn't wince, and he almost respected her for that. Almost.

He laid his other hand around her neck. "Answer my question."

The woman licked where he had broken her lip. "Dreams," she said.

Rath relaxed his grip. "Dreams?"

"A girl—a girl in blue fire." Her eyes narrowed and her lip curled. "Know one?"

The dwarf sighed and released her to flop back to the bench. He leaned back, drained.

Fayne sucked her broken lip. "So you've caught me," she said. "I suppose I dream of wenches after all—but that isn't a fault, aye?" Discomfited as she was, she winked.

Rath understood something about her then: how she used allurement to fight anxiety. He smiled wryly. So he wasn't the only one who demeaned himself in moments of weakness.

He pulled his hand away. "Within three nights," he said, and gestured for her to depart.

If Fayne had gone then, it would have been well, but instead her eyes held him fast. She reached casually across and plucked up his hand. She rubbed it against her cheek, teasing her lips along his thumb. His arm tingled, and his hand looked blasphemously dark against her skin.

Long after she left the table, her touch lingered.

Rath folded the parchment upon which she'd named his mark and slid it into his black robe. He raised the brandy to his trembling lips, but the cool liquid tasted like ash on his tongue. He threw the bottle aside with a hiss.

Even drink did him no good now. She had ruined it for him.

He needed a woman, he knew, but not *her*. Not that faceless creature.

His sharp eyes fell on the serving lass. She had smallish breasts—well enough—and a strong, rounded backside. He wouldn't enjoy it, he knew, but he had no choice. He wouldn't go so far as to say he wanted her, but he knew that he needed her.

Needed to drive his demons away—to forget.

"Girl," he said across the tavern, and she stiffened. He raised the mostly empty bottle of brandy. "Come. Drink with me."

He laid gold on the table.

ELEVEN

§hadovar assassin hides among corrupt merchants!" cried a boy for the *Daily Luck,* hawking his broadsheet on the Street of Silks as evening fell. "Watch denies all rumors!"

"Shadovar spy rumors stupid!" called a rival broadcrier, a bob-haired girl crying the *Merchant's Friend.* She stuck out her tongue at the *Luck* boy. "*Daily Luck* prints idiocy!"

"Does not!" cried the boy.

"Does *so!*"

A disgruntled Watchman came upon the two and hissed them onto the next street. They ran from him, laughing, hand in hand, and—Kalen thought—likely fell to kissing as soon as they were out of sight. Younglings. He shook his head and smiled ruefully.

"I swear to the gods, Kalen," said Bors. "If you keep on delaying us for words with which to woo yon strumpet—when hard coin will damn well do—I shall declare her the Lady Dren."

Kalen surveyed the chapbooks just inside the shop. "Leleera likes to read."

"I suppose we all have our bedchamber pleasures," Bors said.

"Kindly don't share."

Bors grinned.

Kalen coughed into his hand, though it was mostly feigned. The weakness had subsided since yestereve, but he could still feel numbness throughout his body. As on any other day.

They had stopped on the way up the Street of Silks at a shop called the Curious Past, at which Kalen was a frequent customer. The business—which after more than a century was growing to be an ancient treasure in its own right—sold oddities, antiques, and chapbooks about the old world. Kalen scanned the titles of the books stacked on the table as the anxious vendor looked on.

Both were off duty that day, and as he often did on such days, Bors had invited Kalen to his favorite festhall—the Smiling Siren. Mostly, Kalen knew, Bors did so to interrogate Kalen for intimate information about Araezra. Kalen had not seen his superior that day—she had not reported for duty—but he wasn't about to let his worry show more than was seemly.

Kalen tried to put her out of his mind. He studied the wares laid out before him.

Though all the thirty-or-so-page books were romantic in nature, they ranged from the speculative (*The Chained Man of Erlkazar, The Blood Queen of Qurth*) to the historical (*Return of the Shades,* the First and Second of Shadows series), and from the salacious (*Untold Privy Tales of Cormyr: The Laughing Sisters, The Wayward Witch Queen*) to the outright naughty (*Adulteries of Lady Alustra: A Confessional, Seven Sisters for Seven Nights, Torm's Conquests*; this last not a reference to the god of justice, but a lecherous adventurer of the last century).

He also found most of Arita's *Silver Fox* series, up to the eighty-page eighth volume, *Fox in the Anauroch*. Rumors of the upcoming ninth, *Fox and the Blue Fire*, had been the talk of literary circles for some months.

Kalen selected one of the books and handed the vendor five silvers. He slid the book into his satchel and adjusted the thong over his shoulder. The two wore no armor while off duty, but their black greatcoats—hallmark of the Waterdeep Guard—kept vendors from cheating them.

"Well? Which is it?" Bors winked at the vendor's giggly daughter.

"Aye?"

"Which masterpiece shall Leleera be enjoying this night, man?" asked Bors. "Aught with pirates, nay? I've heard the lasses swoon over pirates these days."

"All due respect, sir," Kalen said. "Can you even read?"

"Ha!" Bors clapped him on the back. "Well enough, then."

As they walked to the Siren, a light rain began to fall on what had been a warm day, sending up dust from the cobblestones. It was that time of winter-turning-to-spring when the weather could not choose how to behave. Dust swirled in a breeze that came from the west.

"Sea fog tonight," predicted Kalen.

"Ridiculous!" said Bors. He spread his hands. "You hear this, Waterdeep? Ridiculous!"

Kalen just smiled—and coughed lightly.

With the rain and the approaching eve, business slowed. The street lighters—retired Watchmen, mostly—were about their work, lifting long hooks to hang fish-oil lamps. The streets would grow crowded near the gates, which closed at dusk.

"I don't see," Bors said, munching an apple, "why you bother with lasses of the night, when by all accounts you could tumble a nymph like Rayse for free."

Kalen ignored that. "How are Araezra and Talanna?" he asked quietly.

"You mean yestereve? Bah." Bors sparked a flint and lit his tamped pipe. "Talanna fell—*again*, though at least this time she had the damn ring. Laid up for healing at Torm's temple a few days, but she'll be fine—that girl's tougher 'n bone dragons." He took a deep pull of pipe smoke. "I'm sure the damned *Minstrel* will run a tale in the morn that makes us all look hrasting fools, but no mind."

Kalen nodded. Cellica would tell him about the broadsheets. He never read them himself—he already knew how bleak the world really was. "What of Araezra?" he asked quietly.

"Rayse . . ." He looked down at his hands. "She took yestereve pretty hard, as she always does. Good lass, that one, but hard on herself. Really hard. Thinks she has to be."

Kalen sighed.

"Funny you ask about her, when we're on our way to a *festhall*." Bors clapped him on the shoulder. "Mayhap after we're done there, you'll want to cheer Rayse up, eh?"

Kalen ignored Bors's jape.

They passed under the arms of the Siren—cunningly carved as a blushing, sea-skinned and foam-haired maiden whose gauzy skirts would occasionally billow in the right breeze off the bay. The entry room was cunningly sculpted and painted in a forest scene on one side, a beach on the other. Figures in various states of nakedness seemed to dance off the walls—nymphs, dryads, satyrs, and the like, also knights and maidens reclining and embracing under the boughs of trees.

The images were so lifelike that a small person could blend in by standing still, as was a favorite pastime of Sanchel, the Siren's dwarf madam. Bors and Kalen knew her game, but she startled the Hells out of two young sellswords when she appeared—in thigh boots and a cloak of leaves—from among the trees.

"Sune smile on you." Then, as they almost pissed themselves: "Boy, girl, or common?"

"Cuh-common," said one of them. The other stared at her mostly exposed chest, an impressive edifice considering her stature.

"Love and beauty follow you," said Sanchel. "If you would make your offering?"

The older of the sellswords elbowed the younger, and he drew a purse out of his belt and handed it toward Sanchel. The dwarf shook her head and pointed instead toward a statue of the goddess that stood within a fountain below the stairs. At her gesture, the boy poured the coins into the water, which instantly turned bright gold.

"The goddess is pleased. You are welcome to her hall." Then Sanchel made a bird call and two half-clad celebrants appeared—one lad and one lass. Sanchel pointed each to one of the adventurers. A pause followed, in which the festgirl and festboy appraised the patrons critically, then they nodded and took the young men by the arms.

Sanchel prided herself on knowing the nighttime preferences of her patrons at a glance, and she was right again. The youths looked very pleased at their escorts, and allowed themselves to be led toward the common hall, which would be full of dancing, wine, and song.

Sanchel turned to Kalen and Bors with the smile she reserved for favored regulars. "Good eve, gentles—I see the Watch is treating you well?"

"Hasn't killed us yet." Bors eyed the murals speculatively. "I wonder . . ."

Kalen rolled his eyes. This was one of Bors's favorite games, playing this role.

Sanchel feigned wariness, but her eyes laughed. She knew the game as well and—unlike Kalen—liked it. "Something displeases, honored Commander?"

"I wonder if your practices fall within the scope of the law," Bors said. "Are all your celebrants here of their own will, and given adequate compensation for their arts?"

Sanchel rose to the challenge. "What are you suggesting, sir? All in this place serve Sune—and all want for naught. Or"—she smiled—"did you need to interview one yourself?"

"Mmm, mayhap," said Bors with a grin. He drew out his purse and poured a few coins into the pool. The water glowed. "Clever magic—spares you checking the gold yourself, eh?"

"Just so," said Sanchel. "And yet you pause, my lord. You are uncertain?"

Bors's grin grew wider. "Better make it two," he said, adding twice as many coins to the offering. "Bren and Crin, I think."

Sanchel gave a sweet smile and whistled twice, great trilling bird songs. Kalen wondered if she could speak with birds, if given the opportunity. Two women appeared out of a hidden door in Sune's forest—two dusky-skinned lasses with midnight hair and big, deep black eyes.

Bren and Crin looked identical, though they shared no blood. One, or perhaps both, was a shapeshifter who matched the other. Requests for "the sisters" were common enough—if costly. They smiled at Bors with their full, tempting lips.

"Does this one please you?" Sanchel asked them.

The women looked at Bors Jarthay critically, weighing him with their eyes. Their choosing was the key, Kalen thought. If they did not like the man, no offering was enough, and it would be blasphemy for Bors to coerce or even so much as scowl if they chose "nay."

Oddly, Kalen found himself thinking of Cellica, the only sister he had ever known, and chuckled inwardly at the thought of her in such a situation. She'd probably box Bors Jarthay around the ears, or—failing that, owing to her size—offer him a punch in a more sensitive spot.

Bren and Crin did nothing of the sort. They smiled to one another, then bowed to Bors. "This one," they said together, "half a fool and half a hero—this one always amuses us."

Sanchel nodded.

"Perfect," said Bors with a low bow. Then he smiled boldly and quoted, "Beauty begs joy. The silvered glass smiles, its delight unrehearsed."

The courtesans looked at one another dubiously. Kalen looked at Sanchel, who giggled. Apparently, she understood the private jest.

"Is something wrong, my ladies?" asked the commander, his smile faltering.

"The poesy was not so bad," Crin said to Bren. "Was it Thann, you think?"

"Doubtless," said Bren. "And spoken well, too."

"But my ladies unmake me," said Bors with a small bow. "They have heard this before."

"Of course," said Crin. "It is in *Couplets for Courtiers*, is it not? How does it go, Sister?"

Bren smiled. "Let me see. 'Your lips curve in swift, sweet echo, but this I swear: the mirror smiled first' . . . aye, Commander?"

"Aye, just so."

"Myself, I'd have preferred aught of Thann's 'Gray-Mist Maiden,' " Crin murmured to herself. " 'Let years steal beauty, grace, and youth,' or the like."

"Ladies, I bow to your superior learning," Bors said, bowing low.

"But which is the lady and which the mirror?" pressed Bren—or perhaps Crin. Kalen wasn't certain any more. He wondered if he had been wrong all along.

"I should be most pleased to find out." And with that, Bors emptied the rest of his purse into the water, which glowed brightly indeed. "Might we find a place of privacy, ladies, wherein I might— ah? Ladies?"

Bren was looking at the glowing pool. She clicked her tongue and smiled at Crin. "He would impress us with gold where his poetry fails, Sister."

"How childish," agreed Crin. "Hmpf!"

91

The women stuck out their tongues simultaneously at Bors. They brushed past him toward the commons, seemingly disinterested.

Bors's face fell. "Wait a moment!" the commander cried, and he hurried after them.

Kalen shook his head. The commander was just another man with more coin than sense.

In truth, he did not begrudge Bors Jarthay. Kalen was a man, too, and had the desires of any man. Only the ability . . . Kalen sighed inwardly.

"Sir Dren," Sanchel said. "Have your desires shifted, or is it Leleera again? She has asked for you, should you come around—as you well know."

Kalen turned to her. "Leleera."

"If you wish to marry her," Sanchel said, "that can be . . ."

"No, no," Kalen said. It seemed awkward to claim he and Leleera were merely friends, so he held his tongue. He dropped gold into the pool, which glowed with a radiance more subdued than Bors had wrought with his coin. "As always—an hour longer than the commander stays here. Do not let us leave together."

"As always." Sanchel nodded and gestured to the stairs. "Sune smile upon you."

"Torm bless and ward you." Kalen bowed his head. He paused. "Sanchel—know you a half-elf with red hair, gray eyes, and a quick tongue?"

"If that is your preference," the dwarf said, "we can see if Chandra or Rikkil please you—the eyes would be difficult, but the tongue . . ."

"No," Kalen said, with an embarrassed cough. "Fair eve."

Sanchel nodded and Kalen turned up the stairs, around the image of a great redwood around which dryads pranced.

>———W———<

When he had gone, Sanchel inclined her head to one of the tree nymphs. "Satisfied?"

"Quite."

The dryad pulled away from the wall. It did a pirouette, as though reveling in its sylvan body, and Sanchel frowned. This creature both frightened her and intrigued her with its whimsy.

The dryad plucked a wand of bone from her hair and circled it around her head. A silvery radiance crowned her, then descended to her ankles. Her green tresses turned to bright red curls and her green skin became the particular bronze a half-elf inherits from a gold-skinned elf parent. Her eyes became the perfect gray of burnished steel.

"Which room?" Fayne asked. "From the street, mind—not inside."

"Second floor, third from the north," the dwarf woman said. "When he spoke of the half-elf with gray eyes . . . he meant you, didn't he?"

"Mayhap," she said. "Or mayhap I choose a form to match what he said. It matters little, as you'll say nothing to him—unless you don't care if I tell the Watch certain secrets . . ."

"No," Sanchel said. "Sune smile on you, little trickster."

"Beshaba laugh in your face."

Fayne waved her wand again, and in a blink, she vanished.

Kalen kept his eyes downcast so as not to attract attention or bother other patrons. He would have seen his fair share of attractive sights, but he wasn't there to peruse.

He knocked at Leleera's door and was rewarded. "Enter!" He pushed through.

The room, like most of the pleasure cells at the Smiling Siren, was spacious—sparsely but tastefully adorned to suit the desires of its owner and his or her patrons, whom the celebrant could deny as she wished. Leleera opted for a "queen's chamber," with a stuffed divan, a tightly wound four-poster bed, and even a golden tub. As a full priestess of Sune, she could work the relatively simple magics to fill and heat the bath.

She had a full wardrobe of attire to match the chamber—rich robes, diaphanous silk gowns, and jewelry—along with a fair assortment of martial harnesses, including a thin gold breastplate, greaves, an impractical mail hauberk, and a vast assortment of boots of varying styles and lengths. Warrior queens were popular requests, she had told Kalen—particularly a certain "Steel Princess" Alusair, of late fourteenth-century Cormyr.

The lady herself—who smiled broadly to see Kalen and rose from her divan to embrace him—looked much as a warrior queen ought, with her strong and beautiful features, confident swagger, and honey hued hair, in which she wore dyed streaks of Sune's favored scarlet.

"Kalen!" she cried. "Just in time. I've almost finished *Uthgardt*."

Kalen put down his satchel and sat to remove his boots. "And how goes Arita's debut?"

"Epic," she said. Leleera helped Kalen unbutton his doublet. "I can see why folk love it."

The long-running series, beginning with *Fox Among the Uthgardt*, concerned a heroine from the old world: an eladrin woman called the Silver Fox who couldn't help but plunge into danger with every leap. No one knew the real name of the author—the fancyname "Arita" meant "silver fox" in Elvish—and owing to the volumes' popularity, printers didn't inquire.

"Much wit and banter go with the swordplay, though not *nearly* enough lovemaking. Though"—she pulled the hauberk over his head— "I did enjoy the seduction of the chief."

"Huh." Kalen started unlacing his breeches.

"I suppose there'll be more," Leleera said, slapping his hands away so she could do it. "*Uthgardt* ends in the 1330s, and the Silver Fox is only a young lass. Under forty—but the fey-born age slower than humans, methinks. There are more books, yes?"

Kalen let her pull off his breeches and stood in his linen clout. Leleera looked at his scarred, slightly glistening chest, and he could almost hear her thoughts.

He shook his head. " 'Ware the rules."

"Yes, yes." She pouted. "How many more are there, Kalen? I want to read *more!*"

"I saw *Anauroch* in the shop today, and I believe that's volume eight." He stretched. "Not as many as that other series you like, but each one's twice the normal fifty or so pages."

Leleera wasn't looking at his nakedness anymore, but rather at his satchel. "In the shop?" Her smile widened. "Does that mean . . . ?"

Kalen opened his satchel and produced the book. "One with more bedplay, I'm told."

Leleera gasped. "*Lascivities of a Loveable Lothario*—volume twelve!" She squealed. "Oh Kalen, you naughty, *naughty* knight!" Leleera kissed him on the cheek and plopped down on her divan, feet in the air, to read. She began giggling freely and often.

"I take it that will be sufficient?" Kalen laid the satchel's contents on the bed. Black leathers, a gray cloak—the clothes that fit the man.

" 'You should be flattered, lass,' " she read. " 'Many would give their lives to learn in my bed—many already have.' " She rolled on her back and clasped the book to her chest. "Perfect!"

"Good." He adjusted his sword belt, which felt light without Vindicator. He sheathed his watchsword in the scabbard instead—it was too short, but it still fit, awkwardly.

"Sure I can't tempt you?" Leleera asked. "We could read together." She put her hand on his wrist and if he didn't know better, he'd have sworn she was trying to beguile him.

"Thank you, but no." Kalen kissed her on the forehead and crossed to the window, where he paused. "Leleera—are you . . . are you happy here? In this place?"

She pursed her lips. "When did you start to care about being *happy?*"

Kalen scowled.

"A jest, my friend," Leleera said. "I am content in this place—I serve my goddess, doing that which brings me pleasure. I share her love with the people of this city."

"And that is enough," he whispered. "For you, I mean."

"Kalen." She caressed his cheek, but he could not feel her fingers. He saw her hand move, but felt nothing. "Is it not the same for you?"

Kalen looked away.

"You are a good man, Kalen Dren—but sometimes . . ." She trailed off with a sigh. Then she smiled sadly. "If you want to save someone, why not start with yourself?"

"I don't need saving," he said.

"We'll see." Leleera embraced him and pressed her lips to his. He felt only coldness.

She left him and lay down across her divan. Setting aside the *Lascivities,* she opened *Fox Among the Uthgardt* to the last few pages and began to read silently. Aloud, she murmured, "Oh, *Kalen*—oh, yes—ooh!"

Among other skills, being a celebrant of Sune required substantial acting talent.

Kalen bowed his head to her and she winked.

"Oh, yes—right—*there!*" She flipped a page.

As Leleera moaned, squealed, and read, Kalen donned his helm and opened the shutters. He looked back at Leleera—who writhed in feigned passion as she flipped another page.

Then, without further hesitation, Shadowbane swung out the window into the night.

Just below, watching invisibly from an alley just across Marlar's Lane, Fayne smiled.

"I see you, Sir Dren," she murmured. She pinched her nose. "And smell you, too—do you *ever* wash that cloak?"

With that bit of spying managed, she turned her thoughts to the tale she was writing for the *Minstrel.* The life of a scandal-smith was so demanding!

She slipped away, thinking of the japes she'd use. Ooh, she'd prayed for the day she could burn Araezra Hondyl. And it had arrived, with the blessings of the sun god.

Later—perhaps three bells later—Bors Jarthay listened at Leleera's door to a long and loud chorus of her moans. "Yes!" Leleera cried from within. "Oh, Kalen!"

Bors grinned. "That's my boy."

As he made his way down the curling staircase into the garden in the entry hall, he scowled out the misty front windows at the sea fog that had rolled in. "Damn that man—is he ever wrong?"

He whistled a tune as he left, bound for home.

TWELVE

The city stood hidden in gray night. Selûne had retreated behind deep clouds that threatened rain but did not let it fall. A slight breeze came from the sea to the west and broke against the buildings.

Conditions were perfect for the sea fog that rolled through the streets.

Waterdhavians rarely braved such nights, when the fog hid deeds both noble and vile. On a night like that, the creatures of Downshadow would stay below in their holes, denied the clear sky and Selûne's tears.

Wearing the black leathers and gray cloak of Shadowbane, Kalen perched atop Gilliam's haberdashery. He had not come for battle—for such, he'd descend to Downshadow—but rather for freedom in the surface world. Every tenday or so, if clouds hid the moon, he took time from his task to remind himself of that which he defended: a city he could see but not feel.

"Why not start with myself," he murmured.

Were he a man who could feel as other men did, he might have enjoyed the embrace of so wise a woman as Leleera. He might have tried anyway, were it not for his constant fear of being too rough without knowing it—without *feeling* it. Even had the spellplague not stolen his senses in exchange for strength, he was a man of action. Violence was no more easy to leave behind him than was the mask of Shadowbane.

Enough self-pity. It did not become a servant of justice.

"I don't need saving," he repeated.

He and Leleera were both crusaders. But while she served a gentle goddess who craved only her happiness, he obeyed the will of a dead god who demanded action.

He slid off the roof into the night and ran along the rooftops.

A hundred years ago, before the Spellplague had rebuilt the world, the god called Helm was the patron of guardians and the vigilant— an eternal watcher, who once slew a goddess he loved rather than forsake his duty. Then, because of a mad god's trickery, he had fought with Tyr, the blind Lord of Justice, and fallen under the eyeless one's blade.

The night of Helm's death, in a city called Westgate, a boy named Gedrin dreamed of the duel. Helm perished, but his divine essence lingered. The gods' symbols merged: the eye of Helm etched itself onto Tyr's breastplate with its scales of justice. The blind god's eye glowed, and his sight returned. When Gedrin awoke, he held Vindicator, Helm's sword in the dream.

And thus had begun the heresy of the church known as the Eye of Justice.

Later, plagued by guilt and shame, Tyr fell to the demon prince Orcus, but his powers—and those of Helm—had passed to Torm, god of duty. Gedrin dreamed a second time, and watched the three gods become one. The heretical church he had built began to follow Torm, whom they took to calling the threefold god.

Many years after these dreams—almost eighty years later—in the cesspool of Luskan, a famous knight called Gedrin Shadowbane gave a beggar boy three things: a knight's sword, Vindicator; a message, never to beg again; and a cuff on the ear, that he might remember it.

That boy had been Kalen Dren, the second Shadowbane. And his first vow had been never to beg for anything, ever again.

And how sorely that vow had been tested, so many times.

A cough formed in his chest, and he fought it down. His illness—though he pretended it was worse than it was, in truth— would always haunt him. He had the spellplague to thank for that. From birth, Kalen had borne the spellplague's mark: a spellscar, the priests called it—a different blessing and curse for every poor soul who earned or inherited one. For Kalen, it was toughened flesh and resistance to pain. Any warrior would wish for such a thing but for its accompanying curse: a body increasingly losing feeling, one that would eventually perish.

Justice for the sins of a poorly spent youth, he mused.

He watched as the sea fog shifted, taking on color, radiance, and form. Like much of the spellplague's legacy, this was a rare and unexplained occurrence. Soon, the glowing fog would take on shapes and tell a story, though none could say why.

Kalen eased himself away from the banner pole atop Gilliam's and half-ran, half-slid down the domed roof. Using his momentum, he bent low and sprang from the edge. The magic in his boots—one of the few items he'd managed to bring from Westgate—carried him across the alley and up to the roof of the next building, a tallhouse.

He ran along the crenellated edge, leaping over potted plants and a few squatters who sheltered in the corners of the roofs. Running the rooftops was safer than the street. A seagull, borne on the lazy breezes, matched him, and he balanced on the ledge beside it.

He remembered running the roofs of Westgate with his teacher in the church of the Eye: the half-elf Levia, old enough to have borne him, but who looked as young as he. Her skill was not martial in nature, but divine—priestly magic. Healing and the like.

Kalen knew little of such magic. Aside from his healing touch and the protection given a paladin, he asked little of his threefold god—and begged for nothing. He'd once broken a man's nose for calling Levia a spell-beggar, but he was not sure if he'd done it for her honor or his.

He wished Levia had come to Waterdeep. She was family, Kalen thought. Levia, the only mother he'd ever known—and Cellica, his sister in spirit if not in blood.

Not like the rest of their wayward faith. Kalen did not consider such fools to be his kin.

Gedrin had created the Eye, bringing crusaders from the ranks of the Night Masks—a powerful thieves' guild at the time, ruled by a vampire called the Night King. Gedrin had burst forth from the Masks like a hero digging out of the belly of a beast, and aided in ousting the dark masters of Westgate. Thereafter, they had set out to cleanse the world of evil in all its forms. Gedrin was a zealot, and his faith inspired hundreds to worship the threefold god.

But in time, the purity of the Eye faded, its quest tainted by flawed men in the church—men who used their thiefly skills for personal gain, rather than justice. Gedrin left the Eye, after spending so much of his life in the doomed church, and Kalen, years later, had followed in his footsteps. Both had taken Vindicator, hoping to put its power to use elsewhere.

Kalen felt lost without the sword. It had set him on Gedrin's quest to redeem the world. And though a part of him needed it back, another large part of him approved of its loss. If he had not been worthy of it, was it not the threefold god's will that it choose another wielder?

A low sound perked up his ears. Kalen caught a spire, whirled, and pressed himself flat against the stone, closing his eyes. He heard it again: sobbing. A female voice—somewhere near.

He looked and saw a cloud of mists that glowed blue. That was odd—he had seen colors and distortions in the sea fog before, but never blue. And he recognized the hue—a sickly yet powerful azure, like the inner shade of a flame just before it turned white hot. It was spellplague blue, he realized, just like the spellplague that had changed him.

Unease crept into his fingers, but he heard the sob—more like a plea for aid—again and leaped from the roof. If the Eye would claim him this night, then so be it.

The blue fog was close, only two rooftops away. The near building was a squat noble villa with an open-air garden in the center, and he ran along the wall to stay aloft. Blue fog swirled around him, threatening, and he felt a drive to step forward, to face an unknown peril that might be the end of him. Was it not better to fall now, if Vindicator had abandoned him?

He sprang into the alley, rolling with the fall to come up on his feet, watchsword drawn. It occurred to him only then that carrying the blade would be damning if any Watchmen were to see him, but too late.

The mists seemed empty, but he heard the sob again. The blue glow crackled, electric, deeper in the alley, and he stalked forward.

The mist took on shapes, and Kalen fell into guard, both hands on his sword.

Ghosts appeared out of the mist. He saw two figures—slim men who might have been elves—standing together in a room in some distant land. They were arguing—even fighting, waving misty limbs like blades. Then one vanished into the shadows near a leaning stack of crates. The remaining figure turned to Kalen, smiling.

Another figure appeared out of the mist, this one a woman, her features blurred. The mist man turned to greet her. Without warning, he thrust his fist into her chest and she fell, hands clenched.

Kalen felt a surge of anger, but these were just visions. They meant nothing.

The mist man stared at him. "The sword," the mist man said with a too-wide smile.

Kalen had never heard that the visions of Waterdeep could speak. It chilled him.

Lightning crackled again, blue and vivid, and Kalen turned to search for its source.

When he looked back, both mist men were there, looking at him with hunger. They approached him, hands rising, and he realized they meant to attack. He retreated, but his back was against the wall of the alley.

"Away." As Levia had taught him, Kalen let the threefold god shine against them. He began to glow, warding off the walking dead. "Away!"

But either his power was too weak or these were not undead, for they came forward. Kalen saw the woman climbing to her feet, a bleeding hole where her heart should be.

"The sword," the mist whispered. "The sword that was stolen— the crusader has come!"

Kalen thought, for one horrible moment, that they were talking about him. But these were images of long ago, if not entirely random manifestations.

He struck with his watchsword, but the mortal steel passed clean through them, disturbing the mist with its wind. Their hands passed through his guard and leathers as though they were not there. He felt ice inside his flesh.

"Away," he tried again, but his voice was hoarse.

Weakness was taking him, and he could not even flee. The woman in the mist appeared over him, and he thought she was not beautiful but terrible—she was death embodied.

Then the alley was bathed in blue light. Kalen felt the hairs on his neck and arms rise and he threw himself down just as lightning crackled through the air, scorching the stone buildings. A figure stood before him, surrounded in blue electricity and fire. It was the fiery woman he had seen in Downshadow only a few nights before—whose appearance had saved him from death at a half-orgre's gnarled fingers.

He averted his eyes to keep from being blinded, and the mist creatures fell back. He could see them, just vaguely, bowing and scraping like servants, almost . . . *reverent.*

Then the light went out, and the woman—no longer flaming but still glowing—stood shakily in the center of the alley. Her dizzy eyes met his, and he saw they were startlingly blue.

"*Szasha,*" she said in a tongue he did not know. "*Araka azza grazz?*" Then she sagged.

Leaving his watchsword on the cobblestones in his lunge, Kalen caught her just before she hit the ground. She was so light, barely more than a girl, and little more than skin, bone, and . . . blood.

His gauntlets came away sticky. The girl was naked but for a slimy coating of what looked like black and green blood. He searched for wounds but could find none. Her hair, plastered in the sickly gore, was blue. Everything about her was blue: hair, lips, even her skin.

Then Kalen realized her skin was not blue, but rather covered in glowing tattoos. Runes, he thought, though he did not know them. Even as he noted them, the tattoos began to fade, shrinking into her deeply tanned flesh like ink on wet parchment. He blinked, watching as lattices of arcane symbols vanished, little by little.

Kalen didn't know what to do, but he couldn't leave her.

Her arms tightened around his neck and her face pressed into his chest. "*Gisz vaz.*"

"Very well," he replied, not having the faintest idea what she'd said.

He took off his cloak and wrapped her in it. Then he held her tightly, looked around for mist figures—the fog had begun to disperse—and started off at a trot.

Cellica's stew—left to simmer until morningfeast—was bubbling when he returned to the tallhouse.

"You're back early," the halfling said when he came through the open window. She had risen from her cot, a towel wrapped around her little body, but she didn't look sleepy.

"Did I wake you?" Kalen took care not to hit the strange woman's head against the sill.

"I never sleep when you're—" Cellica's eyes widened. "Who's that?"

"No idea."

Kalen strode into Cellica's room and laid his burden on the halfling's cot.

"She's . . ." The halfling trailed off, touching the sleeping woman's cheek. "She's bone cold! Out! Out! I'll take care of this."

Kalen felt Cellica's will take hold of him and wandered out while she laid blanket after blanket over the sleeping woman. The stranger's uncertain frown became a blissful smile.

Gods, Kalen felt tired. His limbs ached and his armor stank of sweat. The girl was light, but he'd carried her all the way across the city. In that time, her azure tattoos had all but disappeared. Her breathing seemed normal, and she slept peacefully.

"Why lasses run around the night streets naked in this day and age, I'll never understand," Cellica said. "Younglings! Hmpf."

"Mmm," Kalen returned. He was rubbing his eyes. Gods, he was tired.

"Who *is* she?" the halfling asked. Rather than being upset, she was inspecting the woman critically, fascinated. "Your hunting extends to naked ladies in addition to villains and dastards?"

Kalen murmured a reply that did not befit a paladin. He traipsed off to his cot, shedding his leathers as he went, and slumped into bed. He was asleep two breaths later.

It only briefly occurred to him to wonder where he'd left his watchsword.

THIRTEEN

Fayne slammed her fist on the table in the little chamber in Downshadow.

"I should have known." She spat in most unladylike fashion on the array of cards. "Useless. Utterly useless. I should have known you were a perverse little fraud, after you fed me all the drivel about the doppelganger conspiracy."

B'Zeer the Seer—the tiefling who ran this small, illicit "diviner's council" in a hidden chamber in Downshadow, of which only those of questionable honor knew—spread his many-ringed hands. "Divination is an imprecise art, my sweet Satin, and requires much patience."

"Oh, *orc shit*," Fayne said. "Divination hasn't worked right in Waterdeep for a hundred years." She shoved her scroll of notes in her scrip satchel. "I don't know what I was thinking, coming to a pimply faced voyeur like you."

B'Zeer ran his fingers over the cards and furrowed his brow. His milky white eyes, devoid of pupils, scanned the tabletop, and he scratched at one of his horns. "Now wait, I think I see aught, now. Something to do with your father . . . your need to please him . . . perhaps in—"

"I don't need some peeping, pus-faced pervert to tell me about my father, thanks," Fayne said. "I was asking about my dreams—you know, the girl in blue fire?"

"Ah yes, B'Zeer sees and understands. I believe—"

"With all due respect—and that's none—piss off and *die*. I have business to attend to this night, and a tale for the *Minstrel* to deliver to print."

Fayne exploded from her chair, but a hand clamped around her wrist. She looked down, eyes narrow. "Let go of me, or I will end you."

"This may be a touch indelicate, what I ask now," the seer said. "But what of my coin?"

Fayne glared. "No hrasting service, no hrasting coin."

"Call it an entertainment fee," he said. "We all have to eat."

"Piss," Fayne said, "off."

He moved faster than a shriveled little devil man should be able to, darting forward and seizing her throat to thrust her against the chamber wall. She saw steel in his other hand.

"You give me my coin," he said, "or I'll take it out of you elsewise."

She should have expected this. Most women in Downshadow were of negotiable virtue. It was simply part of living coin-shy. Particularly amusing were those monsters that took the form of women and revealed themselves only in a passionate embrace. Justice, Fayne thought.

She smiled at B'Zeer dangerously.

"Hark, Seer—it isn't bound to happen," she said. "I think, if you read your destiny, you'll see only you . . . alone but for your hand."

"So you say, bitch," the tiefling said. "But let us see what—*uuk!*"

The seer choked and coughed, grasping at himself where she had driven a knife through his bowels. Blackness poured down his legs. He mumbled broken words in his fiendish language—harsh, guttural sounds—but he could summon no magic with his life spilling down his groin.

"If it gives you any comfort," she said as he sank to the floor, "I *did* warn you."

Then she left him in his small nook in Downshadow, which to him had become a shrinking, blurry world of heaving breaths, pain, and—quite later—wet darkness.

FOURTEEN

As dawn rose, Araezra sat alone in her private room at the barracks. She slapped the broadsheet down on the table and leaned back in her chair, fuming.

"Watch *fails* to apprehend vigilante in Castle Ward," noted the *Mocking Minstrel,* this particular tale written by the bard Satin Rutshear. "*Clumsy fool* Talanna Taenfeather injured in pursuit while *narcissistic superior,* Araezra Hondyl, parades *half-naked* through streets."

Araezra groaned. The emphasized words were underlined in a girlish hand.

"Open Lord Neverember calls Araezra's actions 'justified,' saying 'I'm sure she acted for the best' . . . in protecting his *bedmate interests* in the Watch," she read. "Neverember was later seen *furtively* arriving at Taenfeather's bedside in the temple of Torm, protected by cloaked men."

Then: "For *misuse* of city taxes to support *nonregulated* religious bodies, see *over.*"

Araezra rubbed her eyes. The quotations were accurate if slanted, and the additions infuriated her. Lord Neverember and Talanna's energetic flirtations were well known, but had never been put quite this way. The casual cruelty left a foul taste in Araezra's mouth. She stabbed her nails into her palms hard.

And of course, Satin quoted Lord Bladderblat, the broadsheet's ubiquitous parody noble.

"On young Hondyl's competency as a valabrar, Lord Bladderblat calls Hondyl 'too pretty for a *thinking* woman, but she's got assets; better she find a blade for 'twixt her thighs than one for her belt—though she can wear the belt to *my* bed, if she likes.' "

That Araezra was presented as the bedmate of a fiction rankled.

And being described as "young"—true, she was just over twenty, but her rank came from her *success*, not her beauty.

This wasn't new to her, this ridicule. She'd often tried to track down "Satin Rutshear," but it was just a fancyname, of course. The *Minstrel* protected its own, and the Lords' command against punishing broadsheet writers and printers stayed Araezra's hand. Violating it would have led to her discharge—but it would have made her feel much better.

"Watch keeps silent on continued threat," Satin went on. "Hondyl has no comment."

In that private, unheard, and thus safe moment, Araezra finally let vent. "Mayhap you might *ask*, Lady Rutshear," she cried. "I'd give you a comment, well and good—then twist your snobby head off your shoulders, you little *whore!*"

She balled up the *Minstrel* and hurled it across the office into the spittoon.

She felt better.

Then she set to repressing her anger into a tight, simmering ball.

Burn her eyes and her waggling tongue, but this "Satin" had the right of it—there was no place for screaming, hysterical lasses in the Guard, particularly not those ranked as highly as she.

This story—and the whole situation it cat-raked with such fiendish glee—was bad enough. If she was going to be humiliated and repri-manded for abandoning her patrol, endangering her men, and landing her second in a bed at the temple of Torm, then at least she could do it with some dignity. The judgmental eyes of the rest of the Watch and Guard, the disapproving glare of Commander Jarthay—they were bad enough.

And where in the *Hells* was Kalen? He hadn't appeared for duty this morn, and she could really use his shoulder to—

Araezra dropped her face into her hands. She wouldn't cry—she couldn't. Crying was for weak-willed women, and she must be strong—for Talanna, if for nothing else.

Don't think about Talanna, fading in and out of life under the hands of those priests.

She looked instead at the sword on the table, and let its silvery masterwork distract her.

It was a bastard sword, well and good, but deceptively light and sharp. Magical, she knew—it had glowed fiercely silver in Shadowbane's hand, and retained this glow even after he'd left it. Now, sitting cool on her desk, it radiated power at a touch—but *balanced* power.

A sword is neither good nor evil, she thought, but that its wielder uses it for either.

Araezra looked in particular at the sigil carved into its black hilt: an upright gauntlet with a stylized eye in its open palm. She'd thought at first it was the gauntlet of Torm, but an hour in the room of records had shown her otherwise: it was the symbol of a long-dead church—that of Helm, God of Guardians.

That god—a deity neither inherently evil nor good—had faded since the old world, like many across Faerûn. She'd read one story of his death at the hands of the then-god of justice, Tyr—who had also perished in the last century. That hardly made sense to her: Why would two such gods make war? And why were they not left to rest?

She found this sword a mystery, a relic of an ancient past. Its symbol—in particular, the eye—stared at her wryly, as though amused by its secrets.

She thought about the gauntlets on her own breastplate—five, for valabrar. Here was only one, for the rank of trusty. But, she noted, the gauntlet adorned both sides of the hilt, making two, for vigilant. And Helm had been called the Vigilant One.

Araezra thought of Kalen, who wore two gauntlets. Something about a ring he wore . . .

But that was ridiculous—with his worsening illness, Kalen could hardly walk fast, much less run. He trained, she knew, and kept his body in excellent condition to stave off the illness he'd told her about—but surely he couldn't outpace Talanna Taenfeather.

She was startled out of her thoughts when a loud knock came at the door. She wiped at her cheeks and was aghast that her hand came away damp. "Come," she said.

The door opened and Bors Jarthay glided into the room, his

face solemn. Standing at attention, Araezra felt a chill of terror and grief.

"Talanna," Araezra said. "How—how is she?"

Bors narrowed his eyes. "Well, Rayse—I don't know the best way to say this . . ."

Tears welled up in Araezra's eyes and her lip trembled.

"She'll be . . ." Bors whispered, "perfectly well."

Araezra's heart skipped a beat. "Wait—what?"

"Healing went fine, and she'll be well," the commander said. "A little wrathful, but generally her precocious, loud, and—ow!" Araezra slapped him. "Heh. Suppose I deserved that."

Araezra slapped him again. "Gods burn you! Why do you have to *do* that?"

He smiled gently. "All's well, Rayse."

"You monstrous oaf!" She wound back to strike again. "Damn you to all the Hells!"

Bors caught her wrist, pulled her to him, and hugged her. "All's well," he whispered.

Stunned, she put her arms around him and buried her head in his chest. Tears came—thankful, angry tears—and she didn't stop them.

"You ever want to talk, lass," he said. "I'm here."

"Just . . . another moment." Then she glared up at him. "And don't think this means anything. With all due respect, you're still a boor and won't be seeing me naked any time soon."

Bors sighed. "More's the pity."

He hugged her tighter.

FIFTEEN

Kalen woke with the kind of splitting headache that comes after one has slept only moments in the space of several hours. He felt as though he'd never bedded down at all. His nose was stuffy and he coughed and sneezed to clear it.

Worse, he was numb all over. He allowed himself one horrified breath before he tried to move his senseless hands. With some hesitation, they rose, and he pressed them to his cheeks.

"Thank the gods," Kalen whispered.

Cellica stood in the room, a bucket of water in her hands. She looked a touch disappointed, and moved the water behind her back. "Well!" she said. "About time."

Kalen groaned.

"Get up, Sir Slug, and come have aught to eat. Our guest has been at the stew all morning, and if you don't make haste, it might be gone." As he started to sit up, she glanced down, then back up at his face, unashamed. "And put those on." She pointed at a pair of black hose, crumpled at the foot of his bed.

Kalen realized he was naked, which made sense. He hadn't donned aught last night.

"*Try* and be presentable for our guest."

"Guest?" he managed as he plucked up the hose, but the halfling was already gone.

The highsun light filtered through his shuttered window, and deep shadows undercut his eyes in the mirror. His wiry chest, with its familiar scars, gleamed back at him. Stubble gone to an early gray studded his chin and neck. Generally, he looked and felt terrible. Pushing himself too hard, he decided.

"Gods," he murmured.

He paused at the door to his bedchamber and fought down a wave of dizziness. His legs felt beyond exhausted. He still hadn't recovered from his flight from Talanna and Araezra.

"Fair morn, Risen Sun," said Cellica when Kalen staggered out to morningfeast—or highsunfeast. She turned to the table with a brilliant smile. "Myrin? This is Kalen."

Kalen realized someone else was in the room—a tawny-skinned young woman who couldn't have seen more than twenty winters, with shoulder-length hair of a hue like cut sapphire, who seemed more bone than flesh. He remembered her now—the woman in the alley from the night before.

"Oh!" She blushed, casting her eyes away from his bare chest.

Kalen grunted something like "well met"—which sounded more like "wuhlmt."

Myrin wore a ratty, sweat-stained tunic and a pair of loose breeches—*his,* Kalen realized. Being far too big, they made her look even more frail than when he had carried her home.

"I hope you don't mind," Cellica said to Kalen. "None of my things would fit her."

"Huh." Words didn't come easily to Kalen in the morning.

The halfling, however, was at her most garrulous just after sleep. "Nothing fashionable, but at least they're clothes." Cellica winked. "Not like you provided any last night."

Kalen grunted and looked to the cook pot, in which the remainder of the morning simmer stew bubbled warmly. He fished a roundloaf out of the box by the hearth, hollowed it out, and spooned in a healthy dollop. The stew had a sharp, pungent aroma from the many spices Cellica had added—she knew his illness stole his sense of taste as well as touch, so she took pride in making food that he could taste. He limped back to the table, sat on the stool Cellica had vacated, and stared across at Myrin.

Heedless of the tears rolling down her cheeks at the heat of the spices, Myrin was eating like she hadn't eaten in years, and seeing how skinny she was, maybe she hadn't. She licked up Cellica's stew with wild abandon, and Cellica brought her another roundloaf while Kalen sat there, picking at his stew. The halfling was smiling grandly, and Kalen imagined she was thrilled to practice her adoptive mother's recipes on someone who appreciated their full taste.

Kalen nodded at Myrin. "So . . . who is she?" he asked Cellica.

Myrin paused in her eating and looked to Kalen. Cellica sniffed.

"Why don't you ask her yourself?" Cellica's manner was sweet, so her suggestion didn't strike him as a command.

Kalen looked at Myrin sidelong. "You can talk?" He winced at Cellica's glare.

"I . . ." she said. "I can talk."

Cellica beamed. "Go on, peach," the halfling said. "Tell him what you told me!"

Myrin looked shyly at the table.

Cellica clapped her hands. "She's a *mys-ter-y!*" she exclaimed, pronouncing the word in excited syllables, like this was a great adventure. "She doesn't know who she is or where she came from—only her name and a few things from her childhood."

Kalen looked at Myrin, who was staring at her bread. "Aye?"

Myrin nodded.

"Naught else?" Like how I found you naked in an alley, he thought, speaking gibberish?

"Kalen!" Cellica snapped at his tone. "Manners!"

Myrin only shook her head. "I remember a little . . . a little about when I was small." Her voice was thin, and her words were oddly accented—old, like something out of a bardic tale.

"My mother—her name was Shalis—she raised me alone. I never knew my father. I was apprenticed to a wizard—his name was . . . I don't remember." She sniffed. "I can see these things, but they seem far away—like dreams. Like I slept years and never woke."

Kalen eyed her tanned coloration. Her complexion was exotic—Calishite, perhaps, though mixed with something else entirely. A whisper of elf heritage was about her as well—not a parent, but perhaps a grandparent. It was clear she would be quite beautiful when she grew to womanhood, but she was yet on the verge.

"Aught else?" he asked. "Homeland?"

Myrin shrugged.

"Was it city or countryside?" Cellica glared and Kalen added: "If you remember."

"City," Myrin said slowly. Her eyes glazed. "It was always cold . . . cold off the sea. Gray stone buildings, sand on the streets. Nights spent locked inside while terrors waited without. They waited, you see—the creatures in the night. Masks of shadows."

Cellica looked anxiously at Kalen, who only shook his head. "What city?" he asked.

"West, it was called," she said. "West . . . aught else, but I don't remember."

"Westgate?" Cellica suggested.

Myrin shook her head. "Mayhap."

Kalen shrugged. "Could be," he said. "I don't know what 'terrors' you would mean—there haven't been anything but men in the shadows of that city for a century, almost. Not since Gedrin and his knights drove the vampires out . . ."

He trailed off as Myrin looked down, her shoulders shaking as though she would cry. Cellica cast Kalen a sharp look, and he sighed.

They sat in silence for many breaths—perhaps a hundred count—saying nothing. Kalen ate a few spoonfuls of his stew, but it was tasteless to him. He drank his mulled cider and tried not to feel so awful.

As he did so, he gazed at Myrin, exploring the contours of her exotic face, trying to figure out where she had come from. She wasn't exactly *beautiful* without that crown of flames she'd been wearing in the alley, Kalen thought, but there remained a certain girlish appeal to her delicate features. Wearing Kalen's old shirt made her look like a child, too—in a dress or even a real gown . . .

Cellica caught him staring. "You've another question, Sir Longing-Gaze?"

Myrin's head shot up and her eyes went wide in expectation.

"Mind your stew," Kalen said to Cellica, harsher than he intended.

Myrin looked back down, blushing. Cellica's wry smile became a chiding frown.

Kalen ignored them both and turned back to his mostly untouched roundloaf, only to find nothing but his spoon on the table. He looked across to where Myrin was contentedly eating his morningfeast with her hands. Curious—he hadn't thought her reach so long.

"Do you need a spoon, peach?" asked Cellica.

"Sorry," the girl said. "I don't mean to be rude—I'm just so hungry." She looked at Kalen's spoon and murmured something under her breath that Kalen didn't understand.

Cellica reached for the spoon as though to give it to Myrin, but it skittered away, rose into the air, and floated to Myrin's hand. She caught it and set immediately to spooning stew to her mouth. Kalen and Cellica looked at one another, then at her.

Myrin, looking nervous in the silence, blinked at them. "What?"

"Lass," the halfling said. "Was that a spell?"

"Of course," Myrin said. "Can't—" She blushed. "Can't everyone do that?"

Kalen and Cellica exchanged another glance. Myrin went back to eating.

Before anyone could say more, there came a loud knock at the door, and Cellica fell off her stool with a startled gasp. Myrin didn't seem to notice and went right on eating. Kalen reached for Vindicator by instinct, and only then remembered he didn't have the blade any more—or his watchsword, for that matter. Bane's breath, where had he left *that*?

"Hark," he said. "Who calls?"

No answer came.

He seized a long knife from the table and reversed it, the better to conceal the blade against his forearm. Cellica grasped the crossbow amulet around her throat and Kalen nodded. He rose, a finger to his lips, and crossed to the door.

He put his left hand on the latch and lifted it as silently as he could, keeping his body shielded by the wall. Then he threw open the door and raised the knife . . .

A familiar red-haired half-elf, clad in a plain leather skirt and vest over a white shirt, leaped over the threshold into his arms. "Shadow, *dearest!*" she exclaimed.

Her lips found his and he could see only the stunned expressions on Cellica's and Myrin's faces.

SIXTEEN

Wheeling around for balance, Kalen managed to break the kiss and breathe.

Fayne seemed undaunted. "Shadow! It's been so *long!*" She hugged him tightly and squealed.

He blinked over her shoulder to the table, where Cellica was staring at him in shock. Myrin looked at him, then the newcomer, then down at her stew—she seemed to shrink on her stool. Cellica looked halfway between angry and wonderstruck.

"Oh, Shadow, we'll have such a *glorious* time at the revel," she said, emphasizing her words breathlessly. "I can't *believe* you have an invitation—I can't *wait* to wear my dress! Oh!"

Kalen could hardly breathe, she held him so hard.

"Kalen," Cellica asked slowly, "Kalen, who is this? What revel?"

"I—*urph*," Kalen said as the woman kissed him again, cutting off any words. This kiss was harder than the first, more insistent, and he tasted her tongue in his mouth.

A little hand tugged the hem of the half-elf's vest. "Pardon, lass," Cellica asked, hands on her hips. "Who . . . who are you?"

"I'm Fayne," the half-elf said, lacing her fingers through Kalen's. "A . . . *friend* of Shadow, here—I mean, Sir Kalen Dren." She winked conspiratorially.

Kalen could only stare when Cellica looked at him. "I don't know her," he said.

"She knows *you*," the halfling quipped. Then, eyes widening: "She *knows?* About—"

"Of *course* I know," Fayne said with a laugh. Then she looked between them and put her hand over her mouth in mock fear. "What, is it a secret?"

Cellica's face turned bright red, and Kalen shivered. "It's not how it looks—"

Kalen saw Fayne glance at Myrin, and she hesitated half a breath. Then she let loose a squeal. "Who's this, Kalen? She's *adorable!*"

Myrin's eyes widened as Fayne rushed to her and hugged her around the neck, then proceeded to fuss over her like a child with a kitten. Myrin stared at Kalen, stunned.

A tiny blue rune appeared on Myrin's cheek, Kalen saw, where Fayne had touched. But before he could comment, a halfling finger poked him insistently and he looked down.

"What's going on?" Cellica looked furious. "Kalen, who *is* this woman?"

"I don't—" Kalen's head hurt even worse than when he had risen. "I can explain."

"Oh." Cellica climbed up on her stool and crossed her arms. "This should be grand."

Myrin looked positively mouselike at the table under Fayne's attentions.

"Better make it *fast,*" Fayne noted, drawing out the word. "Someone *else* is coming up."

Kalen's heart skipped. "Who?"

"A woman," Fayne said. "Very pretty—gorgeous, even. Long dark hair, deep blue eyes. Armed and armored. Five gauntlets on her . . ." Fayne made a gesture across her collarbone and giggled. "Why—" She smiled. "Do you know her?"

"Tymora guard us," Cellica said. "That's *Rayse.*"

"Who's Rayse?" Fayne looked at Kalen jealously. "*Another* lass friend?"

"His superior, Araezra Hondyl!" Cellica said. "You were supposed to report this morn, Sir Snores-a-bed!" Cellica stared, wide-eyed, at Kalen. "What do we—?"

Kalen was in motion, crossing to the table.

Fayne purred at him. "You're quite the man, to have so many—hey!"

Kalen seized her by the arm and hauled her toward a closet, in which hung their spare clothes. He pushed her in, despite muffled protests, and stepped in himself.

"Kalen!" Cellica hissed. "What am I supposed to tell her?"

Kalen shrugged—he couldn't think, except that he knew he couldn't let Araezra catch them.

He shut the door behind them.

Myrin took very close care to stare at her stew the whole time.

She didn't know what was going on—where she was, who these people were, or anything—but just because she remembered nothing didn't mean she was an idiot. She'd seen that red-haired girl—Fayne—and the way she touched Kalen.

Of *course* he's got a lass friend, you fool, she thought. What did you *expect?*

She fancied she could still feel Fayne's fingers on her cheeks—the way the half-elf had prodded at her, grinning all the while. The touch lingered and Myrin felt oddly full, though it was not just from all the stew she had eaten. She felt full in *spirit.*

Maybe it was just Kalen looking at you, she thought. You're such a *girl!*

Cellica looked at her, and her mouth drooped in a sympathetic frown. She threw up her hands. "He's not always so," she said. "Just . . . hold a moment."

Myrin opened her mouth to speak, but she felt a gentle pressure in her ears—a voice that itched at her mind, telling her to remain in her seat. *Magic.* She stayed sitting, wondering.

Cellica got up and started toward the door, which Fayne had left open. In the corridor, Myrin saw with a stabbing curdle in her stomach, stood a very lovely and very angry lady. She had sleek, glossy black hair and liquid eyes bound in a face like that of a wrathful nymph. The woman wore a uniform, but Myrin did not know what sort. Little about this world seemed familiar to her thus far.

"Rayse!" Cellica said. "What a surprise! Won't you come"—the dark-haired woman swept into the chamber past the halfling—"in?"

"Well—" Araezra pulled up short and stared. "Well met?"

After an awkward breath, Myrin realized she was talking to her. "Oh . . . well met."

Araezra looked confused. "I'm sorry—have we met? I don't know you."

"Uh—I'm . . . I'm Myrin." Her fingers curled and her heart thudded. Why did they all have to be so *perfect*? "I'm . . . uh . . ."

Her brow furrowing, Araezra looked to Cellica.

"You probably want Kalen," the halfling said. "He's . . . ah—"

"It's very important," Araezra said. "He was supposed to report for duty this morn, and I haven't seen him." She glared toward Myrin, whose cheeks felt like they might burst into flame. She picked at her blue hair and wished it weren't so straggly.

Myrin wondered if Kalen wasn't some kind of nobleman, or rich merchant, or perhaps the lord of a harem, to have this many lasses flocking to his door. She wasn't certain where she'd heard that word "harem" before—it was floating somewhere in the back of her mind. Elusive, like a shard of a dream that danced just on the edge of her awareness.

Like her mother's face. Like all her memories.

"I'll tell him when I see him," Cellica said. "He's . . . he might be with Commander Jarthay. They were bound for the Siren yestereve. Perhaps they're still there?"

Araezra glanced at Myrin, who tried to shrink smaller. She looked back at Cellica. "You didn't . . ." she said awkwardly. "You didn't happen to read the *Minstrel* this morn?"

Cellica folded her hands behind her back. "No, absolutely not."

"Cellica."

"Well, yes—" The halfling winced. She waved her hands. "But it's horribly unfair! You aren't like that at all. That's just bloody Satin Rutshear."

Araezra smiled and sighed. "My thanks. I—I just have to find Kalen. We need to talk."

Cellica nodded. "I'll tell him when I see him."

The halfling looked at Myrin as though expecting her to say aught, but Myrin had no idea what to say. She couldn't stop staring at Araezra, who was the most beautiful woman she had ever seen—that she could remember, anyway.

Araezra didn't leave. She bit her pretty lip, and Myrin saw her eyes were damp.

Cellica shrugged. "Better have a seat, dear. Would you like cider?"

The armored woman nodded, tears rolling down her cheeks.

Kalen stood inside the closet, hands pressed flat against the sides.

Crushed against the inside wall, every inch of her body just a hair's breadth from his bare chest and loose hose, Fayne blinked at him with her gray eyes. She was about the width of a hand shorter, and he could feel her breath against his bare chest. His lips were level with the bridge of her nose, and he had the unsettling urge to plant a kiss on her forehead. Something about her made him want to kiss her.

She wore a wry little grin.

"Do not," he said.

Fayne smiled and edged a little closer to him, pressing her breasts to his chest and her mouth near his ear. "I wouldn't dream of it." Her tone wasn't girlish at all, but sharp. He felt, uncomfortably, as though all of this was according to her plan.

Kalen bit his lip. "Be still."

"You think your valabrar will hear?" That word confirmed his suspicions—she'd tricked him and knew full well what Araezra was doing there. All of this was her scheme, including hiding with him. "Oh, I promise—no one will hear *anything* we do in here."

A little tingle ran through Kalen. "Why would you fear Araezra finding you here?"

"I've made enough women jealous to know the look."

"Is this a trick?" Kalen asked. "Who are you?"

"Does that really matter?"

"How do you know . . ." He bit his lip. "How do you know who I am?"

"Again, is it meant to be a secret?" Fayne stretched just the tiniest bit, rippling across Kalen's body. Whoever she was, Kalen thought, she knew how to move.

"How did you find me?"

She grinned. "Did you think yourself hidden?"

"Do you answer every question with a question?"

"Don't you?"

Kalen's voice almost broke. "Damn it, lass, I—"

"Hold a moment."

Fayne slid down his chest and belly, startling him. If Kalen hadn't been concentrating on staying quiet, he would have gasped and fallen backward out of the closet.

He heard the rustle of cloth and felt Fayne's head brush his thigh.

"What the Hells?" he snapped.

"Pardon . . . almost . . . ah."

She stretched back up, slowly and languidly, and presented to him a ring of silver, etched with an eye sigil. "Dropped this. So clumsy."

"That's mine," Kalen said.

"Was," she corrected. "Or were you going to take it back?" She pressed her hip against his. "I would love to see you try."

Kalen tried to ignore the threat—and implicit offer. "What could be staying them?"

"Lass talk, I imagine." Fayne shrugged, which made him tingle. "It lets us be alone."

Kalen turned his full attention on her. "Who are you?"

"I told you," she said. "Fayne is my name."

"No, it isn't."

She put her hands on her hips. "And why not?"

"*Feign?* You think me a simpleton?"

"Ha!" she said. "Very well. My true name," she said grandly, "is Feit."

"Really? Counter-*feit?*"

"Damn!" She giggled, a touch of her assumed girlishness coming back.

"Enough." Kalen glared at her. "Unveil yourself, girl, or gods help me, I will burst out of this closet and get us both caught."

Fayne's eyes narrowed. "You wouldn't *dare*," she said.

"I have only embarrassment in front of my superior to fear," Kalen said. "You, on the other hand—I believe you are a thief and a scoundrel and have considerably more to lose."

"Well, then." Fayne dared him with her eyes.

Kalen started to move.

"Wait," she said, throwing her arms around him and holding him back. "Mercy. Gods! Don't get so excited." She held up the ring in the flat of her palm, near her face.

Kalen took it, and while he was distracted, she kissed him again.

He pulled away, thumping his head on the ceiling. Thankfully, Fayne did not follow, just stood there smiling wryly at him.

"Very well, my captor—what would you have of me?" She winked. " 'Ware you don't ask too much—this is naught but our second meeting. I usually wait until the third, at least."

Kalen ignored her and perked his ears—Araezra was still talking, but her voice sounded no nearer than before.

"You call yourself Fayne—very well," he said. "Why are you here? What is your game?"

"My game, dearest Vigilant Dren," Fayne said, "is a mystery by its nature. The hints are in the playing." Still holding him, she pressed her cheek against his chest and purred. "You must be an active man. Not only does it look passing well, but it feels like a *rock*."

"Uh . . ." The numbness in his body wouldn't let him sense her hands.

"Hard as stone." She nuzzled his chest, and he felt a tingle. "I like the scars, as well."

Your chest, idiot, Kalen thought. Keep the thinking in your head!

"Answer my other questions," he said. "You are here for some purpose. Is it coin you want? I have little enough, but it's yours."

"Nothing of the sort!" Fayne looked insulted. "I'm in no such business except"—she shook her hair back grandly—"the business of misery and scandal." Her voice was sweet.

"You must be a writer," he murmured.

"Pique!" Fayne smiled brilliantly. "I don't often tell folk this, but I am, in fact, a writer for a little rag you might know: the *Mocking Minstrel.*"

Kalen narrowed his eyes. "Satin Rutshear," he murmured.

"What a guess!" Fayne narrowed her eyes and licked her lips. "Can you read my mind?"

"No," Kalen said. "She's just the only one wicked enough."

"What charm," Fayne purred. "I like you more and more every breath, Shadowbane."

Kalen gritted his teeth behind a hard smile. What was taking Araezra so long? Why didn't she leave? Fayne was looking at him so directly, so boldly with those deep gray eyes . . . he wondered how long he had before his words—or his body—betrayed him.

"I was hoping to persuade you," Fayne said, "to take me to the revel on the morrow."

Kalen frowned. "Revel?"

><del>w</del>—

"So that's . . ." Araezra said. She'd stopped crying halfway through her story, in no small part due to the aid of a steaming mug of cider from the fire. "That's what happened. It was an accident. Tal . . . Talanna jumped too far and couldn't make it."

"Mmm," Cellica said, nodding.

Myrin, taking the cue, nodded as well, though she had no idea what they were talking about. Shadowbane, though—that was Kalen. She kept her mouth shut.

"I can't understand it," Araezra said. "This Shadowbane seemed—I don't know. He didn't want to be caught, but he helped me out of the pit when he could have run. And when Tal was hurt, he helped her. Do those sound like the acts of a criminal to you?"

Cellica shrugged. "Not at all."

"Then why the mask?" Araezra asked.

"I'm sure he has his reasons," Cellica said. "It's all very romantic, isn't it? Like something you'd find in a chapbook. But I'm sure"—Myrin noted her glance at the closet—"I'm sure that whoever this Shadowbane is, he feels just as badly about Talanna."

Araezra shrugged.

"Talanna . . ." Cellica sipped her cider and asked, cautiously, "She'll be well, aye?"

Araezra nodded. She seemed to catch Myrin looking at her, and her deep blue eyes flicked to meet her gaze. Myrin hid behind her big cider mug as best she could.

"And you—Myrin, aye? What say you?"

"It . . . it all sounds so exciting," she said. "I can't imagine. Um." Myrin took a mouthful of cider, burned her tongue, and choked.

Araezra shifted uncomfortably. "And how do you know Kalen, Myrin?"

"She doesn't," Cellica said. "She's a . . . friend, from Westgate. My friend. Not his."

Araezra pursed her lips. "But you've *met* Kalen, aye?"

"Oh, aye!" Myrin said, and immediately wished she'd restrained herself.

"And what do you think of him?" Araezra asked, looking at Myrin closely.

"He's so—" Myrin looked at Cellica, who was frantically shaking her head. "Kuh-kind," she said. She looked down at the spoon she was fiddling with nervously. "So very kind. *Yes.*"

"*Kind?*" Araezra frowned at Cellica, who grinned helplessly. "Perhaps you know a different Kalen than I do."

Myrin's mouth moved but she couldn't find words.

"Look—gods above, I'm sure I don't want to know," Araezra said. "Vigilant Dren's life is his own, and he *clearly* intends to keep it that way." She stood, leaned over to kiss Cellica on the cheek, and nodded to Myrin. "Coins bright." She crossed to the rack by the window where she'd left her greatcoat.

Myrin leaned toward Cellica. "What does that mean?" she asked. "Coins bright?"

"Traditional Waterdhavian saying. 'May fortune smile,' or the sort."

"Oh." Myrin cradled her mug. "She's so sweet."

The halfling whispered back. "I believe she thinks you're a doxy or some such."

"A what?"

The halfling blushed and shook her head. "Never you mind."

"Cellica," said Araezra from near the window. "Are these blood stains?"

Myrin and the halfling both looked toward Araezra, where she knelt investigating a pair of red marks on the sill and floor.

"Oh, just me," Cellica said. "I mean—I made a pie and set it there to cool, and it spilled a bit. You know how treacherous balancing at the window can be. You know."

Again, Myrin felt that tickle in her ears that indicated magic was afoot. Cellica's voice had an enchantment of some sort about it, that took hold when she was either angry or concentrating on making her words strike. It was working on Araezra, who shrugged.

"Well, then," she said. "Coins bright. Tell Kalen I came to call." She headed out the door.

Cellica breathed a great sigh of relief. After a moment, she crossed to the closet, grasped the latch, and flicked it open.

Kalen tumbled out, the red-haired half-elf on top of him. The halfling put her hands on her hips and looked down at them both.

>===W===<

One breath, Kalen was standing in the closet, practically hugging Fayne, and the next he was on the floor, straddled by Fayne. He blinked up at Cellica, whose face was stormy, and over at Myrin, who looked away.

"Is she gone?" Fayne asked. "*Excellent!*" She bounded up and straightened her skirt. "Well, I should be off. I'll see you at highsun before the revel on the morrow? *Outstanding.*"

"Revel?" asked Cellica. "Tomorrow?"

"Ah." Kalen got to his feet, mumbling. "That scroll I gave you. The one I told you to—"

"You mean . . ." The halfling plucked a small, crumpled scroll out of a pocket and held it up in both hands. "You don't mean *our* revel?"

"*Our* revel?" Fayne asked, mouth wide. She glared at Kalen.

"Please?" Cellica turned her eyes up at Kalen. "The yearly costume revel at the Temple of Beauty on Greengrass—I've been saving coin for just such a windfall. Please—*please?*"

"Ah—" Kalen said. He looked at Myrin, who shrugged.

Fayne put her hands on her hips. "Sweet wee one," she said. "But Kalen's *my* escort."

"Is that so?" the halfling said. Though she reached only to Fayne's belly, she stood just as strong, arms crossed over her breast. "And don't you *ever* call me 'wee.' "

Fayne smirked and crossed her arms. "Well, if you weren't such a *little* thing—"

Kalen was suddenly immersed in the midst of a firestorm that flowed from the women's lips. Their argument was just as loud, just as fast, and just as deadly as any duel he had ever survived—and many he'd run from. The one and only time he tried to step in, they upbraided him so sharply and fiercely that he reeled as though struck.

The situation was a mess. He'd been planning to give the invitation to Fayne just to get rid of her, but Cellica wanted to go as well. If he gave it away, he would never hear the end of it, and if he didn't please Fayne, then gods only knew what would happen.

"Choose one of us," Cellica said, and Kalen felt compelled by that voice of hers. "Choose one of us ladies, right here, right now."

"Aye." Fayne tossed her hair over her shoulders. "That choice should be obvious."

"Only if he dreams of maids half elf, half *giant*," added Cellica.

Fayne smirked. "Unless he prefers lighter fare—girl-children, perhaps?"

Cellica's face went bright red.

The ladies went back to bickering sharply, throwing turns of phrase that would have made the best broadsheet satirists applaud.

Kalen turned his eyes on Myrin at the table, who blushed down at her hands in her lap. She was a buoy of gentle calm in a sea of dueling, querulous words. She saw Kalen looking at her and blinked. Then she smiled gently—demurely—and went back to looking embarrassed.

Finally, head spinning and aching, Kalen closed his eyes and pointed. "I'll go with her."

Cellica and Fayne looked at him, then at his finger.

"You're taking *her?*" Fayne asked, eyes dangerous. "The blue-haired waif?"

Kalen pointed at Myrin. The young woman opened her mouth to speak, but before she could, Cellica grinned widely.

"How sweet! Myrin could use a gown—gods know she can't go on wearing Kalen's things all her days." She sneered at Fayne. "I'm sure we can dress her better than *this* ogre."

Ignoring that, Fayne rounded on Kalen. "Why is she wearing *your* clothes?"

"Better than *you* wearing them," said Cellica. "Though they might fit you, she-whale."

Fayne blushed so fiercely that her face matched her hair. "What?" She investigated her backside. "There's not a drop of blubber there. Unlike certain halflings—"

As they fell to bickering again, Kalen looked at Myrin. Her mouth drooped in a lonely frown and her eyes were cast toward her hands, which were bunched into fists on the table. Kalen watched as she clenched her fists harder and harder.

A splotch of blue appeared on her wrist, then branched into lines of tiny runes—like a sprouting vine of ivy—that spread up her arm.

"Just because I'm not the perfect height for—*cuh!*" Fayne's words ended in a cough.

Grasping her throat, Fayne burbled a cry and slumped, hands clutching her head. She would have fallen, but Kalen caught her. Her hands tightened into claws on Kalen's bare chest.

"What's happening?" Cellica cried, terrified.

Fayne was looking around wildly, a look of sheer rage on her face. She murmured words in a language Kalen did not know and clutched at her forehead as though to smother a fire inside.

Kalen looked to Myrin, who sat at the table staring vacantly at the reeling Fayne. Her skin had sprouted an entire lattice of blue runes growing across her shoulder and down her arm. Her eyes glowed like stars.

Flames leaked from Fayne's hand—dark magic. Her eyes scanned the room as though searching for a foe. Kalen realized she was staring right at Myrin but didn't seem able to see her.

Yet.

"Stop!" Kalen snapped.

Myrin jumped, fell out of her chair, and scrambled against the wall. "Uh?"

Fayne moaned and slumped against Kalen, panting. The agony slipped away from her face, but her anger burned all the brighter. She glared, still seemingly unable to see Myrin.

The hate in her eyes shivered Kalen to his core.

Cellica's eyes darted back and forth between Kalen and Myrin. She seemed not to notice Myrin's eyes or runes—the girl's eyes had been locked on the half-elf. "What was that?"

"Damn," Fayne murmured, touching her head as though it were tender. "Damn me for good and all." She shook her head and looked to the table, where she finally was able to see Myrin. Her lips curled like those of an angry canine, and Kalen half expected to see fangs. But no, her teeth were quite normal.

"Wait," Kalen whispered to Fayne.

She looked up at him, gray eyes slowly draining of rage—and replaced by wariness. "Aye?"

Kalen fell into communion with his threefold god, fingers curling around his gauntlet-etched ring. His hands glowed, attracting Myrin's and Cellica's awed gazes. Healing power flowed into Fayne, easing her breathing.

She closed her eyes and nuzzled her cheek against his hand. "Oh, *Shadow*," she said.

"Kalen," he corrected.

"Hrmm." Fayne moved away—a little wobbly, but that might have been feigned. "If you're taking blue-hair girl, then I'll just have to wait until next time, won't I?"

She winked at Kalen in a way that assured him there would indeed be a next time.

"You don't—you don't have to," Cellica said. "Let me look at you. I've a healer's—"

"No need!" Fayne gave Cellica a winning smile and bent to kiss her on the forehead. "I'll be just fine." She tossed a glare at Myrin. "Just fine."

The half-elf left.

Kalen glanced at Cellica and Myrin. The halfling stood, pale faced, near the door, staring after Fayne. At the table, Myrin looked terrified. Blue runes adorned the left side of her face.

Kalen sighed. "I'll see her home," he said. "Wherever home is."

He grabbed his spare uniform, the black coat of leather and plate with its two gauntlets of rank. Heedless of whether they watched, he pulled off his hose and dressed.

With an *eep!* Myrin blushed and looked away.

Cellica looked hard at Kalen. "Do you know where?" she asked. Kalen shrugged.

"So you really *don't* know her, eh?" the halfling said brightly.

Kalen laced up his breeches and shrugged on the harness straps.

"You . . . you're still taking Myrin to the revel on the morrow?" Kalen shrugged. It hardly seemed relevant.

"Well, then," Cellica said. She smiled.

Myrin pressed her back against the wall and slid down, trembling and hot in the face.

What had she done?

She stared at her hands and her heart leaped. Little blue marks showed vividly against her left palm. She rubbed at them, as one might dirt smudges, but they didn't come off. She pulled up the sleeve of the old tunic, breathing hard. She found more marks traveling up her arm. She scratched hard at her skin, trying desperately to get rid of them, but she drew blood.

She touched her cheek, which tingled. In the small mirror across the room, she saw a vine of blue runes running along her throat and up her face. She sat, rigid in horror, and tried vainly to stay calm. The marks were moving—shrinking.

Soon, they faded entirely, and she could breathe again.

Fayne had gone, she realized, and Kalen—fully dressed and about to follow—was staring at her. His icy eyes glittered balefully. When Myrin opened her mouth, nothing came out. Wordlessly, Kalen strode into the corridor and banged the door shut.

Myrin looked down at her hands. Tears welled in her eyes.

"Don't mind him." Cellica appeared at her side, smiling. "He's just a glowering bastard."

"Really?" Myrin sniffed.

"Yes," she said. "I know what will make you feel better." Her eyes twinkled. "Dresses!"

SEVENTEEN

When she realized Kalen wasn't in the Room of Records either, Araezra slammed her fist on the table. Pain flared and she kissed her wrist to lessen it.

Damn that Kalen—where the Hells *was* he? He wasn't at home, and he wasn't anywhere at the barracks. This, the Room of Records, was his favorite place—it was peaceful and quiet, and he could read. Where could he be?

And who the Hells was that *girl?* Wearing his tunic, with hair like that? Had he brought a girl home from the Smiling Siren?

She felt sick. Everything was going wrong that day—*everything.* Except for Jarthay being so kind, she'd have sworn this was still a nightmare. The commander being sensitive made it seem more a fever dream.

Who *was* that girl? Gods, had Kalen fallen in love with someone else? *Gods!*

In her anger, Araezra hadn't noticed the door quietly opening or anyone entering. Only as she sat there, willing herself not to cry, did gooseflesh rise on her arms. She realized she was no longer alone. "Who's there?" she asked. "Kalen?"

Light vanished from the room and she gasped. The Room of Records had no windows, and with the door shut, it was utterly lightless. Pushing her uneasy shivers aside, she put her fingers to the amulet she and those of her rank wore and whispered a word in Elvish. The medallion glowed with a gentle green light, softly illumining the room around her.

She made out the desk nearby and anchored herself. The candle on the edge of the desk gave off a little plume of smoke from its too-short wick.

"Fool girl," she said. "Scared by a burned-out candle."

She saw another source of light, then, coming from her belt. She froze and reached down, very slowly, to the hilt of Shadowbane's sword. She remembered that it had scalded her hand before, but the hilt was no longer warm to the touch. Instead, it felt cool and comfortable. *Right.* Light leaked around the edges of the scabbard and she drew it forth, gasping in awe at the silver shimmer that fell from it.

"Gods," she murmured. She cut the blade twice through the air, marveling at the way the light trailed. It felt so efficient—a killing weapon, beautiful and deadly.

Then she thought she saw movement against the wall. "What was—?"

She crept forward, Shadowbane's sword held before her like a talisman. She approached, letting the circle of light creep closer and closer to the wall, until—

Nothing.

Nothing had moved—it was just a Watch greatcoat hung on a peg by the disused hearth.

Araezra loosed a nervous breath.

Then a man was there, leaping inside her guard. She gasped and tried to slash, but he was too fast, batting the sword out of her hands. The weapon spun end over end toward the door and clattered to the floor. Her attacker seized her by the throat and hip and crushed her against the wall. She could see, by the dim, flickering light of the sword, that it was a smooth-faced dwarf. His features were flawless, making him look all the more monstrous to her eyes. She knew his name—remembered Kalen mentioning a beardless dwarf.

"Arrath Vir," she squeaked.

"I am pleased that you know me," the dwarf said. "It means you might be useful." He fixed her eyes with his own. "Tell me—who is seeking me? A name."

"Piss—*urk!*" He pressed his arm tighter against her throat, cutting off air.

"Know that you are mine to slay on a whim." His eyes bored into hers. "You are powerless. The Watchmen in the barracks—all those swords and shields sworn to serve this city. All those men who hunger for your beauty. All of them mean nothing to you now."

Her face felt as though it would burst from the pressure within. As though he sensed this, Rath eased his arm enough that she could breathe.

"All the years spent cultivating your life—everything you learned as a child, all the pointless loves and hates that have defined who you are. All of it ends, here and now, at my whim." He smiled gently. "You will die at my hands, no matter what you do now."

Araezra gasped but could not speak. She could barely breathe.

"Aye," he said. "But you've a choice. Aid me, and I shall make your death a painless one. Do not, and I shall not."

Araezra looked over Rath's shoulder.

"What say you?" The dwarf eased his grasp so she could just choke out words.

"Pick . . . it . . . up," Araezra said.

Rath looked back, and there stood Kalen Dren.

→W←

Kalen had trailed Fayne through the streets as best he could, but she was like a devil to follow. She would vanish around a corner and appear elsewhere, a dozen paces to one side or another. Eventually he lost her entirely.

Perhaps it was good riddance—to be free of whatever scheme she'd concocted for the revel—but in truth, no small part of him *wanted* to see her again. To finish what they'd started.

But duty came before beguiling lasses who showed up at his door unannounced, and so he made his way to the barracks. Araezra was not in any of her usual haunts—her office, the commons, the training yard—and Kalen was a little relieved. He didn't feel like facing her, and if duty had called her away before he got the chance, then so be it. After Talanna had been hurt, he didn't feel like he could lie to Araezra anymore.

He reached the unlatched door of the Room of Records—just a little ajar, so he could see inside—and froze. Rath was inside, holding Araezra captive.

At first, neither of them noticed his appearance, so he kept to the shadows and stood, unmoving, in the doorway. He was not wearing Shadowbane's leathers and cloak, but the Guard uniform was black and he could use that to his advantage. He called upon the lessons he'd learned first in Luskan—how to stand still and silent—and thought hard.

Kalen's instinct was to strike, but he suppressed it. Rath held Araezra at such an angle that if Kalen stepped forward, the surprise could prove fatal for her. With his training as a thief, Kalen could kill the dwarf in one, fast blow, but he could not cross the room without one or the other noting him. The silver glow of Vindicator illuminated the room enough for that.

Neither could he cry out for guards—as Araezra would surely die in the confusion. And if he went to get aid quietly, he would be abandoning his friend to death.

He had to do something, though. He had—

He had no sword. The scabbard at his belt was empty.

How had he forgotten that? He had dropped the blade when he brought Myrin back, and never retrieved it. He'd even walked past the barracks armory on his way, coughing and feigning weakness as always. He could reclaim Vindicator, but surely moving the light source would alert Rath.

Think, he told himself. *Think.*

But nothing came. He was the weakling Kalen Dren who could barely hold a sword, much less fight with it. There was so little he could do. The dwarf had been too much for him at his prime as Shadowbane, armed and on even ground. If he attacked now, in any way, Rath would kill them both. If it were just himself, he might take Tymora's chance, but it was *Rayse.*

He felt helpless. He could not attack, could not flee, and if he revealed himself . . .

That was it.

Making sure to hunch as usual, Kalen stepped forward, out of the shadows, and coughed—softly, but distinctly.

Araezra's eyes danced with stars, but she clearly saw a figure step out of the shadows and into the silvery light: Kalen! His hand was not a dagger's length from Shadowbane's sword.

"Pick . . . it . . . up," she said.

Rath looked, and a smile spread across his face, particularly at the stooped way Kalen stood, and his empty belt. He only smirked as Kalen stood over the silver blade.

"Touch that steel," Rath said, "and I snap your commander's neck."

"Valabrar," Kalen corrected, in his damnably precise manner.

What are you doing? Araezra thought at him.

"Speak thus, again," Rath said. "I do not understand."

"She is a valabrar. To explain"—Kalen gestured to the two gauntlets on his breastplate—"two, for vigilant. Araezra wears five for a valabrar. One would be a trusty, three a shieldlar—"

"Silence," the dwarf said. "If you wish this *Araezra* to live, down any weapons you carry, shut the door, and do only as I say."

Kalen inclined his head, the way he did whenever an instruction was given. Not taking his eyes from Rath, he slid the door quietly shut. He spread his hands to show them empty.

"Kneel," Rath said. "There—where you will block the door."

Kalen did so without argument, sinking to his knees.

Araezra wanted to scream at him. Burn him, what was Kalen *doing?*

The dwarf smiled at Araezra, and she could smell the brandy on his breath. "What a finely trained mastiff you have," he murmured.

"Let him go," Araezra said. "Don't hurt him. I'll do whatever you want."

"Such as?" A bemused fire lit in the dwarf's eye, as though she had reminded him of a private jest. "What could you possibly offer me?"

"Me." The word tasted like wormwood in her mouth. "I'm beautiful, did you not say it?"

Rath smirked.

Then he hauled Araezra away from the wall and threw her to the floor near the desk as though she were an empty tunic. Her head knocked against the stout darkwood and her vision blurred. She reached to pull herself up, but the dwarf caught her hand—her sword hand—and twisted it. A crackle of bones sounded and her wrist exploded in pain. She uttered a screech that did not reach any volume, because he kicked her in the belly and blew any air from her body. The scream became a wet sob.

Kalen was saying something.

The dwarf looked at Kalen then. "I did not hear you, trained dog," he said.

"You should flee this place," Kalen observed in his indifferent manner. "You can accomplish nothing here."

The dwarf lunged across the distance between them and stood over Kalen, one hand grasping him by the brown-black hair that hung messily in his eyes. "Why, dog?" he asked. "Do you offer me a threat?"

Kalen's eyes did not leave Rath's, and he shook his head. "Only a fact," he said. "You are in the heart of our barracks, and a cry will call more Watchmen than you can defeat alone."

Araezra realized Kalen was distracting Rath. She flexed her wrist—broken, but she'd trained left-handed as well. She could still wield a sword, albeit poorly. She looked to the silvery blade on the floor. But it was nearer Kalen than herself, and he could not fight, could he?

Would he? She wondered.

"You can slay both of us, but you cannot silence both of us at the same moment." Kalen continued. "Thus, if you kill either of us, the other can cry out and you will die."

The dwarf did not blink, but the look on his face told Araezra he had counted the guards he had bypassed. "Why not call for them now?" he asked.

"Our bargain," Kalen said. "You leave this place and do not harm either of us, and we will not cry out. No one need die."

Araezra gasped and coughed, as her breathing once again became normal. "Kalen . . ."

He ignored her and stared at Rath, who seemed to be considering.

Then the dwarf's fingers touched the edge of Kalen's jaw, caressing it softly and gently—like a lover, and like death. "Very well, dog," said Rath. "But I want to hear you *beg*."

Kalen cast his eyes down.

"Beg for mercy," Rath said with a cruel smile.

When Kalen spoke, his voice hardly rose above a whisper. "Please," he said. "*Please.*"

"Kalen . . ." Araezra couldn't believe it. The Kalen she loved did not beg.

Rath sniffed. "You call yourself a man, and yet you take the coward's path," he said. He looked at Araezra. "Your mastiff is not a hound, my lady, but a mongrel bitch."

Kalen's eyes, gleaming pale at Araezra, seemed very, very cold in that silvery light.

Araezra rubbed her bruised throat. "Choose, dwarf," she said. "I have a good scream in me yet, and weak as he is, I've no doubt Vigilant Dren can muster such a cry."

Rath looked from her to Kalen and back. Then he snorted.

"Very well." He hauled Kalen up, and to his credit, the man barely coughed. "Know that your cowardice falls beneath the weakest pup, for even such a cur can fight when cornered."

Kalen did not answer.

"Have you nothing to say?" asked the dwarf.

Kalen only stared at Rath. Araezra felt a trembling anger build within her.

Then Rath was gone, nearly flying down the hall. Kalen slumped to the floor, but he caught himself before his face struck the stone. Araezra saw his eyes, bright and furious and icy, gleam at her. Then he started to cough.

In an instant, as though that sound had given her strength, Araezra pushed herself to her feet. "Guard!" she cried, loud as she could. "Watch, Guard—to arms! Intruder!"

A great clamor of feet and steel arose in the rooms around them. Folk were coming, summoned by Araezra's cry. Araezra looked at Kalen, so weak and sad, lying there. She reached down. "Up, Vigilant."

He took her hand and climbed up shakily. "Are you hurt?" he asked.

She shook her head, furious words building in her throat.

Kalen coughed. "Gods, Rayse, I didn't want you to get hurt. You know that."

"Spare me." Araezra shook her head, too angry and hurt to spend soft words on him. "I don't need anyone to protect me—especially not a coward."

Kalen cast his eyes down.

Araezra took Shadowbane's sword—it felt warm to the touch but did not burn her—then ran into the hall to muster the Watch.

Kalen stood shaking, wounded deeper than any sword could have cut.

He'd given everything to save Araezra. He had broken his greatest vow to himself, never to beg. And still, she had turned away from him. He had seen the contempt in her eyes.

He was less than a man to her, and he had pulled her low as well.

A coughing fit came upon him then, bubbling up like a cruel reminder of his failure, and he fought it down—in vain. He coughed and retched and spat blood into his hand.

That blood and spit could easily have been Rath's blood on his hands. The temptation had been so strong—to trick the dwarf into vulnerability and plunge a blade into his liver, kidney, or heart. Like a backstabbing thief, or like an assassin. The way he would have done in Luskan. But that would have sullied his vows, and the paladin in him would not allow it.

He lifted his hands to heal himself at a touch, but his powers did not come forth.

He realized why, and the understanding struck him like a slap across the face.

All this time, he had protected Waterdeep—this city of faceless citizens—and protected those he loved and cherished. But he could not do it at the cost of his own principles. He could not compromise the deepest commitment of all: to himself.

So that he might continue in his duty, he hadn't revealed himself after Lorien, or after Talanna had been hurt. The threefold god had not punished him for that. But when he hadn't revealed himself today, he'd chased away his only friend other than Cellica.

Although Araezra was alive, he knew he had acted wrongly. The

Threefold God had taken his powers for sacrificing his duty to himself for his duty to others.

He saw that he must do both—fight for the city, and fight for himself and those he loved. He would prove himself worthy.

He swore it.

EIGHTEEN

To prepare for the revel, Cellica took Myrin to a dress salon called Nathalan's Menagerie—named, Cellica explained, for the elf noble who was the owner.

Lady Ilira Nathalan owned a number of such shops across Faerûn, which did their part in supplying—and in many cases creating—the fashions of the day. Patrons tried on styles amid cages filled with exotic birds and flowers. The gowns, sashes, and shoes were rich in quality but low in cost, which, Cellica explained, was the reason behind the Menagerie's success.

"I don't know how she does it," Cellica said as she gestured to gown after gown for the attendant to take for her, "but some lucky goddess must watch over her supplies. Her prices always undercut her competitors. Nobles usually have their own seamstresses as a matter of pride, but Ilira caters to merchants and other wealthy folk who don't have signets stuck up their—heh." Cellica smiled wryly. "Better dresses, too, though don't let the nobility hear that."

Myrin watched as a pair of lovely middle-aged human women draped a series of gowns over their chests, admiring the colors in the mirror. An attendant—whom Myrin realized must be a half-orc, owing to her small tusks and gray skin—watched impassively. Her hair was a brilliant pink that could not be natural. It reminded Myrin of her own blue hair, which she pawed at idly.

"Ninea," said Cellica, tugging at Myrin's arm and pointing to the half-orc. "Just watch."

One of the customers framed a request to Ninea the half-orc, who touched the woman's shoulder briefly. The effect was as sudden as it was impressive: the woman's skin took on a brilliant golden sheen, astonishing her companion, who gasped and broke into tittering.

"Gods!" Myrin said. "That's amazing!"

"Simple magic," Cellica said. "Ninea has a spellscar that lets her alter colors to match her whims. Temporarily, of course." She continued breezing through gowns. "Certainly you could find cheaper attire elsewhere, but the quality is hard to defeat." She selected her tenth and eleventh. "Perhaps it's goodness rewarding the same."

"Aye?" Myrin hadn't selected a gown—she was remembering Kalen's glare.

"Aye," Cellica affirmed, taking down her twelfth. "Lady Ilira's a patron of the Haven of the Scarred, for those run afoul of spellplague or other magical maladies—a consortium of priests and healers. I'm a member."

The halfling frowned at a conservative brown gown Myrin was looking at and led her away. "It'll be a costume revel," she said. "Most of these are a particular lady from history—that one must be a Candlekeep ascetic. Boring as old rat tails!"

"What?" Myrin was standing shyly to the side, grasping her right elbow behind her back and burrowing her left foot into the floorboards.

"Pay it no mind, dear," said Cellica. "Let's find another that suits you better."

"Oh?" Myrin behaved around the finery the way a mouse must in a hall full of cat statues. She was terrified she would perish under the assault of silk. "Can . . . can we afford this?"

"Of course! We halflings have a way with coin. Just none of the priciest, eh? Ooh!" Her eye fell on a rich cloth-of-silver gown. She spoke with a halfling attendant in a language Myrin didn't understand, winced, then nodded. The gown went into the attendant's already full arms.

The half-orc woman with the bright pink hair brushed past Myrin. While the attendant was dexterous enough, Myrin's inherent clumsiness almost knocked her over. The half-orc had to catch her by the hand and ward her off. Ninea's hand sparked against hers. "Ooh, sorry!" Myrin said.

The woman started to respond, then shook her head, seeming faint.

"Ninea?" asked the halfling attending Cellica and Myrin. "Be ye well, lass?"

"Aye," said the half-orc. Her hair, Myrin saw, was fading from its sharp pink to a dirty brown. "Just weary, methinks."

"Well, ask Ilira if you can go early, aye?" Cellica's voice carried a touch of compulsion.

"Aye." Ninea gave Myrin a curious look. "Aye, I'll do that."

The half-orc wandered to the back of the salon, looking ill.

Hesitantly, Myrin selected three gowns—a gentle, deep blue affair with gold trim, a conservative green with silver chasing at the bodice, and a sleek black garment. She didn't particularly want any of them. She pulled Kalen's worn tunic tighter about her body. She liked how it smelled—it felt like Kalen was embracing her. Why did he have to be so *handsome?*

Stop it, girl, she thought. You don't even know who you are. You shouldn't worry about men—particularly ones who *hate* you!

She hoped Kalen didn't hate her, after what she'd done—accidentally—to Fayne.

But what *had* she done?

As they made their way to the mirror-walled fitting room, Myrin spotted Ninea near the back of the Menagerie. The woman she spoke to was slim and elegant and beautiful, with long midnight hair and delicate pointed ears. An elf, Myrin thought, but there was something . . . otherworldly about her. Looking at her made it hard to breathe.

"Lady Ilira herself," Cellica said, poking her head around Myrin's waist. "Aye—you're thinking she can't be mortal. She's an eladrin, lass—they're all like that."

"Eladrin?" Myrin frowned. She'd never heard this word before.

Cellica shrugged. "High elves, eladrin, all the same to me." She took Myrin's arm. "Come—you'll see her again at the ball, of course."

"She's coming?" Myrin hadn't thought there might be nobles there, but of course there would be. Good thing she would be in costume, otherwise she'd be too afraid to show her common face. Around such a creature as Lady Ilira, she would feel even worse.

"Every year!" Cellica said. "It's a tradition."

Myrin blinked then hurried to follow. She felt self-conscious trying on the gowns with the aid of an attendant, but the way Cellica casually flung clothes around made her relax. The attendants measured them, then waited for a decision. The dresses would be altered later, to be picked up in time for the revel.

"The dance between Ilira and Lorien is traditional," Cellica said. "Every year, she and Lady Lorien dance at the height of the ball. No two ladies are closer friends than that pair, and—so the gossip says—it's more than that." She tossed a slinky green gown over her shoulder, and the attendant barely caught it. "But never we lesser mortals mind."

Myrin blushed, though she couldn't say why.

"And who . . . who will Lady Ilira dress as?" Myrin asked. If she stood on her toes, she could just see the elf woman over the mirrors, surveying her salon.

"Probably no one." Cellica shook her head. "She always wears black, and lots of it," she said. "Dull, I know, but she's so elegant." She leaned in close to Myrin. "Some say she does it in mourning for a lost love, but I rather think it's to hide something. Unsightly tattoos or scars or the like. Some say she has one on her back—and that's why she never wears her own backless gowns—though I think there's a reason she always wears long gloves, let me tell *you*."

"How do you know all this?" Myrin asked.

"One of us has to keep up with the news in the city, and godsknow Sir Shadow isn't going to do it." Cellica shrugged into a silver gown and admired herself. "And I like gossip."

Myrin smiled and looked at her feet—thinking of Kalen.

The attendant returned with a woven basket in which lay two gowns. "If you would be pleased," she said, "the lady suggests you try these."

Cellica frowned at the gowns. "Who—?"

"Lady Ilira," said the attendant. "She saw you in the Menagerie and thought these colors and styles might serve. Fitted per your measurements. Perhaps . . . a happy coincidence?"

Curious, Myrin looked across the room. Lady Ilira was gone. She seemed to have vanished into the shadows. It gave her a chill.

"Ye *gods*." Cellica held up a scarlet gown, human-sized. She eyed Myrin devilishly.

"I don't think—" Myrin started, but Cellica wouldn't accept such an answer. She disrobed timidly while Cellica drew on a gold gown.

Myrin had to admit the red dress looked fine. It was sleek, it was daring, and it was bright without being gaudy. And the cut was perfect—it hugged her waiflike curves in a way that was not at all waif-like, but neither was it loose. She almost thought she looked pretty.

"Perfect for your skin!" Cellica nodded.

Myrin looked at her shimmering skin in the mirrors. In the soft lighting of the salon, it glowed a deep tan like polished betel wood. She blushed.

"The blue doesn't really serve," said Cellica. She stood on a stool, straining up to finger Myrin's shoulder-length hair. Myrin flushed and tried to look away from the mirror, only to remember she was surrounded by mirrors. "It's a lovely blue, and all, but it's . . . blue."

Myrin's insides tingled. "What . . . what *would* serve?"

"Well," Cellica said, "this one's an evening gown worn by the legendary Lady Alustriel of Silverymoon, who—as one of the Seven Sisters—had silver hair to her waist. If we could just get Ninea over here. Shame, as she charges such hard coin for—"

And just like that—as Myrin watched in the mirror—the scraggly blue hair spun and swam like the currents in a whirlpool. In a breath, it turned to rich, burnished silver and fell to her waist.

Cellica's eyes widened. "Now that . . . that's impressive." She looked for Ninea, who had disappeared out of the store, then leaned toward Myrin to whisper. "Can you do aught for me? I'd love . . . I'd love a good crimson, if you wouldn't—"

"I don't even know how I did it for me." Myrin blushed. "I could try—"

"No, no!" Cellica said, turning white. "It looks too glim for such a risk. Keep it that way."

Myrin frowned. Then she realized something. "You wanted crimson? Like Fayne's hair?"

"Ha! Hark—how the day wanes!" Cellica picked nervously at the gold dress. The color flattered her well and the gown was cut with gods' eyes to show flashes of sunbrowned flesh on her slim belly. "This one, then."

She whistled, and their attendant glided over. The halfling didn't seem surprised to see Myrin's silver hair.

"I think we've decided," Cellica said, and Myrin realized she wanted to be away from the salon as soon as possible. Was it something she had said?

"Please, my lady, to have these as well," said the halfling girl, presenting two parcels bound in waxed string. "Less elegant—more practical, but fine. A gift, for gracing the Menagerie."

Cellica blushed furiously. "We can't accept these," she said.

But the attendant shook her head. "Lady Ilira mentioned aught of a debt," she said. "She spoke of a 'shadow that wards'?" She shrugged. "She said you would understand."

Cellica and Myrin shared a long, curious glance. Then the halfling smiled. "Very well, but we pay for these in full." She gestured to her gold gown and Myrin's scarlet.

The attendant shrugged. She looked at Kalen's borrowed tunic and breeches and tried to hide her disdain behind her kerchief.

Cellica murmured a laugh. "Better just toss those out, I think."

The attendant nodded and took up the old clothes, averting her nose. Myrin watched the clothes in her arms and felt Cellica's eyes. The halfling smiled at her mysteriously.

"Cheers, peach," Cellica said, squeezing her hand. "No reason to fret—he did promise to take *you* to the revel, not that other stripling."

"But—"

"Kalen, for all his faults, is a man of his word." Cellica winked. "Don't you forget that!"

When Cellica turned away, Myrin wiped at her cheek and noted in the mirror a tiny blue rune on her wrist, glowing softly. It hadn't been there when she'd entered the salon, but it was there now—a bright little spot that filled her with nervous dread. It felt warm to the touch and didn't fade no matter how long she looked at it.

Myrin looked where Lady Ilira had stood, at the back of the Menagerie, but no one was there. She saw only a shadow on the wall, which flickered away as though someone—unseen—had moved.

"Come, lass!" Cellica called. "Delay too long, and I'll just have to buy another!"

NINETEEN

Fayne rose late the following morn, in her rooms above the rowdy Skewered Dragon in Dock Ward. She was alone, and every bit of her ached.

Awakening from reverie alone in her own bed was in itself cause for concern. She hadn't spent more than a dozen nights alone in all the years since her mother's death. She normally required only a few hours of the trancelike rest—only half what she had just spent. She must have felt truly awful, to fall into bed by herself and rest the night through.

Perhaps she had even spent some of the time in real *sleep*—ye gods. Maybe she was wearing a half-elf's face too much.

She recalled that the owner of the Dragon had questioned her gruffly when the carriage had dropped her off, but she'd waved him aside, along with the catcalls of patrons. She'd ignored the sneers of the serving girls—saucy wenches who sold their charms as openly as drinks—and managed to climb up to her chamber before collapsing into bed.

She examined the damage in the mirror. That blue-headed snip had muddled her mind, adding worry lines around her eyes and lips. She'd often wondered what it would feel like, being struck by dark magic—gods knew she'd done it often enough herself.

"Hit me with my own power, eh?" she murmured. "*Children.*"

All in all, totally unacceptable, she thought. She set to work. She would just touch up a few details of her appearance.

She caressed the invisible pendant that hung at her throat. It faded into sight and gleamed as she harnessed the magic—complex, powerful things for which her wand was not quite suited. It wasn't that she *couldn't* cast the shaping ritual with the wand—it just didn't feel right to her. It was better for quick castings, particularly illusions and dark, fey-touched art. It had come from her mother, who had been a talented witch of the fey path. The amulet, on the other hand—her patron had built it precisely for this sort of ritual, which was more wizardly than warlock.

She thought she should see Kalen today. Fayne hoped the man was suitably in agony over the wounds she had sustained in his tallhouse. She might suggest that he could make it up by taking her to the revel instead of Myrin, thus furthering her plan.

She left shadows under her eyes, so as to make herself appear a little more vulnerable. She knew Kalen liked the gray eyes, so she made them shine. She slimmed her image slightly, and made her face just a bit more darling—her nose, in particular, seemed a bit too long, so she made it small and delicate.

More like Myrin's nose, she realized, and she stuck out her tongue in disgust.

Her amulet had been a gift from her patron on her fortieth name day (gods, how long ago that seemed!), and coincided with her learning how to change her face. First, she had used the wand's illusory powers, but her patron had taught her how to perform a ritual that would make the changes deeper, harder to dispel.

Finished, she stepped back to admire her handiwork. This was the face she would wear this day—Greengrass, the festival of spring. It wasn't what she'd call beautiful, exactly, but a proper seduction was accomplished according to the desires of the man or woman seduced. She winked at the mirror, glad of her false face. A blessing no one could see the real one—she didn't spend so much effort hiding it in vain.

Her face and body made up, Fayne selected suitable attire for the Watch barracks: mid-calf gray dress with open front, laced black bustier cut with slits on the flanks to reveal slashes of lacy red underslip, matching scarlet scarf for the cold, wide leather hat for any rain, and her favorite knee-high boots with dagger-length heels.

None of them cheap, but none of them rich—quite what she thought Kalen liked.

As she dressed, she smiled at the revel-ready garments hanging in the wardrobe, carefully selected for the occasion. She would have quite the laugh at that private jest—most of her best pranks were personal.

She threw on a weathercloak to hide her outfit, whisked her way out the Dragon around a few highsun brawlers and patrons waving for her charms, and hailed a carriage.

Vainly, Kalen had hoped that by the next day, Araezra would have calmed herself about the Room of Records and they could talk. But he hadn't seen her all morn, and when he'd asked, a gruff Commander Jarthay had told him she was out on duty. Kalen didn't need the subtle, tight pitch of the commander's words to know things would be tense with Araezra.

He hadn't wanted to go home, so he'd spent the night at the barracks and eaten among the Guard. Thankfully, no one bothered him. His notorious indifference was good for that, at least. That morn, he had tried to work in the Room of Records, but every time he looked up from the ledgers, he would see Rath holding Araezra helpless or hear her choked whispers. Eventually, he moved outside to work in the warm, sun-filled courtyard.

Greengrass was the first day of spring, and the weather treated Waterdeep to warm days, cold nights, and frequent rain. Kalen disliked autumn and spring, with their long shadows and false warmth: he preferred the commitment of summer heat or winter chill.

In the yard, he left the ledger untouched and began a letter to Araezra, trying to explain what he had done. He paused now and then, to listen to the sounds of training in the court.

A cluster of Watchmen had gathered to watch a practice match between two of the youngest and most handsome members of the Guard: Aumun Bront and Rhagaster Stareyes. The latter was the more handsome thanks to his elf heritage (the legacy of a scandalous, hypocritical indiscretion on the part of his elf supremacist father, Onstal Stareyes, with a serving lass in Dock Ward). The men circled each other, stripped to the waist and sweaty, padded swords swishing.

They sparred under the unimpressed eye of Vigilant Bleys Treth, whom Kalen had done his best to avoid these last days. He didn't much like the man (the feeling was mutual), and Treth had seen Shadowbane on the night Talanna had been hurt. He might recognize Kalen.

The other guard who might have known him—Gordil Turnstone—was there, too, sitting on a bench. Though he was ostensibly watching the sparring, Turnstone was dozing.

Bront cut over and high and Stareyes replied with a plunging block. It could have become a counter to the belly, but the half-elf held the parry too long. Finally, Stareyes broke the parry and cut in from the opposite line, then reversed again, striking from both directions in sequence. He feinted right and attacked left. In rhythm, Bront tried to parry right, and the half-elf dealt him a sharp rap on the left side with his blunted blade.

The watchers clapped and Stareyes flashed his winning smile. Bront cradled his bruised side and gave Stareyes a rueful grin.

Kalen watched them surreptitiously over his spectacles. A part of him wished he could lord his prowess before an audience, but the needs of his disguise prevented it. He'd learned that lesson in a harsh manner during his time as an armar, before Araezra.

He thought about the flaws in Bront's style, and it must have shown on his face. Treth was watching him with a sneer. Kalen averted his eyes.

"Dren," Treth called. "Care to teach us aught?"

The congratulatory chatter in the courtyard fell silent, replaced by whispers.

Kalen said nothing, only looked at his parchment and quill. He had paused before telling Araezra the truth. He could see the unwritten sentence: "I lied to you, Rayse."

Did he dare? Would she understand? Or would she continue to hate him, not only for humiliating her but for lying to her as well? Not to mention that Araezra would be honor-bound to arrest him as a dangerous vigilante—or would she keep his secret?

He shook his head. He hadn't given her any reason to trust him.

A gloved hand seized his book of notes—with it the letter—and tore it from his hands. He looked up, calmly, to see Bleys Treth gazing down at him with that same cocky smile.

"Come, Dren," he said. "You've not graced the yard in some time.

Spar with Stareyes, and show us your style." He winked lewdly. "Now that Rayse's attentions are elsewhere, you've the chance, aye?"

Though Treth was older, almost twenty winters over Kalen, they were the same rank in the Guard: vigilant. But Treth had been a master swordsman for hire, a sellsword for nobles, and he bore an aura around him that had made him quite popular. "The Dashing Jack," the older Watchmen called him—a name he hated. His looks had faded little with the years, but his smile still melted hearts.

He took pride in his charms, and in his skill. And like many warriors past their prime, Treth saw the need to assert his dominance among the "young pups," as it were.

Kalen saw no reason to stand in his way.

"I've work to attend." He refused to meet Treth's eye. "Perhaps when I am at leisure—"

"I'm sure"—Treth dropped the ledger in the dirt—"this can wait."

Kalen looked up at him and around at the silent training yard. The folk—Guard and Watch alike—watched the confrontation intently.

"Vigilant Treth," Kalen said. He coughed. "You know I can't—"

"Fleeing behind your weakness of the flesh, eh?"

Kalen looked around once more, seeing uncertain, expectant faces.

The Watch and Guard knew of his illness only in part. Certainly none knew he pretended it had grown worse than it truly had. It had been months since he had wielded a sword while wearing a uniform. But when he had . . . Those who had served with him knew of his ferocity, and he saw in the eyes of those gathered that tales had spread.

"I must decline," Kalen said.

"Then Rayse told true," Treth whispered in his ear. "And you *are* a coward."

That stabbed into Kalen's chest like a searing knife. It struck not because of his own ego—though he confessed there was some—but because of the truth in Treth's words.

He shouldn't do anything to risk revealing himself, but everything was going so very wrong. And Kalen was angry.

"Very well, Dashing Jack," said Kalen, invoking the man's hated moniker.

Treth sneered.

Kalen rose, stiffly, and stepped to the center of the yard. He heard gasps at first, then applause. Rhagaster Stareyes saluted and took a high guard with his padded blade.

Kalen took the weapon handed him by Bront, who smiled. Kalen shrugged.

"Tymora's luck on you," said Treth—mostly to Kalen. "Begin!"

They circled each other slowly, the ring of Watchmen backing away to give them room. The half-elf skipped from foot to foot, keeping himself loose. Kalen flexed his legs. The front of his thighs felt as if they bore heavy pads, but the sensation was merely his numb flesh.

Stareyes came at him with a plunging cut that Kalen knocked aside easily. He coughed and sidestepped, not holding the parry or countering.

Stareyes turned back toward him. "To you, sir," he said.

Kalen shrugged—and attacked high. He didn't move fast—he didn't have to.

From his hanging guard, Stareyes parried high. He could have countered, but as Kalen had expected, he didn't. Rather than pull back, Kalen ran a hand along the length of his own sword, caught the end of his blade, and twisted to set the edge near the hilt at the half-elf's throat.

A gasp passed through the yard.

"You hesitated to reply," Kalen said. "You don't need speed—just readiness." He pulled back a step and set his sword against Stareyes's raised blade. "You just parried. Now stab."

Stareyes, blinking, pushed forward, and the padded blade punched into Kalen's belly.

"A counter in every parry," he said. "Do not hesitate, but commit yourself."

The half-elf shook his head. "But my parry needs to be—"

"Firm, I know," Kalen said. "Trust yourself to set a strong position, and there is no way the other blade can hit you."

He demonstrated, slapping his blade against Stareyes's parry. With the guard wide enough, his blade could not reach Stareyes's arm.

The gathered watchers—who had grown in number, Kalen saw—murmured agreement.

Treth laughed. "Try a master, Sir Dren." He tossed his hat and black watchcoat to a junior Watchman, then unbuttoned his uniform and unlaced his white undertunic to the belly.

"The winner goes with Rayse to the ball tonight at the Temple of Beauty," said Treth.

Coughing, Kalen nodded grimly. He'd known it would come to this.

Treth sneered. Gray-black hairs bristled along his chin and neck.

Kalen shrugged. He handed the sword to Stareyes with a nod, then brought his fingers up to the buttons of his uniform.

Apparently, an attractive form—such as the one she had donned in the Skewered Dragon—was more a hindrance than a help in a barracks filled with wandering eyes.

Fayne had arrived at the barracks earlier, and now wore the illusory form of a junior Watchman whose name she hadn't asked. She could have done so, but why bother? The boy, who had been only too eager to follow her into the stuffy Room of Records, now slumped senselessly under a desk, trapped by magic that bound his mind into a relentless nightmare. Fayne had invoked the power in her wand, taken his face, and gone out into the warm sunshine. She found Kalen in the courtyard, just in time to see him handily defeat a rather handsome half-elf with dark hair and the most beautiful eyes.

Fayne made a mental note to visit the barracks more often.

Then a good-looking man of middling years—Vigilant Treth, she heard a Watchman whisper—challenged Kalen, and they proceeded to disrobe in the middle of the yard.

Fayne had to restrain herself not to squeal. She wasn't a gambler, but she *loved* cockfights.

She shared in the collective intake of breath when Kalen stripped off his shirt. His body was covered in scars—knife cuts, arrow holes, burns. Some of them, Fayne recognized: the finger-shaped lines on his forearm were the spellscar burns he had suffered in Downshadow the night they had met. His tightly woven muscles carried not a drop of fat.

Treth was a whip-wire of a man, like a curled snake, ready to lunge. Kalen, on the other hand, was a wolf. Fayne saw it in his movements and the way he stood—and the way he glared.

Her cheeks grew warm, and she cursed herself for a brainless child.

The men faced each other across the courtyard. Sneering, Treth held his steel low. Kalen held his high, and coughed. Part of his disguise, Fayne realized.

Then Treth lunged toward Kalen, fast as a striking viper, and Kalen caught his spinning, shifting cut with a solid, low-hanging parry. The padded swords thumped.

Treth pulled back and struck again, reversing, and Kalen parried easily. Where Treth attacked wildly, with great sweeping slashes and flurries, Kalen's movements were quick and precise—conservative. It was obvious to Fayne—who knew as little about swordplay as a stray kitten—that Kalen was better. But could he win, and still maintain his mask?

That held Fayne's interest—that, and Kalen's glimmering skin. Mmm.

They came together again, and again. Every time, Treth attacked, lunging fast, and every time, Kalen warded him off. He didn't press—he was holding back.

They broke apart for the eighth time, and Treth, hopping from foot to foot, grinned madly. "Don't say you grow weary yet, youngling," he said. "I'm enjoying this."

Kalen dropped a hand to his heaving chest. It curled into a fist.

Treth came again, his lightning strike harder—more brutal. He hammered into Kalen's high guard, both hands on his sword, and Kalen compressed toward the ground.

Then the older man dropped a hand unexpectedly from his sword and punched at Kalen's face. Fayne bristled at the injustice, but Kalen seemed to have expected it. He grappled his left arm around Treth's and threw their flailing swords wide. They wrestled, each trying to push the other away, and finally half a dozen Watchmen rushed forward to pull them apart.

Fayne saw that the watching horde had grown—sixty or more folk were in the yard. Some commotion arose at the gates, but she couldn't see what it was.

Treth thrust, but Kalen moved so suddenly and quickly that the crowd gasped. He attacked high into Treth's attack, locking blades. The clash of steel rang blasphemously loud.

Kalen punched forward to shift his blade under Treth's and inside his guard. Treth's arm was hopelessly twisted and wide. Kalen grasped the older man's throat.

"Low guard," Kalen said. "Surely you know better than that."

A cry came from the gates and both of them looked, startled.

Fayne saw a girl—she realized, after a heartbeat, that it was Myrin—with a shimmering red gown and a wild, perfect sweep of silver hair that fell to her waist. She was as a magical apparition—so unexpected that the courtyard gaped at her.

Kalen hissed as Treth broke the hold and wrenched away. Kalen tried to follow, but Treth lashed out hard across his unprotected face with his padded blade, making a sound like a hammer on wet wood. Kalen's head snapped back and he fell, like a cut puppet, to the dirt.

"Kalen!" Myrin shrieked. She shoved past black-coated forms as she ran to him.

Treth stood over Kalen. He blew his nose on his hand then spat in the dust. "Well struck, Dren." He jerked his head at Myrin. "Now I see your weakness, Rayse's hound."

Kalen only glared at him, blood running from his nose. As he sat on the ground, coughing and retching, Fayne reflected that he must be as fine a mummer as she.

"What the Hells is this?" shouted a voice. Fayne recognized it from a past misunderstanding as that of Commander Kleeandur. Kleeandur was much like Bors Jarthay—whose tastes in women Fayne knew quite well—but older, harder, and less amusing. She'd crossed him before and come out the worse for it. She retreated behind a pillar as the commander strode into the yard.

Kleeandur grasped Treth by the arm. "What the Hells are you about, Vigilant?"

"Commander," Treth winced. "I can explain—"

"Caravan patrol for two tendays!" Jarthay shouted. "At half pay."

Fayne stuck out her tongue. What kind of vengeance was *that?* She would get Treth much worse than that for daring to hurt Kalen.

Since when do you care? she asked herself. You're just using him, anyway. Aye?

Kleeandur turned on Kalen, who lay coughing in the dirt. "And you, Dren," he said. "Brawling in the yard—goading him like that. Suspension without pay for a tenday."

Fayne almost screamed at the injustice of it, but Kalen only coughed and nodded. Kleeandur strode away, beckoning Treth to follow him. The man sneered at Kalen and went.

Myrin arrived at Kalen's side and fell to her knees beside his sweaty, dirty form. "I'm sorry!" she cried, patting dust away from Kalen's head and shoulders. "I didn't mean—"

"Not your fault," Kalen murmured. He smiled at her, and his eyes sparkled.

Fayne shivered. Those . . . that . . . *gods!*

She realized then that her illusion had slipped away. No one had yet noticed, all eyes intent on the duel. Fayne didn't even care, until a small voice beside her asked, "Fayne?" She looked, and there was Cellica, peering up at her curiously. The halfling had entered with Myrin and picked her way through the crowd to Fayne's side. "What are you about?" Cellica's frown was suspicious.

Mind racing, Fayne grinned broadly. "I . . . ah . . ." Then her plans shifted in a heartbeat. "Cellica! Just the lass I was searching for. I have a small proposal for you—a favor that you might pay me, if you're interested."

Cellica's eyes widened. "Aye?"

TWENTY

As they climbed down from the carriage before the Temple of Beauty and joined the fancifully dressed revelers waiting outside, Kalen admitted to himself that he was not pleased.

But when he looked at it honestly, he had no one to blame but himself. He'd known this was a mistake. How had he let Cellica talk him into this?

"Give me one good reason why you *shouldn't* go as Shadowbane," she said.

When Kalen had given her seven, Cellica frowned. "Well . . . give me one more."

In the end, Kalen privately suspected she'd used the voice on him.

"Kalen?" Myrin asked at his side, calling him from his thoughts. "Is aught wrong?"

"No," he said, taking the opportunity once again to admire how the red gown and silver hair suited her. She looked uncomfortably womanly, rather than girlish. He hadn't said anything, of course, but that didn't stop him thinking it.

Mayhap that was why he hadn't argued against Cellica more effectively.

Don't let yourself be distracted, he thought. You can survive the night. It's just a ball.

He hoped there wouldn't be dancing. Graceful as he might be, he was a soldier. He knew nothing of the world of courtly balls or dancing.

They entered through the foyer, decorated with images of the Lady Firehair and her worshipers—beautiful and graceful creatures, all. Fountains shaped like embracing lovers trickled wine. Windows of stained glass depicting scenes from Sunite history let in the radiance of the rising moon. Guests were gathered, laughing and flirting with rose-robed priests and priestesses. This, Kalen could handle. Only a ball, he thought.

"Sorry again," Myrin said. "About yestereve—I didn't mean to hurt anyone."

Kalen shrugged.

"I thought for sure you'd bring Fayne," said Myrin. "She's your . . . ah?"

"No." Kalen looked at her blankly. "I know her about as well as I know you."

"Oh." Myrin held his arm a little tighter. He could have sworn she added, "Good."

"Saer and Lady—if you'll enter the grand courtyard?" A pretty acolyte gestured to a set of open golden doors carved with the visage of the goddess.

"Courtyard?" Kalen murmured, but he couldn't argue with Myrin's brilliant smile. She took his arm and pulled him along.

At least *Myrin* was happy.

>———W———<

Fayne was fuming. Kalen had taken that little chitling—not a real woman like herself.

The carriage started to turn onto the most direct thoroughfare, Aureenar Street, but Fayne wasn't about to lose a single moment of style. Ostentation made her feel better.

"Keep around!" Fayne snapped to the driver. "Up to the Street of Lances!"

The man in his pressed overcoat tipped his feathered hat. "Your coin, milady."

Since she had the carriage already, she might as well prolong her rich procession.

The carriage broke away from the loose train of vehicles and swerved northeast. Fayne smirked out the window, surveying the streets, the jovial taverns, and the folk walking.

Cellica, sitting across from Fayne, fidgeted her thumbs and chewed her lip. Their ride had included a visit to Nurneene's for masks, and the halfling wore a plain white eye mask with her gold gown. She'd added a lute to represent a bard Fayne had never heard of, but apparently halflings knew their own history quite well.

"How long will this be?" She looked at Fayne anxiously.

Fayne laughed. "Enjoy it, little one! Not every day working lasses like us ride in style."

"I appreciate you inviting me along, Fayne." The halfling smiled halfway. "I'm just worried about—" She peered out the window.

"Oh, don't fret!" Fayne insisted with a girlish smile. "I'm sure your jack can handle himself. That little wild-haired girl didn't look so vile." A touch dangerous, mayhap—but that was intriguing, rather than off-setting. If only the little scamp weren't interfering!

"No." Cellica smiled, apparently at the thought of Myrin. "No, she isn't."

Beshaba, Fayne thought, what is it that makes everyone cling to such pathetic waifs?

They continued north on the Singing Dolphin thoroughfare and turned east on the Street of Lances. Fayne grinned at onlookers, whose responding stares she chose to interpret as jealous. They turned south again on Stormstar's Ride. At the end of the street, they saw the Temple of Beauty.

"Ye gracious gods," Cellica murmured, eyes wide. She reached across for Fayne's hand.

"Shiny, eh?" Fayne took Cellica's hand automatically, and the halfling clutched her tightly.

Sune's Waterdeep temple was best approached from Stormstar, Fayne thought, and particularly at this time of evening, when the last rays of the setting sun fell upon its ruby towers and gold-inlaid windows. And from the look on Cellica's face, she was right.

The great cathedral, palace, and pleasure dome towered over the noble villas alongside, shining like a beautiful star of architectural brilliance. Soaring towers and seemingly impossible buttresses made for a façade of true grandeur, which masked an open-air ballroom from which the sounds of revelry could be heard even from far away.

The halfling smiled wanly all the way until the carriage let them off.

"Aye?" Fayne grinned. "Pleased?"

But Cellica said nothing—she looked at her feet nervously.

The iron-faced dwarf attendant at the door looked at their invitation—which Fayne had forged—without any suspicion, then eyed them appraisingly. It was uncommon that two women came to a revel together, but hardly rare. "Who're you lasses supposed to be?"

"Olive Ruskettle!" Cellica peeped, then she went back to staring at the temple.

The guard nodded—he seemed at least to have heard of the "first halfling bard"—then looked at Fayne. He handed back the scroll. "And you, lass?"

"Aye?" Fayne gestured down—black leggings tucked into swash-buckler boots, billowy white shirt and black vest, scarlet half-cape and matching dueling glove—and flipped her magic-blacked hair. She grinned through her scarlet fox mask. "I'm not . . . *famous?*"

The guard shook his head.

"Good," Fayne said, and she kissed the dwarf on the lips. "Tymora's kiss upon you!"

They skipped inside, arm in arm, Fayne pulling Cellica along.

"Your names?" the herald asked Kalen and Myrin inside the courtyard. Music wafted across the open space from minstrels near the central staircase.

Kalen hadn't thought about such a question. "Ah—"

"Lady Alustriel of Silverymoon," Myrin said without hesitation. Smiling beneath her gold mask and crown, she took Kalen's arm.

The herald nodded. He peered at Kalen's ragged old armor with a touch of distaste. At least Kalen had let Cellica buy him a new cloak. "Of course, your ladyship."

He stepped forward and called to the assembled, "Alustriel of the Seven, and escort."

Heads turned—apparently, dressing as such a famous lady was daring—and Kalen felt Myrin stiffen. But most of the masked or painted faces wore smiles. There was even applause.

Myrin relaxed. "Good," she said, clutching her stomach.

"Outstanding," Kalen agreed, though he wasn't sure he meant it. She smiled at him in a way that made his chest tingle.

In the courtyard, Kalen and Myrin looked out over a sea of revelers dressed in bright colors and daring fashions. Kings and tavern wenches mingled and laughed around braziers, and foppishly dressed rapscallions flirted with regal queens and warrior women. Muscular youths in the furs and leather of northern barbarians boasted over tankards of mead, eyeing dancing lasses dressed in yellows and oranges, reds and greens, like nymphs and dryads. The dancers whirled across the floor while musicians struck up a jaunty chorus on yartings, flutes, and racing drums.

The ballroom was open to the night sky, and though the season was cool, braziers and unseen magic kept the courtyard comfortable—teasingly so, inviting revelers to disrobe and enjoy the headiness of Sune's temple. And, Kalen noted, some of the revelers were doing just that.

They had arrived in time to witness the finale of a dance between two ladies. One—their hostess, Lorien Dawnbringer—wore gold accented with bright pinks and reds. The other, a dark-haired elf clad in sleek black, was unknown to him. They whirled gracefully, in perfect balance, arms and legs curling artfully. Most of the nobles were watching their dance, enraptured, and when the women finished and bowed to one another, the courtyard erupted in applause and cheers.

Lorien, panting delicately, bowed to the gathered folk. The elf smiled and nodded. They joined hands and bowed to one another. Then Lorien turned up the courtyard stairs and climbed slowly, turning to wave every few steps, as the elf lady disappeared into the throng of nobles.

Myrin tensed at his side. "The *dance!*" she cried. "We didn't miss it, did we?"

"What?" Entirely too much dancing was still going on, Kalen thought.

"Lady Ilira Nathalan," said Myrin. "And that priestess—Lady Lorien."

Several nearby lordlings and ladies rolled their eyes at her outburst.

"Nay, nay," said a youthful man at their side. He wore the simple but stylish robes of a Sunite priest. "You've not missed it. They dance again at midnight—Lady Lorien will return to dance with Lady Ilira, as the sun with the night. In the middle-time, enjoy yourselves."

"Oh," Myrin said. She smiled vaguely.

The acolyte took Myrin's hands and kissed them. "Let me know if there is aught I might do to aid in this," he whispered with a sly wink. Myrin blushed fiercely.

The priest took Kalen's hands and paid him the same obeisance, to which Kalen nodded.

When the acolyte had gone, Myrin's eyes roved the crowded nobles, as though searching for someone. She found something far more interesting. "Food, Kalen!" Myrin gasped. "Look at all the *food!*"

"Yes—let's . . ." Kalen swallowed. The spectacle dizzied him. "Let's go there first."

Banquet tables around the yard were stacked high with the bounty of the realm. Myrin found sweetmeats and fruits, honey and melon and tarts, breads of a score of grains carved in the shapes of animals, wines of a hundred lands, cheeses of dozens of creatures.

While Myrin piled her plate high, Kalen scanned the party. Merriment filled the courtyard: the murmur of a thousand conversations, laughs, and whispers in out-of-the-way corners where intimate encounters waited.

Damn, Kalen thought, seeing the lovers in their half-hidden alcoves. He glanced at Myrin—at her slender posterior as she bent to inspect some cheeses—and blushed. Amazing what a difference a proper gown made to Myrin—that and the silver hair, which went so perfectly with her skin like polished oak. The red silk forced Kalen to see her for the woman she was, and that scared him as much as pleased him.

A thought occurred, then, and Kalen shuddered. Gods—she might ask him to *dance.*

To distract himself, he tried to recognize the costumes. Kalen was no student of history, and he did not recognize all the masks and manners, but he remembered a few heroes from the chapbooks he had bought and occasionally scanned. Mostly, he knew them by their salacious parodies—little about their true lives—and it made him feel even more awkward.

Kalen stood stiffly, trying to quell a wave of panic that had begun in his stomach and threatened to engulf the rest of him. Too many folk—and too much Myrin.

Were she here, Fayne would have a great laugh about this, he had no doubt.

The herald's next call perked Kalen's ears. "Ladies and lords, the Old Mage and escort, the Nightingale of Everlund," he cried. "Representatives of the Waterdhavian Guard."

Kalen froze at the words and turned slowly around.

"Kalen?" Myrin asked, her mouth half-full, but Kalen didn't acknowledge her.

Instead, he stared at the woman he least expected to see: Araezra, walking the halls on the arm of Bors Jarthay. It was the tradition of Watchmen to wear their arms and armor to costume revels—for instant use if needed—but to alter the garb with a tabard or cloak that could quickly be discarded in the event of trouble. Araezra's tabard depicted a stylized bird in purple embroidery. She carried a shield painted with the same bird, and she'd dyed her hair a lustrous auburn.

He told himself he should be keeping his distance, since she was one of only a few who could recognize Shadowbane. Kalen ducked behind a knot of nobles praying she wouldn't see him.

Fortunately, Araezra was distracted by something Jarthay had said. The commander had shirked tradition and opted to dress as a buffoonish sort of wizard in a red robe and an obviously false beard. He looked more than a little drunk; in fact, as Kalen watched, Jarthay took a swig of something from a flask crudely disguised as a pipe.

"A moment," Kalen murmured toward Myrin. Then he cut into the crowd, looking for a mercyroom or a broom closet or at least an alcove where he could lose the tell-tale helm. He could escape—he could . . .

When a hand fell on his arm, he whirled, thinking certainly it was Araezra.

"Behold, the day improves!" a woman said. "Unveil yourself, man—and don't try to lie about your name, for I'll know."

The noblewoman in question—barely more than a girl, Kalen saw—wore a tattered black gown and must have enchanted her hair, for as he watched, it writhed like a rustling nest of silver vipers. Her gown was cut cunningly and scandalously, with more gods' eye slits than dress. He knew her apparel from stories—the legendary Simbul, the Witch-Queen of Aglarond.

"Choose your words with care!" the girl said with a confident sneer beneath her half mask. "I've been taking lessons from the greatest truth-teller in Waterdeep, Lady Ilira herself! I can hear lies in a voice or read them in a face . . ." She snaked her fingers across his mask. "That is, I *could* read your face if you'd be so good as to unmask yourself." Her hand retracted and she grinned at him—much like a cat grins at a mouse. "For now, a name will do."

Kalen stumbled in his head for a reply. "But lady, my name—"

The girl smirked at his consternation. "I don't mean your *true* name, good saer," she said. She gestured to his outfit. "I mean, who are you meant to *be?*"

That didn't make it better. He didn't have an answer for that, either.

"Lay off him, Wildfire." The venomous lady's voice behind Kalen's back saved him, and he felt something take hold of his arm. "I saw him first!"

Wildfire. He knew that nickname. He didn't remember the girl's true name, but Lady Wildfire, heir of House Wavesilver, was infamous for one of the sharpest tongues in Waterdeep. Kalen remembered Cellica telling him considerable gossip about her, and wished he'd listened more. As it was, he'd heard enough to thank the gods someone had saved him.

Until he looked around.

Kalen gawked at a petite woman dressed in a gown composed of black leather and webbing—not much of either—that barely covered her most precious family heirlooms. Her skin was tinted black and her hair was snowy white. Her skin matched her garments perfectly, especially her thigh-high boots with heels as long as fighting dirks, giving her a height to match his. She fingered the handle of a whip wrapped around her waist.

It took Kalen a breath to recognize her: a drow priestess of the spider goddess, Lolth. He knew she wasn't really a drow, as she'd made no attempt to disguise her human features. This did not surprise him: lordlings and lordlasses were quite vain. The whip didn't match, either—it made her look more a priestess of Loviatar, goddess of pain.

At his side, Kalen heard breath catch and saw The Simbul's eyes light up with fire that was anything but magical.

"Perhaps you saw him first, Talantress Roaringhorn—but I *claimed* him first," Lady Wildfire said in a low, dangerous hiss. "I'm surprised to see you, after last month's scandal. If I recall—the Whipmaster and his . . . *whip?*"

Kalen knew Lady Roaringhorn as well—Cellica had mentioned aught of such a scandal, though he remembered no details. He did recall that these noble girls *hated* each other, and competed in all ways—for the best salons, fashion, marriage, anything that could be fought over. For Waterdeep entire, if it was on the table.

"A misunderstanding," Talantress said tightly.

"Mmm. Aye, you leather-wrapped tramp," Wildfire countered.

"Kindly note my utter lack of surprise," Talantress said, "that you're so crude."

Wildfire hummed—almost purred—at Kalen. "Mmmm. Buck-toothed tease." She shot a glance at Talantress.

"Ah!" Talantress glared. "That will be quite enough, slut of a dull-eyed dwarf!"

"Gutter-battered wick-licker!" Wildfire put her fingers to her lips and licked them.

"How unwashed!" Talantress's wrath had almost broken through her calm face, but she seemed possessed of as much self-control as Araezra. Her lip curled derisively. "I wonder about those tales in the sheets about all those sweaty dockhands that loiter around Wavesilver manor. I'm sure they're very helpful with your . . . *boat.*"

"That's more than enough!" Wildfire's eyes flashed. She looked to Kalen. "We'll let Lord *Nameless* decide."

"What?" Kalen goggled.

Wildfire caught up his right hand and wound herself into his arm; her smile could cut diamonds and her glare was positively deadly. If The Simbul of legend had half that sort of menace, no wonder she'd kept Thay so terrified so long. "Choose," she said coldly.

Talantress curled herself around his left side. Kalen was almost glad he couldn't feel much, or all that magic-black skin would drive him to distraction. "You'd better choose *me*, or you'll regret it," she whispered. "I'll make personally sure."

"Choose *me*," Wildfire purred in his other ear. "I'm much more fun than she is." Her tone shifted from suggestive to commanding. "And my uncles are richer—and employ more swordsmen to throttle fools who spurn me."

"Ah," Kalen said, his mind racing to match his thundering heart.

"Ninny!" Wildfire said. "You want *me*, aye saer?"

Talantress grasped Kalen's other arm. "He's dancing with *me*."

"Me!" Lady Wildfire hissed.

All the while, Kalen watched as Araezra wandered toward them. He couldn't get away, not with the ladies fighting over him. He was trapped.

"You should spare yon knight, ladies," said a gentle voice behind them.

The soft and alluring voice—strangely familiar—froze him in place like a statue.

"Ilira!" Wildfire's eyes widened, and she curtsied deeply. Her beautiful face broke into a genuine smile. "So good to see you."

"Lady Nathalan." Talantress gave her a false smile. "We did not ask *your* opinion." Her tone was that of a noble addressing a lesser—an upstart merchant, whose only honor lay in coin.

"Apologies, young Lady Roaringhorn. I only meant to warn of knights who wear gray and walk lonely roads." A velvet-gloved hand touched Kalen's elbow. "Like this one."

Kalen turned. Lady Ilira—the eladrin he'd seen dancing with Lorien—stood just to his shoulder, but her presence loomed greater than her size. Perhaps it was the weight of years—like all elves, she wore a timelessness about her that defied any attempt to place her age. Her face hid behind a velvet half-mask that revealed only her cheeks and thin lips.

Her pupil-less eyes gleamed bright and golden like those of a wolf, with all the tempestuous hunger to match. Those eyes had seen centuries of pain and joy, Kalen thought. Wisdom lurked there, and a sort of sadness that chilled his heart and shivered his knees.

Ilira wore a seamless low-cut black gown that left her shoulders and throat bare but otherwise covered every inch of her body, highlighting and enhancing her skin. Her midnight hair was bound in an elaborate bun at the back of her head. She wore what he thought was a wide black necklace that broke the smooth expanse of her breast. He realized quickly that it was not jewelry—she wore naught of that but a star sapphire pendant looped around her left wrist—but rather a series of black runes inked in her flesh, which gleamed as though alive.

She had asked him a question, Kalen realized. He also realized he'd been staring at her chest, and his face flushed. Not for the first time, he thanked the gods for his full helm.

"Is this not so, Sir Shadow?" Ilira asked again.

Why was her cool, lovely voice so damned familiar? Where did he know it from?

"It is," Kalen said, because he could say nothing else.

Lady Wildfire laughed and clapped her hands, delighted to see Lady Ilira proven right. Talantress scowled on Kalen's other side. "Spare us your poetry, coin-pincher," she spat. "I'm taking him to dance now—unless you plan to steal him yourself?" She sneered at Lady Ilira. Her voice might have been that of a serpent. "But surely you wouldn't be interested—surely you'd not sully yourself with us mere *humans*."

Ilira smiled and released Kalen's arm, the better to focus on the drow-glamoured girl.

"If I were you, Talantress Roaringhorn," Ilira said, "I should not fight battles that cannot be won—particularly over those whose worth is not measured in *noble* blood." She winked at Kalen.

"You mean—he's not *noble*?" Talantress peered down her nose. "How unwashed."

"Tala." Ilira laid a gloved hand on her arm. "Is not your *precious time* better spent finding a suitable mate for resting 'twixt your nethers? Aye, I believe your *time* grows short." The emphasis she put on the words struck Kalen, but he hadn't the least idea what she meant.

By the way her face turned white as fresh cream—despite the glamour that painted her skin black—Talantress certainly did. Her lip trembled and she gazed at Ilira in shock before she stumbled away. Several lordlings turned to gawk as she scrambled ungracefully through the throng—and thus did those men earn slaps or harsh words from their feminine companions.

Kalen looked back to the ladies, who shared a smug smile. "I cannot dance," he said.

"That hardly matters, saer, if the Lady Ilira partners you." Wildfire laughed. Then she turned her wicked smile on the elf. "If she beats *me*, of course."

"Oh?" Ilira turned to the girl and raised one eyebrow.

"What boots it?" Wildfire put her hands on her hips and set her stance. "I love common men as well as nobles." She smirked at Ilira. "I shall fight you for him! Choose the game."

"Very well." Ilira nodded serenely. "You are a brave and bold student, Alondra," she said. "But let us see how *good* a student you are. You will tell me whether I speak a lie or the truth, and if you are right, he is all yours." She winked at Kalen. "Gods help him."

Wildfire straightened her shoulders. "I accept!"

Ilira closed her eyes and breathed gently. Serenity fell in that moment, and the dancers and gossipers and servants around them grew hushed and seemed far away.

The elf opened her eyes again, and they seemed wet. "I wear this black in mourning," she said. "For my dearest friend, who was taken from me long ago through my own cowardice."

Wildfire looked positively stunned, as though Ilira had smitten her with a mighty blow.

"Oh, my lady," she said. "I'm so sorry—I did not know . . ."

Ilira looked away. "It seems you believed me," she said. "Aye?"

Wildfire nodded solemnly, and Kalen saw tears in her eyes. The rest of her face revealed nothing though, and he marveled at what must be self-discipline like iron. Like Araezra.

Ilira smiled. "What a pity." With that, she led Kalen toward the center of the dancers.

"What?" Wildfire colored red to the base of her silvered hair. "*What?*"

But they were safely protected from any fury she might have wrought, blocked by a living wall of nobility clad in the finest costumes and brightest colors coin or magic could buy. And on Lady Ilira's arm, Kalen could see no one else.

It completely escaped him, moreover, that a dance with her might attract exactly the sort of attention he didn't want.

"Olive Ruskettle and . . ." the herald looked at Fayne, who just smiled. "Escort."

Arm in arm, Cellica and Fayne looked out into the courtyard full of revelers and song. The dancing—the music—the colors—the gaiety! Cellica, in a word, *loved* it.

"I'm so glad you came by an invitation," the halfling said. "Funny you didn't dress as anyone in particular, though. I was sure—"

"Pay it naught," Fayne said, her eye drawn to the dancers in the courtyard. She stiffened, as though she saw someone familiar.

"What?" Cellica asked, straining to see, but everyone was too tall. "Who is it?"

"No one," Fayne said. "No one of any consequence."

"One moment." Fayne let go of Cellica's arm and skipped away through a mass of nobles—roaring drunk and dressed as fur-draped Uthgardt barbarians.

"What? Wait!" the halfling cried. "Fayne!"

But Fayne was gone, leaving Cellica lost in a forest of revelers. With a harrumph, she started looking for Kalen or Myrin.

Not bothering with the servants' stairs, Fayne made her way immediately to the grand staircase that led to the balcony on the second floor. There she'd find the rooms of worship and splendor—where her mark waited, preparing for her dance at midnight.

On the way, she nestled something amongst the statues of naked dancers that flanked the stairs. The item was a small box her patron had given her—a portable spelltrap—into which she had placed an enchantment of her own, one of her most powerful. The item gave off only a faint aura when inactive, and with a courtyard full of woven spells and the temple wards, no one would notice until it was tripped. And by then, enough chaos would be caused.

Two jacks, descending the stairs hand in hand, looked at her askance, but she just nodded. "Sune smile upon you," she said.

They replied in kind and joined the throng.

Fayne, managing to keep herself from giggling like a clever child, strung the privacy rope between the statues' hands and nodded to the watchmen, who smiled indulgently and knowingly. Just a reveler off to some tryst.

Oh, yes, fools—oh, yes.

Fayne skipped up toward Lorien Dawnbringer's chamber. No guards milled about—why would they, when all were below, at the revel?

Fayne knocked gently, and a womanly voice came from within. "Who calls?"

Then Fayne remembered, and swore mutely. She had almost forgotten—dressed in these ridiculous clothes—a face to go with the attire.

She ripped off her fox mask and passed her wand over her body, head to toe. She shrank herself thinner and a little shorter, her face slimming and sharpening, and she became the elf to whom this outfit belonged—the one Fayne remembered in her nightmares.

Fayne always committed herself fully, throwing herself into danger with wild abandon.

The door opened, and Lorien peered out, blinking in genuine surprise. "Lady Ilira?"

Fayne gave her a confident wink, then she leaped into Lorien's arms. She kicked the door closed as they staggered inside.

TWENTY-ONE

"It was a trick," Kalen said as Ilira led him toward the dancers. "What you told her."

"What, saer?"

"It was both true and false," Kalen said. "Your face is covered, and I couldn't tell from your voice or your eyes, but I saw it in your throat. You lied, in part, and told true in another."

"How intriguing, good Sir Shadow." Lady Ilira looked at him with some interest. "When you become more . . . *familiar* with moon elves such as myself, you will note that our ears tell lies more clearly than anything else."

Kalen's heart beat a little faster at the thought of becoming familiar with this woman. "Will you solve the mystery, then?"

"I did lose my dearest friend long ago," she said. "But I do not dress in black for him."

"A half-truth, shrouded in lie." Surprisingly, he could feel her hand—very warm—in his.

"Like a paladin shrouded in night," she said. "Light hidden in twilight, aye?"

A song was ending—a gentle Tethyrian melody, with decorous dancing to match. Kalen knew styles of music—he had once romanced a traveling bard of Cormyr—but dancing was quite beyond him. He hoped he did not disappoint the graceful elf.

As though she read his thoughts, she smiled again. "Never fear, saer—I shall teach you."

Lady Ilira released his hand—he felt the loss of her touch keenly—and presented herself before him. She offered an elegant, deep bow, which Kalen returned.

They waited for the applause to die down and for the lordlings to select new partners. Most of this was according to rote, already long established. Many envious glances fell on Kalen and Lady Ilira, who was clearly one of the most beautiful and graceful ladies in the ballroom. In particular, one sour-faced elf lord was glaring at him. That one wore a long false beard and black robes, making him look like a dark sorcerer. Gloves of deep red velvet gleamed, and Kalen could see his fingers tapping impatiently. Kalen felt unsettled.

"Ruldrin Sandhor," she said. "I imagine he does not like to see me dance with a commoner. But I dance with whom I wish—I always have."

Kalen smiled wryly. "How did you know I was not noble, lady?" he asked.

"The way I know *I* am not." She chuckled. "It is obvious."

"Your husband does not make you noble?" Kalen offered. "Lord Sandhor, mayhap?"

"Oh, good saer." She showed him that she wore no rings over her gloves. "No husband."

Then she took his hands and placed his right on her hip and kept his left hand in her right. "You are fortunate," she said. "As a man, the dance is easier."

The bards played the first few strains of what sounded like a vigorous refrain, then paused to give the dancers a chance to pair off in preparation.

With her left hand on Kalen's shoulder, Lady Ilira reached up for his brow, and his heart leaped at the thought that she might remove his helm and kiss him—but her hand only touched his mask. For some reason, he thought of Fayne, and wondered where she might be.

"Who are you thinking of, I wonder?" she asked as they bowed to one another.

That snapped him back to the ball. "Ah, no one . . ." Kalen floundered.

"Fear not—I am not jealous," Ilira said. "Your face is hidden, but I can see your eyes well enough." She grinned mischievously. "Keep your secrets as you will."

Her exotic eyes—pure metallic gold without iris or pupil— were unreadable, but he sensed her wisdom—and playfulness. "Indeed, lady."

They danced. The steps were foreign, as he'd feared, but not difficult. He credited his movements to the superior skill of Lady Ilira, who was without a doubt the finest dancer he could have imagined. She flowed through the movements, letting her skirts and sleeves trail like wings as though she were flying. Her shadow seemed to dance independently of her, with the same movements but in different directions, but Kalen reasoned that was a trick of the light.

After the first tune, there was applause and the dancers bowed. He seized the opportunity to remove his gloves and stuff them in his belt. Hands shifted and partners moved, but Lady Ilira seized Kalen's arm and held him steady, her eyes like yellow diamonds binding him in place.

With more confidence than the first time, he laid his bare fingers on her hip. Without his gloves, he tried and failed to feel the silk of her gown; all he could feel was the heat of her flesh beneath. Maybe he was touching her too hard—he had no way of knowing—or maybe she was pleased. Regardless, her whole body reacted to his touch, sending tingles up his arm. She was like an immortal creature—not at all human or even elf. A spirit.

They danced again—this time to a Sword Coast tune more forgiving of missteps.

"What was it you meant, touching Lady Roaringhorn?" Kalen asked.

"My good knight, your mind wanders Downshadow, to think of me touching Talantress."

Kalen fought to keep the heat out of his cheeks. "I mean about her 'precious time.'"

"I happen to have heard of a tiny enchantment." She looked at him knowingly. "Secrets are coin, saer—interested in buying one?"

Kalen smirked. "If I'm to keep mine, you'll keep yours."

She nodded serenely.

The minstrels began another song—this one much faster—and rather than let him go, Lady Ilira grasped Kalen harder. It was a Calishite rhythm, he realized—a dance of passion and heat, more akin to loveplay than innocent dance. Watch horns blared in his mind, and he repeated to himself that he could not dance, but his feet didn't listen, and his hands—*well*.

He'd thought her skilled before, but now—with such a tempestuous dance—Lady Ilira was wonderful. Her leg wrapped around his, bringing heat into his cheeks, and she turned around him so gracefully, so expertly, that he might have thought them destined to dance together. He saw her eyes flash; she couldn't have failed to note the steel strapped to the insides of his thighs.

Then she whirled up, pressing herself hard against him, arms around his neck, lips almost against his ear. He felt the whole of her, and he tingled.

The dance lulled, allowing for folk to stand.

"Well, good saer," she whispered in his ear. "You're full of hidden dangers."

Kalen didn't flinch. "Care to search them out?" he whispered back.

She pressed her lips to the mask of his helm: kissing the shadow, not the man. Then she said—aloud for the benefit of the dancers nearby, "Keep your dagger in your breeches, goodsir."

Kalen couldn't help but smile.

The dance built to a furious tempo that he could hardly follow. He felt more and more as though he were merely there to allow Lady Ilira to show herself, and show herself she did. All eyes in the hall fell upon her, and all but the most vigorous dancers stopped to watch.

Kalen wondered about the runes tattooed across her collarbone. What did they mean? He realized they were Dethek, the script of dwarves. Why would an elf wear dwarven runes?

Ilira whirled and met him once more, and he caught her in a fierce embrace. They spun together once, twice—then he held her bent low like a swooned woman as the song ended. Their eyes met, and she smirked at him—mysterious, alluring, *dangerous*.

As the hall erupted in applause, her expression became a wide grin—the first genuine smile he'd seen her wear. Kalen couldn't help but sigh, pleased.

Ilira made him think, oddly, of Fayne—how he wanted to see her smile like that.

Ilira rose and laughed, curtsying to the crowd in an elegant fashion. She smiled and waved, and blew a kiss at the sour-faced silk merchant she'd pointed out earlier, Lord Sandhor. Kalen did little more than stand stiffly and wait for her to return. She did so, bowing to him as was proper.

"What have you lost, Lady?" Kalen asked.

Her smile instantly vanished, replaced by a dangerous cold. Unconsciously, Kalen's hand twitched toward one of those knives he'd been thinking of just breaths earlier, but he reined his impulse.

"Your tattoo." He nodded to the runes inked along her collarbone. "*Gargan vathkelke kaugathal*—Dwarvish, aye? I know only *vathkel*—lost. What does the rest mean?"

He raised his hand toward her chest. He didn't intend to touch the tattoo, but perhaps he did—he couldn't feel anything. His thoughts were suddenly distant—only the warmth of her body pressed against his, the sweet lavender perfume of her hair, the cool velvet of her gloves . . . he wanted—he *yearned*—to know how her skin felt.

But Lady Ilira broke away from him, hand reaching halfway to her chest. Her eyes like burnished gold coins were far away—distant and sad. "No," she said, and he could have sworn before the Eye of Justice that he saw tears in her eyes. "Good saer, my thanks for the dance."

"Wait, I did not mean—" he said.

"Your pardon, boy," said a velvety smooth and dagger-sharp voice behind him. The robed elf—Sandhor—slid past him and seized Ilira's gloved hands in his own. "Does this human offend, my twilight dove?" He glared back, down his impressive nose.

Ilira blinked over Sandhor's shoulder at Kalen, and for an instant, he thought her eyes were pleading. Then she assumed a brilliant smile and put her hand on his shoulder.

"Ruldrin, heart, just in time—" They swept into the dance. "I've been meaning to discuss your latest donation to the Haven."

"What donation?" Ruldrin favored Kalen with a cruel smile over Ilira's shoulder.

"Exactly," the elf woman said sweetly.

They whirled away, leaving Kalen stunned and very alone amidst the other dancers.

He saw, over the whirling gowns, a face framed by red-dyed hair: Araezra. "Gods," he murmured, and ducked away. With that display, she must have seen him and recognized the outfit. Yes, she was coming his way. *Idiot.*

He was making his way back to Myrin when he smelled something strange—something burning. He looked at his hand, and saw—mutely—smoke rising from his fingertips. The tips of his fore and middle finger were blistered and bleeding.

When had *that* happened?

><=====W====<

"Hmm-*mmm*," Fayne moaned, lounging in one end of Lorien's golden bathtub. "Perfect."

The priestess, ensconced at her own end, watched Fayne with a serene smile on her face. Her cheeks were rosy in the candlelight reflected off the warm water.

"Dancing next?" Lorien asked. "Our appointed arrival at midnight cannot be far off."

"Just," Fayne said, stroking one of Lorien's long, slender legs. "Just a little longer."

The priestess smiled and closed her eyes. Fayne hadn't been certain this would be the right course—seduction, her favorite method—but it was certainly paying off thus far. And if she enjoyed it a little herself, all the better! Time enough to dispense pain after pleasure, aye?

Careful, she thought. *You'll sound like that Roaringhorn girl you humiliated last month.*

The memory made her giggle. The *whipmaster*. She had rather liked wearing such a big, muscle-bound form. It had felt stupid and thick, but oh so enjoyable—particularly after.

Lorien saw her smile. "What are you thinking of?"

"A jest—nothing." Fayne in Ilira's form giggled again. "You?"

Lorien stretched and drew herself out of the bath, gleaming and perfect. The light glittered off her soft curves. Fayne told herself to remember that effect, to use some day.

"Many things." Lorien crossed to a divan and drew a ruby red robe around her lovely body. "Things about you—and about us."

"Oh?" Fayne pressed her breasts against the edge of the gold tub and grinned. "What?"

"First—" Lorien lifted from the divan an ornate, golden rod. "Have I shown you this?"

"And what might *that* be for?" asked Fayne, still blissful.

Lorien smiled. "Revealing secrets," she said. "From a false face."

Fayne didn't understand immediately, and that proved her undoing. "What do you—?"

Lorien gestured languidly. "Come." Her word was powerful and inescapable.

The hairs rose on Fayne's neck—a magical attack. Fayne's will hammered at the command, but her body was already caught. She stood, trembling, and wrenched herself out of the bath. Against her will, her body began walking toward Lorien.

"I don't understand," Fayne said. "Heart, what are you—"

Lorien shook her head. "Whatever you are, creature," she said, "Ilira and I love each other well, but you misunderstand our relationship. A pity for you."

Fayne's mind whirled. "I felt . . ." she tried. "I felt it was time to . . . My love, don't punish me for my haste! I only wanted to take us to another ledge, my darling one!"

Lorien rolled her eyes. As Fayne stood before her, Lorien gestured for her to kneel, and Fayne did so. "I can't decide," she said, "whether you are one of my enemies, or one of hers." She shifted the golden rod from hand to hand. "Which is it, child?"

"Dear heart," Fayne gasped. "I don't understand what you mean."

"Show truth," Lorien intoned in Elvish, and tapped Fayne on the forehead with the rod.

Fayne screeched, loud and long, as magic ripped away from her, shattering her illusions and deceptions. They faded in sequence: first Ilira's face, then the conjured black hair, then the alluring features, then—as her skin prickled and stretched—her entire shape began to shift, back to—good *gods*—back to her true self. Something that was certainly not a half-elf.

Lorien gasped. "One of Lilten's creatures," she said. "Ilira warned me."

Those names. Ilira, the woman Fayne hated, but the other. How did she know . . . ?

Fayne looked at herself, at her black-nailed fingers and alabaster skin. Her tail slapped her legs. Not her real body—not now! She pawed at her garish pink hair and screamed.

"Gods." Lorien put out a trembling hand, reaching toward Fayne's head by reflex. "That explains everything. I'm sorry, child. I didn't—"

There came a rush and a snickering sound, and Lorien's head snapped back. Fayne looked at her, confused.

For a heartbeat, Lorien stood there, bent backward, standing erect.

Then she fell in a geyser of blood from her opened throat. The priestess slumped to the floor, twitching and dying.

Rath stood near them. He had struck and sheathed his blade in a single movement.

"What?" Fayne's mind barely functioned. "I thought . . . you said you never use that."

The dwarf looked down at her as one might look at a child. "For those who are worthy," he said. "And those for whom I have been paid."

Fayne stared numbly at Lorien—at the blood spreading around her face—and could not think. The priestess's eyes blinked rapidly, and she tried to speak but only gurgled. Fayne's stomach turned over and she felt like vomiting into the golden tub.

Rath turned away from Fayne in disgust. "Clean yourself. Put your mask back on."

Fayne grasped her head, which was reeling. Magic drained the vitality from her limbs, but those limbs shifted, their deathly pallor replaced by the smooth warmth of her half-elf body. She felt her teeth—normal once more—and sighed in deep relief. It was only an illusion and would have to last until she could perform her ritual again, but it was enough.

She rose on shaky, weak legs. Rath didn't help her.

Finally, her ugly self hidden, she could think clearly again. The enormity of Rath's actions struck her, and she gasped.

"You stupid son of a mother-suckling goat!" she screamed at the dwarf as she wound a white towel around her nakedness. She pointed at Lorien, who lay dying on the floor. "She wasn't supposed to die—I didn't pay you to *kill* her!"

Rath shrugged. "You are welcome."

"You beardless idiot!" Fayne's face felt like it would explode. "*Who asked you?* Who asked you to step in? I had everything under my hand, every—*urt!*"

The dwarf seized her by the throat, cutting off words and air. Choking, she could not resist as he forced her against the wall and pinned her there with his arm. Her weak fingers could only flail at his ironlike arm.

"Her, I took coin to kill," Rath whispered in her ear. "You, I slay for free."

Fayne gasped as light entered her vision.

TWENTY-TWO

Kalen found Myrin surrounded by a crowd of admirers—young noble lads who were taking turns trying to get the silver-haired girl to dance. She kept giggling at their flattery and answering their increasingly bawdy compliments innocently. While her gold crown-mask hid her face, Kalen thought he saw understanding and bemusement in her eyes.

"Kalen!" she said as he approached, and the noble lads looked around.

Kalen flinched—she shouldn't use his name when he was trying to keep a low cloak.

The lads puffed themselves up against him, but one sweep of his icy eyes and they turned to easier sport elsewhere. At least the damned Shadowbane getup was good for something tonight.

Myrin threw herself into Kalen's arms. "Hee!" she said. "I'm having such a—*heep!*—*marvelous* time." She ran her pale fingers along his black leathers. "Dance with me."

Newly confident in that regard from his dance with Lady Ilira, Kalen thought at first to accept. Then he thought better of it, owing to the scent of flowery wine on her breath. From that and the slur in her speech, Kalen could tell Myrin was quite drunk.

"There you are!" said a familiar voice. Cellica appeared out from under a banquet table.

"How did—how did you get in here?" Kalen asked.

"Fayne brought me," Cellica said. "Haven't you seen her?"

"Fayne?" Kalen furrowed his brow inside his helm. It was hot and hard to think in there—good thing Cellica hadn't seen him dancing, or she'd start blaming that for any . . .

"Aye," the halfling said. "Little red-headed half-elf dressed as a swashbuckler . . . maybe you didn't notice her while you were dancing with that elf hussy. Who was she, anyway?"

"Uh." Kalen flinched. He remembered Cellica speaking of Lady Ilira, usually in glowing terms. Perhaps it was for the best that she hadn't recognized the woman.

Cellica stared up at him, tapping her foot. "Well?"

"Well what?" Kalen flinched away from Myrin teasing at his mask.

Cellica looked at the intoxicated woman in his arms.

"Eep!" Myrin said, and she giggled.

"Oh." Kalen hitched Myrin up and set her down on the table with a bump that made her giggle. "I wasn't doing—"

Cellica just narrowed her eyes, and Kalen sighed.

At that moment, a scream split the night, cutting through the music of the minstrels. The murmur of conversation, jests, and laughter died a little, and nervous titters followed the scream, as though it were a jape or prank played by some noble lass with more drink in her than sense.

Myrin shivered. "Kalen, I don't think I like this ball any more."

Louder screams followed—screams of someone being tortured in the rooms above—and the revelers could ill laugh it off. "Fayne," Kalen said, recognizing the voice.

Cellica went white.

"We need to get up there," Kalen said.

Kalen saw a pair of guardsmen start up the grand staircase, only to meet a crimson flash. Black, froth-covered fangs appeared in the air, gnashing and tearing at the first guard. The others paused, horror-stricken, and disembodied mouths struck at them, too. Ladies screamed and panic broke around the stairs as the spell struck celebrants and revelers at random. The other guards employed to watch over the revel could not get through the crush of bodies.

"Not the stairs," Kalen said, and Cellica nodded.

The screams died, but chaos was in full bloom. Revelers scrambled this way and that, shouting and shoving. Kalen saw noblemen arguing, terrified, hands on their blades, and he knew a brawl was imminent.

Abruptly, another cry came—loud and wrenching—from the

midst of the dancers. Kalen looked, for he recognized the voice: Lady Ilira had backed away from Lord Sandhor, clutching at her throat. The elf merchant stepped toward her, casting the shadow of his cloak around her, but she shook her head to whatever he was saying. She vanished into him, as though she had stepped *through* him. She did not appear out the other side.

Wide-eyed, Kalen looked at Cellica, and the halfling nodded.

"Kalen?" Myrin asked sleepily. "Kalen, what's going on?"

"Have you your murderpiece, wee lady?" Kalen asked, drawing the daggers from their sheaths against the inside of his thighs. Where Lady Ilira's leg had wrapped, he recalled.

Cellica gave an impish smile and drew out her necklace, with its little crossbow-shaped charm. "Always." She spoke a word in an ancient language, and the medallion grew to fit her hand. She wound the crossbow with two quick twists of her wrist. "And don't call me 'wee.' "

Kalen boosted the little woman up on his shoulders and bent his knees.

"Kalen?" Myrin's face was pale. She seemed sober—and frightened. "Where—?"

"Wait." Kalen cupped her chin and rubbed her cheek with his thumb. "We'll be back."

He scooped up Cellica, hopped onto the banquet table, and ran. When he reached the end, his boots gleamed with blue fire and he leaped for the edge of the balcony. He caught it with one hand, hoisted Cellica up, and swung himself over the rail.

>———W———<

Myrin's hair rustled in the wind of Kalen's jump. He and Cellica flew up and away, toward the balcony where the screams had come from. Many revelers looked up, startled, and shouts renewed. Men argued, shouted, and shoved.

She wondered what magic let him jump like that—leaving a thin trail of blue flame.

Myrin only watched Kalen as he flew, and silently cursed herself.

"Of course he didn't kiss you, you ninny," she said, fighting the tears. "You get drunk and throw yourself at him? How pitiful!"

Then Myrin gasped as a lordling slammed into the banquet table beside her with enough force to crack it. The man who had shoved him—a cruel-faced man in a black cloak—turned to leer at Myrin. She gaped and fought for air, frozen at the suddenness of his appearance.

"Kalen!" she moaned.

"Coward!" the nobleman cried. He lunged from the table and punched the cloaked man in the face. The rogue staggered back, snarling, and reached for a blade.

"Are you well, my lady?" the lordling demanded of Myrin.

"Uh," Myrin said. She couldn't think. She didn't know what to do.

Shoving her under the cracked banquet table, the lordling pointed a wand at his advancing foe and fired a blast of green-white light. The spell struck the man hard like a hammer's blow, staggering him, but he only smiled and straightened once more.

"Run, my lady!" the lordling said as he looked at his wand angrily. "Run—"

Then the word became a cry of pain as the rogue ran him through.

Myrin could only stare, horrified, as the man kicked the body off his sword. She knew that the blade would come for her next, but she could only crouch, paralyzed in terror.

The murderer squinted around, as though trying to see her. That didn't make sense to Myrin, who hadn't moved. She was sitting right before him, not a pace away, just under the table.

The sword flashed through the air, prodding this way and that as though searching for her. She cringed as far back as she could.

The murderer growled in frustration. He rose and ran back into the melee.

Myrin was puzzled. Why wasn't she dead? Hadn't the man seen her sitting before him?

Dazed, Myrin looked around, then crawled across the floor to escape her hiding place. She gasped when she looked down—her hands had changed color to match the stone floor. She held them up in front of her and her skin changed tone and pattern to blend with the room. Myrin panicked and grabbed hold of a nearby crimson drapery to haul herself to her feet—and her body immediately flushed crimson to match the fabric.

What was happening to her?

She rubbed at her reddened arms and saw that a trail of blue runes like ivy had crept up the inside of her forearm. She slipped back to the floor and sat, wrapped in the velvet drapery.

She didn't understand—she couldn't think. Why had she had so much wine?

Looking around the courtyard, she saw that at least twenty men and women in black cloaks—like the man who had attacked nearby— had appeared in the courtyard, attacking revelers. Chaos swept the courtyard, leaving cries of pain and terror in its wake.

A chill passed over Myrin, as though a door had opened nearby and let in a wave of cold air. She saw her skin shift again, back to its usual tan, and the blue runes faded from her arms. Whatever that chameleon magic had been, it was leaving her.

A face bent down to peer at Myrin. "Excuse me, young mistress."

Myrin turned where she sat, and a shiver of fear passed through her. "Y-yes?"

The woman was very old, but Myrin wasn't sure how she knew this. The rounded figure standing before her was rather youthful—even lush, with a heart-shaped face surrounded by vibrant gold curls. Her emerald gown, under a jet black cloak, was perfectly in fashion.

Myrin had the distinct sense the woman wasn't alive, though that couldn't be.

"I am Avaereene," said the woman. "Your jack seems to have abandoned you, and I thought you might be in some distress. May I aid you?"

"Oh, no," Myrin said. "Kalen's just gone away for a moment. He'll be—"

But the stranger was raising her hand. Myrin sensed, too late, the pulse of enchantment within the woman's arm, which beat with its own inner heat. Its proximity tickled her senses like the aroma of a steaming platter of hot sweets.

"Sleep," the woman said, in a language Myrin understood without knowing how.

Darkness swallowed Myrin.

The woman who'd called herself Avaereene lifted the girl fluidly. The young body was light, yet she felt a little dizzy—her power diminished around this girl, somehow. She knew the blue-headed waif had power of some kind, but she didn't know what it was.

No matter. She had more than enough strength for this purpose.

She tucked the sleeping girl under her cloak and whispered a spell to shroud them. Her cloak dimmed and bent the light, hiding them from view. A fog appeared in the air, shrouding half the courtyard in mist. In a few more moments, the temple would be one great brawl, and she and her followers could slip away.

Her employer would be most pleased.

Kalen swung up onto the balcony, where Cellica hopped down and they cast about for the source of the screams. Kalen heard loud, harsh words from the half-open door to the nearest chamber. He pointed, and Cellica dashed to the door, crossbow up and scanning for a target. He padded after her, thankful she'd made him wear his leathers after all.

What they found in the chamber, neither of them could have expected.

Lorien Dawnbringer lay dying upon the floor near a great golden tub. She choked and sputtered and tried to speak, but only blood came from her throat. Bent over her, cradling her as she bled, was Lady Ilira. She seemed to blend into the shadows of the golden tub, as though she had melted from them just heartbeats before.

"No," Ilira moaned. "No, no, *no!*"

Her gloved fingers caressed the priestess's face. Lorien did not seem able to see her, and could only cough, sputter, and finally go still.

Ilira, her face in shock, opened and closed her mouth several times but could not speak. Then she lowered her lips, tentatively, to Lorien's forehead. She shook as though from strain at the effort. Then, gently, she kissed the priestess's pale face.

Kalen expected something to happen, though he did not know why. Nothing came to pass but the gentle sound of her kiss.

Then, as if a wave loosed within her, Ilira threw back her head and screamed, loud and long—an elf mourning cry unknown in the lands of men. She bent and kissed Lorien's face again—kissed it over and over, washing it with her tears. She cried out in Elvish, but Kalen could not understand. She tore off her gloves and pressed her hands on Lorien's cheeks as though she'd never touched them before, as though her skin could bring life to death.

All eyes remained on her, but Kalen became aware of someone else in the room. His gaze flicked to the side, where he saw a thick figure in the shadows. It was Rath, pinning a squirming, mostly naked Fayne under his arm. Both of them looked rapt at Ilira's display.

"Hold and down arms!" Kalen cried. "Waterdhavian Guard!"

"Ka—!" Fayne gasped.

Rath slammed her head against the wall and Fayne slumped to the floor, unmoving.

TWENTY-THREE

Ilira was the first to move. Rather, *she* remained still, but her shadow moved.

Kalen realized, to his horror, that her dark reflection did not match her—it was great and broad, like a hulking warrior. It moved of its own will; though Ilira knelt, still and trembling, her shadow reached toward the dwarf with clawed hands meaning to rend him apart.

Suddenly, Kalen recognized it—from Downshadow, the night he had followed Lorien. The shadow must be bound to protect both women.

Then Ilira was in motion. She screamed a war cry of fury and leaped—not toward Rath, but backward, toward the wall. Kalen watched as she melted into the shadows, then appeared next to the dwarf and tackled him to the floor. Her hands fumbled at his black robes, and the two rolled and bounced across the silk carpets.

"Fayne!" Cellica cried, and she ran to Fayne, who lay unmoving.

Her voice snapped Kalen into motion. He lunged toward Rath and Ilira, daggers wide.

Rath got two feet under Ilira and heaved, sending her flying toward Kalen. He braced himself to catch her, but she twisted in the air, landed lightly on his chest with both feet, and kicked off, turning a somersault and landing on her toes near the dwarf. She lunged at Rath, hissing like a serpent.

Driven backward by the collision, Kalen fell to the floor. He coughed and kicked his legs around, pushing himself to stand. What he saw paralyzed him for a heartbeat.

Ilira's shadow had fallen upon Rath. It stood like a living man—a giant of a man. Its features were blurry, but Kalen could see torturous pain etched on its face. With a soundless cry, it tore at the dwarf with its black claws.

Rath eluded its blows, eyes wide. He danced backward and around the room, running around the tub and leaping over divans and dressers. The shadow pursued, relentless in its assault. Rath ran up a wall, kicked off, and dropped behind it, right hand across his belt on his sword. The creature turned—or rather, turned itself inside-out—and grimaced at Rath out of its back-turned-front. The dwarf began to draw steel.

"*Elie en!*" Ilira screamed, and she pounced on him like a cat. Her bare hand grasped his wrist, holding his sword in place.

Flesh sizzled and the dwarf screamed. Kalen smelled it before he saw the smoke rising from Rath's wrist. His flesh burned under Ilira's touch as though by incredible heat. Great red welts appeared and blood dripped to the floor. Bubbles of skin collapsed into blackening burns.

A spellscar, Kalen realized—Ilira's power was to unmake flesh at a touch. That explained his burned fingers, her dress and gloves, the way she recoiled from contact. Never would he have suspected it of such a lady—so fair, yet so monstrous as well.

Kalen understood, in a flash, what had happened with Lorien—why Ilira had cried out after she had touched the priestess. Lorien's flesh had not burned at her touch because the priestess was dead. Only the living suffered the burns. Like Rath.

The dwarf struggled to escape, but the hand he laid on her forearm scalded in the same fashion, and he cried out in pain. His eyes were filled with horror and his voice turned to a squeal.

"*Elie en, ilythiri,*" Ilira said, her words soft and cold. She leaned in to kiss him.

The dwarf flinched, Kalen saw, sparing his lips. Ilira's kiss fell instead on his unprotected cheek, and the smoke of burning flesh wafted around their faces. Rath cried out and beat at Ilira, trying to break her hold, tearing her black gown. The elf hung on, clinging to him with her arms and legs like a spider as he burned under her touch and shrieked.

"What's she *doing?*" Cellica screamed. She cradled the unconscious Fayne and pointed her crossbow at the duel but did not fire, unable to sight a clear target.

Kalen shivered to watch Ilira's attack. Even the shadow seemed to pause in its fury, standing back to let her kiss the dwarf with her burning lips. The creature recoiled, seeming to cower as though ashamed. Rath cried out over and over, wordless.

"Hold!" Kalen cried, but to no avail. He knew the fury on Ilira's face. This was not a woman who would stop until she killed or was killed herself.

He ran at the pair, daggers held low and wide, and the shadow lunged into his path. He cut at the creature, but as he expected, his knives passed through the black stuff of its body as though through heavy mist, causing no injury. Mortal steel could hardly touch a creature from beyond their world. If only he still had his paladin's powers, he could harm it.

The beast lashed out with its claws, and Kalen knew better than to parry. He danced aside, weaving, trying to get around the creature rather than through it. It was huge and powerful, but as Kalen guessed, not fast or nimble. He could dodge its strikes as long as he stayed fast and low. Cowardly, perhaps, but it kept him alive.

Fight like a paladin, he thought. Prove to the threefold god that you are worthy. Have faith that your strikes will harm it, and they will.

But growing up in the cesspool of Luskan, Kalen had never trusted to faith. The center of his being was wrought of cold practicality, hardened by a thousand strikes and hard blows. Thanking the gods again he had worn his leathers rather than his Guard arms, he moved in the tight, efficient dance of elusion and avoidance that had marked his days as a thief.

Yet he couldn't get past the shadow. It was too strong a guardian—a perfect mate to its mistress, this elf noble with her hidden scars. He pulled back to face it levelly, and held up his daggers to ward it back. The creature ceased its attack and stared at him, and he had the distinct sense that he was gazing at a guardian just as devoted as he.

He hefted a knife to throw. He thought it might pass through the shadow and strike Ilira, distracting her from Rath. He hated the dwarf, but he needed to stop this.

Then Ilira groaned as the dwarf punched her solidly on the ear—at the same instant, the man-shaped shadow drew back as though struck.

The elf reeled away and Rath rose, his half-blackened face dripping blood. He touched it and winced. His bare hand came away bloody and sticky.

With anger that was the stuff of nightmares written on his face, the dwarf reached down with his unburned hand and pulled his sword free. The blade glittered with its perfect, keen edge.

Kalen had seen such blades on the Dragon Coast, among tradesmen from the east. Katanas, they were often called—light, efficient, and delicate.

Rath crouched to lunge at the shuddering woman. His grimace calmed a little as he focused himself into the blade. Then he leaped.

Kalen darted in front of him, daggers crossed, and caught the sword high.

The slender sword shrieked against his crossed steel, and Kalen thought for one terrible heartbeat that it would shear through them and into his chest. But the steel held, and Rath pressed only another instant—face wrought in agony and rage—before he pulled the sword back, dropped low, and kicked Kalen's legs out from under him. Kalen fell back, colliding heavily with Ilira and falling in a tangled heap. Flesh burned—Kalen's own—but he could not stand. He looked up, saw Rath's sword, and knew he could not block.

A crossbow bolt streaked toward Rath and he swept his blade up to slap it aside.

Cellica! Kalen saw the halfling near the door, standing protectively over Fayne, who was coughing her way back to awareness. The shot had startled them all—broken the rhythm of the battle. Cellica glared at Rath banefully and reloaded her small crossbow.

Eyes wild with horror, the dwarf touched a trembling hand to his face and moaned. Not bothering to sheathe his sword, he leaped through the open window.

Kalen grasped Ilira to pull her away, but the bare flesh through her ruined gown burned his fingers. It felt distant, that burning, but still powerful—he felt the death inside her.

Ilira moaned and struggled. "No!" she cried. "You're letting him escape!"

Kalen tried to respond but she slammed a knee into his belly and he slumped to the floor, gasping.

Ilira glared at her shadow, and the creature nodded. Ilira said nothing, only closed her fists tightly. As though in response, the creature melted into the floor and swirled around her feet, joining with her. She stood, panting and heaving, half naked in her torn gown. Blood—Lorien's and Rath's both, Kalen realized—dripped from her hands.

She glared down at Kalen with a fury and a hate that only an elf—with untold ages stretching behind her and ahead—could know. He crawled backward on the floor, inching away from a lioness that could pounce at any instant. She knelt, meeting Kalen eye to eye, considering.

Two Watchmen burst through the door, swords drawn. "Hold!" they cried. "Down arms!"

The swords pointed first to him, as the man with steel, then at Ilira. Kalen thrust a warding hand toward Cellica, and she cradled Fayne against the wall, hiding her. He opened his hands, daggers hooked between palm and thumb. He rose slowly, trying not to provoke Ilira.

"Hold and talk truth!" cried one Watchman. "What happened here?" His gaze roved to the corpse of the priestess, then to Ilira, kneeling with bloody hands and wrists. "Merciful gods!"

The elf turned baleful eyes toward them and they winced.

"Hold!" the armored man said. "Down arms! Down . . . hands!"

Uncaring, Ilira rose and started toward the window, but Kalen moved to block her.

"Stay, Lady," Kalen said. "None of us are certain what happened here."

"Calm yourself," Cellica said with her suggestive voice. Turning against her will, Ilira raised her hands to her ears, her face contorted. "Stay calm, Lady—calm . . ."

With a roar, Ilira threw her hands out wide. "Enough!" She gave Kalen a sharp glare, and words died on his tongue as though her will had struck him a solid blow. Her eyes glowed gold-yellow from within the shadows that enwrapped her like mist. Darkness roiled in her—a cruel, terrible darkness.

Her shadow did not follow her movements. While she stood calmly, it thrashed and clawed on the floor, as though in agony.

Then she laughed—half crazed, half terrified. The mocking cackle—perfect and terrible as the voice of a singer drowning in madness—chilled him to the bone. "You want to pierce me, is that it?" the elf asked, her words wry. She glared at the Watchmen and ran her bloody hands along her hips, pulling the silk gown up past her knees. Her gaze grew alluring and dangerous. "You and any of a thousand men—little boys with your swords."

Shadows lengthened—the Watchmen shivered. Kalen saw them looking at her writhing shadow, their faces white as cream.

"Lady." Kalen lowered his daggers. "Lady, no one will harm you."

Ilira shook her head dazedly, and some of her darkness fell away as though the shadows that surrounded her were tangible.

"I am Waterdeep Guard," Kalen said. "Calm yourself, and we shall—"

"Shut up!" she snapped, startling him. Angry tears burst forth to stream down her face. "Stay away from me. Away!"

Kalen raised his steel once more. "Lady Ilira, please—"

She loosed a strangled cry of rage and pain, then ran toward the window. Lunging forward, Kalen shouted at her to stop, but she ran straight into the wall—or would have, had not the shadows swallowed her. He staggered to a halt, startled and disbelieving. She had cast no spell—used no magic that he knew of.

"A shade," said one of the Watchmen. "Did you see her eyes? Lady Ilira's a *shade!*"

"Gods above," said the other. "No other explanation—hold!"

When Kalen moved, they perked up and leveled their war steel at him.

Kalen put his hands out wide—peaceful. He looked to Cellica and to Fayne, whom the halfling clutched near the wall. An ugly bruise was seeping across Fayne's face where the dwarf had struck her.

He realized Fayne was looking hard at where Ilira had vanished, and her eyes twinkled.

You and any of a thousand men . . .

Kalen shivered. If Kalen didn't get Fayne out soon . . .

The Watchmen were pointing steel at them.

He had no choice.

He raised his hands to the sides of his helm.

TWENTY-FOUR

Boots sounded on the steps without, and Cellica saw Kalen shake himself from his stupor. She heard shouts from outside and a great clamor, but her eyes locked on Kalen.

"Hold!" said the Watchman, but Kalen ripped off his helm. Fayne inhaled sharply.

"Vigilant Dren!" They scrambled to salute.

"Care for this mess," he said. "I'm sure she won't be back, but 'ware Ilira's hands—they burn." He started to don his helm, then stopped. He added, "Her kiss, too."

"Sir!" a Watchman cried. "What passed here? Who killed—"

Kalen shook his head, and Fayne realized that he didn't know. When he arrived, Lorien was already dying, and Ilira had been closest to her.

Fayne's heart raced. What did he think had happened?

Kalen gestured to Fayne and Cellica. "These two are with me."

One Watchman stiffened and nodded. "Sir," he said. The other was openly weeping over the slain priestess. "We'll ward this place, as you command."

Kalen returned their salute then pushed past them, out the door onto the balcony. He carried his helm. Fayne opened her mouth to speak, but Kalen's cold eyes froze her tongue. She snatched up her clothes, which lay next to the bathtub, now wet from all the commotion.

Cellica followed Kalen to the balcony, and Fayne held her hand tightly. With the other hand, Fayne tucked the towel around her body with some degree of modesty.

"You showed them your face!" Cellica hissed.

"No choice," Kalen said. "We needed to get out of there before Rayse arrived." He looked pointedly at Fayne.

Fayne goggled. Revealing himself seemed so stupid, yet Kalen had done it for her? Why would he do something like that? Had the world gone mad, or just her?

You're losing your mind, her inner voice noted. Again.

Chaos boiled up in the courtyard of the Temple of Beauty. Brigands had appeared as if from the air and began a brawl that had since turned the place into a mess of shouts and steel. As they watched, noble ladies screamed and ran from hot-headed duelists. The room was half filled with mist, confusing the fighters into hacking at everything that moved.

"Myrin," Kalen and Cellica said at once.

The name was like a knife in Fayne's belly. What use had they for the doe-eyed stripling? Hadn't Kalen compromised himself to protect Fayne, just now? Didn't he fancy Fayne?

Oh, gods, *did* he? Fayne wasn't sure if she was pleased or terrified.

Fayne's head hurt and she grew fearful, as she always did in confusing situations. Kalen was acting on instinct and passion, not cold rationality, and that was unpredictable.

"Where is she?" Cellica asked.

Kalen shook his head. His rumpled hair swayed in front of his eyes.

"Wait—" Fayne started. "Wait a breath—tell me . . ."

But Kalen whisked her up in his arms, naked and all, and shoved her against the wall in an alcove, pressing himself firmly against her. She coughed, sputtering, but then he kissed her to still her lips and she ceased struggling. Then she was *certain* she'd gone mad.

He broke the kiss, finally, parting them by a thumb's breadth.

"Well met to you as well," she managed.

"I did that to shut you up." Kalen's eyes were cold. "What were you doing there?"

"I—" she said. "You don't understand . . ."

Kalen scowled. "Never mind," he said. "You'd only lie anyway. Just . . . just shut up."

"You could kiss me again," she thought of saying, but stopped with a shiver. Kalen's face was hard and his eyes were those of a warrior. Those of a killer.

No use being ingratiating or alluring. She would just keep her mouth shut for now.

A woman in armor ran past, and when they heard the muffled voices inside Lorien's chamber, they recognized Araezra Hondyl.

"Gods," the valabrar said. "What happened?"

"Murder—gods above!" a man said. "Lady Nathalan . . . oh, gods, her closest friend!"

"Did you see it? You saw the murder?"

"Nay, but . . . Vigilant Dren. He was here, you could . . ."

"Dren?" The valabrar sounded shocked. "Kalen Dren, my aide?"

"Time to go," Cellica murmured. She'd wedged herself into the alcove near Kalen's leg, and she darted out.

Kalen, shoving Fayne roughly along, followed her around the balcony to look down into the chaotic courtyard. Cellica was looking for Myrin, Fayne realized. Kalen was just glowering.

"Are those yours?" Kalen demanded, waving at the intruders.

Fayne could only shake her head, completely at a loss. Whoever had sent these men to the temple, it hadn't been her.

Near the entrance, Kalen saw a knot of guardsmen and Watchmen rallying around Bors Jarthay. The commander—whose drunkenness had been mostly an act—knocked one man out with his handflask pipe and drew a surprisingly long blade out of his billowing shirt. Commander Kleeandur was there too, barking orders to cut off exits and trap the chaos inside.

"I don't see her!" Cellica cried.

The more Watch that arrived, the fewer rogues remained. But the nobles began dueling, and that perpetuated the brawl. Lady Wildfire, surrounded by a dozen noblemen fighting over the right to protect her, tired of the commotion, brained one of the lordlings with her jeweled purse, and fled of her own power. Talantress Roaringhorn was conspicuously absent, and dozens of nobles cried out in search of one another amidst the din.

Kalen saw black-garbed figures slipping out of the court-yard, hooded ladies in their grasp. They moved south into the temple plaza.

Cellica followed his gaze and pointed at the kidnappers. "What are you going to do?"

Kalen pushed Fayne roughly at the halfling and took his helmet in his hands. He slid it over his head.

"Kalen, you have no sword," the halfling said. "You can't—"

He pulled the daggers from his belt. He looked across the courtyard as though judging the distance to one of the high windows.

"Wait, Kalen!" Fayne caught his hand, and he glared at her. His eyes burned. She swallowed a sudden rush of fear. "You . . . saved my life," she said.

"You stupid girl!" Kalen slammed his fist, dagger and all, into the wall beside her head. The blade rang against the stone, deafening her. "What the Hells did you think you were doing?"

Fayne was stunned. "Kalen, I—"

"Shut up. I'm tired of it," he said. "You're a spoiled child playing games. Just a stupid fool who thinks there aren't consequences to your pranks—that people don't die."

"Kalen," Cellica said, casting her eyes down, her cheeks reddening with embarrassment.

Fayne trembled. "Please don't," she said. "Please, Kalen—I'm sorry!"

But Kalen's eyes were cold. "Begone," he said. "I want nothing to do with you. Now, pardon," he said as he locked his helm in place, "but I have someone worthwhile to save."

He ran for the opposite end of the courtyard, leaping from table to table around battles, his enchanted boots guiding him. Screams went up in the courtyard from startled nobles, and a few wary Watchmen fired crossbows in his direction. The bolts cut through his cloak and one cut open his left arm, but he did not falter. When he gained the far window, he paused and looked back—his colorless gaze cut into Fayne. Then he turned, cloak swirling, and was gone.

Fayne, shocked, pulled herself away from Cellica. She drew out her wand—the wand she could use to hide herself from the world, as she had always done—and glared.

"I'm sorry," Cellica said. The halfling rubbed her hands together. "Kalen . . . he—wait!"

The halfling staggered as Fayne turned her gaze on her and whispered a word of dark magic. Cellica pawed blearily at her face and seemed unable to see Fayne, who had pulled away and hurried down the stairs toward the brawl. Her longer legs meant Cellica could not catch her.

As she went, she growled. "Didn't warn me about *this*, Father."

Avaereene paused when they had run two blocks, to see how many of her men followed. It didn't matter—she held the wealthiest prize in her own arms—but every noble lass taken prisoner was more coin for the Sightless.

She was pleased to see that a dozen had escaped, carrying half that many girls among them. Not all of her men had made it, but desperate men were plentiful in Downshadow she could always hire more.

The lead man stopped at her side. He carried an unconscious Hawkwinter in his arms, head hooded, moaning up a squall through her gag. Though the face was hidden, Avaereene knew all the nobles in Waterdeep by figure as well as face. She had an excellent memory.

"Where, mistress?" asked her lieutenant.

They were panting from exertion. Avaereene wasn't breathing hard—she wasn't breathing at all, as she hadn't had to for almost a century.

"The sewers—keep a low cloak," she said. "I shall follow with haste."

The man nodded and directed the other stealthy kidnappers to follow him. Downshadow men, all of them, and useful enough, even if scarred and ugly.

"Hasn't the spellplague warped us all?" she murmured. She thought of the horror lurking inside her and grinned. "Some more than others."

Avaereene stepped into an alley, where she found her employer stepping out of a bank of shadows. His cowl hid most of his face, but she knew he was a half-elf. And while he was not dead, neither was he alive. He was something like her.

"Well accomplished," he said, indicating the girl in her arms. "Give her to me."

"The gold, first." The blue-headed girl started to moan in her arms as Avaereene began to draw the life from her like a sponge from a pool of water. "Or she dies."

His face held no emotion. "Very well." He gestured, and a pouch appeared from his sleeve, heavy with coin. His black eyes never left the girl's face.

Instinct told Avaereene to grasp the reward while it was there, but pragmatism stayed her.

"Such a curious thing," Avaereene said. "To pay so much for a girl with no family or connections. I do not even know who she is, and I've spent more than a century in Waterdeep."

Her employer reached out silently and stroked the girl's temple with his gloved hand.

Then he looked up, over Avaereene's shoulder, and she swore she saw his face for half an instant. His lips had drawn back in a hideous grimace, and his teeth seemed very long.

"Shadowbane," he hissed, more like a serpent than a man. "Damn that sword!"

"What?" Avaereene asked, but he was gone as though he'd turned to dust.

He had not taken the sleeping girl, but he had snatched the coins back from her. Avaereene snarled in anger and resolved to slay the first thing she saw.

A pair of her thieves came upon her. "Mistress?" one asked. "Mistress, what—"

Avaereene tossed the first one aside with a flicker of her will—he shattered against the alley wall. That made her feel better, and appeased the hungry magic within.

She thrust the sleeping girl into the arms of the other one, who looked frozen in terror, and peered down the street. Sure enough, a man ran toward them, glittering steel in his hands, gray cloak trailing behind him. He followed on the heels of four more thieves carrying three noble girls.

"Kalen," the girl murmured as she stirred in the thief's arms.

TWENTY-FIVE

Well met," Kalen said as he caught the nearest thief by the arm.

The man turned and Kalen drove both daggers into his chest.

The thief stiffened, blinked rapidly several times, then fell with a choked gasp as Kalen—hands free from the blades he left in the scoundrel—caught the woman he carried.

No time. He set her aside, ripped the curved sword from the thief's belt, and ran forward.

Ten paces farther, two men carried a bulky noble lass in a green gown between them. They cursed and fumbled, pushing her back and forth. Finally, the smaller of the men—an ugly, warty dwarf—took her, and the freed thief—a half-orc—turned to face Kalen.

The brute bristled with metal nails that stood out from his skin like ghastly pierced rings or jewels. The half-orc hefted a stout buckler on his left arm and a length of barbed chain in his other hand, and opened his mouth to challenge.

Kalen didn't slow—he leaped to twice the half-orc's height in the air, driven by his boots. The brute looked up as Kalen hissed down toward him, sword plunging, deadly as a hawk.

The half-orc interposed his buckler between himself and the airborne knight. Kalen's thrust, backed by all his weight, shattered the stout wood—but snapped in two as well. The half-orc howled in pain as shards of wood flew into his face, putting more shrapnel in his flesh than before. The broken scimitar blade tumbled away.

The half-orc, infuriated, swung his chain at Kalen, who interposed his left arm. The chain enwrapped it greedily, barbs barely short of striking his helm. The slashing razors would have split his face open like a boiled egg. The barbs sank instead into his flesh, deep enough that he could feel them prickle. The chain-wielder grinned and Kalen realized his misfortune.

"Tymora—" Kalen managed, before the half-orc jerked the chain and slammed him against a building. Pain swept through his stunned consciousness, and he sank down.

The half-orc wrenched him over and he flopped like a limp doll to the cobblestones. The impact ripped through him, but he was still alive and still conscious.

"Stlarning Watchman." He also growled a few Orcish words Kalen knew to be curses.

"Come!" shouted the dwarf, pausing near the half-orc and struggling to hold the kidnapped girl. "No time!"

"Wait," said the bruiser, and he reached down to seize Kalen's neck.

The noble girl, by chance, kicked the half-orc in the shoulder and his attention wavered.

It was just a heartbeat, but it was enough.

With a roar, Kalen rammed the jagged, shorn-off hilt of the thief's scimitar into one half-orc ankle. The creature howled in pain and faltered on his feet. As the brute teetered, Kalen wrenched the hilt upward and jammed it into the half-orc's groin. Black blood spurted forth and the creature gave a high-pitched squeal like a stuck pig.

Kalen rose, the half-orc's discarded chain hanging from his arm, and faced the dwarf thug who held the struggling girl. Kalen looked down at the chain, the barbs cutting into his arm. Without wincing, with barbs ripping out his flesh, Kalen unwrapped the chain.

This second thief looked somehow familiar.

"Wait!" he said, putting up his hands as though to surrender. "It's you! Shadowbane!"

Kalen hesitated. He recognized this one from Downshadow—this was the dwarf he'd let flee. Apparently, he hadn't learned aught.

The dwarf thrust his forearm forward, and a tiny arrow concealed in a handbow in his sleeve streaked through the air. Kalen batted it aside with the barbed chain.

Kalen leaped forward and split the dwarf's chin with a rising right hook. The thief slammed into the wall and Kalen caught him. With an expert twist of his wrist, he wrapped the blood-soaked chain around the dwarf's neck and pulled. The ugly man's eyes bugged, making his face even more hideous.

The noble girl had managed to free her hands and doff her hood and gag. "Thank—" She saw the strangling thief, saw the way Kalen spat and growled like a murderous wolf, and she froze, horror-stricken. "What—what are you *doing?*"

Kalen ignored her. The dwarf fought for breath and Kalen pulled tighter on the chain.

The noble lass put her hands to her throat, found a scream, and split the night with her terror. Then she fled, shouting for aid.

Not all saviors are angels, Kalen thought. And not all killings are pretty—or quick.

The thief sputtered and slapped at him impotently.

"Kalen," came Myrin's voice, whispering seemingly on the night's mists. She spoke softly, yet he could hear her as plainly as if she stood next to him.

Was this truly her voice, or his imagination? Did that matter?

Kalen released the chain, let the dwarf collapse retching to the ground, and ran.

The night had grown misty of a sudden, and Kalen knew magic was at work. The thieves were hiding their escape, trying to throw him off, but Myrin's voice led him.

He saw another kidnapper who carried a barefoot girl over his shoulder. Kalen outran him and dived, slamming into the man's back. Kalen rolled so the thief did not fall on him and hoped he had picked the right direction to catch the captive. Sure enough, she landed atop him, and wild silver-white hair tumbled down.

He pulled off the girl's hood, and the shocked eyes of Talantress Roaringhorn stared into his. The magic that changed her skin black had failed, leaving her flesh very pale, but her hair was still long and white. She managed to spit out her gag, and she blinked at him, confused.

Then a smile spread across her face. "My . . . my hero!"

Kalen growled in frustration and thrust her aside. Her captor had risen and was plunging a rapier down at his chest. Kalen rolled away, then back against the blade, wrenching it out of the thief's hand.

He kicked the man's legs out from under him, toppling him to the ground. Kalen rose and put the man out with a kick to the jaw.

"Kalen!" came Myrin's cry—louder this time. Talantress hadn't seemed to hear it. Kalen turned toward the source of the sound and saw a greenish glow: magic.

Kalen seized the thief's fallen rapier. He coughed, opened his helm halfway to spit blood, then sealed his mask. He strode on.

"Wait!" Kneeling, Talantress caught his hand and held him back.

Calmly, Kalen snaked his hand around and unbuckled his gauntlet. It came free, and Talantress hit herself in the chest with it and fell on her overprivileged rump.

"Wait!" Talantress cried from the ground. "Come back right this breath!"

He continued his run, hobbling a bit more slowly after the punishment he'd endured. Young Lady Roaringhorn got up and gave chase, but he paid her no mind. He plunged into the mists, following Myrin's voice and the green glow.

The fog swelled thicker than before, but Kalen pressed on. He was nearing the source, he realized, but he quickly lost his bearing and swam, blind. His body was aching, his lungs heaving, and his heart raced to put him down. He clutched his left arm, which was in agony. He felt as if the half-orc were sitting on his chest.

"Not yet, Eye of Justice," he hissed through clenched teeth. "Not yet."

He channeled healing into himself, praying that he had proven himself once more worthy, but no power came. He gritted his teeth and pressed on.

Kalen stumbled through an empty, gray-black world. Mist swirled around him.

"Myrin!" he choked. He felt that he would fall at any breath.

"Kalen," came her voice, leading him forward. "Kalen . . ."

He staggered ahead, stolen rapier ready for any attack, but found only mist.

"Show yourself!" he challenged. "Cowards!"

As though in response, the mist parted, and Kalen saw a woman from whose cupped hands the mist flowed. A green glow suffused her fingers—magic. Beside her stood a thief who looked more terrified than anything else, and in his arms was a limp girl in a red dress.

"Something's countering my casting," the woman murmured in a deep, rasping voice that didn't match her slim body. She seemed an ordinary human woman, but the voice was that of a beast. "It's the girl. Somehow, even dazed, she's—"

"Then we stop her!" The thief drew a hooked dagger and raised it over Myrin.

"No, you fool!" the woman roared.

Kalen ran forward and stabbed the thief through the chest. Stunned, the man looked down at the blade, then at a panting, heaving Kalen. He toppled, loosing Myrin as he went.

Kalen dived to catch her. She weighed little in his arms and he cradled her tightly.

An arcane word, in a voice like a grinding gravestone, stole his attention. He looked up at the woman to see her gloved, clawlike hand reaching for his face. A finger touched his brow.

Power seized him—cruel power that sucked the life out of his limbs. Lightning arced through Kalen, lashing every stretch of bone and sinew, stealing the strength from his muscles. He fell to his knees.

"Well," the woman said in her corpselike voice. "This is what happens, Sir Fool, when you cross wills with the most powerful wizard in Waterdeep."

She raised her hands and began to chant a spell that Kalen could only imagine would be his doom. Flames and shadow flickered around her hands, like the fires of the Nine Hells.

And so it ends, he thought.

His eyes blurred and he sank toward peaceful sleep.

Myrin's eyes opened and blue light flooded the alley.

TWENTY-SIX

In the strange flash of light, Myrin saw Kalen first, kneeling and helpless, and then the woman—the dead woman wearing the false face—looming over him.

"No," she said in a voice she hardly recognized as her own. She lunged forward and grasped Avaereene by the arm, trying anything she could to stop the slaying magic. She wanted to steal the magic away, rip it from Avaereene so it could not touch Kalen.

And she did exactly that.

The fires darting around Avaereene's fingers faded, flowing instead into Myrin's hands, which lit with fierce blue light. The wizard opened her mouth and stammered.

Oblivious to what she was doing, lashing blindly, Myrin struck Avaereene with her will. A flash of brilliant red and black flame erupted, and the woman slammed backward against the wall with a chorus of crackles and snaps. Bricks cracked and turned inward.

Myrin stared down at her hands, horrified and awed. Blue runes spread down her forearms, almost covering her skin. Power electric filled Myrin's body, making her shiver and shake. The fog boiled away around her, evaporating in the heat coming off her body.

"Damn you!" Avaereene hissed in a voice from beyond the grave. "You do not know what you do, child. This is my own power! How are you—?"

"Shut up!" Myrin shrieked. The stolen magic punched Avaereene in the chest, shaking the building behind her. Holes burst in the wall, and Myrin saw into the common room of a tavern through the cracks.

Avaereene hardly seemed hurt by the blow, but her eyes went wide. Then they turned blood red and began to leak sanguine tears.

"How are you doing this?" she roared in frustration. "You're just a child!"

Myrin merely pointed her hands, loosing bright, hungry flames like nothing she had ever seen or imagined to tear at Avaereene. The wizard screamed in agony and fear. Her skin shivered, then began to bubble and boil. Around her, the bricks glowed red, sizzled, and shook as though caught between an anvil and a smith's hammer. Her black cloak and gown started to smolder and unravel, and soon she was naked. Her entire body quaked and rotted before Myrin's eyes, but the wizard could not scream against the pressure of Myrin's spell. Her eyes were livid and terror filled.

A smile spread across Myrin's face and a thought came unbidden— a thought in her voice but not hers: *this will teach her.*

Then Myrin heard a new sound: a gagging, rasping sound from the ground at her side. She looked down and saw Kalen coughing and retching. He tore open his helm, and she saw him vomit blood onto the cobblestones. "Muh-Myrin . . . stuh-stop . . ."

He looked up at her and she gasped. His skin shivered like Avaereene's, and his eyes were shot through with red. Tears of blood leaked onto his face.

Myrin looked around and saw others gagging and retching—folk inside the tavern, and some who had come forth to watch or help. Gods—what was she doing?

The force holding Avaereene against the wall lessened, and the old woman sucked air into her lungs. She looked down at her withered hands, then touched her face. She screamed.

Myrin turned and clapped a hand to her mouth, shocked. Gone were the beautiful face and body—they had rotted into a withered corpse. Worse, her form had been crushed against the tavern with such force that she had somehow melded with the building's skin. Bricks grew out of her like massive, chunky warts. The red eyes that glared out were not dead, nor were they alive. Myrin recognized the woman's true body, that she was—Myrin didn't know where the word came from—a lich. An undead horror.

"My face! My body!" Avaereene shrieked. "You will die for this, girl!"

The wizard's form had been a magic-wrought falsehood—the corpse embedded in the wall revealed the truth. Myrin's magic had undone years, perhaps decades of delicate spellwork that had achieved the beauty the lich wanted for herself. Complex castings, and probably painful.

Avaereene barked a sharp word. Myrin recoiled, but it was no attack. Hissing in pain and anger, the lich vanished, taking part of the wall with her—and leaving aught of herself too.

With a sick cry, Myrin closed her eyes and fists. She willed the magic to vanish.

It didn't.

Dark fire rolled out of her, uncontrolled. Myrin screamed for it to stop, but it was alive in its own right. It danced around her, gleefully consuming whatever it touched.

She could not stop it.

"Myrin," came a voice, cutting through the chaos.

It was Kalen, his form blurring as though it fought to maintain consistency. His gauntleted hand grasped her tightly—strange, that the right hand had a gauntlet and the left hand was bare. she reached for his bared hand, but she remembered what her touch had done to the lich. She drew back, horrified.

"Myrin, you have to stop." Kalen's voice was calm, his eyes filled with blood.

"I can't!" she cried, and barely jerked her face away from his in time to send her words into the air and away. The force of her voice struck a spire on a nearby building, which tore free of its mounting and fell—horribly—toward them.

Kalen seized Myrin in his arms and threw them both aside. Sharp stone shattered into the cobbled street where they had been standing. Kalen held Myrin with fingers hard and cold as coffin nails.

"Stop!" he cried. "Stop this now!"

Myrin moaned and the ground began to shake. Buildings trembled around them and began to wrench themselves apart. Blue-white flames burst out of loose stones and bricks, which started rolling as though to put themselves out—or to delight in destruction. Folk screamed around them, gagging on what Myrin prayed were meals and not blood or worse.

"Calm," Kalen whispered. "All's well. You must calm yourself."

"I can't!" Myrin sobbed. Her body was shaking, far beyond her control.

His eyes bored into hers, shrinking her world to the size of two orbs. She saw her face reflected in his eyes, saw that almost every finger-length of her skin was scripted with blue runes. They told her a story, and she could almost read them.

"Calm," Kalen whispered again. His face was close to hers, but not touching. His lips hovered over hers, not kissing. "Please."

Slowly—so slowly—Myrin's heart slackened its race. Her screams and sobs subsided and her breathing slowed. The buildings ceased their shaking and the blue flames flickered out and died.

Finally, finally, the blue haze faded, and they were alone in the street, Kalen lying atop her, holding her, protecting her from the night—and from herself.

He wasn't moving, she realized.

"Kalen?" she asked. "*Kalen!*"

"Uhh," he groaned and rolled off, coughing. "Not so . . . not so loud."

Myrin could have kissed him, but men loomed over her, and she looked up. Thieves and kidnappers had come to harm them. Many were wounded or bruised, attacked by Kalen in his pursuit or wasted by the spell chaos. Kalen's eyes glittered and he closed his helm's faceplate, preparing to fight again.

No. Myrin would stop this. Words came unbidden to her lips.

Kalen knelt on the ground, coughing and trying to rise. "No," he said. "No—don't do it."

"All's well." She touched his helmed face with a loving hand, which yet glowed blue. "This is mine," she said. "It's only magic."

"Only . . ." Kalen coughed and retched. "*Only* magic?"

Myrin spread her hands and began the chant. This time, no blue runes crawled onto her tanned skin. This was a spell, whose words were written on her heart, though she had not known them until now. The power felt pure—untainted by the horrid darkness she had channeled from the lich woman. Somehow, she had drawn Avaereene's power, but it was too much—she couldn't control something so strong.

Never again would she draw powers like that. Never again.

"Begone," she said, magic crackling about her fingers.

The men hesitated.

"Begone!" she cried, and conjured fire arced up and burst from her hands.

The thieves didn't have to be told a third time. They turned and fled.

Myrin let the power subside and die, then breathed out in a rush. She felt so tired—so very drained. She sat down next to Kalen. His breath came raggedly and his face was bloody, but his eyes were bright and sharp as diamonds.

She wanted so much to kiss him, but a part of her feared to do so. Instead, she pressed her forehead against his. "I . . . Kalen, I . . ."

His eyes widened and he thrust her away. She saw, as her backside hit the cobbles, his reason.

The thief who'd held her—the one Kalen had stabbed—was crawling toward them, a hooked blade in his hands. The edge dripped with a purple smear that Myrin knew was poison. Kalen's rapier—still inside him—scraped along the stones with a sickly hiss. Blood ran from his mouth. Pain and hatred filled his eyes, from which dripped red tears.

"Bitch," the thief rasped as he limped toward Myrin. "Stick you good, I will—"

His dagger fell. It would have struck Myrin's chest, but Kalen lunged in front of her and grappled with the thief. Myrin watched, stunned, as they wrestled, the knife pressing ever closer to Kalen's unprotected face. Then the knife cut across his cheek and she screamed.

The thief's eyes flicked to her, and the distraction was all Kalen needed. He slammed his open helm against his attacker's face, sending him reeling. He punched out with his gauntleted fist, hitting the man in the same place and shattering his nose. Before the thief could flee, Kalen caught hold of his wrist. He wrenched, and the man screamed as his arm snapped.

"Kalen, stop!" Myrin wept.

At her cry, Kalen looked up, and the thief punched him in the jaw, knocking him down. The man limped away, coughing. Kalen stumbled after him, his hands curled into claws.

"Stop! Please!" Myrin cried, weeping big tears that ran down her cheeks. The man had attacked her, yes, but she had to stop Kalen. He was not a beast but a man—she wanted a *man*, not a monster.

At her words, Kalen turned and caught Myrin in his arms. And though she knew they were both falling down beaten, she felt perfectly safe.

"Shush," Kalen murmured. "It's well—all's well."

"Gods . . ." Then Myrin's heart leaped. "All's *well?* Kalen—you've been poisoned."

She lifted her fingers to touch the slash across his cheek, where the venomed knife had cut him. Greenish black veins had appeared there and spread beneath his skin, the poison working through his blood. They already covered half his face. Myrin had no idea how she could see it—she knew she shouldn't be able to.

Then, as she watched, the poison began to recede. The veins became pink once again, little by little, and the blackness shrank until it vanished entirely from beneath his skin.

He looked as surprised as she felt. "My blessing," he said.

Myrin felt power unlike her own—divine, rather than arcane—fill him. His bare fingers joined hers against his cheek, and she watched as they shimmered white with heat, so bright she could see his bones. The light spread from his fingers into his skin, and the cut turned into a sharp scar. He gasped in relief and surprise.

"I don't understand," Myrin whispered, yet somehow she did understand. A god had saved him.

He shook his head. "Helm—nay. The threefold god," he explained. "He . . . he isn't finished with me yet." He hugged her tighter and his head dipped against her shoulder.

Myrin let loose a deep, terrified breath. She feared Kalen had succumbed, but she could feel him breathing. Tears welled in her eyes.

She and Kalen held each other in the empty street. They would have to move along soon, she knew—before the Watch came—but for now, they could just rest together.

Above them, far above them, a light rain began to fall.

At the top of the cracked tavern, a half-elf woman moved out of the moonlight, trailing a mane of scarlet hair.

TWENTY-SEVEN

W hat's the matter, child?" asked her patron over ale at the Knight 'n Shadow.

Fayne couldn't tell him the truth—didn't *know* the truth. She didn't understand the source of the discontented hollow in her chest. She thought she'd feel better with it done. But now . . .

They sat in the shadowy lower level, in the last hour before dawn. It would be darkest out now, or so the saying went, but the darkest time in Waterdeep occurred not in the city at all but below it, when the hunters of Downshadow returned from a night spent above, pillaging and raiding and doing what they loved best.

Fayne used to love this time, but now . . . she felt nothing but sadness. And anger.

"That damned dwarf stlarned it up." Her ale tasted sour—like goblin piss—and she pushed it aside. She gestured at a serving girl to bring wine. "I had Lady Dawnbringer—I had the situation fully in control and he just . . . *damn!*"

She slammed the heel of her palm down on the table. The loud bang attracted the notice of a few fellow drinkers, but her patron's magic made them look away. As for the man himself, he merely listened to her without speaking.

"No one was supposed to die," she said. "And *she* wasn't supposed to get any kind of vengeance. Her lover was supposed to leave her, not *die*." She scowled. "I'm glad that hrasting pisshole Rath got scarred—served him well for taking matters into his own hands."

Her patron watched her levelly, his easy smile betraying nothing. If he agreed or disagreed, she had no idea. She hated that about him, at times. With that face, he could bluff a dragon out of its hoard, or a god out of her powers. The bastard.

She hated feeling so weak when she sat across from him—hated the way he stared at her, weighing her, like both a prized horse and a petulant child.

That was the way Kalen had looked at her—as a child.

"My sweet?" her patron asked. Fayne looked up, startled. "What are you thinking about?"

"Only how I'm better than *her*," Fayne said, as much to herself as to her patron.

Though Fayne hadn't named her, her patron must have known who she meant: the bitch who styled herself Lady Nathalan. After what Fayne had done this night . . . well. At least Ilira Nathalan's anguished face should chase away Fayne's nightmares about that night eighty years gone.

"Ah." Her patron gazed at her closely. "And yet, something is amiss. What is it?"

"Naught." Fayne downed her bowl of wine and waved for another. "Tell me this, though—it was a brilliant plan, aye? If Rath hadn't come, I'd have ruined Lorien for her, right?"

She saw her patron's wry smile—saw his eyes glowing dimly in the light, as though he enjoyed some private jest. Now it was his turn to grow quiet. "What?" Fayne asked.

"Just reflecting," he said, "how like your mother you are."

Any other day, she'd have taken that for a great compliment.

Fayne sniffed. "What do you mean?" she asked, false bravado in her voice. "That I am proud? Regal? Competitive? Perhaps"—she flipped her hair back—"beautiful?"

He waved a gloved hand and laughed once. "Why not?"

She glared across the table. "Speak plain, fate-spinner."

"As you wish," he said. "She was all those things and more, but she was also flawed. You have shown a similar weakness, but rather than frustrating, I find it endearing."

Fayne bristled. "My mother," she said, "had no weaknesses."

He shrugged, and she saw a quiet twinkle in his eye. "As you say."

Those three little words cut her legs out from under her. They reminded her that she was just a foolish child who had never really known her mother—not as her patron had.

Sometimes, she truly and utterly hated this man. Loved him, of course, but hated him too.

"If you're going to mock me, at least be plain," Fayne said. Her lip trembled.

"Very well," he said. "Your mother . . . if all did not go exactly as she had planned, victory was dust to her. I see the same drive in you, my sweet child."

"That's ridiculous," she said, her voice breaking. "I'm pleased. See how I—"

He reached across the table and laid a hand on hers, cutting off her words. She felt a fearsome heat in his fingers, as though fire coursed in his blood. She stared at him.

"In the end," he said, "did you not succeed at destroying her—this Lady Nathalan?"

The name struck her like a blow, but Fayne felt only a deep, irresistible sadness. "I—I suppose, yes, but—" Fayne wiped her cheeks. "Damn you, I'm *pleased!*"

"Then why are you crying?" he asked. She looked down, and there was a white kerchief in his dainty, perfect hand, the runes for L.V.T. stitched into the corner in red thread.

She ignored his handkerchief and wiped her nose with her hand. "It's not relevant," she said.

Illusions could hide tears, anyway.

"As you say." Her patron smiled patiently, his eyes unreadable. "Don't worry—folk do not change. Killer or hero, angel or whore, no one ever changes. We only wear different faces."

Fayne shivered. She fixed her patron with a cold glare. "You must really hate her."

"Who?" he asked, tucking his kerchief into his colorful doublet.

"*Her.*" Fayne ground her teeth. Who else could she mean? The yellow-eyed whore—the woman who had destroyed her life—she who had taken the only thing she held dear in the world.

He was going to make her say it, she realized. Might as well accept it.

"Ilira," Fayne said, the name like bile in her mouth. "You must hate her as much as I do."

"Ah."

Fayne swore under her breath, remembering. She'd seen such pain on that damned face—and yet, it hadn't soothed her. Now she was not sure what to feel.

Her patron reached across the distance between them and laid a lithe hand against her cheek. She felt his awful heat over her scar—felt again the cutting bolt across her face.

"Do I hate her? No." His eyes were burning pits of molten gold. "Quite the opposite."

Fayne opened and closed her mouth several times. "I don't understand," she said.

"No." His eyes seemed very sad for a moment. "No, I don't expect that you do."

He drew away. She felt as if something had been cut from her—as though an axe had taken her arm, leaving a stump that tingled impotently.

"You wouldn't," he said. "Not yet. Not for several centuries, I don't think."

Anger rose from where it guttered in her belly—the rage let her ignore her doubts. She had always used it to protect herself from herself—that and guile.

Her words were cool and sharp as steel. "Treating me like a youngling?"

"No," he said. "Just someone who is missing the relevant experience."

"That being?" Fayne stretched sinuously. "You'd be hard pressed to find something I haven't . . . experienced." She wet her lips in one long stroke.

The casual flirtation made her feel better. She was no child to be dealt a chiding.

He smiled. "Where were we?"

"The next mark." Fayne leaned across the table, putting her nose alongside his.

"No holiday?" her patron asked. "No rest for the misery-maker?"

"Never." Fayne shook her head and kissed him on the tip of his nose.

"Careful," he said. "You've a place, young one. Remember it."

With a sigh, she leaned back and crossed her arms, pouting. "Tell me one thing."

"Yes, dear one?" he asked.

"Who hired the dwarf to kill Lorien?" she asked. "It wasn't me—so who was it?"

He grinned and did not answer.

Fayne scowled. "Well—who sent Avaereene and the Sightless? You must know *that*."

"Ah yes, lovely Avaereene. Heavens save us from spoiled, sharp-tongued girls!" He winked at her. "Present company excluded."

Fayne smirked. Present company excluded, her curvy *backside*.

"It seems an old friend of mine," her patron said, "one with whom I used to play a game of"—he waved as though thinking of the proper word—"*wit*, say, has decided this city holds an interest for him. Something suitably intriguing—and dangerous, for what it can do."

He yawned and waved. The serving lass brought two more bowls of wine. Her patron winked in thanks, and Fayne saw a shiver pass through the poor girl.

"You were saying, old one?" she teased.

He rolled his eyes. "Naturally, I determined what it was—this plaything my friend has discovered."

"And I'm to obtain it first," she guessed.

"Indeed—tonight, if possible." He raised his hand. "You'll need this."

Seemingly out of the air, he conjured a small pale gray stick, about the length of his smallest finger. He squeezed it once and it lengthened to about twice the length of his hand.

It was a wand, Fayne realized. It didn't feel any more powerful than her mother's wand—the one she carried now—and she had no idea what it was for.

"It isn't my fashion," she said. "So this must belong to someone else."

Her patron smiled. He pulled a pink quill and ink bottle from somewhere and was wrote a single word on a scrap of parchment. He contemplated his writing plume for a moment, then released it into the air, where it vanished. "Though I must tell you the sum total of this one's powers."

"Yes, yes, give it here," Fayne said. When her patron frowned, Fayne batted her lashes. "Please?"

He slid the parchment over and took up his wine as Fayne read the name. She stared.

"You—you must be hrasting *jesting* me." Fayne read it again and blinked at her patron.

He chuckled. "I see the irony is not lost upon that clever mind of yours."

"Oh." A sharp-toothed grin spread across Fayne's face. "Oh, no. Not . . . not at all." She peered at him, eyes glittering. "Why the interest—I mean, for your friend?"

"For that, I must tell you a story, dear child, of long ago—of this very city."

Fayne leaned forward, chin on her hands. Her whole body was tingling, her mind racing. This would be fun.

"The story of a great mage who wanted to stop the spellplague driving the world mad—only he had one impossible barrier." Her patron took up his wine.

"He was already mad."

TWENTY-EIGHT

Unexplained magical disaster strikes Sea Ward!" called a broadcrier for the *Vigilant Citizen*. He was the loudest in the main streets. "Dozens wounded, priests at work."

"Watchful Order baffled as to cause!" shouted another. "Quoth the Blackstaff, 'It could have been worse—*much* worse.'"

"Watch seeks rogue spellcaster! For his protection, and for ours!"

Kalen and Myrin walked south past the criers on Snail Street. She clutched him tighter as they passed the ones who spoke of the spell chaos in Sea Ward yestereve, which seemed to be most of them. Kalen could feel her fingernails even through his glove, which spoke to what a ruin the previous night had left him. He would never tell Myrin that, though—she carried enough guilt already.

"You didn't mean it," Kalen murmured.

Myrin kept her silence, but Kalen saw tears in her eyes.

"Noble daughters kidnapped, ransom demanded!" shouted the broadcrier for the *Daily Luck*. "Watch following all leads—a dozen knaves in custody." Then, because it was a gambling sheet, the crier added: "Place your bets on the search, win fifty dragons!"

"Roaringhorn heir seeks mystery knight," called the crier for the *North Wind*. "Avows true love—offers hand in marriage! Lordlings line the streets."

Horns sounded in the dawn, bidding the gates to open and the day's business to begin. Kalen had come to Dock Ward to search for Fayne. He had treated her unfairly, he knew, and wanted to make amends.

He told himself it was only that—only a matter of honor.

Despite protests for her safety, Myrin had insisted on aiding. Privately, Kalen suspected the girl worried Fayne had been a casualty of yestereve.

"Imposter noble murders Sune priestess!" the broadcrier for the *Mocking Minstrel* called, startling Kalen. The voice was strangled. "Menagerie Salon ruined! Watch declines comment."

"Boy," Kalen beckoned him over. "Speak."

Tears filled the boy's eyes. "Oh, goodsir and lady," he said, pulling off his hat. "No one was a finer friend of us common-born than the poor lady."

"Lady Lorien, you mean?" Myrin asked.

The boy shook his head. "Lady Ilira," he corrected. "She gave coin to folks like me pa, who's hurt by magic and can't work. It's come out"—he pointed to his wares, to a tale halfway down the page— "come out that Lady Ilira was the one *founded* the Scarred Haven, a body of kindly ones who . . ." He shook his head and pointed to the lead article of the *Minstrel*. "Don't read this tale, m'lord—'tis cruel to one who did so much for us all."

"We all do what we must." Kalen handed the boy a gold dragon and took the broadsheet.

"As you will, m'lord." The boy smiled at the gold—far more than the broadsheet cost—then wandered down the street, crying his wares.

"What is it?" Myrin asked. "You saw how upset the boy was—why read—?"

"That's Fayne," Kalen said, pointing to the name on the broadsheet.

"Satin Rutshear?" Myrin giggled at the name, but Kalen grimaced. She blushed. "Sorry."

"At least we know she's alive," Kalen said.

Myrin smiled hopefully.

"Or at least," Kalen murmured, "she was when she gave this to the *Minstrel* to print."

Myrin's smile faded.

Kalen began to read. The boy had told him true—the gossip-ridden tale was sharp and biting, witty and entirely unfair. Exactly like Fayne.

Lady Ilira Nathalan, it reported, was a creature of cruel, murderous depravity. A search of her villa by the Watch had revealed—much as

Satin had long suspected it would—evidence that Lady Ilira had been stealing from her competitors and, indeed, was an assassin. Private papers showed she had been in the employ of the Shadovar, under the name Shadowfox, one of their most effective assassins. She'd killed dozens of folk before the turn of the century—and, possibly, more recently as well—and used the bloody coin to build and support her Menagerie and the dummy organization, the Haven for the Scarred, which masqueraded as a charity. The Watch and mercantile bodies were now working to dismantle those bodies.

"That . . . that can't be Fayne's writing," said Myrin. "That's horrible! Lies! That can't . . . that can't *be*, Kalen."

But Kalen remembered Lady Ilira's hands covered in Lorien's blood—remembered the way she'd lunged at Rath and burned away half his face with her kiss, and the cruel passion in her eyes when she'd dared the Watch to *pierce* her.

He shivered, and Myrin put her arm in his as though to warm him. He smiled at her, but he didn't feel the slightest comfort.

>———W———<

They spent the day looking for Fayne—to no avail. Aside from the broadsheet that proved she was alive—or at least had been that morn—they found no trace of her.

As dusk fell, Waterdhavians returned home for evenfast—and though Myrin kept silent, Kalen heard her stomach gurgle. They had eaten little: only a simmerstew at dawn and handpies at highsun. They should go to a hearth-house, Kalen decided.

Likely Cellica was cooking even now, but Kalen couldn't yet return to the tallhouse and face her reproving stare—not after he had been so harsh with Fayne.

He felt every bit as guilty as Myrin did, he realized, but for a different reason—she had simply lost control. What Kalen had said . . . he'd meant every word, and regretted each one.

Kalen took Myrin to the Bright Bell, just south of Bazaar Street on Warrior's Way in Castle Ward. He didn't often eat at hearth-houses, but this one he liked. While not elegant or exotic, the food was good and plentiful and the place was frequented by plain folk—those people of Waterdeep whom he fought every night to defend from shadows they could not see.

Being around these folk let him think and relax, though he did not know any of them. That struck him as odd for the first time: for a defender of the folk of the city, he rarely spent any time with them. Most of his talk and time were spent with the Guard, the Watch, or Cellica, who, like Kalen, was not from the city. Though his looks and speech marked him as blood of the Sword Coast, he was yet a foreigner. Waterdeep, with all its adventures and splendors, was no more home than Westgate had been—or even Luskan, before that. He no longer had a home.

Myrin, for her part, loved the Bell. She stared about its tight labyrinth, crowded nooks, and choked dining alcoves with the innocent wonder of an explorer. She hearkened close to the loud buzz of chatter and jest that vibrated through the walls, and though the thick, smoky air made her cough, she was smiling as she did it. She seemed to have forgotten her worries with the proximity of folk and the promise of food. She seized Kalen's gloved hand and held it tighter and tighter as a servant led them to a table, deeper in the hearth-house.

Several times, Myrin stumbled and almost fell on one of the many trip steps between chambers that changed level slightly from room to room. Kalen caught her each time, as he knew the perils, and each time she lingered a little longer in his embrace before pulling away with a laugh.

They sat in a curtained alcove on the second floor of the Bell. A tall, thin servant wiped the table clean with an ale-stained rag as they sat. Then he stood waiting, and Myrin looked at Kalen awkwardly, out of her depth.

"You have the courses written?" Kalen asked.

The servant smiled and handed them printed menus—grand, elegantly scripted affairs on thick parchment. Myrin's eyes widened at the lists and she began reading immediately, fascinated.

In addition to a thick warming stew and fresh bread, Kalen ordered a pie of fowl while Myrin opted for boiled tahllap noodles with fresh vegetables and goat cheese. She tried a weak mulled wine, and Kalen requested a small glass of zzar for himself. The night was cold, and he felt like strong drink. The taste of almonds was intense enough to touch his numb tongue.

Myrin particularly liked the first-spring strawberries that came before the meal, and Kalen was glad to let her have all of them. He rather liked her little smile and the way she closed her eyes as she set each one against her lips to savor the taste. Once, she caught him looking and blushed.

He looked away and sipped his zzar. It had a bite that warmed his insides.

"You should tell me about yourself," she said. She blushed again. "A little, if you like—I just remember so little about myself, and I'd rather we spoke than sat in silence, aye?"

Kalen shrugged. "For instance?"

Myrin looked at her food. "That woman—Rayse. She's . . ."

"My superior in the Guard," Kalen said.

Myrin colored. "She's . . . she's very pretty."

"Yes." Kalen fell silent.

Myrin was flustered. "I'm sorry—I didn't mean . . ."

Kalen shrugged. "Nothing else binds Rayse and me," he said. "There was once, but that was some time ago."

Myrin shook her head. "I didn't mean to ask—that was improper."

"All's well." Kalen reached across the table to touch her chin.

Myrin looked up, startled, then smiled.

Kalen realized what he had done and retracted his arm. "Never you mind."

She started to speak but the words became half hiccup, half belch, and she covered her mouth, giggling. Kalen looked back at his food. He wished she'd stop doing that—he knew what Fayne meant, now, when she'd called Myrin "adorable."

"Kalen," Myrin said. "About today. About Fayne."

Kalen stiffened and wondered if she could read his thoughts.

Myrin looked down at her empty soup bowl. "I know why I'm seeking her, because she might be hurt, but why are you doing it?"

Kalen sipped his zzar. "Personal business," he said.

"Oh." Myrin bit her lip. She radiated disappointment like light and heat from the sun.

"Not *that* personal," Kalen said. "I . . . last night, I said something to her that was cruel and unfair. I need to beg her pardon." That was at least *part* of the truth.

"Oh." Myrin didn't ask anything more, but her eyes lingered. Kalen ordered another zzar.

"Will you tell me?" Myrin asked. "Cellica told me only a little. What passed, last night?"

He shrugged. "It's not important."

Myrin's eyes fell and she said nothing. Kalen's reply seemed to have displeased her. He might have spoken again, but their food arrived, steaming and delicious. As always, Myrin fell to her plate with relish, as though to make up for years of fasting. Kalen ate only half-heartedly.

"Speak," Myrin said. "Tell me something—anything about you!" She smiled sweetly.

Kalen *wanted* to speak, but there were too many things he did not want to say—either to her, or to himself. About Fayne. About Lorien and Lady Ilira. It left him uncertain.

As she ate, he started speaking. Not of Fayne, or Ilira, or Lorien, or anything about Waterdeep at all. He spoke about Shadowbane.

He told her, in quiet tones that would not be overheard, of his quest. He spoke of his training in Westgate and of Levia, his teacher. He told her of the Luskan of his youth, when he and Cellica had stolen and begged for their meals, or used her voice when she could. How in his eighth winter he had met Gedrin Shadowbane—the Night Mask turned paladin, founder and leader of the Eye of Justice—who had changed his life.

Kalen told Myrin of the oath Gedrin had exacted from him—never to beg again—and he spoke tightly of Vindicator, bequeathed to him and now in the hands of Araezra.

"Perhaps she is more worthy of it," Kalen murmured.

Myrin looked up, wiped her eyes, and laid her hand on his wrist. "You protected me," she said. "You have your powers back. Should you not have your god's sword back, too?"

Kalen smiled. "As the Eye judges," he said. "If I am worthy, it will come back to me. If I am not . . . then may it bring Araezra victory in her aims. I hope she honors it as I tried to."

Myrin drew her hand away. "It must be well," she said. "Having a god to serve. I don't know what god I served—if I even had one."

They sat in awkward silence, and Kalen was aware that Myrin was looking at him from the corner of her eye. She had stopped eating, and without knowing why, Kalen could sense she was upset. Was it something about her memory?

"Kalen," Myrin asked finally, "why do you do this?"

He looked down at his drink.

"If I don't," he said, "then who will?"

Myrin kept her eyes on him. "Who was that man I saw yestereve?" she asked, barely whispering. "When the villain was running and you hurt him anyway—just to hurt him?"

Kalen understood why she was upset. "That man attacked you," he said.

"But he was fleeing," Myrin said. "He would have run away, but you gave chase. You hurt him, when you didn't need to. Why?"

Kalen shrugged. "You wouldn't understand."

"Stop it!" Myrin touched his hand. Kalen felt a little tingle, electric, beneath his skin. Her eyes were very bright in the candlelight. "This isn't you—you aren't so cold."

Kalen opened his mouth, but a delicate cough arose near their table. The servant had returned. He hovered, looking awkward. "I'm sorry, I didn't mean to interrupt."

Kalen loosed Myrin's hand, and the girl looked embarrassed.

"Not at all," Kalen said. He reached in his scrip for coin. "We're finished, I think."

Other diners called for the servant, who nodded to Kalen and Myrin and left.

Kalen turned back to Myrin. He wished he could tell her everything—all the awful things he had done as a younger man—but he knew that would erase her smile. And that . . . he couldn't bear to do that.

>——W—<

"Mayhap we should buy me a weapon," Myrin said on their way back to Kalen's tallhouse. Her arm was linked in his, and any tension from the evenfeast had passed.

"Why?" Kalen examined her critically. Despite having eaten like a ravenous dog for two days, the girl was thin and light, almost frail. She didn't have the muscle or constitution for a duel at arms. "You have *me*."

She blushed. "But when you aren't there—like at the ball," she said. "A weapon for me to defend myself with, rather than with—you know." She waved her fingers.

"Like what?" Kalen asked. "A sword?"

"A dagger," Myrin said. "Small, light, eminently fashionable." She mimed patting the hilt of a blade sheathed at her hip and grinned. "Easy."

"Daggers are more difficult than swords." Kalen shook his head, which was clouded with zzar. He wasn't accustomed to strong drink. "Most of knife fighting is grappling," he said in response to her disbelieving look. "You don't have that sort of build."

Myrin crossed her arms. "I still want one."

Kalen paused in the street and shrugged. He drew the steel he usually kept in a wrist sheath. Myrin's eyes widened when she saw the knife emerge seemingly out of the air, and he passed it to her. As she marveled at it, he unbuckled his wrist sheath and secured it on her belt.

"Take care with that," Kalen said. "I'll be having it back."

"For true?" Myrin sheathed the blade reverently. "You'll show me how, someday?"

Kalen shrugged.

Myrin smiled and held his arm tighter as they walked on.

A cool drizzle began to fall when they reached Kalen's neighborhood, and he covered Myrin with his greatcoat. She wore a canvas shirt and skirt of leather, warm and practical, but no cloak. They reached the tallhouse and Kalen nodded to the night porter, then waved Myrin inside first. She blushed and giggled and picked up her skirt to cross the threshold.

They climbed two flights of stairs to his rooms and found the door unlocked. Cellica sat at the table, working on Shadowbane's black leather hauberk, stitching the rents. She looked up from her work and smiled. No matter what disaster befell, the halfling always smiled.

"About time," she said. "You two love whisperers had a pleasant day? I can tell you mine's been a crate of laughs." She threaded the needle through the leather and pulled it closed.

Kalen colored and Myrin giggled.

"I'm weary," the girl said. "Is it well if I sleep in your chamber again, Cele?"

"Kalen's bed's bigger," Cellica said.

Myrin flushed bright red. "I . . . I, ah . . ."

"Don't get giggly, lass," Cellica said. "I meant that he'd take the floor again." She batted her eyes at Kalen. "Won't you, Sir Shadow?"

Kalen shrugged. The ladies had shared a bed the first two nights, but after the ball—the third night—he'd given Myrin his bed. "Of course."

Myrin hesitated. "I think Kalen needs his bed. He hasn't fully recovered, you know." She bit her lip and looked at the floor.

Kalen didn't understand this at all. He just needed sleep—it mattered little where.

Cellica stared at her a long time, then smiled, as though picking up some subtle jest. "As you will—you're quite warm." The halfling shrugged. "I'll join you in about an hour. Soon as I finish." She clipped the thread with her teeth and rubbed the stitched breastplate with her delicate fingers. "Merciful gods! One would think you'd learn to dodge more blades and arrows."

"I'll remember that," Kalen said, his voice dry. His head ached and he rubbed his temple.

Myrin grinned and winked at the halfling, who winked in kind. Whatever conspiracy they had hatched, it was cemented. Myrin walked toward Cellica's room but did not let go of Kalen's hand, pulling him along. She opened the door but did not go in, nor did she release Kalen.

They lingered for a moment. Kalen looked over his shoulder, but the halfling seemed not to notice them. Myrin was digging the ball of one foot into the floor.

"We'll find her, Kalen," she said. "I know it."

He shrugged. Then, because it wasn't enough, he spoke: "Yes."

Myrin clasped one arm behind her back and looked at the floor shyly, then up at Kalen. Something unspoken passed between them—something that neither could say.

"Good e'en," Myrin said at length, awkwardly. She went inside and closed the door.

Kalen stood blinking for a breath, then he turned to find Cellica's eyes on him. "What?"

"For a man who reads faces and listens for lies every day . . ." The halfling trailed off.

Kalen rubbed his temples and limped toward his room. "Good e'en," he said.

He stepped inside, shut the door, and pulled off his doublet, which he tossed to the floor. He crossed to the basin and mirror and splashed water on his face. Vicious bruises and stitched cuts rose on his muscled frame. The deepest ached, despite his numbness.

Tough as he was, he had to admit the accumulated hurts of the last few days were taking their toll. All he wanted was to sleep until he no longer hurt.

He saw something move in the mirror and turned.

She lay in his bed, blanket pulled up to her nose. Her pale skin glittered in the candlelight and her red hair seemed almost black. Her eyes were wide and mischievous.

"Well met, Kalen," Fayne whispered. She smiled. "Coins bright?"

TWENTY-NINE

Y ou're here," Kalen said, and he stretched. Though he didn't expect
a duel, he didn't turn his back on her and checked the dirk at his
belt. He made no hasty moves, and didn't let his eyes linger on her
curves under the blanket. "Cellica let you in?"

"Yes." Fayne bit her lip, her smile chased away by his cold voice.
"And no. She doesn't remember I'm here. I warded us"—she nodded
to the door—"against sound."

"You—" Kalen winced at the zzar ache in his head and rubbed his
stubbled chin. "Are you wearing anything under that blanket?"

Slowly, Fayne lowered the blanket to reveal a thin white ribbon
around her throat, from which hung a black jewel. Then she raised
the sheet back to her chin.

"Ah." Kalen coughed and kept his gaze purposefully averted.

Fayne rolled her eyes. She sat up and lowered the blanket to bunch
around her. "This is stupid, I know, and I'm a fool to come here, but
I just have to say something, Kalen. You don't ever, ever have to see
me again afterward, I just have to say it."

Kalen walked near the bed but remained standing. "Then say it."

Silence reigned between them for a moment. They looked at one
another.

Kalen had seen Fayne nearly naked at the temple, but that had
been different. A battle, when his blood was up. Now, her skin seemed
smooth and soft. She was so very vulnerable, deprived of clothing.
She seemed younger and lighter—fragile.

Like Myrin.

As though she could read his thoughts and wanted—*needed*—
to turn his mind to her, Fayne opened her mouth and the words
gushed forth.

"I . . . oh, Kalen, I've made a terrible mistake," she said. "A woman

227

is dead because of me—because of my pranks. And . . . and I wanted to tell you that I'm sorry."

Kalen broke the gaze and looked toward the window. "Don't," he said.

Fayne's eyes welled. "Kalen, please. Please just let me say this."

She sat upright and edged closer to him. When he stepped away, she stayed on the bed, peering up at him.

"You were . . . you were right about me," she said with a sniffle. "I *am* just a silly girl who doesn't think about the hurt I cause. My entire life, all I've done is lie and ruin. I have a talent for it, and the powers to match, and that was how I made coin. All I've ever done is scandalize folk—some honest, most dishonest—for gold." She wiped her nose.

"Sometimes I did nobles and fops, sometimes people of real importance—merchants, politicians, traders, foreign dignitaries. Whatever they believed or fought for, I didn't care. I know—I was a horrible wretch, but I didn't care."

She sniffed and straightened up, looking at him levelly.

"I . . . I was doing the same thing with Lorien and Ilira and I didn't mean anyone to get hurt." She cast her eyes down. "You believe me, right? I didn't mean—"

Kalen kept his silence but closed his hand on the hilt of the dirk he wore at his belt. The dirk was a cheap, brute object without the elegance of Vindicator, but it could kill just the same. He'd spent the day searching for Fayne, but he hadn't realized that it had been equally a matter of anger as concern.

He didn't know how he felt.

"Explain why I should believe you."

"Why would I lie about this?" Fayne asked.

"I do not know—but you *are* lying." Kalen fished in his satchel and pulled out the folded *Minstrel*. He pulled it open and set it on the table. Then he drew his dirk and slammed it through her false name, pinning the broadsheet down. "Explain that," he said.

She bunched the blanket around herself, rose, and padded toward him on bare feet. "Oh, Kalen!" She flinched away from the broadsheet as though from a searing pan on a fire. "That . . . that *creature* killed my mother. I—I just wanted to cause her pain, that's all. But I never meant anyone to die—that was Rath's doing."

"How do I know you didn't hire him?"

"I'm telling you the *truth!*" Fayne cried. "You saw him try to kill me. He would have done so, if you hadn't come!" She sobbed. "I didn't want anyone to die."

"I don't believe you." He put his hand on the dirk—simultaneously gesturing to the broadsheet and offering a quiet threat. "Why write that? You *know* who killed Lorien."

"I . . . I was upset, Kalen!" Her eyes grew wet. "You don't understand! I was there when she killed my . . . I *saw* it happen! I hate that woman, Kalen—I *hate* her!"

She ripped the *Minstrel* off the table, tearing it against his blade, balled it up, and hurled it to the floor. Her scream that followed nearly shook the room.

Kalen flinched and looked to the door, but Fayne had spoken true. Had it not been warded against sound, Cellica would have burst in.

"So why not kill *her?*" Kalen asked. "Why Lorien, and not Ilira?" He stepped closer to her, so he could seize her throat if he wanted.

"I don't—I don't *like* people, aye," Fayne said. "I hate them. I hate everyone, especially her—but I don't hate enough to murder. That isn't me, and . . . and I have to make you see that."

"Why do I matter so much?"

Fayne wiped her eyes and nose. "Because I can't—not with you. I can't lie to you or trick you. You always know—you *always* know." She sobbed again. "It was so, so frustrating at first, but—there's something between us, Kalen. And it's something I can't understand."

Kalen looked into her eyes. How rich they seemed—bright, wet pools of gray cloud in her half-elf face. How earnest and true.

"I have to know, Kalen." She made a visible effort to compose herself, grasping her hands tightly in front of her waist. "Is . . . is what we have real? Can that really happen between two people who meet only for a moment? I've never loved any . . ." She trailed off and stared at the floor. She stomped angrily—frustrated. "I don't understand! It's not—it's not *fair!*"

"Fayne," Kalen said.

"You!" she cried. "The one man I can't have—the one man I should flee—but I can't leave you. Even now, as I stand here naked before you—you, who chastised me, who rejected me, who threatened to arrest me, and I can't leave—I can't just forget you."

Tears slid down her cheeks, and he couldn't have spoken if he tried.

"I need to know if I love you, and if you love me," she said. "I need . . . I need something real in my life of shadows and lies. Does that make any sense? Can't you understand?"

Kalen looked away when she met his eyes. He weighed her words and body language, probing for a lie, but found nothing. This was the truth, as far as he could tell.

Hers was a life of shadows and lies, he thought. Like his own life.

"Oh, Kalen," Fayne said. "Say something . . . say anything, just *please*."

Kalen turned toward her. "It isn't true."

Fayne's body went rigid, as though his gaze had turned her to stone. "What isn't true?"

"That a woman died because of you," Kalen said. "You didn't send Rath to kill her."

Fayne inhaled sharply.

"I believe you," Kalen said. "Your game was thoughtless and wicked and took Lorien off her guard, but it is not your fault—"

Fayne threw an arm around his neck and kissed him hard. It caught Kalen off guard and he staggered back a step. He could feel the pressure and could taste her lips on his, even with the numbness. The blood thundered in his veins, and he could feel his heart beating in his head.

"No." Fayne pulled away. "No. I'm sorry. I just . . . I had to. I'm sorry."

"What is it?"

Fayne went to reclaim the clothes she'd left on his bed. "You love her," she said.

"Ha." Kalen shook his head.

"Ha?" Fayne scoffed. "That girl practically hurls herself at you every moment you're together—it's in everything she does. She adores you—the sight of you, the thought of you. She loves you, you idiot. And you"—her eyes narrowed—"you love her, too."

He shook his head. "I do not."

She paused and looked at him curiously, warily. "You're sure?"

She stepped toward him, and he could feel heat growing within—lust for her and for the duel. It would always be this way with her, he thought.

"What do you feel, then?" she asked. "What do you feel, right now?"

It came to him, the perfect word. Kalen smiled sadly. "Pity."

Whatever Fayne had expected, that surprised her. "You pity her?" Then her voice became colder. "You pity *me?*"

"Myself." Kalen shook his head. "She makes me wish I were a better man."

Fayne flinched as though he'd slapped her. "That sounds like love to me."

She started to turn but he caught her wrist. "No," he said.

"No?"

He shook his head.

"Well thank the Maid of Misfortune," Fayne said, raising her jaw proudly. "I was starting to think you didn't fancy me anymore."

The sheer, unflappable confidence in her eyes—the mock outrage and scornful words, the shameless flirtation—all of it made Kalen smile. The bravado of this woman astounded him.

Fayne was not like shy and thoughtful Myrin, but bold and conceited, utterly convinced of her own allure. And as arrogant as Fayne was, Kalen had to admire her. She was unchanging, immovable, *perfect* in her imperfection.

He told her what he hadn't told Myrin—what he never would have dared tell her. He wanted to stop himself but couldn't.

"I am sick, Fayne."

She stared at him, as though judging whether he spoke true. Finally, she nodded.

Kalen went on. "When I was a child, I felt less pain than others did. My fingers are scarred from my teeth"—he spread his hands so she could see—"as are my lips." He licked his lips and pursed them,

231

so she might see the marks. "I just—I just didn't feel it."

Fayne nodded, and her gray eyes grew a touch wider.

"I would have died, but for the scoundrel who took me in and raised me, among a host of other orphans," Kalen said. "He taught me how to inflict the pain I couldn't feel—how to use my 'blessing' for my benefit. Or rather, his."

"Sounds like my father," said Fayne. When he paused, she waved him on. "But this is your story—pray, continue."

"I found feeling eventually, but long after my skin had hardened. At six, I shrugged off stabs that would have left a man weeping on the floor."

Kalen watched Fayne's eyes trace the scars along his ribs and chest, some of which were very old. Each one, Kalen remembered well.

"I killed my master when I was just a child," Kalen said. "He was a cruel old man, and I had no pity for him. More pity I had for the older orphans he had hurt over the years—though I reserved the most for myself, understand."

Fayne nodded. She understood.

"I was a thief, and a mean one," he said. "Folk had done things to me—terrible things—and I had seen far worse. So when I hurt folk—killed them, sometimes—I didn't think anything of it. I used my blade to get coin—or food. Or if I was angry, as I often was. I was born hard as steel, and I only got harder."

He almost wanted Fayne to say she was sorry—as though she could take the blame for all the world and offer atonement. But she merely watched him, listening patiently.

"Without my master, I was forced to beg on the streets—to sell my services for food or warmth. I met Cellica shortly thereafter, and she became like a sister to me, but my master had done his work and I was stone not only on the surface, but inside."

"Cellica grew up in Luskan, too?" Fayne glanced toward the door. "She seems too soft."

Kalen shrugged. "She was a prisoner," he said. "Escaped the grasp of some demon cult."

"A cult?" Fayne looked troubled. "What kind of cult?"

Kalen shrugged. "Cellica didn't talk about it much, and I didn't ask," he said. "I met her by chance, and she set my broken arm. Healing hands."

"Mmm." Fayne nodded. "She was a good friend?"

"I hated her, too, at first," Kalen said. "As soon as my arm healed, I hit her, but only once." He grinned ruefully. "She put me down faster than you could say her name."

Fayne giggled. "You wouldn't think it, to look at her."

"Tough little wench," said Kalen, and Fayne shared his smile.

Then he paused, not wanting to tell her the story of Gedrin or of obtaining Vindicator, and in truth it did not matter. That would instill a touch of nobility to his story, and he did not feel noble. He was awash in his brutal past.

"When I was eight years of age, I . . . I made a mistake. I did something terrible, and my spellscar returned in full force. I couldn't move at all."

He tried to turn, but she held his hand tighter and didn't look away. Kalen set his jaw.

"I was frozen, locked in a dead body that felt nothing, but saw and heard everything. It was like my childhood sickness, but returned a hundredfold. A man grown would have gone mad, and perhaps I did—not knowing when or if I would ever move again. I couldn't even kill myself—only lie there and wait to die."

His hands clenched hard enough for him to feel his fingernails, which meant they would be drawing blood. Fayne watched him closely, consuming every word.

"I prayed—to anyone or anything that might hear," he said. "I prayed every moment for true death, but the gods did not hear me. They had abandoned Luskan and everyone in it."

"You were a man of *faith?*" asked Fayne. Her voice was respectfully soft—almost reverent. "An odd choice for a beggar boy."

He shrugged. "Cellica didn't follow the gods either—her healing was in needle, thread, and salve. But she believed in right, and she definitely believed in wrong. And though letting me die might have been kinder, as I thought, she told me every day that she would help me, no question. She loved me, I came to realize, though I had no understanding of it then.

"She kept me from starving. She cared for me when anyone else would have left me for dead. I hated her for that—for not letting me die—but I loved her all the same. She would feed me and clean me and read to me—but other times, she would just sit with me, talking or silent. Just be with me, when I had nothing else.

"And eventually—finally—I began to pray for life. Just a little bit of life—just enough to touch her cheek, hold her, thank her. Then I could rest." Kalen brushed a hand down Fayne's cheek. "Do you understand?"

Fayne nodded solemnly. "What happened?"

"Nothing," Kalen said. "No god came to save me—no begging brought life back into my dead body. I was alone but for Cellica, and she could not fight for me. I had to fight for myself."

Fayne said nothing.

"I stopped praying," Kalen said. "I stopped begging. Once . . ." He trailed off.

He breathed deeply and began again.

"After I escaped my master but before my mistake—when I was a boy of eight winters, begging on the streets. Someone once told me not to beg. A great knight, called Gedrin Shadowbane."

Something like recognition flickered across Fayne's face—the name, he thought.

Kalen continued. "He didn't ask me why I begged—nothing about my past, or who I was. He didn't care. He just told me, in no uncertain terms, that I was never to beg again. Then he struck me—cuffed me on the ear so I would remember."

"What a beast!" Fayne covered a grin with her hand and her eyes gleamed with mirth.

Kalen chuckled. "It was the last thing anyone said to me before I fell paralyzed," he said. "And as I lay unmoving, hardly able to breathe or live, I realized he was right. I stopped praying for someone else to save me, and fought only to save myself. Not to let myself die. Not yet—I would die, I knew, but not yet." Kalen clenched his fists. "Then, slowly—gods, so slowly—it came back. Feeling. Movement. *Life*. I could speak to Cellica again. I told her what I wanted—to die—and she cried. If I had begged her, she would have done it, but

I would not ask that of her. She pleaded with me to wait—to give it a tenday, to see if it got better."

He closed his eyes and breathed out.

"It did. Slowly, with Cellica behind me every moment, I recovered," Kalen said. "But I knew it was only temporary. When we had the coin to hire a priest, he told us I still bore the spellplague within me—a spellscar festering at my core. Perhaps I'd had it from birth."

He flexed his fingers.

"Some bear an affliction of the spirit, mind, or heart—mine is in my body. The numbness will return—is returning—gradually, over time. And with it, my body dies, little by little." He shrugged. "I feel less pain—less of everything. And though it makes me stronger, faster, able to endure more than most men, ultimately, it will kill me."

Kalen looked toward the window at the rain hammering the city.

"I had a choice," he said. "I could waste my life dreading it, or I could accept it. I followed the path that lay before me. I accepted Helm's legacy, and followed the Eye of Justice."

As though his voice had lulled her into a trance from which she was just waking, Fayne blinked and pursed her lips. "Helm? As in, the god of guardians? The *dead* god of guardians?"

Kalen said nothing.

"I don't know if you know your history, but Helm died almost a hundred years ago," Fayne said. "Your powers can't come from a dead god—so what deity grants them?"

Kalen had asked himself the same question so many times. "Does it really matter?"

Fayne smiled. "No," she said, as she leaned closer to him. "No, it doesn't."

She caressed his ear with her lips, and her teeth. Kalen could just feel it—enough to know what she was doing—which meant she was probably hurting him. He didn't care.

She dipped a little and bit at the soft spot at the end of his jaw. She pressed her cheek to his, letting her warm breath excite the hairs on his neck.

Through it all, Kalen stayed still as a statue.

"I know you can feel this." Fayne's eyes were sly. "I wonder what else I can make you feel. Things that little girl couldn't dream of— things your mistress Araezra doesn't know."

Kalen smiled thinly. "Only," he said, "only if you give me something."

"And what," she asked, kissing his numb lips, "is that?"

"Tell me your name," Kalen said.

Fayne stepped back and regarded him coolly. "You don't trust me, even now?"

He shrugged.

"Very well. Can't blame you, really," Fayne said. "Rien. That's my real—"

Kalen shook his head. "No. It isn't."

"Gods!" Fayne laid her head on his shoulder and pressed herself hard against him, kissing his neck once more. He felt her sharp teeth, which meant they must have drawn blood. She wiped her lips before she drew away to speak to him, so he could not know for certain. "Rien is my true name, given me by my mother before she died."

"And it means 'trick' in Elvish," Kalen said. "No need to trick me."

She swore mildly, still smiling. Then she nibbled his earlobe and breathed into his ear. He knew his senseless skin awakened and went red, but he could not feel it.

Kalen sighed. "You can stop lying," he said.

"Eh?" Fayne clutched his lips hard enough for him to feel—hard enough to draw blood.

"You don't have to pretend to love me," Kalen said.

With a last, lingering kiss on the corner of his lip, Fayne pulled away and faced him squarely. His eyes glittered in the candlelight.

"How dare you," she said, half-jesting and half-serious.

"All this," Kalen said. "This is just an act. Isn't it?"

Her face went cold and angry, shedding all pretense of jest. "How *dare* you."

Fayne snapped up her hand to strike him, but he caught it and held her arm in place.

"That time," Kalen said, "your anger told the truth."

Fayne said nothing for a long time. Kalen put his hand on her elbow and though he held it only lightly, he might as well have bound her in iron.

"It's still that girl, isn't it?" Fayne accused. She raised one finger to point at him. "It's that little blue-headed waif with her tattoos you fancy, isn't it?"

She drew the bone wand from her belt and flicked it around her head. An illusion fell over her, cascading down like sparks to illumine her form, which shrank and tightened, billowed out a scarlet silk gown, and became Myrin.

"Is this what you want?" came the soft, exotic voice. Fayne in Myrin's image knelt and pressed her hands together. "Please, Kalen—please ravage me! Oh, ye gods!" She caressed herself and moaned. "I just can't *stand* the waiting, Kalen! Oh, please! Oh, take me *now!*"

Kalen shrugged. "This is beneath even you."

"Even me, eh? You have no idea how low I can sink," Fayne said with Myrin's voice. "Wouldn't you like that, Kalen? To see your little sweetling as *wicked* as I can be?"

"She's far too good for me," Kalen said. "For any of us."

"And I'm what—a perfect fit?" She flicked her tongue at him. "You disgust me."

"No," Kalen said, "I don't."

"Oh?" Fayne crossed her arms—Myrin's arms—and regarded him with an adorable pout.

She took out her wand again and broke the illusion. Her half-elf form reappeared, wavered over something darker, then settled. It was brief, but it made him wonder . . .

"Why, O wise knight of shadows," she said, "why don't I hate you?"

"Because you're like me," Kalen said. "A lover of darkness."

Fayne stared at him another moment, anger and challenge in her eyes. Every bit of him burned—wanted him to lunge forward and grasp her, wrench the blanket from her body, throw the paladin aside and free the thief at his heart.

"I should go," she said finally. "You and I . . . she's the one for you, Kalen, not I. She is better for you." Fayne made to leave, but Kalen stopped her. This time, his grip was firm.

"I know well what's better for me," Kalen said. "And I want you instead."

Fayne blinked at him, wordless.

"Show me." Kalen ran his fingers along her cheek. "I want to see your face."

He saw the shift in her stance, could almost feel every hair on her body rise. He felt her bristle, the way a lion might just before it pounces. "But you do see my face," she said, her tone dangerous. "I stand here before you, no illusions."

"That's a lie," Kalen said. "I've taken my mask off for you—take yours off for me."

He still held her by the wrist. Could he feel the blood thundering in her veins, or was he imagining it? His grip lessened.

"Run," Kalen said, "or take off your mask. Choose."

"Kalen, you can't—" she said. "Please. I'm frightened."

Perhaps I *am* cruel, Kalen thought. But Gedrin had taught him the value of pain, with that clout on the ear. Pain reveals who we truly are.

"You want it to be real, then choose." He shook his head. "I won't ask again."

Trembling, Fayne looked at him for three deep breaths. He was sure—so sure—that she would run. But then she drew her wand from her belt with a steady hand. He saw the tension in her body, practically felt her insides roiling and tossing like a rickety boat in a god-born storm, but she stayed calm.

She was like the thief he had been, he thought.

"Very well," she said.

She passed the wand in front of her face and a false Fayne slid away like a heavy robe, leaving her naked before him. Her true face took form—her skin and hair and body. All her lies vanished, and she was truly herself. Regardless of her shape, she was just a woman standing before a man.

Kalen said nothing, only looked at her.

Finally, Fayne looked away. "Am I . . ." she asked, her voice broken. "Am I really so repulsive?"

She tried to run, but he caught her arm once more. "Your name," Kalen said. "I want your name."

Fayne's eyes were wet but defiant. "Ellyne," she said. "Ellyne, for sorrow." Her fists clenched. "That's my name, damn you."

"No." Kalen looked down at her, his mouth set firm. "No, it isn't."

Fayne's knees quaked. "Yes, it—"

Then he kissed her, cutting off her words.

He kissed her deeper.

The blanket slipped down to the floor and her warm body pressed against him.

THIRTY

Cellica must have dozed at her work. She awoke at the table, needle and thread in hand, to the sound of muffled sobs.

The tallhouse rooms were not large—only a central chamber five paces across that served for dining and sitting, and two smaller rooms for slumber. Cellica's room, from whence the sobbing came, was small by human standards, adequate for a halfling. It boasted a window—Kalen, in one of his rare thoughtful moments, had cut it out of the wall.

Myrin was crying, she realized. But why?

"Kalen," she murmured.

Cellica slipped down from the chair and padded over to Kalen's door. She peered through the keyhole, much as she expected Myrin must have—

She looked just long enough to see Kalen's back, a pair of feminine arms wrapped around it, and knew instantly what had happened. She pulled away and her face turned into an angry frown. "Kalen, you stupid, *stupid*—"

She hurried to her chamber. Sure enough, Myrin was clad in her red gown again, though it was now much rumpled. She sat in the corner, compacted as small as she could manage, and bit her knuckles. She smelled of honeysuckle—Cellica's favorite and only perfume.

"Oh, peach, peach," Cellica said. She crossed to Myrin and embraced her. "It's not your fault. You know that, right?"

Myrin sobbed harder and leaned her head against Cellica's chest. Where their skin touched, Cellica felt a tickle of magic.

It wasn't difficult for the halfling to connect events. Behind the closed door, Myrin had doffed the more practical attire they'd received at the Menagerie in favor of the red gown, which she'd asked Cellica to mend and clean earlier that day. Armed with that—and Cellica would confess readily that she looked a true beauty—and a bit of Cellica's perfume, she'd padded out to Kalen's room.

But Fayne had pounced on Kalen first.

Cellica cursed the man. How could he be so blind? Myrin had been throwing herself at him ever since that morn when they met. No wonder nothing had ever come of Kalen and Araezra. Cellica was surprised Rayse still *spoke* to the dumb brute.

"There, lass, there." Cellica stroked the girl's hair. "Kalen's just an idiot."

Myrin wrenched away. "No, he's not!" she said. "You know he isn't. Shut up!"

The halfling blinked, stunned by her outburst, and leaned away. She tried to speak, but a compulsion in Myrin's words had stolen her speech.

My voice, Cellica thought. She took my voice?

The girl's anger turned to a sob. "He doesn't love me," Myrin said. "I thought maybe he followed me from the ball because he loved me, but . . . but . . ." She sniffed and wiped her cheeks. "He followed because it was his duty, because he was guarding me. That's all."

"But that's not true," Cellica said. "I've never seen him look—"

"Go away," Myrin said. "Take your false hopes and just *go away!*"

Cellica found herself rising to her feet without thinking. Her conscious mind wanted to stay and talk, but her body obeyed without her consent.

It was the *voice*. Cellica's own command, but from Myrin's lips. How was this possible?

"Go away and go to sleep," Myrin said. "Here." She handed Cellica the blanket.

The halfling closed her door softly, leaving Myrin alone in her chamber. She wandered, increasingly sleepy, into the kitchen and main room. She felt so tired, as though she had run fifty leagues that day. Just a little—

She slumped down on the floor and was snoring before her chin hit her chest.

>=——w—=<

"Mother!" Fayne gasped, waking with a start, that one word on her lips.

Merely a nightmare, she assured herself with some disgust. She'd been sleeping again.

Fayne leaned back, her naked body glistening with sweat, while the world drifted back. A sparse tallhouse chamber. A plain bed. A man sleeping beside her, head nestled in her lap. Her tail curled around him like a purring cat, restlessly flicking back and forth.

Who was this man, and why did she smile when she thought of him?

She remembered the dream. An elf woman screamed and tore at herself to fight off a horror that existed only in her mind. A gold-skinned bladesinger without a heart moaned on the rough, slick floor. Fayne's own mother, dark and beautiful and dead, lay impaled at her feet. The cold, bone wand in Fayne's tiny hand sent pain through her arm and into her soul.

And the girl—Fayne had seen the girl wreathed in blue flames. The girl flickered into being just as Fayne's mother's magic burned her from the inside out.

She looked down at the muscled, scarred man who embraced her naked thighs and slept. Kalen, she remembered.

Then it all returned, chasing the nightmares away once more. She whistled in relief.

Gods, she hated sleeping. So barbaric. It limited more pleasant activities, anyway.

Fayne slipped out of Kalen's embrace and left him on the bed alone. She smiled at him for a moment before shaking her head. "Belt up, lass," she chided. "You're going all giggly."

She emptied the chamber pot out the wall chute—again, a barbaric necessity—and sat on the cold floor for a moment, collecting herself. Then she rose and stretched.

The moonlight that leaked through the window would not last long—dawn was coming, and she had best take her leave soon. She opened the shutters and put her face out into the cool Waterdeep night. She breathed deep the refreshing breezes off the sea and let loose a peaceful, contented sigh. Then she shut herself back inside.

She reclaimed her clothes—plain leathers, slightly shabby and worn. They weren't the ones she remembered wearing there, but she was used to that feeling. When most of one's wardrobe was illusory, one's basic clothes often varied.

Illusion . . .

She realized something and crossed quickly to Kalen's mirror, which hung on the wall over a small basin. The water was tepid when she trailed her fingers through it, but the mirror was more important.

Her true face blinked back at her.

"Gods," she murmured, caressing her pale skin. "Did I really sleep in *this?*"

She ran her fingers across the scar along her cheek—pushed back the rosy pink hair that obscured it. The scar, from a crossbow bolt, ached, as it always did that time of night.

"This just won't do," she said. "Can't go scaring children, now can we?"

She made to draw her wand from her belt, then stopped. That was for cosmetic changes. Her true body—she really needed to hide that.

She invoked her disguising ritual with the aid of her amulet. Her flesh shifted like putty. The pink hair turned back to her familiar half-elf red, her sharp features smoothed, her ears shrank and rounded slightly, and her wings and tail vanished.

"Now, then," she said.

Over this she slid an illusion, one that suited her. Simply because she felt like it, she made herself look like her mother: a beautiful sun elf with eyes like tar pits and lips like rubies. A gauzy black gown spun itself out of the air around her thin limbs.

It was exactly as Fayne remembered her mother, in the few years they'd had together before the crossbow bolt that had given Fayne the scar on her cheek.

Fayne crossed to the door, opened it as silently as she could, and stepped into the outer chamber. She heard Cellica snoring and saw a sleeping bundle slumped in the center of the room. Fayne smiled gently.

Then she heard a whisper of leather on wood, and she looked just in time to see Rath rushing her out of the shadows. She did not have time to speak.

>⸺W⸺<

Once again, Cellica awakened to what sounded like Myrin weeping. "Gods," she murmured, brushing away the stickiness of sleep. She'd had such vivid and bawdy dreams, too.

The first light of early dawn crept through the windows. An hour would yet pass before the sun peered over the horizon. The city lay quiet.

Cellica heard shuffling sounds and stifled sobs from her own bedchamber.

Thinking of Kalen, she lifted her crossbow from the table. Mayhap she'd shoot him for being such an idiot and sleeping with the wrong woman.

She paused to look again through the keyhole into Kalen's chamber. She braced herself for what she would see, but he was alone and unmoving on the bed.

Blushing a little, Cellica tiptoed toward her room. She heard a stifled moan, then something crashing down, like a chair, and the hairs on her neck rose.

The halfling slid the door open a crack and stopped dead.

On the bed, illuminated by the moon, was a struggling Myrin in a nightgown, two hands tying a cloth around her mouth to gag her. Those hands belonged to a black-robed dwarf—the one they had seen in Lorien Dawnbringer's chamber: Rath. Half his face was a burned wreck, but she knew him.

"Don't move," Cellica said, mustering as much command voice as she could.

The scarred face blinked at her, holding Myrin on the bed with one hand. "Child . . ."

"I'm not a child." Cellica aimed at his face. "And if you think this is a toy, you're damn wrong." Her hands trembled. "Kalen!" she cried. "Kalen!" He would hear that, she hoped—unless his wall suddenly blocked all sound, or some such nonsense.

"Calm yourself, wee one," the dwarf said. "I am unarmed."

As if that mattered, Cellica thought. From what Kalen had told her, he could kill them both with his bare hands, if only he could move. Her voice had trapped him.

"Don't call me wee, orc-piss," Cellica snapped. "Take her gag off."

"I wouldn't," Rath said. As he could not otherwise move, his eyes turned to Myrin. "This girl is dangerous."

"Do it!" Cellica hissed. "And where's Fayne?" She raised the crossbow higher. "What have you done with Fayne, you blackguard?"

"Cellica," came a voice.

A shadow loomed out of the corner, and Cellica turned to find—*her*.

Of all the nightmares she might have imagined, she never would have expected this one. A specter from her past—from before she and Kalen had gone to Westgate, from when she had been slave to a demon cult. One she had never told him about, and one who had haunted her every nightmare through all the years in Luskan and since.

The golden elf lady with the eyes of darkness.

"You," Cellica said, terrified.

The woman paused, considering. Then, finally, she smiled. "Me."

A dagger flashed and pain bit into Cellica's stomach. Her legs died and she slumped to the floor. The world faded. She heard only Myrin's muffled voice crying her name.

THIRTY-ONE

Kalen must have been weary—and indeed, he hadn't slept until shortly before dawn. He awoke near highsun—rested, thirsty, and ravenous.

He was mildly surprised Cellica hadn't awakened him—perhaps with an ewer of water, as was her habit. In a way, he was disappointed he wasn't waking up dripping wet. He would have seized Cellica's pitcher and drank the rest of its contents, he was so thirsty.

Kalen felt around the bed next to him, but Fayne was gone. In truth, he wasn't surprised. A woman like that couldn't be kept abed all night *and* half a day. And had she stayed, she certainly would have awakened him in the morning—he knew that for a certainty.

The desires of that woman—that *creature* . . .

"Growing up like that—hated and beaten and unloved," she said, her wide, silver, pupilless eyes gleaming at him. "It muddled you—ruined you for mortal women, did it not?"

"Yes," he gasped. Her magic heightened his senses and her hands burned him through his hardened skin. Her lips, oh gods, and her teeth . . .

Her sharp-fanged grin widened. "Good."

Kalen shivered at the memory.

He pulled himself from his cool, tousled bed and stretched. It smelled like her. Her scent was everywhere, sweet and intoxicating and wicked.

In the mirror, his face had a short forest of brownish bristle, which he would leave to grow. Fayne had giggled when she touched his rough chin.

The previous night blurred in his mind—he had an eye for detail but his awareness had ruptured against her. She existed to him as a forbidding yet alluring ideal—a memory of pleasure and shadowed pain.

"You have to tell me if I'm hurting you," he had told her.

"Why?" had been her reply.

She whispered a word in his ear that filled him with shuddering agony. He fought through the dizziness to kiss her harder. His fingers dug into her flesh, wrenching a gasp from her lips.

"I can't tell my own strength—I can't always feel everything. You have to—"

"You misunderstand." Nothing about her smile was innocent or confused. "*Why?*"

He shivered again and the image faded.

There had been pain, yes, but none of it physical. It had been in their hearts. Things had broken that had needed breaking.

He shook his head to clear it. He wandered, in only his loose hose, to the door.

In the main room, all looked much as it always did. But he saw immediately that the coals that kept the simmer stew hot through the night in preparation for the morn had gone out, yet the pot still hung over them.

Kalen frowned. Had no one eaten today?

And—when he entered the room fully—he discovered an oily red-black puddle spreading across the floor, coming from the other bedchamber.

Instantly, Kalen was on alert and listening. He heard weak, haggard breathing and recognized it immediately. Heedless of an attack, he hurried to Cellica's room.

The halfling lay within. Her middle was a mess of red and she was paler than chalk. Kalen would have thought her dead if he hadn't seen her chest moving, just barely.

"Cellica," Kalen said, kneeling beside her. "Gods. Gods!"

The halfling's eyes opened and her lips parted. "Well . . . met. Coins bright?"

Kalen cupped her face. "Cellica," he said. "Sister . . ."

"Look at this, Kalen." One feeble hand indicated the black mess that soaked the front of her linen shift. "Killed me, Kalen. Knife cut all my insides. Poisoned. Too much for you."

Kalen's fingers lingered over her breast. He knew she was right. The wounds were too deep, and puckered black by poison. He couldn't heal her—not with his meager powers.

But he had to try. He had to.

He cupped his hand around his ring and closed his eyes.

Eye of three gods, Helm, Tyr, Torm, whoever you are—hear my prayer.

"No, Kalen—even if you'd come four hours gone . . . it's too late."

"Shut up." Kalen gripped his ring tightly, driving the symbol of Helm into his skin. He had sworn he would never beg, but he would beg for any god who might heal his sister . . .

"Don't do it, Kalen," Cellica said. Her suggestive voice was cracked, broken, but still made him pause. "Not for me."

He looked into her eyes and tried to speak through a choked throat. "Let me save you."

"You can't." She shook her head. "Save it for her. The dwarf . . . he took her."

Rath, Kalen realized. "Who?" he whispered. "Who did he take?"

"Myr . . . Myrin."

Cellica shook her head sharply, prompting a series of heaving, gagging coughs. Kalen thought she might spit forth shards of glass. "And Fayne."

"What about her?" Kalen coughed, burying his mouth against his arm. "Did you see her?"

Cellica shook her head. "I saw—" Her eyes widened as though afraid. "Not important."

"I don't understand," he said. Anger suffused him.

"I know—" Cellica clutched his arm hard. "I know that look in your eye."

"Cellica," Kalen said. "Cellica, I swear to you. I will find him, and when I do—"

"Please don't," she said. "Don't make me die listening . . . to dark words." Tears filled her eyes. "If it takes . . . me dying to remind you—to save you from . . ." She gestured feebly, as though to indicate the world entire.

"You're not going to die," Kalen said.

Cellica grinned wanly. "Just remember who you are."

Kalen swallowed. "I'm nothing. Just a shadow of a man—not fit for—"

"Shush." The halfling rolled her eyes. She reached for his face and slapped him lightly on the cheek. "You idiot."

Then blood poured from her lips and she gasped for air. Kalen held her tightly, felt her heart hammering in her chest. "Remember," she whispered.

"I—" Kalen squeezed her hand tighter. "I will, but you'll be right here to remind me."

"So charming." She smiled dizzily. "Always so—"

And then her eyes quaked and saw nothing.

THIRTY-TWO

The world swam back gradually, in layers of gray and black.

Myrin struggled for several moments to remember who she was, and even longer to reason out where she was: a darkened chamber with a stone floor and walls. A slim shaft of sunlight fell through a high window, lighting the chamber dimly. Overhead and all around her, she heard a great clicking and whirring, as though from some sort of mechanism—grinding stone and metal against one another.

Fayne sat next to her, looking up at the ceiling and murmuring softly. A bruise colored the right side of her face, and something was wrong with her left arm—it hung oddly from her shoulder.

"Fayne?" Myrin tried to ask. Something lumpy and soft filled her mouth.

"Oh good, you're awake," the half-elf said. She was not gagged. "I'm almost . . . there."

Fayne's hand slipped out from behind her. Myrin heard a fleshy pop, and Fayne's arm shifted back into its socket. Her stomach turned over.

Fayne looked around and reached toward Myrin. "Now," she said, "promise not to cry out or try any magic—something the dwarf might hear?"

Myrin nodded.

Fayne removed Myrin's gag. "Kalen will come to rescue you soon, I think," she said. "I left him a note, and I don't think he knows how to give up." She ran her fingers through her hair.

"What's going on? Who was that gold woman?" Myrin asked, hardly daring to speak. Then she struggled against her bonds. "Why aren't you untying me?"

"Don't be silly—we can't *both* escape," Fayne said. "If we do that, Rath will get away—and you want him to pay for Cellica, right?"

"I suppose." Myrin didn't want anyone else to be hurt. "But won't he hurt me when he finds you gone?"

"I don't think so," Fayne said. "He's been paid to take us alive, I think." She patted herself as though searching for something. Her hand settled over her belly. "Here it is."

"What?"

Myrin watched as Fayne drew from her bodice a shaft of gray-white wood about twice the length of a dagger. It didn't look at all familiar and Myrin had no idea what it was.

"Wait." Fayne moved to put it in Myrin's hand, but paused. "I can only give this to you if you promise you'll be careful, and only use it when the time is right."

"I promise," Myrin said. "But what is it?"

Fayne slipped the item into Myrin's manacled hand and she knew its touch instantly, though her mind had no memory of it. A wand—*her* wand.

Fayne slid it gently into the sleeve of Myrin's nightgown. "Remember your promise—only if you think you can defeat Rath." Fayne stood.

"Yes," Myrin said. She longed to feel the wand again, but she could wait. "Hold—"

Fayne had turned to leave. "Aye?"

"Can't you stay with me?" Myrin asked. "Can't we fight him together?"

Fayne knelt down again. "Child—"

"Don't call me a child," said Myrin. "I'm not that much younger than you. Maybe five or six winters—no more."

Fayne's eyes glittered. "Are you sure?"

"Yes," Myrin lied. She wasn't, now that she thought about it. "But what's more important, I know what you said."

"Oh?" Fayne looked dubious.

Myrin narrowed her eyes. "You said Kalen would rescue *me*—and I also know you aren't unbinding me and putting the wand in my hand because you think I might use it against you. Now why would you do that—unless you were afraid of me?"

"Not convinced by my performance, eh?" Fayne smiled and

gestured to the manacles she'd discarded. "I'm afraid you're right. I'm an opportunist, Myrin—and I see my chance. It's nothing personal, you understand."

"This is about Kalen," Myrin accused.

Fayne looked genuinely surprised. "Why would you think that?"

"You're leaving me here," Myrin said, "so I won't fight you for him."

"Would you?" Fayne knelt before Myrin, her hands a dagger's length from Myrin's bonds. "Would you fight me for him?"

"Yes." Myrin stared her down, looking right into her gray eyes.

Fayne stared back, that same ironic smirk on her face. "You'd be wasting your time," she said. "Kalen's a killer—a hard, brutal killer. He'd never love a softling like you."

"He's different now," Myrin said. "He's changed."

Fayne shook her head. "Folk never change," she said. "They just wear different faces."

Myrin shivered at the words. Her mind raced. "If fighting you for Kalen is useless," she reasoned, "then you would as well release me. So why don't you?"

Fayne shook her head. "You're a clever girl. But I can't do that."

"Why not?"

"I have reasons, I assure you."

"I'd like to hear them."

Fayne said nothing, only leaned in to kiss Myrin on the lips, in a gesture that was as sisterly as it was mocking. It lingered, becoming warmer, but Myrin felt trapped—paralyzed as though by a spider's venom.

Dimly, she felt Fayne freeze taut as well. Her hands clasped ineffectually, as though she was trying to escape the kiss but could not.

It felt strange. She'd never kissed a woman—that she remembered, anyway—and it stirred odd, tickling feelings on the back of her neck and down deep in her stomach. She wanted more of Fayne—to drink Fayne in, absorb her into herself.

Myrin saw, reflected in Fayne's widening eyes, blue runes spreading across her forehead.

When Fayne's lips touched hers, Myrin saw her clearly—saw *inside* her. She couldn't say how—as with the lich woman and her magic, Myrin simply saw and did not question.

She was in an underground chamber, she realized, smoky with torches and the reek of burning flesh. She could see no more than half a dozen paces around her.

An elf woman in leathers stood a few steps from her. She looked familiar, and Myrin knew her: Lady Ilira, only younger. Young enough that she could see the difference, which for an elf meant seven or eight decades, mayhap ten. She held a crossbow pointed at Myrin—no, at *Fayne*.

Myrin realized she was watching this through Fayne's eyes.

"Where is she, Cythara?" Ilira's voice burned her ears. "Where is the child?"

Myrin felt strong hands grasp her shoulders. "What child?" a woman's velvet-dark voice asked over her shoulder. "I hold none but my own daughter. Why—lost one of yours, did you?"

Myrin saw Ilira shiver in rage.

"By the Seldarine—don't fire!" a man cried from behind Ilira. "You'll hit her child!"

Myrin looked: a tall, handsome, gold-skinned elf, clad in shimmering mail, with a sword that gleamed in the torchlight. The sword should have pulsed with magic, but she felt a pressure she recognized as a magic-killing field radiating from the elf. A spell he had cast. *Bladesinger*, she thought, though she had no idea what the word might mean.

She understood that he had meant her—Fayne. She had a sense of feeling childlike. If Ilira was almost a century younger here, how old was Fayne? What *was* Fayne?

Myrin looked up through Fayne's eyes at the woman holding her protectively. *Mother*, she realized: a gold-skinned elf, half-dressed in a sweaty black robe. She could have been twin to the bladesinger, were it not for her cruel beauty. Shadows danced in her eyes.

"Kill me if you will, slut, only let my daughter live," Fayne's mother said to Ilira, with a cruel smile. "You see, *I* can have a child, while you are barren, no matter how my brother ruts you. I am well pleased with that and can die smiling."

Ilira gave a strangled cry and would have fired, but the bladesinger stepped in the way.

"Twilight, please!" the elf lord begged. "Please—she's my sister, and she has a—"

"That is *not* a child, Yldar," Ilira said. "That is a demon. A *demon!*"

Myrin felt white-hot loathing for Ilira wash over her like a wave and knew it was Fayne's hatred. It suffocated her, and she could not move.

The bladesinger put his arms out. "You'll have to kill me, too. I'll not move."

Ilira grasped his arm to pull him aside, and Myrin-as-Fayne saw smoke rise where their skin touched. Yldar's flesh *burned,* and yet he stood firm. They both looked startled by Ilira's use of her power, and she quickly let go.

"How can you defend her?" Ilira cried. "She murdered your betrothed!"

"That was an accident," he asserted. "She meant to kill—"

"Don't you see?" Ilira cried. "She's controlling you! She's controlled your life since you were a child. She rules you now, though you refuse to see it. She—*Yldar!*"

The bladesinger had fallen to his knees, clutching his chest. Ilira reached for him, then flinched away as though her touch might kill him. She looked at Fayne's mother. "Stop it!"

Myrin looked up to see a bloody mass in her mother's hand. A heart, Myrin knew—Yldar's heart. She realized Yldar's attention had waned, and his counterspell with it.

"Flee," her mother said, "or he dies."

"Do not do this, Cythara," Ilira said. "He is your brother. You saw how he—"

"Only that he stood between us," Fayne's mother said. "Now you owe him your life—don't waste his. *Flee.*"

Myrin heard the imperative—the magical command in that word—but Ilira fought to hold her ground. Myrin saw something move in the shadows behind her—thought she saw a face—but it was only for an instant.

"Flee." Cythara squeezed the heart in her hand and Yldar, still moaning, screamed loud and long. "I won't say it again."

Ilira, tears streaking her face, rose to go. "You win, Cyth." She turned her back.

Myrin could feel Fayne's mother smile.

Then she heard a click and felt a sharp slash across her cheek. She screamed in Fayne's youthful voice and fell. As Fayne fell, Cythara looked down at the crossbow bolt that had sprouted between her breasts. Myrin realized Ilira had fired behind her back, under her cloak.

Blood—bright red blood—trickled from the corner of Cythara's mouth and she fell.

Something caught Myrin: Ilira had appeared, seemingly from the shadows. Their skin touched and Myrin's flesh tingled but did not burn, as had Yldar's. She wanted to speak—Fayne wanted to speak—but the elf only set her down and ran to the bladesinger, who was coughing and trying to sit up.

Myrin looked at Cythara's corpse. Blood leaked around it—hot, sticky fluid that cooled to tacky sludge. Her open eyes stared. Yldar's heart had vanished from her hand, and she lay like some stripped, crumpled doll. Abused by the world, humiliated, and discarded like refuse.

Myrin felt hot inside—Fayne burning with anger, crawled to her mother's body.

Stop, child, came a voice in her head. *You cannot.*

But she didn't listen. She drew Cythara's wand—a shaft of bone—from her mother's limp hand and turned it toward Ilira's back. The woman was fussing over Yldar and wouldn't see the attack.

Stop, Ellyne, commanded the voice—and she knew it was distracted. A battle was going on, somewhere, between the speaker and some shadowy foe. *It is too powerful for you.*

Myrin leveled the wand and uttered syllables in a language she couldn't possibly know. But she recognized them, horribly, as the tongue of demons.

"*Your worst fear*," she said in those black words. "*Your worst fear to unmake you!*"

Searing pain swept through her, burning every inch of her body. She fell to her knees and screamed as the horrible power ripped from her and struck the woman she most hated.

And Ilira straightened, back suddenly taut as a wire, and turned toward her. She did not see Myrin, but something between them. Her mouth spread wide in a terrified **O**.

"No!" she screamed. "No—I don't need you! *I don't need you!*"

Blood trickling down her face, Myrin—Fayne—Ellyne—whoever she was—laughed.

She saw something else, then, behind them—a girl, clad in blue flames.

Myrin.

Herself.

⊰—W—⊱

The vision ended as Fayne wrenched herself away from Myrin. Fayne lay shuddering on the floor, her hands pressed to her temples.

"Lady Ilira," Myrin murmured. "Lady Ilira killed your mother. That's why you wanted to hurt her. That's why—"

"What?" Fayne shook her head. "What are you blathering about?"

"I was there—I saw you get cut. Right there." Myrin looked hard at Fayne's cheek, and sure enough, a scar faded into existence along the smooth skin.

Mutely, Fayne raised her hand to the scar. Her lip trembled. She was afraid.

Myrin understood what Fayne wanted. More than that, she understood what Fayne *was*. She saw the depths of her game—saw the darkness in her heart. "What happened to you?"

Fayne shook her head. She pulled a bone shaft from her belt—the wand from the vision, Cythara's wand—and slid it across her cheek. The scar smoothed out and vanished.

"Whatever you saw, it doesn't matter," Fayne said. "It has nothing to do with you."

"I saw *you*. Saw what you are. Ah"—Myrin shivered—"what are you?"

Fayne laughed—and in that moment, all the tension went out of her. "Oh, stop it—you're so cute when you're scared." She nuzzled her thumb into Myrin's cheek.

Despite herself, Myrin had to smile.

"You don't have anything to worry about." Fayne traced her fingers down her cheek. "This is one of my rare noble moments."

"Noble?" Myrin blinked.

"Indeed," Fayne said. "The very existence of our world is at stake, and you can save it."

Myrin narrowed her eyes. "How?"

"Simple, my dear," Fayne said with a smile. "You can die."

Myrin laughed, but the nervous sound died away. Fayne's face was mortally serious.

"You . . . you're not jesting?"

Fayne shook her head. "No, tragically. Your very existence is a threat to yourself, everyone around you, and perhaps all of Faerûn."

Myrin was stunned. "But . . . but I haven't done anything!"

"No," Fayne said. "But you will."

"You . . . you can't kill me for something I *might* do!"

"Will," said Fayne. "I didn't say might. *Will.*"

"Tell me what it is!" Myrin said. "I won't do it—I promise!"

"No. I'm sorry, but it's inevitable. You can't stop yourself." Fayne shook her head sadly. "You might do it by accident, or more likely some villain or other will use you. You come across an archmage or one of the plaguechanged . . . sooner or later, you will absorb something too powerful for you to control."

"I don't understand." Myrin's heart was racing. "What do you mean, absorb?"

"Never mind. The point is that the power inside you is simply too dangerous for you to exist," Fayne said. "Thus, I'm going to take you to someone—someone who can contain you safely, without destroying the city in the process." She touched Myrin's cheek, a little more guarded this time, as though fearing another vision. "Don't worry—you might not have to die."

Tears were streaming down Myrin's face. "Why are you saying this? I'm . . . I'm just a girl. I hardly even have any magic! You can't possibly . . ."

"You're a goddess," Fayne said.

Myrin's eyes went so wide they might have popped. "I'm . . . what?"

"No, no, that was a jest." Fayne tried to stifle her laughter with her hand. "Honestly, you should have seen your face."

Myrin wasn't laughing.

Fayne's expression grew grave once more. "To be accurate, you've got a goddess *inside* you—or, more truly, the death of one," she said. "Metaphorically speaking, you're carrying death, little one—the death of the old world. Just like all the other spellscarred. Like Kalen. Like Lady—" Her eyes narrowed. "Like that *whore*."

"I—I don't—what?"

"It's complicated." She pursed her lips. "You're all spellscarred, but you, Myrin, are far more interesting than any of them. Your powers . . ."

"But what are they?" Myrin almost wept. "What do I do?"

"This is delightful," Fayne said. "You really don't know, do you?"

Myrin shook her head, tears welling in her eyes.

"Very well," Fayne said. "I'll tell you, but only because I fancy you well."

"What?" Myrin choked on the word. Tears rolled down her cheeks.

Fayne bent as though to kiss Myrin, then recoiled, thinking better of it. "Let us begin this way," she said, catching Myrin by the chin. "You remember the lich, in the alley, when you were kidnapped, yes?"

"Yes, I—but I chased her away. I didn't—"

"Silly girl." Fayne batted Myrin across the chin, almost playfully—the way a cat might. "You didn't honestly think that power was *yours*, did you?"

Myrin's lungs heaved and she could barely speak. "I . . . I don't understand."

Then Myrin wept for true—terrified, confused, and frustrated. Had the world gone mad? She was just Myrin—little more than a slip of a girl, with hardly any magic to her name. She wanted her mother—whose face she didn't even remember. That made her weep more.

"Oh, sweetling, don't—I'll be plain, I promise."

Myrin was crying, and damn it if Fayne was going to stop her with anything less than divine revelation.

Fayne smiled. "Remember when we first met?" she asked. "I fussed over you, then later, you struck me with that spell? The one that hurt me and stripped my strength?"

"What—what of it?" Myrin asked between sobs.

"That was *my* spell," Fayne said. "Stolen out of my head."

The words froze Myrin, and she looked up, stunned.

Fayne raised her hand, murmured a few words, and Myrin felt the same pressure in her mind as she had used to strike Fayne in Kalen's tallhouse.

Myrin stared, heart hammering, as Fayne knelt and picked up the gag.

"Please," Myrin said. "Please—I need to know more!"

Fayne scoffed. "Only this," she said. "Folk never change. Do not forget that."

"Fayne, plea—!"

Fayne shoved the gag back in Myrin's mouth with enough force to knock her over. By the time Myrin recovered and looked up, the half-elf was gone.

THIRTY-THREE

The sun dipped outside his window. Dusk fell quickly, and mist flowed into Waterdeep once more. No strange glowing patches would appear that night, though—only calm, expectant fog to shroud the city, hiding the unpleasant things that needed to be done.

The faltering light slanted across the blood-stained floor that Kalen had done his best to clean.

Though Kalen didn't feel like eating, he forced himself. However much Cellica had spiced it, the cold stew tasted like soggy paper. In part, it was his curse; in part, it was fate.

The dwarf was giving him some time, and he was glad of that much, at least.

He'd taken Cellica to her adoptive family in a hired carriage. They'd accepted the body with tears and sobs. Kalen hadn't been able to face her adoptive siblings and stood aloof. Philbin, so like a father, had whispered a silent prayer for vengeance. Kalen had nodded silently.

Now, Kalen sat wearing the armor Cellica had repaired, rolling his helm between his gauntleted hand and his bare one. He had only one gauntlet, after that noble stripling had taken his second away. He was supposed to do this alone, weakened, without his full armor or even his sword? Impossible, he thought, and yet, he had no choice.

He looked again at the scroll on the table—the note that had been affixed to his door with a dagger. *His* dagger, that he had given Myrin the night before.

> Shadow,
> Rath is making me write this.
> Come to the Grim Statue at midnight or he will kill us.
> Come alone.

He says he may just kill one of us and maim the other. He says you can pick.

–E

Kalen ran his hand across his grizzled chin, thinking. Why had Rath spared him? And, above that, did Rath know he was Shadowbane?

The dwarf could be toying with him, but Kalen did not think that Rath was the sort to play games with his prey. He must have known Kalen was in the room, helpless and asleep. If he'd known Shadowbane slumbered nearby, he could have slain him easily, or awakened him so they could duel on the spot. And if he didn't know Kalen was Shadowbane, he would have had no hesitations about killing him in his sleep.

For the life of him, Kalen could not puzzle out why he was still alive.

Then he realized: Fayne.

Fayne must have done something to spare his life. Perhaps she convinced Rath that Kalen knew Shadowbane, and could deliver the letter. Perhaps she *begged* Rath not to kill him—perhaps she offered him lewd favors in return . . .

Kalen grimaced and clenched his fist.

Or perhaps he did not owe Fayne his life at all, but owed it rather to Rath himself. The dwarf came from a monastery—he knew great discipline. Perhaps he would have thought slaying a helpless man to be dishonorable. And leaving Cellica to die hadn't been?

"Twisted sense of honor," Kalen murmured, but in truth, he was hardly in a position to judge. Would his own code make sense to anyone besides himself?

It had made sense to Cellica, he thought.

He shook his head. Thinking with his heart was a weakness he could ill afford.

Surely Rath would have obtained healing, but likely the scars on his wrist would stop him fighting with his sword hand, or perhaps compromise his technique. That was an advantage for Kalen—a strength. He passed the helmet to his right hand, in its steel gauntlet.

Kalen did not have Vindicator—that was a weakness. He passed the helm to his left hand.

Rolling the helm back to his right hand, Kalen thought he was the stronger—strength.

Rath had proven, though, that his skill more than compensated for Kalen's strength—weakness. He rolled the helmet to his left.

Kalen wore armor that allowed him mobility—strength.

Rath did not need armor and seemed not to tire, while Kalen had to carry the weight of his leathers—weakness.

Kalen had the threefold god—strength.

They almost matched for speed, but Rath was just enough faster—weakness.

Rath had Fayne and Myrin, while Kalen had no bargaining power—weakness.

Rath had picked the dueling ground—weakness.

And, most important, Kalen was dying of spellplague—*weakness.*

Kalen was holding the helmet in his unarmored left hand. He hefted it, as though trying to dispel his doubts, then shook his head.

Going into this duel was tantamount to falling on his own blades, but he had to try.

"If I don't," he murmured, "then who will?"

The words he had shared with Myrin.

He felt the familiar chill at the base of his neck that told him he was not alone—someone stood just outside his door. Had Rath chosen to kill him by stealth after all?

He lifted his helm and slid it on, fastening the buckles with distinct, if muted, clicks.

Then he was up, dagger in his hand, facing the door. It burst open, as if by cue, and a woman in black coat-of-plate armor stood before him. In her hands was a hand-and-a-half sword that dripped with silver fire.

"Waterdeep Guard!" she cried. He knew her voice.

Araezra.

Shadowbane turned to the window, but a red-haired woman sat on the sill, hands at the hilts of twin knives—Talanna. "Lost your other gauntlet, have you?" she asked. *"Shadowbane?"*

Kalen pressed his lips firmly together—they would know his voice.

"Down arms and doff your helm," Araezra commanded. "In the name of the city."

He looked for another way out. Cellica's window, perhaps, but that was a small fit. He could try his luck with Araezra, but a dagger would be as nothing against Vindicator. He might escape with a wound, but he could hardly fight Rath while hurt.

"Do it now," Araezra said. "Down arms and unveil yourself!"

He dropped the dagger, which stabbed into the floorboards, there to quiver. He made no move to unbuckle his helm.

"You're making a mistake," he said as gruffly as he could, to hide his identity. "I've done nothing illegal or—"

"The time for masks is past, lad," said Talanna. She hefted her blades dangerously.

He thought desperately but could find nothing. He nodded.

"Slowly, then," Araezra said. "Unveil yourself—slowly."

He put his hands out, showing them empty—his left hand bare, his right hand gauntleted. Then he reached up and opened the clasps of his helm and pulled it off. He watched Araezra's face and saw the hope in her eyes fade. And with it, his own hopes.

"I *knew* it!" Talanna clapped the blades of her daggers together and grinned. She looked at Araezra, who grimaced angrily. "I told you, Rayse—didn't I tell you?"

Kalen blinked. "What?"

"Kalen." Araezra lowered Vindicator, setting the point against the floor. "I tried so hard to believe it wasn't you. Even up until I knocked on your door, I thought there would be an explanation." She shook her head. "I didn't think you would lie to me, but you did."

"I'm sorry," he said. "You were never supposed to know."

Araezra's eyes narrowed. "Never supposed to know? You think me a dullwit, then?"

Kalen blinked.

"All those stories we heard," Araezra said. "About the gray knight who feels no pain? And the colorless eyes. You think I don't know your eyes, Kalen? We've . . ."

She looked at Talanna, who grinned. Araezra nodded toward the window, as though directing her out to give them privacy, but Talanna only shrugged, feigning ignorance.

With a scowl, Araezra looked to Kalen. "It was only circumstantial, until that night in Downshadow—when you saved first me, then Tal. We were chasing you, and you came back for us anyway. You didn't want to be caught, but you didn't want us hurt. You're always like that—taking care of us whether we want it or not."

Kalen looked at the floor. He supposed it was true. "I never meant to offend."

"And the ball," said Talanna. She grinned. "Rayse told me about the ball."

"What about the ball?" Kalen asked. He thought he'd hidden himself well enough there.

Araezra waved. "When all the panic started, Shadowbane appeared and picked up *Cellica*, of all folk, and leaped up—" She trailed off.

"We're sorry," Talanna said. "That's why we've come—because of Cellica." Kalen opened his mouth, but she continued. "Of course we heard. Her family was just concerned about you, Kalen. They sent word to the Watch, and we requested to go along for the task."

"So, now," Kalen said. "You've come to arrest me?"

Talanna laughed.

Araezra didn't look so amused. "Aye, or so the ten Watchmen below think," Araezra said. "You're a dangerous vigilante, Kalen. We came up alone to talk to you, and they're under orders to follow if either of us shouts. But since we know you and love you well, we came to see if you would come peaceably."

"What happens now?" Kalen looked at the dagger stuck in the floor. He was fast, he knew—could he knock Talanna to the floor before she could put two daggers in him?

"We arrest you," Araezra said. Then she shrugged. "On the morrow."

Kalen blinked. "What?"

"Assuming, of course, you're still in the city," Talanna said. "But why would you leave? Waterdeep is the city of splendors—everything you could ever want is here, aye?"

Araezra shifted her boots.

"We worked out a wonderful tale," Talanna said. "We found you, agony-stricken, inconsolable. Plying that indefinable charm of yours, you lulled Rayse and I—"

"Mostly *her*," Araezra noted.

"—into lowering our guard," Talanna continued. "Then you sprang from the window and fled!" She grinned. "Naturally, the story will vary around the Watch for months, and I expect you'll have charmed us both into bed and escaped while we were searching for our trousers, but nevertheless!" She sighed grandly. "Ah, such is the legend of Kalen Dren!"

Araezra groaned.

Talanna sheathed her daggers and stepped toward Kalen. "Here," she said. "Take this." In her hand was her golden ring of carved feathers. "I've had my fill of high places."

"It was a gift," Kalen said. "Won't Lord Neverember be offended?"

"He can always buy me another." Talanna shrugged. "I owe you a debt for saving me."

It was pointless to argue. Kalen did not don the ring, but laced it into the sleeve over his bare hand, so he could use it at a heartbeat's notice.

"I am sorry for this," he said. "I love you both well, and I never meant to hurt you." He looked especially at Araezra. "I mean . . . hurt the Guard."

Talanna laughed. "Surely you jest! Your exile from the city will be the cheeriest bit of news the Guard's had in ages." She winked at Araezra. "It means some certain lass has become free game once again."

Red in the face, Araezra looked ready to strangle Talanna.

"What are you talking about?" Kalen asked.

"Are you that dull?" Talanna asked. "For months, Rayse has been free of suitors because everyone thought that you two—"

Araezra's cheeks were burning. "Shouldn't you be going, Kalen?"

He smiled weakly then said, "I have aught to do, first."

"Does this have to do with Cellica?" Araezra asked gently. "If so, let the Watch—"

"I can't," he said. "I'm sorry—I can't tell you. I must do it alone."

Araezra sighed. "You always seem to have to be alone," she whispered.

Kalen donned his helm once more and secured it in place. "Araezra—I'm sorry."

"I know," Araezra said. "Just—one thing."

He turned toward her, thankful for the helm that hid his anxious expression. "Aye?"

"In the Room of Records," she said. "When Rath was holding me prisoner, and you came in. You . . . you did what you did, broke your vow, to protect me, didn't you?"

Kalen didn't trust his tongue, so he just nodded.

She stepped forward, snaked her arms about his neck, and pressed her lips to his cold, shining helm. "Thank you," she murmured.

He smiled inside his steel mask.

Then she slapped him lightly, causing his helmet to vibrate and his ears to ring. "I don't need you making decisions about what is best for me," Araezra said. "I can make those myself."

"Yes, Araezra."

"*Rayse*," she corrected.

Talanna rolled her eyes. "No wonder you two didn't last."

Araezra reversed Vindicator and handed it to him. As she did, her hand lingered on his. She gazed into his eyes, and he into hers. He knew she wanted to say much, but both of them knew she could not say it.

"I will miss you, Vigilant Dren," she finally said.

"And I you," he said, "*Rayse*."

She smiled widely, as though he'd paid her the finest compliment in Waterdeep.

"Now, go do what you must," she said. She straightened and her face turned stony. "Farewell, and remember—begone by the morrow. You have one day."

Talanna winked at him. "One day," she repeated. "Then I get to chase you down."

Kalen nodded, turned, and leaped out the window. He hit the roof of the building across the alley, rolled to his feet, and broke into a run.

He would need only one night.

THIRTY-FOUR

Rath meditated, waiting for nightfall.

Fayne had sworn Shadowbane would get the note, and that he would be punctual. The woman had subsequently fled—while Rath had gone in search of food for them—but no matter. The human was the more important, and Fayne's absence meant one less distraction.

He'd drunk three bottles of brandy the night of the revel, when the elf woman had scarred him. He'd paid for all the healing he could afford, but the marks were still there. He'd drunk until he couldn't see them in the mirror anymore. And he'd paid for whores who wouldn't wince to see his face. The next morning, his employer had come upon him as he lay aching from liquor and burns and women.

Now, he would wait for the next move in this game. And he would be sober.

He breathed in and out, in time with the ticking. He'd listened to the clock for a long while—it helped him to focus and align his breathing with the world around him. It was off, he thought, but only slightly. Craftsmen would be required to fix the clock soon—on the morrow, perhaps. After this business was concluded.

The girl fidgeted again, distracting him.

He'd brought her food. He'd even ungagged her long enough to pour soup down her throat—slowly, so as not to choke her. He hadn't unbound her wrists—no need. He'd helped with her toilet so that he didn't have to untie her. She'd nearly died of embarrassment, but he'd just stared at her with the same bored expression until she yielded. There was nothing erotic about it.

Even as he meditated, he was aware of her staring at the back of his head. What a curious creature. At least her fear kept her quiescent enough.

Finally, when he found his thoughts settling too much on her, he opened his eyes and turned his head. She quickly looked away, but he knew she'd been staring at him.

He sighed. Feeling the lightness in his ready joints, he rose and crossed to her. "I will not harm you, girl," he said. "I have not been paid to slay you. If you are hurt, it will be accidental and as a consequence of your own actions." He frowned. "Understand?"

She nodded. From the way she flinched when he turned his head toward her, he could tell the mangled half of his face frightened her. That brought a twinge of anger, but he suppressed it.

"I will remove this," Rath said, touching the gag in her mouth. "But you must promise you will not scream or attempt any magic. There will be consequences. Yes?"

She nodded, and her eyes looked wet.

The dwarf sighed, then pulled the gag out of her mouth. She gasped and coughed but made no loud sounds. This was good.

She looked at him, lip trembling. "What—what are you going to do with me?"

Rath frowned. "Just hold you here for a time. Nothing more."

"Are you—are you going to . . . ?" Myrin trembled and edged a little away.

"Humans." Rath rolled his eyes. "I would swear by any god you could name that you are the most despicable, insecure, bastard blood in the world, but I know the ways of my own kind and find them worse." He shrugged. "You have no dishonor to fear from me."

"Why not—" Myrin swallowed hard. "Why not unbind me? Am I a threat to you?"

"No," he said, perhaps faster than he should have.

She pursed her lips. "You fear me?"

"I fear nothing," Rath said. "I have nothing to fear from you."

"Prove it." Myrin puffed herself up as big as she could in her frail body. "Unbind my hands. If you have nothing to fear from me."

"Hmm." Rath couldn't argue with her logic. "Why do you want them unbound? You cannot escape."

"Uh." Her eyes widened. "My wrists hurt."

Rath said nothing, only reached around to do as she asked. She hadn't lied: the ropes had left red welts on her wrists. He pulled away and let her rub her skin.

"There," said Rath. "Satisfied?"

"Yes." Myrin brought a wand of pale wood from behind her back and thrust it under his chint. Rath felt sparks hissing out of it.

"Hmm," the dwarf said.

Myrin stared at him, her eyes very wide. She breathed heavily.

"You should do it," Rath said. "I have slain many—men and women both. And children."

Myrin breathed harder and harder. Rath could feel her heart racing, see the blood thudding through her veins on her forehead.

"Do it," Rath teased.

The girl inhaled sharply.

Then he slapped the wand away and swatted her head at the temple with his open hand, as one might stun a rabbit. She collapsed to the floor limply. Lightning crackled and died.

"Wizards," he murmured, rolling his eyes.

THIRTY-FIVE

On nights when Selûne hid behind a veil of angry clouds, the streets of Waterdeep became much like those of Downshadow below. Moon shadows deepened and buildings loomed. Even the drunk and foolish had the sense to lock their doors against unseen frights. Few but the dead walked such nights. Even Castle Ward, protected by the Watch and the Blackstaff, was risky after dark—particularly on a night like this.

But Waterdeep's darkest nights knew something Downshadow never could: rain.

Water cut against Kalen's cloak like a thousand tiny arrows. Every drop was a command to reverse his course—every one a despairing word. His body told him to lie down and die. The spellplague was taking him, he knew.

Kalen took the crumpled note out of his pocket and read it again. This was surely a trap, he thought, but he had no choice.

In particular, he thought of Myrin. Fayne could care for herself, certainly, but Kalen could not abandon Myrin. Powerful as she might be, she was still a lost, confused girl. And if her powers overcame her control, no one could predict what destruction might follow. He'd barely stopped her that night after the ball.

And Rath had to answer for Cellica's murder—he would see to that.

Kalen knew that even if he failed, Talanna and Araezra would hunt down the dwarf, but that gave him little comfort. The Guard could do little more than avenge him, and vengeance would mean little to his corpse and less still to Myrin and Fayne, if Rath killed them.

No, he would go, no matter the obstacles—no matter the rot inside him. He would not fail. One last duel—that was all he needed. Just this one last fight.

He opened his helmet and vomited into the gutter. Passersby hurried along.

He staggered down the alley near the Blushing Nymph festhall, which led to a tunnel into Downshadow near the Grim Statue and whispered under his breath.

"I will make an emptiness of myself," Kalen murmured against the rising bile in his throat. "A blackness where there is no pain—where there is only me."

He shuffled past rain-slicked leaves and unrecognizable refuse. His head beat and his lungs felt waterlogged. The fronts of his thighs were numb—he felt as though he wore heavy pads beneath his leathers. If he hadn't worn such heavy boots against the rain, he'd have thought his toes frostbitten. His hands were steady, but that was scant comfort. Dead flesh was steady. His stomach roiled.

"A blackness where there is only me," he said again.

He repeated the phrase until the aches subsided. They did not leave him—not fully—but they faded. He would not recover, he knew. Not if he did this.

"Every man dies in his time," he murmured. "If tonight is my time, so be it."

His hands felt dead as he wedged his fingers under the lip of a metal plate, uncovered beneath the alley's debris. The reek did not offend him, for he could hardly smell it. The trap door had been used that night, he knew—it was loose. It awaited Downshadowers who prowled the rainy streets, and would for hours hence. Creatures of shadow risen from below. What was he, but a shadow come from above?

A shudder, worse than ever before, ripped through him, and he curled over, hacking and coughing. He wedged his helm open and spat blood and bile onto the metal door. It dripped onto the cobblestones and swirled with the rain.

When the fit passed—he had half expected it would not—Kalen righted himself and gazed at the rusty ladder that led into the shadows beneath the city.

"Eye of Justice," he prayed. He didn't beg. "Be patient. I am coming soon."

He wiped his mouth and began to climb down.

Downshadow felt surprisingly empty that night. Its inhabitants saw night in the world above as their due, when they could dance or duel at whim, love or murder at their leisure. Those with eyes sensitive to light could walk freely in the streets, and a heavy rain or a mist off the western sea would hide their deeds, be they black or gray.

No space was emptier on such nights than the plaza around the Grim Statue: a great stone monolith of a man on a high pedestal, his head missing and his hands little more than stubs of stone. Tingling menace surrounded the figure, filling the chamber with quiet dread. A careful onlooker would see tiny lightnings crackling around its hands at odd moments.

Kalen knew the legend that this had been an independent and enclosed chamber designed as a magical trap. However, the eruption of the Weave during the Spellplague—as story would have it—caused the statue to loose blasts of lightning in a circle continuously for years. The walls had been pulverized under the onslaught, making the twenty-foot statue the center of a rough plaza.

Eventually, the lightning had subsided as the statue was drained of its magic. In recent years, lightning flashed from the statue only occasionally. The surviving walls, a hundred feet distant from the statue, marked the danger zone of the statue's destruction. The ramshackle huts and tents of Downshadow extended only to that limit, and most of those were abandoned. Only a fool or a fatalist would live so close to unpredictable death.

A favored game among Downshadow braves was to approach the statue as closely as possible, taking cover behind chunks of stone, to see where their courage would fail them.

Kalen stood at the edge of the round plaza, scanning the neighboring hollows and warrens for any sign of his foe. He saw little movement in the dead plaza, but for a pair of figures that stalked through one of the broken passages nearby.

Then he saw Rath step into the open from behind the remains of a blasted column twenty paces distant. His hands were empty, his face calm and emotionless. He wore his sword on his right hip, as Kalen had hoped he might. The dwarf's right hand was wrapped thickly in linen.

"I thought you wouldn't come," said the dwarf. "That her note wouldn't bring you."

"You were wrong." Kalen put his hand on the hilt of Vindicator but did not draw. He knew the tricks of the Grim Statue—knew how its lightning could be random, but it almost always triggered in the presence of active magic. If he drew his Helm-blessed sword . . .

"I am pleased," the dwarf said. He made no move to draw.

Kalen saw that Rath's face, while not as horrible as on the night of the revel, still showed evidence of burn scars across its right side. His left side was unchanged, and Kalen could tell from his stance that he coddled the burned side. Proud of his looks, Kalen thought. He would remember that. If he could find a way to make the dwarf emotional, it could be an advantage.

"Agree to let them go if you kill me," Kalen said. "They mean nothing to you."

A flicker of doubt crossed Rath's scarred face. Then he shrugged. "What is this *if*?"

"Agree," Kalen said.

Rath shrugged. "No," he said. "Your little blue-headed stripling has another use to me."

Kalen didn't like that reply, but it wasn't a surprise. He shivered to think of the possibilities.

"What will you do next, dwarf, after I am dead?" Kalen had approached within ten paces, and the two of them began to circle. "Do you have other vengeance to take?"

Rath sniffed. "I kill for coin—vengeance means little," he said. "But I do know of hatred." He smiled, an expression made unpleasant by his ruined face. "Two guardsmen. Araezra Hondryl and Kalen Dren—they will die as well."

Kalen smiled, reached up, and pulled off his helmet, showing the dwarf his face.

Rath's eyes narrowed to angry slits. His hands trembled for only a moment. He was realizing, Kalen thought with no small pleasure, how deeply and completely he'd been fooled.

"Well," the dwarf said. "I suppose I need slay only one other after you."

Kalen smiled and put his helm back in place. He circled Rath slowly, keeping his hand on Vindicator's hilt and one eye on the statue.

"You should draw your sword this time."

"If you prove worthy of it," said Rath. "This time."

Kalen was so intent on letting the dwarf strike first that when Rath finally moved, it almost caught him off guard. One moment, Rath was circling him peaceably, and the next he was lunging, low and fast and left, where Vindicator was sheathed. Only reflexes and instincts built up over long years on mean streets sent Kalen leaping back and around, sword sliding free of its scabbard to ward Rath away. Vindicator's fierce silver glow bathed them in bright light, making both squint.

But Rath didn't follow. Kalen saw him dancing back, and felt his hairs crackle just in time to see the Grim Statue slinging a bolt of green-white lightning at him. Kalen couldn't dodge and only barely brought Vindicator into the lightning's path. He prayed.

Kalen felt the force of the blast like a battering ram, blowing him back and away from the statue. He tumbled through the air, trying vainly to twist and roll, and landed outside the plaza in a gasping heap. Lightning yet arced around him, and he twitched and hissed as it faded. If Rath had come upon him then, Kalen would have had no defense.

But the dwarf was merely standing over him when Kalen could finally move again, a wry smile on his face.

"What glory would I gain," asked the dwarf, "if I let some relic of another age vanquish you, the mighty Shadowbane? Come. On your feet."

Kalen coughed and spat and started to rise—then slashed at Rath's nearest leg. Laughing, the dwarf flipped backward and waited, a dagger-toss distant, while Kalen rose.

"Draw your steel," Kalen said, brandishing Vindicator high.

"You have done nothing worthy," said Rath.

"Then come to me with empty hands, if you will," Kalen said, taking a high, two-handed guard. "I tire of your child's games."

That seemed to touch Rath, for his neutral smile faded. He streaked toward Kalen like nothing dwarven. Kalen cut down, dropping one hand from the sword.

Steel clashed, followed by a grunt of pain.

Rath danced back, and Kalen coughed and struggled to stay on his feet.

The dwarf reached down and touched a dribble of blood forming along his right forearm. He looked at the cut curiously, as though he had not been wounded in a long time and had forgotten what it was like. Kalen gestured wide with the dirk he had pulled from his gauntlet, gripping it in his bare left hand. He let himself smile wryly inside his helm.

"I underestimated you, paladin," Rath said. "I shall not make that mistake again."

The dwarf reached for his sword in its gold lacquer scabbard and untied the peace bond. He closed his eyes, as though in prayer, and laid his fingers reverently around the hilt.

"You know what an honor this is," said Rath. "To find a worthy foe."

"I do."

The dwarf drew the sword in a blur, opened his eyes, and lunged.

Kalen almost couldn't block, so fast was the strike. Rath's steel—short and curved and fine—screeched against Vindicator, but both blades held. The speed stunned Kalen enough to slow his counter, which might have taken out Rath's throat if he'd been faster.

Instead, the dwarf leaped away, then lunged back, slashing. He did so again and again, moving so fast and gracefully that Kalen could hardly follow him with his eyes and parried almost wholly by touch.

Kalen worked his muscles as hard as he could, bringing the steel around to foil Rath's strikes, trying always to catch his slender sword between his own blades, but to no avail.

They exchanged a dozen passes before Rath fled, down the hall to the great cavern. Kalen gave chase, and might have lost everything when Rath came at him suddenly. The dwarf could reverse his motion as though by will, in defiance of momentum or balance.

Kalen parried the blow with his dirk, but he felt Rath's blade slit open the leather over his bicep. He took a wider guard—a narrower profile. He tried to bring Vindicator around, but hit nothing as Rath flowed away from him, running along the wall of the corridor. The dwarf plunged into the tunnels, and Kalen followed.

They ran from corridor to corridor, slashing and scrambling forward. Their swords sparked, trailing silver lightning through the halls of Downshadow. Rath struck a dozen times with his blade, but Kalen parried every attack—with sword, dirk, or gauntlet. Each time, Rath bounded away and Kalen cursed, panted, and followed. Lurking creatures scurried out of their way as the men ran and fought, roused from hiding by the duel. The combatants ran on, heedless.

"A darkness where there is only me," Kalen whispered through gritted teeth.

Rath vaulted off a nearby wall and slashed down hard enough to break through Kalen's guard and ring his helmet soundly. Instead of following through, he leaped away and continued the chase. Kalen grunted and sped after him.

"Why do you keep fighting, Shadowbane?" Rath's calm voice showed no sign of strain. "I can see you tiring—feel you slowing."

Kalen said nothing, but ran on.

They ran between crumbling chambers. The magic of Kalen's boots drove his leaps high and far, but the dwarf still eluded him. The dwarf seemed able to run along the very walls if he wanted.

They broke into the main chamber of Downshadow, with its tents and huts, lit by the dancing firelight that flowed across the ceiling. Inhabitants clustered around cook fires erupted in curses, then fled the path of the avenger and his quarry. Vindicator's silver glow made them bright, shining warriors as they chased each other.

They plowed through the heart of the encampment, leaping over cook fires and around startled natives. Hands reached for steel or spell but Kalen and Rath flew past without pause. They knocked down tent poles, sent stew pots flying, and generally wreaked chaos across the cavern. Rath struck Kalen several more times, but his leathers held. He could not land a single blow on the dwarf, but felt certain that when he did, Rath would fall.

"What will it take?" Rath asked as he vaulted up a wall, caught an overhanging ledge, and swung over the side, seizing higher ground.

Kalen jumped after the dwarf, grasped a broken handhold—his gauntlet screeching—and swung himself up. He caught a narrow metal pole that lay between the ledge and the wall—a waste pipe for the Knight 'n Shadow, he realized, which perched in the cavern wall just above their heads.

He swung himself around the pipe like an acrobat, once, twice for momentum, then he let himself soar, feet first, up onto the ledge. He twisted in midair and landed on his feet, panting, knees bent, sword wide. He looked up at a huge stack of crates and barrels, above which hung the low platform of the tavern. Near Rath stood a small shack, balanced precariously on numerous long splints for legs, where workers would clean the tavern's rags and dump the waste water.

As Kalen landed, Rath scurried to the shed, slashed through two of the supports, then climbed up the side of the shoddy building, pausing to look down.

As the dwarf watched from atop the platform, Kalen grasped his left arm, gritted his teeth, and tried to still his raging heart.

"Wait, Helm," he demanded, calling upon his dead god. "They need me."

"Still you refuse to fall," said the dwarf. He stood, in perfect balance on the platform railing. "What admirable valor—foolish, but admirable."

The groan of buckling wood warned of danger, and the supports of the platform splintered and collapsed. The dwarf launched himself again, flipping and sailing through the air—leaving behind a collapsing storm of wood, stone, and water.

Kalen barely threw himself aside before the shack shattered against the narrow ledge, which itself started splintering. Choking on dust, he tumbled backward.

Rath was there, sword dancing like a steel whip, and it was more luck than skill that let Kalen block. He parried with his off hand, but the sword screeched against his blade and wedged the dirk free—it spun off into the cavern. Rath stabbed, but Kalen kicked his feet out from under him. The dwarf scrambled away before Kalen could get Vindicator in line.

"This will end only one way," Rath said.

He leaped out into the cavern and Kalen jumped after him, falling toward a sea of Downshadow folk who had joined in pursuit of the two crazed duellists. The dwarf bore down on one orc-blooded man and raced across the heads and backs of several others. Kalen crashed down in a knot of folk, sending three or four to the ground, then pushed himself up. He shoved his way through the crowd, holding Vindicator high and muscling the folk aside.

"Move, citizens!" he cried. "Waterdhavian Guard! Stand aside!"

That might not have been the best cry, for several lumbering forms—stirred by anger against that very organization—moved to block his path.

"Damn." Kalen bent his aching legs and sprang up.

His boots carried him up and over the intervening figures, following Rath. He landed badly and stumbled to the cavern floor, face first. Vindicator slipped free, but he recovered it in a roll to his feet. He charged after Rath, who was heading along the corridors toward the Grim Statue. Not attacking—just fleeing. Luring him.

Gods, Kalen thought—was he going toward the place where he'd hidden Fayne and Myrin?

Kalen burst into the plaza just as the statue's hands started glowing. He saw Rath standing before the statue, smiling. The dwarf sheathed his sword and spread his hands.

Whatever Downshadowers had been chasing them stopped at the edge of the cursed plaza, loathe to run into a trap.

With a grunt, Kalen charged.

The first lightning bolt was easy enough to dodge by rolling, but the second came too quickly. He tried to deflect it with Vindicator as before. Fortunately, the blast was at a sharp angle, and the bolt bounced from the enchanted steel into the ground, there to be absorbed harmlessly. The force drove Kalen to his knees, and he threw himself behind a boulder, panting.

"Come, then." Rath stood atop the headless statue. "I wonder if you'll be in time."

Rath leaped up, and Kalen watched as he vanished into the air, as though entering a pocket in the darkness above the statue's head. He saw the shadows wavering, and knew the dwarf had found a portal of some kind. But where did it lead, and how long would it stay open?

Though he knew it was a trap, he had no choice.

Kalen darted out from behind cover. He dodged a lightning bolt with a roll, then leaped over a second blast to grasp the statue's wrist. The figure's heat caused his hairs to rise as lightning gathered, but his eyes stayed on the unseen portal above its head.

He jumped and prayed it was yet open.

Lightning flashed.

THIRTY-SIX

Kalen felt a sense of incredible space, as though he had been trapped somewhere cramped and now floated in the open sky. His mind reeled and he wavered on his feet.

Something hit him while he was dazed from his journey. He felt it coming only an instant before it struck and grasped the nearby wall by instinct.

Two feet collided with his face like the lance of a charging jouster. The force sent him arching back, and pain stabbed through his arm as he fought to retain his hold. His helm shrieked as it tore free of his head and flew off, out into the Waterdeep night.

Rain lashed him as he hung weightless over empty space. He saw the lights of Waterdeep far below, and what could only be the palace roof. He realized the portal had led to the small chamber at the top of the Timehands, the great clock tower.

The temptation rose in him to let go—to sail off into the night and fall like an angel with broken wings. He was tired and beaten, choking with spellplague. The strength it lent him was fading, and soon, he would die. Why not let go? If he hung on, he would hurt more.

He hung on.

He swung into the tower, both feet leading, and kicked only air. He landed on his back with a crack that sent shockwaves through his insides, below his numbed flesh. Broken and bruised bones, he could feel.

He lay there and listened to the loud, deliberate clicks of the clock mechanisms working all around him. Without his helmet, the noise was so loud he could barely think. His heart beat countless times between each click. He vaguely saw an open stairwell, where candlelight filtered up.

Up, he thought—up. *Up.*

He spat blood onto the floor and hefted himself to a sitting position. He looked everywhere for his assailant, but Rath must have vanished into the shadows. Waiting.

Kalen expected the dwarf to strike at any instant, but nothing happened. He climbed to his knees, ignoring the complaints from every ounce of his flesh, aching for him to lie down.

"Why don't you come?" he murmured. "Here I am. Waiting."

But he knew the answer. The dwarf didn't want to kill him on his knees.

Up—*up*.

Kalen swung one foot flat onto the floor. He could feel nothing in his body. His arms and legs were dead wood to him and moved only accidentally. He had nothing left.

"Kalen?" said a voice, cutting through the chamber. *Myrin*. "Kalen, can you hear me?"

He murmured something that might have been "aye."

"I'm here! Please! Come—" Then Myrin seemed to realize, and he heard her strangled gasp. "No! No—go away! Leave me here! Begone!"

Kalen paused, thinking perhaps Rath had seized her, but then he saw the girl. Tiny blue runes glowed like candles on her skin. He pushed Vindicator in her direction and saw that she was alone, curled up against a corner of the clock room. Runes glowed beneath her eyes, which glittered in the swordlight. He stood and limped to her, fighting to move every pace.

Myrin shook her head, pleading with her eyes that he turn away. He kept coming, though it would kill him. When she saw he would not stop, she sobbed incoherently.

He reached her side and set Vindicator on the floor. He wrapped his dead arms around her and rested his bloody chin on her shoulder. She was shivering.

"Peace," he whispered, shocked at how hoarse his voice sounded.

"It was Fayne!" Myrin moaned. "She said—she said such horrible, horrible things." She shivered. "Oh, gods, Kalen! I'm—gods, all those people!"

"Peace."

"But you don't understand. I'm sick! I'm carrying something that—Fayne said—"

"Stop." Kalen put his fingers across her lips. "Fayne lied."

Myrin stared at him, dumbstruck and frightened and wrathful all at once. Her eyes pooled with tears, and Kalen could see blue flames deep within them.

"Truly?" Myrin asked. "Oh, Kalen—truly?"

Even as Shadowbane, Kalen Dren had never lied. Deceived, yes. Left words unspoken, yes. But flatly lied? Would he be lying to Myrin in that moment? He did not know.

"Yes," he said.

Myrin turned in his arms—held him as tightly as her thin limbs could—and kissed him.

To Kalen, she felt like fire—a wrenching, sucking fire that drained his body. He gagged, breaking the kiss, knowing he would die in that instant. Myrin just held him, weeping.

Then, something returned to him. Life, vitality, strength—it was like healing magic, but painful, and it was pain he could truly *feel*. He couldn't speak—couldn't think—just held Myrin as she held him, weeping and sobbing. Everything else faded, leaving them the only beings in an empty world.

Then it was over, and they were just holding one another, alone in a tiny chamber at the top of the grandest city in the world. A great sense of space spiraled around them, and Kalen felt weak and vulnerable and very small indeed. But he was strong enough for Myrin.

Kalen pressed her head against his chest, holding her as she sobbed, and fancied that he could feel her hot tears soaking through his clothes. Or was that only phantom feeling?

"How touching." Rath appeared around the clock apparatus. He held his thin sword wide. "And now that you're on your feet, I can kill you."

Kalen let go of Myrin and directed her back to the wall. She didn't move. "Myrin," he said. He could barely manage a whisper.

"No," she said and rose to her feet. "You're not hurting him."

Rath shrugged. He pulled something from his belt. A grayish white stick of wood. "I told you I would not kill you, girl," he said. "But there would be consequences to your—"

Myrin thrust out her hand and the wand wrenched itself from Rath's grasp. It flew between her fingers and crackled with magic. "Begone!" she cried.

A bolt of freezing amethyst light streaked past Rath as he twisted aside. It slammed into the wall, blowing hunks of stone in every direction and sending lines of frost crinkling across the stone. The dwarf looked at the patch of ice, then at Myrin, his face an arrogant mask.

"No more!" Myrin declaimed words of power and twirled her wand. "No more!"

Rath started dodging, but the bolt of force that shot from her wand stabbed him in the shoulder. The dwarf cursed, faltering in his dodge, and Myrin cried out in triumph.

As though he'd been waiting for just that moment of distraction, Rath lunged at her.

Kalen moved. Vindicator caught the dwarf's blade and pushed it harmlessly wide.

As Rath barreled in, a victim of his own momentum, Kalen whirled and dealt the dwarf a left hook to his burned face. Clutching at his wound, Rath tumbled back.

Kalen drew a circle with the Helm-marked sword, and a ring of silver runes appeared in the air. Their holy radiance sent Rath staggering back, and Kalen saw Myrin's face bathed in his threefold god's light. How beautiful she appeared.

Kalen and followed Rath.

They fought along the floor and off the walls of the small chamber, blades ringing and scraping. Kalen felt new strength—new fury—flooding his limbs. He felt everything, as though the numbness had fled him. He had no need of inner darkness to hide his pain, for it was gone. Rage coursed through him and he fought tirelessly. Vindicator blazed with light as he struck the dwarf's blade, knocking Rath back.

Rath weaved his blade and spun, and Kalen slashed at him. Their swords clashed and sparked, silver fire trailing. Kalen cut wide and punched around a parry, but Rath danced seemingly along the ceiling, flowing along slashes of Vindicator.

They cut through gears and pulleys, and once Kalen slammed into a bell, setting it to ring the dawn. Waterdeep would awaken many hours before dawn this day. In his fury, he didn't care.

Myrin shouted more words of power and multicolored stars burst into being in Kalen's eyes, dazing him. Rath might have struck in that moment, but the dwarf, too, staggered.

"That isn't helping," Kalen hissed, as he and the dwarf recovered in the same breath.

As Rath fell into a defensive stance, Kalen stabbed high. The dwarf ducked and turned a flip backward, kicking Kalen's hand up. The glowing bastard sword spun up into the darkness.

Rath twirled back, kicked off the wall, and lunged forward, sword leading—and hit air where Kalen had been standing.

Kalen leaped after Vindicator, caught it, and slashed down. He cut open the back of Rath's robe.

Kalen landed two paces from the dwarf, and they stared at each other.

Then Rath leaped back, avoiding a beam of frost from Myrin's wand.

"Stop!" Kalen cried, but it was too late.

Myrin's face was drawn and haggard, and she collapsed to her knees. Blue tattoos sprouted all across her skin, as though the runes were taking over her body. Her wand sagged toward the floor. She stood near the room's window, where the portal had deposited Kalen.

As Rath surged to her, blade low, Myrin pointed the wand with her shaking hand.

A burst of flame emerged from her wand and struck Rath's sword. The blade turned red almost instantly, and Rath hurled it at Myrin. The girl gasped and dodged, and the glowing blade flew out the window.

The dwarf's iron hands caught Myrin by the throat and wrist, holding the wand wide.

"Stop!" Kalen said. He held Vindicator level, pointed at Rath.

"Take another step, Shadowbane," Rath said, tapping his fingers on Myrin's cheek.

"Kalen!" Myrin croaked. "Just cut through me if you have to! I'm not important!"

"Myrin," Kalen said. "Myrin, don't be afraid. I'm going to save you."

"What Fayne said, Kalen! I'm not—*gkk!*"

Rath squeezed her throat tightly enough to cut off air. The knight waited, breathing hard, never taking his eyes from the dwarf's face.

"I wonder." Rath regarded Myrin for a single heartbeat then looked at Kalen. "Which is more important to you—justice or her?"

Kalen said nothing. Vindicator dripped silver-white flame like blood onto the floor.

The dwarf grinned. "Let us see."

He hurled Myrin out the window. She screamed and fell away, arms whirling vainly.

Kalen ran and leaped, sword leading. Rath slid a step to the left, his hands raised, but the knight went past him into the night.

Lightning flashed and an awful screech, as of metal on stone, joined the thunder.

THIRTY-SEVEN

Rain tore the night to shreds, and lightning bathed the high clock tower in light bright enough to match the day.

Kalen hung from the tower, his right hand on the hilt of Vindicator—which he'd wedged between two stones. A struggling Myrin hung from his left.

"You idiot!" Tears fell from Myrin's eyes as she beat at him with her free hand, trying to break his grip on her wrist. "Just let go of me!"

"Stop that," Kalen said. He swung her a little one way, then back the other way, like a pendulum—like the amulet on Fayne's breast . . .

Rath's head appeared in the window.

Kalen kept swinging Myrin, wider and wider. Her feet kicked at the rain-slicked tower stones, but Kalen knew she wouldn't find a hold. There was no ledge between them and the palace roof below. Only Vindicator kept them aloft.

Kalen gritted his teeth and pulled. Myrin swung over open air—and back the other way.

"What are you doing?" she cried. "Are you insane?"

Kalen kept swinging her. Wider—wider. "Listen to me," he said.

"Just drop me!" she sobbed. "I don't want to kill all those people—"

"*Listen,*" Kalen snapped. Myrin gaped. "The ring . . . laced in my sleeve. Put it on."

Myrin moaned. "Just let me go!"

"*Put it on!*" Kalen roared over the rain and thunder.

Then Vindicator shook. Myrin bounced and shrieked, and Kalen gasped at the strain. He looked up, and standing on the broad hilt of his sword—and his gauntlet—was Rath. The dwarf had scrambled down the wall nimbly as a spider and perched on Kalen's sword. Rain streaked around him.

"Interesting plan," the dwarf said.

Kalen couldn't spare a glance at Myrin, but he felt her taking the ring from his sleeve. He prayed the dwarf wouldn't notice.

"I don't imagine my standing here hurts you—you can't feel it, can you?" Rath raised one foot, keeping balance. "But even nerveless fingers can't hold you up when they're crushed."

Kalen gritted his teeth against the storm and the pain in his straining arm. "Make an emptiness of myself . . . in which there is no pain . . ." He kept swinging.

Rath stomped.

Kalen felt it—less than he should have, but no amount of spell-plague could mask the jolt of a broken forefinger. Just one finger—the dwarf was cruelly accurate. Kalen swung and almost fell, but kept a hold. Myrin gave a cry halfway between a scream and a sob.

"Put . . . it . . . on," Kalen hissed at Myrin.

Rath grinned. And crushed his middle finger. One at a time.

Against the slipping agony, Kalen shut his eyes. "No pain—only me."

He kept swaying, swinging back and forth as though he might hurl Myrin to safety—as though any building was near enough or high enough. He could not reach the palace wall from this angle, and his hand was slipping.

"Kalen!" Myrin cried. "Just drop me! You can—"

"Put it on!" he shouted.

"Put what on?" Rath saw the ring and sneered. "Humans. So romantic, even to the end."

He crushed the third finger, almost sending Kalen down. Only by the Eye's grace . . .

Kalen coughed harshly. "Have you got it?" he managed.

Fear clouded Myrin's face. She was swinging away from the tower. "Yes, but—"

"Good."

And he let go of her.

Myrin swung to the side before she started to fall, her eyes wide and her face startled. Her expression changed to shock, and then heart-break. She drifted into the rain and vanished without a sound.

The dwarf frowned. "I don't under—" Rath started to say, but Kalen, continuing his swing, hauled himself up and grasped the dwarf's ankle in his free hand. He planted both feet on the slippery tower wall.

"Fly," Kalen dared him.

With a fierce kick, he wrenched Vindicator free.

For one horrible, perfect instant, they were gliding, falling a little as if they had tripped. Vindicator was arcing, end over end, through the air beside them.

Then Kalen's guts rose up into his throat, and the two combatants were streaking down, wrestling in the air. The dwarf punched him soundly across the face and the world blurred. He held on.

They ricocheted off the palace roof—crashing hard, bones snapping—tumbling madly like dolls. Kalen tried to jump but the dwarf held on. Kalen rolled and wrestled and prayed and . . .

Hit.

THIRTY-EIGHT

For a long time, nothing existed but darkness.

Darkness, and rain like knives.

Then pain—sharp, stabbing agony that came from every broken limb and ounce of flesh. He had survived the fall—somehow, crashing against roofs and shattering almost every bone in his body.

Rath awoke on the cobbles of Castle Ward, in the shadow of the palace, and coughed up blood before he breathed. This magnified the pain a hundredfold. He couldn't feel his body. He was—

Alone.

That couldn't be. Shadowbane had fallen with him. They must have hit something else—some building. Otherwise, Rath surely would have died.

But who had landed on the stone first? Who had borne the brunt of the fall?

Rath saw a silhouette emerge from the mist. No—he saw the sword first. Saw the silver flames rising from it, the fog boiling away. Shadowbane, he thought for a moment, but . . .

It was Myrin. She walked toward him, the sword held awkwardly in her frail hands. Blue runes covered her skin, but they were fading as she strode forward. Her magic was unraveling, leaving only mortal hatred in her eyes.

"Taking vengeance," Rath said. He burbled. "I slew him and you avenge him. Fitting."

His sword lay on the cobbles, where it had fallen from the window. The hilt, still sizzling from Myrin's fire spell, sent up steam as rain fell on it. It was only a hand's length from his grasp.

A black boot fell on the hilt. Rath looked up.

Shadowbane loomed over him—stooped, bent, but not broken. His damp cloak draped around him. His helm dripped black rain.

"Kalen," Myrin whispered.

He reached toward her with his unbroken hand.

Myrin's face softened. "Kalen, no."

He curled his fingers, beckoning.

"Kalen, please. He's a monster, but he doesn't—you don't have to—"

Kalen said nothing—only held out his hand.

Myrin looked at Rath once more, then put the hilt of Vindicator in Kalen's hand.

"Turn away," Kalen said.

Myrin shook her head.

"Turn."

"No!" Myrin backed away. "I want to see what you are. What *we* are!"

Kalen looked only at Rath. He focused on the dwarf silently, ignoring Myrin's heaving breaths. Then she turned away and darted into the mist, vanishing into the night.

"For Cellica," Shadowbane said, as though in explanation.

Rath smiled, tasting blood in his mouth.

Kalen wrapped both hands around the hilt gingerly, reversed Vindicator, and held it ready to plunge into the dwarf's throat. He paused, his eyes unreadable.

"What will it be, knight?" Rath did his best to smile. "Vengeance . . . or mercy?"

Kalen coughed once and steadied himself.

"Justice."

The sword screeched against the stone.

THIRTY-NINE

Lunatic swordsmen cause havoc in Downshadow!" the broadcrier was yelling at the entrance to the Knight 'n Shadow. "Same culprits suspected in damage to Timehands! Watch . . ."

He trailed off and gaped at a gray figure standing before him—bare headed, bare handed, clad toe to chin in black leathers. Bandages wrapped his right hand and a sword was sheathed at his belt. In the dawn light, his brown-black hair was glossy and his chin dark with stubble. His eyes burned like light off snow.

"Boy," he said to the broadcrier. He took a hand out of the scrip satchel at his waist—in it gleamed five gold dragons. "Do you want these?"

The broadcrier had seen so much coin before, of course—this was, after all, the City of Splendors, where coin was king and blood was gold. But never had he owned that much wealth himself.

The boy nodded. The knight handed the coins over, and they quickly disappeared into the broadcrier's belt pouch. Then, his bandaged hand shaking, the knight unbuckled the black-sheathed sword from his hip and held it out as though presenting a gold scepter.

"Hold this for me." The knight nodded to the tavern. "When I collect it from you again, I shall give you twenty more dragons."

"And—" The boy shivered. "And if you do not?"

The knight smiled. "Then wear it well, and do not try to run from it as I did."

The boy nodded and took the knight's sword in his hands. It pulsed with inner strength—neither good nor evil, only powerful. Waiting for a worthy hand.

Without another word, the knight strode past the boy.

Fayne waited for him, legs crossed on the table. She was in a good mood.

She didn't care about being private or unnoticed; she wore her most beautiful red-haired half-elf face and her most revealing black and red harness, which was more leather straps than fabric. A dozen men had come to her with propositions, but she'd casually ignored each of them until they'd gone away. She'd had to fend off one with a charm to make him run away in terror. After her display of magic, no one bothered her.

She was waiting for one man, and one man alone. She hadn't slept that night, and neither had he, she knew. This would be their last meeting.

He came, just as she had anticipated, at about dawn, when the street lamps were being doused and the shadowy dealings in unused alleys gave way to legitimate business in the streets. The Knight 'n Shadow was mostly empty at dawn, though a few Waterdhavians had come for morningfeast before going about the business of the day.

He was dressed in leathers but carried no sword and wore no helm. His brown stubble defined his strong, tense jaw. His right hand was bandaged. His left was bare.

"Last place you expected this, eh?" Fayne asked.

"On the contrary," her visitor said. "Drinks and sly glances are your favored weapons. Why should I expect anything less than your element?"

"Mmm." She nodded to the two goblets of wine on the table, one before her and one before an empty chair. "Drink? 'Ware, though for—"

Kalen seized her goblet—not his own—drained it in a single gulp, then sat down.

Fayne blinked at him, then at the goblets. He'd ruined her game, and it offended her.

"My apologies," Kalen said. "Was one or the other meant to be poisoned?"

"Very well," she said, keeping the anger he'd roused off her face. "We don't have to play this game, if you don't want."

Kalen shrugged, then belched in a way rather unbefitting a paladin.

"So you beat Rath," Fayne said, tracing her finger along the lip of her empty wine goblet.

Again, silence.

"And I suppose you know about Cellica," she said. "I imagine the dwarf told you *I* stabbed her, did he? I thought he might. That *was* the plan, after all."

"He did not," Kalen said. "But I had guessed."

"Poor puppy." Fayne grinned. "Surely you didn't believe all that romantic nonsense about me *loving* you."

Again, Kalen said nothing, but Fayne could see the vengeful wrath behind his eyes.

"Ah, Kalen." She smiled at him. "I knew—I knew the moment you went after the girl instead of me at the revel—that we would never work together."

He spoke, his voice grave. "Threatening to turn you in had naught to do with it?"

Fayne laughed. "No, no, silly boy—in my circles, that's just flirtation. No." Her eyes narrowed. "You just don't understand my very humble needs."

"Needs?" Kalen's bloodstained teeth glittered at her. The look of it intrigued her.

"Yes—your heart, body, mind, soul—everything." She flashed her long lashes and feigned a kiss. "Is that *really* so much to ask?"

"I might have given it," Kalen said. "Before you killed Cellica—I might have given it."

"And what of Myrin, eh?" Fayne asked.

She seemed to have struck him to the quick. Kalen looked down at the table silently.

"Ah, yes, the girl between us," Fayne said. "And how fares yon strumpet?"

Kalen slammed his fist on the table, drawing wary glances. "Don't insult her," he said low. "A creature like you couldn't possibly understand her."

"I'm sure." Fayne didn't bother looking around. "She's not with you now?"

Kalen shook his head.

"You let her go," Fayne said, clasping her hands at her breast. "Oh, how romantic! You really are such an insufferably good man—and an arrogant boor, besides." She sneered.

Kalen did nothing but stare at her.

"You just *have* to make decisions on behalf of those around you, without consulting them," Fayne said. "Rejecting that slut of a valabrar, for instance, so as not to hurt her. Deciding Myrin would be happier without you. Telling yourself it's to protect *them*, and not yourself!"

"I do what I must," Kalen said.

"Gods defend us!" Fayne threw her hands up in the air. "The arrogance! The conceit!"

"I know Myrin," Kalen said. "And I do not deserve her."

Fayne couldn't contain her laughter. This was just too much.

"People never change," she said. "Once a thief, ever a thief. Once a killer, ever a killer. Too much to expect you might stop hating yourself." She blew him a kiss. "But what if Myrin wanted you anyway?"

"I wouldn't let her."

"How perfect!" Fayne said. "Oh, Kalen, the gods endowed you in many ways, but wisdom of the heart was hardly one of them."

"Whoever she is," Kalen said, "whatever she is, whatever folk have done to her—Myrin deserved none of it." His eyes blazed. "She is better than me—better than all of us."

"Spoken like a man who knows nothing of women."

Kalen shrugged.

"Ah, Shadowbane, the arbiter of justice—but you're working without all the evidence, love," said Fayne. "You don't know what that girl is. If you did, and you had the slightest love for good and justice, you'd march right out of here and take her to the Watch—or the Tower." Fayne grinned. "Why not do that now? Or are you afraid they'd take her away from you?"

Fayne saw Kalen's hand clench, but the knight restrained himself.

"But no—you don't need anyone else." Fayne winked. "You're always alone, aye?"

She could see Kalen trembling as he looked down at the table.

"You really do love her, aye?" asked Fayne.

"You know I can't," Kalen said angrily. "She hurts me too much, just by looking at me."

"You idiot." Fayne laughed. "What do you think love *is?*"

A timid barmaid stood at the edge of the room, and Fayne rolled her eyes and waved to her. Soon, tankards of ale came, and they raised them to each other, even toasted and clinked the tankards together and smiled. By all appearances they were merely young companions, dressed in the garb of sellswords, sharing drink and conversation.

Through it all, the goblet of wine before Kalen went untouched.

"What are you thinking about, lover?" Fayne asked.

"I am thinking about how this will end." There was no warmth in his eyes.

"Then you will not object to assuaging my own wonders," Fayne said.

He shrugged with his tankard.

"First question," Fayne said. "Why did you drink my wine rather than your own? Had you decided what manner of wench I am—one who would expect to be trusted?"

Kalen gestured to the full goblet. "I could drink this," he said. "Or shall we talk more?"

Fayne's smile didn't falter—she wouldn't give him a hint as to her scheme. It was far too delicious. "We should talk, and you should answer my question."

"I knew," Kalen said. "Because I know *you*, Fayne."

"I suppose you do at that—in a certain sense." She winked lewdly then composed herself. "Second question—you knew I was crooked. How?"

"Lady Dawnbringer," Kalen said.

"Ah." She nodded. "But that didn't let you save Cellica. So you must not have been certain. You didn't know Rath was mine?"

"I suspected," Kalen said. "I saw the way you looked at Lady

Ilira—the triumph in your eyes. Was *anything* accidental about that night?"

"Well struck," Fayne said. "What I told you was true—the whore killed my mother, and nothing pleases me more than hurting her. I didn't pay Rath to kill Lorien, but I don't care that he did. The only part I lied about was whether I would have killed her myself." She smiled. "Yet still you let me share your bed, even after you knew I was bent. I don't suppose you really did love me? Just a touch?" She batted her eyes at him.

"No more than you did," he replied, his eyes never leaving hers.

Good, that was good. All his attention fixed upon her.

"Glad my true face didn't steal your virility," she confessed. "But I'm so terribly curious—make love to many of my kind, do you?"

"I like my lasses wicked." Kalen shrugged. "But I've never known one quite like you."

"Mmm. Good." Fayne laughed lightly. "Not wielding your paladin's sword, I see." She gestured to his empty belt. "You murdered Rath in cold blood?"

"And if I did?"

"Then I can see why Myrin has left you." She reached across the table for his wrist but he drew away. "Ah, Kalen! You and I know too much darkness for a soft thing like her."

"Yes," Kalen murmured. "I suppose we do."

She narrowed her eyes. "Are you—and this is my last question—here to fight me, rather than claim me for your own?"

Kalen said nothing.

Fayne sighed. "Of course. Well—it would have been joyous, saer, but I can't say as I disagree. You and I were not meant for one another. Irreconcilable philosophical differences."

Kalen shrugged. "I suppose this is where I ask how you intend to kill me." He gestured to the wine goblets—hers empty, his full. "I suppose one of those was poisoned."

"Mayhap." Fayne looked him up and down. "You seem to be alive."

"This likely would have been some game of yours," Kalen continued. "You'd suggest we both drink, and let me choose which wine to take for myself. You just had to decide which I would drink—and poison that cup." He gestured to them. "Apologies if I spoiled your plan."

"And I apologize for insulting you earlier," she said. "Mayhap the gods did endow you with some brain after all—just not enough. You've missed one little detail." When Kalen narrowed his eyes warily, she laughed. "I'll tell you for free—a free lesson in Waterdeep, aye?"

"What could you teach me, Fayne?"

"Every thief," she said, "knows that the first rule of thievery is misdirection."

When Kalen frowned, Fayne gestured to his chair. The paladin reached down tentatively, as though to scratch an itch, and felt one of the tiny, poison-coated needles that were stabbing into his legs, buttocks, and back—needles Fayne had placed there an hour gone.

The irony, she hoped, was not lost on him. Because of his sickness, he'd not have been able to feel them pierce his flesh when he sat down, and by then it was far too late.

"Farewell, lover," Fayne said. She gathered her feet off the table and stood. "I would have liked to share a tumble with you again, but . . . we never would have come to pass." Then, dipping low to give him one last eyeful down her bodice, she claimed his wine goblet and drank. When she was done, she licked her lips. "You and I are too much alike, and yet not enough."

She started to go, but Kalen laid his bandaged right hand on her wrist. The hand was shattered—only partly healed—and had no strength to stay her, but she stopped anyway.

"You're sweet," she said. "But with that much poison in you, you won't even be wakeful but for a few more heartbeats—and your heart will stop in a ten-count. Hardly time for—"

He started to rise. He came away from the needles, leaking trickles of blood, and rose before her like a black specter. She saw, in the folds of his stained gray cloak, the edge of a watchsword, which he drew into his bare left hand.

"There's—there's no way you could fight off that poison," said Fayne. "Unless—"

"Unless I managed to restrain myself"—he rose fully to his feet and kicked the table aside—"took Rath to the Watch instead of killing him"—with a flick of his wrist, he laid the watchsword across her throat—"and retained the favor of my three-faced god."

And thus speaking, Kalen began to glow with silver-white light, as though his skin itself was aflame, as though a deity had chosen that moment to smile upon him—and gaze through him. In the face of that divine radiance, the other patrons stared, transfixed.

"Well." Fayne trembled a little bit, then smiled. "Well played, Kalen—you really are a cold-hearted bastard." Her eyes flicked down to the steel he held at her throat, then up to him. "And you saved your soul to spend on me? I'm flattered."

He looked at her impassively.

She smiled bewitchingly. "I've waited many years for someone as clever as you—a foe who could defeat me. I'm glad he was so handsome, too."

Kalen's eyes were cold.

"Come now, lover—don't you want me?" She stepped forward, letting his blade cut a tiny red trail along her throat. She purred. "Don't you want to *hurt* me? I've hurt you, haven't I—killed your little sister and chased off your blue-haired tart?"

Her face was almost against his. Only the sword, keen enough to slit her throat with a twitch of Kalen's arm—one false step—stopped her from kissing him.

"When you think about that," Fayne said, "when you look at me—you don't have even just a *little* hate in your heart?" She tapped Kalen's chest. "That big, strong, *dying* heart?"

Kalen tightened his hand on the sword hilt.

He shoved her back. She fell to the floor and looked up at him, eyes and hair wild, sneering as he stepped forward. Her heart was pounding and she knew this was the end.

"No," he said. He sheathed the sword at his hip and turned his gaze aside.

Fayne trembled. She didn't dare move—he could whirl and open her throat at any instant. But he just stood, silent and still. Death might as well have taken him as he stood—his sickness crept up and slain him. She panted on the floor behind him, blood trickling down her heaving chest from the wound she had inflicted on herself.

Fayne rose. She dusted her leathers and smoothed her hair.

"Well, then—farewell, Kalen, though I don't expect you will." She winked. "Cellica's dead, Myrin has undoubtedly left, and you just pushed away the only other woman who could have made you happy. But I suppose you'll always have the memories."

She started to walk away.

"Fayne," Kalen commanded. "One last question."

She turned. His back was to her. "Yes, lover mine?"

"What's your real name?"

She pursed her lips. "I told you, it's—"

He whirled and smashed her nose with a left hook. She landed on her backside, dazed and dizzy and coughing.

"Just because I don't hate you," Kalen said, "doesn't mean I'm letting you go."

Fayne tried to retort, but her face exploded in pain.

Kalen pulled a set of manacles out of his belt. "You and Rath might just share a cell," he said. "Perhaps you'll have a nice conversation about how you betrayed him—but I doubt it."

Fayne only moaned on the floor, clutching her bloody face.

"No clever quip?" Kalen sheathed his sword. "Fayne, I'm crushed."

Drizzling blood from her broken nose, she smiled up at him with surprisingly sharp incisors. Her eyes drifted up his frame, lingering in places.

"I've had better, you know," she said.

Kalen smiled. "So have I."

FORTY

Fayne hadn't stopped smiling all day.

She'd smiled silently when the Watch stripped her of her possessions, including her mother's wand and her ritual amulet, crippling her magic. She'd pressed herself hard against each of them in turn, inviting with her eyes, but none of them had taken her offer. Pity.

She'd smiled silently when they asked for her name—then again when the stuffed peacock from the Watchful Order of Magists had threatened to call the Blackstaff to interrogate her personally. He didn't realize that the red-haired half-elf was a false face, though, so he had not tried to break her transmutation. Thank Beshaba for small blessings.

She'd smiled silently, regardless of how much it hurt, when the gray-faced priest of Ilmater set and bandaged her broken nose. She did lick his hand once, because it amused her. She loved the look in his eyes—desire warring with faith.

The Watchmen, the mage, and the priest probably got the impression she was laughing at them, but that wasn't true. Granted, she had not the slightest esteem for the Watch, but today, she felt like laughing only at herself.

Only after they led her into her cell, dressed in her blood-spattered doublet and breeches, and after the door had slid shut behind her, did she finally give voice to the laugh that had been building inside her. It was all so amusing. She was the one, after all, who had trusted a paladin.

She laughed loud and long for quite a while, until the other prisoners—cutpurses and swindlers, hungover nobles and the like—slapped the bars, trying to get her to be silent. But it was just so funny, this whole ludicrous situation, and she was the lead comedienne.

"Oh, Ellyne, Ellyne," she mused. "You're such a gods-tumbled fool! Such a *fool!*"

The Watchman on duty thought she was simply mad, and he made the mistake of asking her to be silent. That man—a bulbous-nosed fellow of thirty winters or so—became the target of her lewdest and sharpest barbs. She threw herself into her mockery with a passion, pantomiming the jests and prompting more than a few cheeks around the prison to redden.

For she was Fayne, the Trickster of Waterdeep, and who would she be if she weren't the center of attention?

The Watchman gave up and stopped paying attention to her after a while, and she turned to tease her fellow deviants. Rath dwelt among the prisoners, sitting silently—mostly wrapped in bandages—in the cell opposite hers. He said nothing, no matter how she teased him.

After an unsuccessful hour of teasing anyone and everyone, Fayne grew bored. And thirsty, too. Not for the pond-scum water they'd given her—which she'd emptied on the guard's head—but for good brandy. Enough to make her face stop hurting.

Another hour passed. Having run out of breath to voice her japes and too proud to beg outright for attention, she contented herself with fuming at times, weeping at others.

Then, in the space of a heartbeat, all went silent.

Her sensitive ears could no longer hear the quiet murmur of the Watchmen at the front of the prison. She looked around, and her fellow prisoners all seemed asleep—or dead. Her heart started racing. What had happened?

"Aye!" she called. "Water, sirs! Please, goodsirs?"

No response.

The door swung open at the end of the hall, quiet and calm as soft death, and her heart almost froze. What was coming for her?

She sensed a presence—someone standing not a pace away from her at the door—and she shrieked and fell to the floor. She scrambled backward on her hands and feet and cowered against the wall.

Then came laughter.

"Mercy, child," a familiar voice said out of the air. "You *are* just like your mother."

A figure materialized before her, invisibility fading around it.

Relief flooded Fayne when she recognized her rescuer. "Gods," she said. "Did you leave me here long enough?"

The gold-skinned elf clad in the loud garb of a dandy swept off his plumed hat and bowed to her. He wore a bright rose pink shirt with dagged lace at the wrists, and his ebony overcoat was trimmed with complex gold swirls on the sleeves. Over this he wore a red half cloak that fell to about his waist, below which he wore white leather breeches. The outlandish garb might have seemed foppish or puerile on someone else, rather than dashing. She suspected, though, that he could wear anything and not fail to dash.

"Truly, Ellyne, you do me such dishonor," her patron said. "I was merely seeing to affairs of my own—I was quite unaware of your unfortunate circumstances."

"Hum." She didn't believe that for a heartbeat. "You've the key?"

Her patron lifted a ring of twenty keys. Then, as Fayne knew he would, he selected one completely at random and fit it in the lock. It turned, and he made a show of gasping surprise.

"You're impossible," Fayne said.

He shook his head. "Just lucky."

Her patron swept in as though he owned the city, and perhaps with good reason; privately, she suspected he was one of the masked lords who did exactly that.

"How positively *dreadful*." He pointed to her face. "Shall I avenge your honor, love?"

"No, no." Fayne's voice was made ugly and hollow by the broken nose. It rankled her, not being beautiful. "I prefer to do that myself."

"I thought you might." He leaned across the doorway, blocking her path out the door. "My darling little witch, I really must rebuke you."

"Oh?"

"For breaking the first rule of proper villainy," he said.

"Misdirection?"

"Point." Her patron smiled. "Very well, the *second* rule of villainy," he corrected.

Fayne spat on the floor indelicately. "And that is?"

"Never do anything yourself." He smiled and bowed. "Hirelings and minions, child! That way, you've no chance being caught—and their antics are always amusing."

Fayne crossed her arms and pouted. "Which am I, a hireling or a minion?"

"Oh, *tsch*." He kissed her on the forehead.

She pushed past him and started walking down the corridor. He stepped out and, as an afterthought, wove a bit of magic over the lock so that it would work only occasionally. He grinned at the mischief that particular cantrip would cause.

"Hold," he said.

"Aye?" She turned and fell to her knees as a wave of power struck her, pulling apart her disguising spells one by one. It felt like Lorien's rod on the night of the revel, but harsher. The power was not gentle, and Fayne felt every bit of its intrusive touch.

When it was done, she coughed and retched on the ground, reduced back to her true form, with its pale skin, hair the color of his doublet, and gleaming eyes of silver. She had long elf ears and delicate features, leathery wings, and a long tail tipped at the end with a spade-shaped ridge of bone. She glared at him with her fiendish eyes.

"This is my punishment?" Her bright red tongue darted between her too-sharp teeth.

He shrugged. "No hiding for a tenday," he said. "You allowed that paladin to use you because of your insecurities. I won't have that—not in a child of my blood. So deal with your weakness."

"Well." She stretched and yawned.

He blinked—he truly hadn't expected that. "Already? You are content?"

At least one person thinks I'm pretty, Fayne thought, but she didn't say that.

"Mayhap my true face is not so bad." Fayne rose, slowly, and stroked her hands down her silky hips. "Mayhap you should wear your own—or am I the brave one?"

"Mayhap you're not as smart as I," he corrected. "Who's the one with the broken nose, who spent half a day in a Watch cell crying her eyes out?" He averted his gaze. "Your punishment stands—until you remember your place."

"*Hmpf!*" Fayne stuck out her tongue.

He laughed. "Gods know I've made mistakes like yours, and mostly for the same reason." He patted her head. "Love is the sharpest sword of all."

Fayne swore colorfully.

Her patron winked. Then he handed her the amulet and bone wand.

"And what did you do," Fayne asked, "to correct those mistakes?"

"Oh. A bit of this"—he waved three circles in the air—"a bit of that." He put his hand on the hilt of his rapier. His white-gloved fingers caressed the starburst guard. Then, as though its touch had reminded him, he looked at Fayne with affectionate, twinkling eyes. "*She* made the same mistake many times."

"My mother?" Fayne asked. "Cythara?"

He smiled knowingly.

"Not that again," Fayne said, rolling her eyes.

"I speak with all sincerity," he said. "You remind me of your mother at your best—and at your worst. She made many mistakes of the heart—at your birth and at her death. You see?"

Fayne only nodded. She wondered why he wouldn't say her mother's name. He probably found it painful. A weakness, perhaps?

As they left the jail, the binding spell that had frozen the Watchmen expired, and they bolted upright, searching in bewilderment for their prisoner. Fayne almost started to cast a hiding spell of her own, but of course, her patron had prevented that.

She was, after all, his best and most important asset. She could trust him—at least, until her usefulness to him ended.

The bonds of blood, Fayne thought.

As they were leaving, cloaked in invisibility magic, Fayne mused over the one question that she'd been dying to ask—and could, now that this phase of his game had ended.

"Would you permit me to ask a question?"

"I would certainly permit you to *ask*."

"The dwarf," she said. "*You* paid him to kill Lorien."

Smiling, her patron waved one casual, delicate hand.

"*Lilianviaten*," she murmured, speaking his name.

In Elvish, it meant something like "master fate spinner." Lilten, she knew some called him. Also the Last Heir, though he'd never explained that to her. Mayhap he would, in a decade or so—perhaps a century.

It mattered little, Fayne thought. He was the only man she could trust in the world: trust to love her and betray her with equal frequency.

She wouldn't have it any other way.

She pressed. "So Rath was yours all along? Why didn't you tell me?"

"For my play to work, I had to make your reaction *real*, didn't I? And I knew you'd just ruin the whole game." He smiled wryly. "You should have seen your face."

Fayne started to ask, but then she understood it all—all of his plan, down to the smallest detail. How he had used her to manipulate events, and let her think he cared about her vengeance on the Nathalan bitch.

"Myrin," she said. "Myrin's the whole game—always has been."

"And?" Her patron waved her on.

"And now she's alone, undefended . . ." Fayne scowled. "You bastard!"

He flicked a lock of gold hair out of his eyes. "That's me."

Fayne couldn't help but laugh. It was so deliciously obvious—so simple—and so perfect. She could only pray to Beshaba she had half this sort of canniness when she came of age—and that the opportunity to pay Lilten back for his deception would arise soon.

"So . . . the game went according to your desire?"

"Of course." He stretched and yawned. "The next move is mine to make."

"I could help you with the rest of the game." Fayne nuzzled close to him—half like a solicitous child, half like a lover—and purred. "I promise I'll play by your rules."

"That's kind of you, but no." He shrugged. "Luck is with me—as she always is."

Of course, Fayne thought. She should have known—being the high priest of Beshaba, the goddess of misfortune, had its advantages.

And he was treacherous—she must never forget that. He'd served another god before, in the old world: Erevan Ilesere, if she remembered correctly, one of the faded Seldarine. Lilten the Turncloak: the apostate high priest, who had abandoned his god in favor of his bitter enemy.

She wondered when he would betray Beshaba in her turn.

Fayne hugged herself close to his arm, pressing her breast against his side. "You're sure you don't want me?" she purred.

"Quite sure, my little fiendling," he said. "This is *my* game, and I've dealt myself a shining hand at it."

She leaned up to kiss him on the cheek. "You're such a bastard, Father."

"Indeed I am, Ellyne, indeed I am." Lilten winked and returned the kiss. His lips burned like the fires of the Hells. "But you—you are as trueborn as I could make you."

Fayne blushed.

EPILOGUE

Myrin wasn't there when Kalen returned.

He hadn't really expected her to be, though he had hoped.

Too much had passed between them, and she had seen the cruelest and worst in him, as he had seen it in her. And yet, he had held out hope that mayhap, just mayhap . . .

A parchment letter—wrapped around Talanna's ring—was waiting on the empty, scarred table. That table reminded him of Cellica. How many times had he lain there while his adopted sister stitched his wounds? How many times had they sat together to mend Shadowbane's armor?

But it was Myrin's table, too, where he had first seen her, eating stew. Everything in the tallhouse had her on it—her scent, her smile, her memory.

The letter was brief. There were gaps, where many things went unsaid. It sounded of her and smelled of her, that sweet perfume of her bare skin. She'd crossed things out, and the ink had run in places. The parchment was dry, but he could see water stains. Tears, he realized.

As he read, all he felt was persistent cold.

> *Kalen, I'm sorry.*
>
> *I keep thinking [smudge] this wasn't supposed to happen like this. Mayhap I would wait for you, to be yours and to live out the rest of our story with you. Gods know I wanted [smudge]*
>
> *But life doesn't work like that. I need to find my own way—I can't have you make my choices for me. And until you see that [smudge] Here's your ring back, by the way.*
>
> *Farewell.*

I hope you find what you're looking for—and that I do too.
—M

Kalen sat a long time, looking down at the letter in his hand. He let the aches and sharp reminders of the past days settle. He felt them more keenly, since Myrin had touched him—had kissed him—though he didn't know why.

A tremor of sadness passed through him. It might have been a sob, if he'd not been weighed down by so many years—so many scars earned in service to the memory of a long-dead god—that he could not weep. So much pain, inflicted and suffered. When would it be enough?

He realized, almost immediately, that it didn't matter.

She was asking him to make a choice that went against everything he was, or had ever been. He couldn't make that choice, and she knew it. That was why she had left.

If he followed her now—if he rose and limped out the door and tracked her down—would it be to set things right, or would it be for her? What would he say to her?

He moved to crumple the note and toss it in the bin, but he saw more words scrawled on the back. He smoothed the parchment with shaking hands.

> *I wasn't going to say this. I scratched it out on the front, but you deserve to know.*
> *I did something to you, Kalen—I can't [smudge] I can't feel my hand well, as I write this.*
> *When I kissed you, I took some of your sickness from you. I absorbed it. I didn't do it on purpose, it just happened. [smudge] I think you're going to live. Just a bit longer. Some of my life for some of yours. Call it [smudge] a fair exchange, for bringing me to life at all.*
> *You don't owe me.*

Kalen blinked. He stared at the letter for several pounding heartbeats.

He was out the window before the letter fluttered to the floor.

ONE DROW · TWO SWORDS · TWENTY YEARS

A READER'S GUIDE TO

R.A. SALVATORE'S

THE LEGEND OF DRIZZT®

"There's a good reason this saga is one of the most popular—and beloved—fantasy series of all time: breakneck pacing, deeply complex characters and nonstop action. If you read just one adventure fantasy saga in your lifetime, let it be this one."

—Paul Goat Allen, B&N Explorations on *Streams of Silver.*

Full color illustrations and maps in a handsome keepsake edition.

The New York Times BEST-SELLING AUTHOR

RICHARD BAKER

BLADES OF THE MOONSEA

"... it was so good that the bar has been raised.
Few other fantasy novels will hold up to it, I fear."
—Kevin Mathis, d20zines.com on *Forsaken House*

Book I	Book II	Book III
Swordmage	**Corsair**	**Avenger**
	March 2009	March 2010

Enter the Year of the Ageless One!

FORGOTTEN REALMS®

Richard Lee Byers

The Haunted Lands

Epic magic • Unholy alliances • Armies of undead
The battle for Thay has begun.

Book I	Book II	Book III
Unclean	**Undead**	**Unholy**
		February 2009

Anthology
Realms of the Dead
Edited by Susan J. Morris
January 2010

"This is Thay as it's never been shown before . . . Dark,
sinister, foreboding and downright disturbing!"
—Alaundo, Candlekeep.com on *Unclean*

Forgotten Realms, Dungeons & Dragons, Wizards of the Coast, and
their respective logos are trademarks of Wizards of the Coast LLC
in the U.S.A. and other countries. ©2009 Wizards.